Trolls Don't Do Kung Fu

John McCrudden
Text Copyright © 2012

All rights reserved. No part of this publication may be produced, or stored in a retrieval system, or in any form or by any means, without the prior permission in writing of the author, nor otherwise circulated in any form of binding or cover other than that in which it is published and without a similar condition including this condition being imposed on the subsequent publisher.

ISBN: 978-1-291-31157-0

The sculpture featured on
The front cover is titled
Troll Scenting Christian Flesh.

Created in 1896
By
Niels Hansen Jacobsen

Dedications

To my family that allowed me to enjoy my fantasy books.

To Mark Jaeger the real Uffe Jægerblod.

And to all my Danish friends in that little bit of Ireland in Fredericia called the Generalen.

To Kennet the secret Nisse King.

Lastly but not least, Erika and her husband who made me very welcome in their Camp site where I wrote most of this book.
Hindsgavl Camping
5500 Middlefart
Denmark

Prologue

The sun kissed Earth, as the Trolls say, in a glorious and clear frosty morning. From my balcony overlooking the lake I can see as far as the snow-capped mountains that line the horizon north and east. A deep breath to take in the air, sharp and invigorating; it would be a crisp clean day to enjoy, if it did not happen to be the eve of my execution.

My own actions brought me to this splendidly sad place and I blame no one but myself for my present condition. Never did I believe that I would be able to plan my last day alive.

After the weeks of intense media attention given to my Courts Marshal, today is a rather peaceful, quiet day. This day is my last and I decide to spend it in reflection upon the journey that brought me here, to ponder the events that led to this sad end. One last precious day left to me, before they come to call at my cell door. Yes, I am afraid. In one very short day, I will face my death. I wanted to die an old man, in my own bed, with my wives and family around me.

When I say my cell, I do not want you to think my captors cast me into a dark and fearful dungeon, my cell is far from that. In reality, the rooms that I call my cell are sumptuous apartments fit for even that of a royal Nisse prince such as me. An invisible heat-retaining barrier splits my north balcony, I can enjoy the freezing temperatures outside and a single step takes me back behind the invisible barrier to the warmth and comfort of my spacious apartments within.

Often I have faced battle and many times, I have faced death and the Ferryman's barge. One of the things I often thought about, through my life as a soldier was, what I would do if I knew it was the last day of my life. Of the many scenarios that I could possibly think of, mostly in the company of a large bottle of fine Blackbush whiskey and numerous beautiful fae nymphs, I do not believe that I ever imagined I would spend that last day recounting my story to prevent a war between our two worlds. A war we on Earth Prime started and one that I carried out against my own race with devastating effectiveness. Dad would have been proud of my many successful campaigns, if I had not been fighting my own army of the United Federal Europe.

My captors have gone to the extent of furnishing the apartments with nisse sung furniture in the style of my own country and I must admit they are very much to my taste.

Alien to my native decor are the imagers that watch me, and the large plexi-glass screens through which I watch the world. They act as windows to the marvellous panoramic views of the frost dusted winter countryside that surrounds the palace; they are also video screens on which I am able to view the multitude of television channels beamed around the globe and through the inhabited outposts within our solar system. Most of the terran channels carried the televised courts marshal my captains and I had the dubious privilege of attending, as guests of His Catholic Majesty's Federal Government. There was no real question to the verdict. I was as guilty going in as I was coming out.

I really could not find fault with the trial, United Federal European justice being blind was seen to be done in full view of the world's attention, as well as by those representatives from the courts of the Emperor King Kennet and the Troll King Ullrick. It is ironic that I say my world, as if I am a native of Sol. I am not. Born and grown to manhood on Earth Prime I feel that this world, a world we so arrogantly call, Earth Prime, the world of my birth, is now so alien to me.

With my father serving in the Euroforce, I was born in the UFE military birthing centre just outside Paris. I left planet side only twice in my first eighteen years of life, the first, a weeklong vacation to the Lunar Disney Pleasure Dome when I was eight years old, an expensive celebration for my formal church baptism. At fourteen or fifteen years old, I cannot recall exactly, I went on a school field trip to the crater Ptolemaeus to visit the ancient Tlixtic ruins buried underground. This vast subterranean city was the first solid proof of Xeno civilisation and was the United Federal Europe's finest treasure.

From that ancient city, entombed in vast airless caverns under the Ptolemaeus crater for millennia, scientists came across clues to other cities in ancient alien texts discovered on a type of plastic parchment that, although preserved in the vacuum of the airless moon nevertheless seemed to be indestructible. The scientists decoded and translated, those texts that led our UFE extra-terrestrial taskforce to other buried cities silent and entombed on Mars, Venus, Io and Ganymede. Those cities held treasures of technology that brought to our civilization miracles of technology that we would have taken thousands of years to discover. The shining star of those ancient gifts to humanity was a form of subspace travel that put the stars within our reach and allowed us to export those products of earth we held in abundance: people, garbage and war. The creation of controlled hyperspace wormholes allowed space to be folded in accordance to Saint Einstein's Holy Laws of Special Relativity and travel from one end of the portal to the other happened instantly no matter the amount of space between the portals in hyperspace, the portal coordinates drawn together, all a person did was simply step through the portal to the other side.

UFE engineers funded by the Holy Virgin World Lottery Fund and UFE state grants from Britain, France, Germany and Russia, spent three years sealing the rifts in the shell of the ancient moon city and the atmosphere they recreated from the vast ice deposits deep beneath the crust. I spent three glorious weeks bouncing and leaping around that city exploring all the museums and interactive displays. I had my photograph taken beside the statues of the insect like Tlixtic inhabitants on this once great city, long gone, their disappearance still a mystery to us. Every type of sport I played had a hilarious dimension when played in one-quarter gravity. I took a few lunar rides on the old style buggies they used when settling the planet and four moonwalks in that desolate landscape of our local moon.

My brothers and I were army brats. Dad was a senior Euroforce NCO, and then a Sergeant Major for as long as I can remember. He served all over the European commonwealth worlds. Unlike most military families, dad insisted that we stayed in one place, so while he soldiered through the quadrant, we stayed in our comfortable married quarter's habitat in Euroforce St Patricks barracks in our native Ireland. The Euroforce barracks in Ballymena, County Antrim in the UFE State of Ireland was where I knew my childhood, we had everything we wanted and we needed for nothing. We grew up as a close-knit family even though dad spent most of the year away on some distant world.

There had been a member of my family in the Euroforce and before that, the British army since the creation of the Scottish Black Watch regiment in 1715. Yes, mum and dad ensured that we had a very ordinary domestic life. I have mixed feelings about that. While I am grateful for a stable childhood, I spent most of my young life yearning to go space side and soldier across the cosmos as my father had done before me, and his father before him.

As I said, the discovery of that alien technology buried for millennia on sites around our solar system gave European Scientists the breakthrough they needed to achieve a type of travel far beyond their reach. It the technology did not break Saint Einstein's Holy Laws of Relativity and it was not actually faster than light travel but the warping of space which allowed us to travel through subspace to instantly emerge many thousands of light-years away.

The technology was excellent for placing these portals between far-flung cities of the earth. The portals made inhospitable places like the Sahara and Gobi deserts liveable. Permanent portals took very little energy to sustain and in most of the hotter areas, solar panels powered the portal points there.

There was a massive portal in Regents Park London that permanently linked to Central Park New York. Citizens would walk up to the Customs and Border Security officers and their robotic scanner and sniffer droids. People would have their I.D. implants scanned and walk through to the other side in a moment. Using these portals humankind could move food in an instant from places of plenty to places of famine. Portals sprung up in most cities and towns allowing instant and affordable travel for all.

There were problems and resistance from airlines and shipping companies but there was no contest between them and the cheap and instant transport offered by the portals, in the end they had to comply. Most aircraft became redundant and the massive seafaring liners and city-sized ocean ships became obsolete. Portal devices popped up on the Moon, Venus, Mars, Ganymede and Io. For the first time, travel into space was possible for the average person and many flocked to this new frontier.

Man, or more accurately, UFE man reached out and colonised the far reaches of our solar system and for the first time, there was a sustained effort to terraform Venus into the new earth we so desperately needed. Europe solidified and became the strongest superpower; there was an amicable civil divorce from the American Empire when the United States fractured under the stress of financial hardship caused by continual excesses and greed. That is when the USA became the fourth most powerful superpower.

We placed portals out in orbit around our earth and through them built massive orbiting cities far above the atmosphere. Most of the cities built like giant wheels, provided earth like gravity to the people who took up habitation on those orbiting cities. With the portals open permanently, for the first time we had people who lived in space and worked on earth. Five of the fifty orbital cities that could be seen from Earth Prime were built like giant disks, to these were sent those that volunteered to live in a weightless environment, many of whom were wheelchair bound on earth, they lost their obvious disability in a no gravity environment and became equal to the able-bodied of that city. While they were able to use the portals to visit or return to Earth at any time, most chose to remain there in their preferred world.

The most exciting ability of this technology allowed for the opening of a portal one way without a portal at the other end. The first experiments were very successful with our engineers pinpointing sites on the planets and moons of our solar system. Problems arose when they set their sights further afield. They could not accurately pinpoint targets more than ten light-years away, and although an impressive distance, it was minute compared to the distances between the stars. The further away they aimed the less accurate they became. Soon the distance became so great that they gave up trying to aim accurately.

Space is a big place and for the most part, they opened one-way portals in the vast nothingness between the stars. In the end, they would just aim in the general direction of their desired target. If the portal opened in space, they would send through probes and robots to build a space habitat and construct a portal there. If a portal opened on a planet, the chamber that contained the portal was shielded and reinforced with force fields, within the chamber lived numerous robots that could operate in almost any environment. This high level of security kept harmful gasses and other deadly materials from gaining access to the chamber. Robots sent through the portal would probe the alien environment. If the environment proved satisfactory to our needs, a second more complex set of robotic probes went through. If they sent back positive results, a military expeditionary force was dispatched to secure the foothold on that world and build the other side of the portal.

The most important and significant discovery happened quite by accident. We found out that day that all of our monsters were quite real. During one slow evening, the technicians followed their boring script set to dial the various target areas decided by the overseeing committee. One young man midst the monotony of the graveyard shift thought it would be amusing to enter the expression ∞ for infinity into all six coordinate vectors for a portal opening.

To everyone's shocked surprise the portal opened in the area what we now call New Paris, right in the middle of the annual elvin mulluck chariot races. It caused mayhem amongst the elvin and the animals within earshot. The Tlixticians designed the portals to emit a high-pitched buzzing and ultrasound vibrations that discouraged animals from crossing the boundaries without supervision. The sounds deafened the elves and the racing mulluks bolted everywhere. It was a Felix Culpa of epic proportions.

The happy accident caused a massive stable gateway to Sol. We could not turn it off even if we wanted to. There were always gateways to Sol, right back in the time before time, gateways existed, humans were blissfully unaware of them and they remained under the strict control of the trollish race of the world of Sol. Since time began, they were closely guarded secrets and used primarily by the fae of Sol to travel to Earth Prime and the inevitable encounters with us humans. These encounters sometimes accidental, sometimes with a faeian purpose for good or ill, gave rise to the legends and folktales of faeries, trolls, elves and all of those other fantasy creatures of our myths and legends.

Our world that we so arrogantly called Earth Prime saw that all those faerie tales were based on truth and there was a real place where trolls, ogres, faeries and elves lived ordinary lives, untouched by the corrupting hand of humanity. While humanity took its wars to the heavens, it also took to stripping Sol of its natural resources, so desperately short on our own world. While our world's population was around 24 Billion not including those colonies out in our solar system and amongst the stars, Sol's population was estimated to be under one billion. Earth saw Sol as a prime candidate for pioneers and settlers to travel to Sol and claim land for their farms and homesteads. No one asked the natives of Sol for permission.

* * *

There would be months and sometimes years when dad was away soldiering, he loved the adventure and I believe because mum and dad spent so much time apart they made their time together special. My parents had a long and happy marriage and I am glad that dad was not here in person to see me end this way. It would have broken his fierce and patriotic heart to see me shot for treason. My father spends his last few years cloistered away in his lunar Euroforce retirement complex; the quarter gravity allows him the freedom from the lack of movement he would suffer here on a 1G planet like Earth Prime.

My brothers all excelled at school and I am very proud of what they have achieved. All I could manage at school was a comfortable if middle-of-the-road B minus, never lagging behind yet neither a shining star. My only big success was to follow my father into an army career.

One of my fondest memories and the one I will take with me to face the firing squad, was the look of pride on dad's square-jawed face. He sat with my ever so proud mum, resplendent in his best blues and a chest full of medals while they watched me march on to the parade square after completion of my Pegasus Company training at Euroforce Brize Norton. Just as in school, so in my Parachute Regiment recruit's course, I was a comfortable middle-of-the-road soldier. I remember my recruit sergeant, Sergeant Matthews' comments. "A promising recruit who fell well short of his full potential." I wonder what Sergeant Matthews or even my father, a retired Regimental Sergeant Major would say now. I certainly pushed all the way, when it came to fulfilling my potential.

In the morning when the sun kisses the earth, when the first rays of light shine upon that place where I am to die, I will face a military firing squad, the shooters, I am informed, are Paras detailed from my old regiment. I smile a little; for at least I have little hope they will miss.

I do accept that which I did was treason and betrayal of my oath and my duty as a Euroforce officer; I feel caught between deeply regretting my actions and yet feeling proud. One comfort is that I face my end in the company of my two loyal and most trusted captains, firm friends and loyal companions from the first to the last. I bet Jenser will try to bravely shield us and stand in front of me to face the firing squad, while Dixie I know would hide behind us both if he was not tied to the post.

In a way only a soldier would understand, I am grateful to General deBretton-Gordon the courts martial chief judge, he allows us to face this firing squad side by side, as we stood so often in battle, in the uniform of our beloved parachute regiment. He will allow us to wear the badges of rank we held at the time of our betrayal of our home world and the UFE military expeditionary force to Sol. I know that when the time comes we will face that firing squad without blindfolds; we are soldiers and we will be soldiers to the end.

They tell me that I am already a legend and in the three decades I spent on Sol, I will be remembered in the histories of both worlds. I so miss my wives and children and I do not know how they or I will deal with this separation. They grieve for me as I do for them. I deeply love them all and my hope and most heartfelt wish is that none of my sons will attempt to avenge my execution, as is their royal prerogative but strive to bring a lasting peace not only between Earth Prime and Sol but also amongst the peoples and creatures of Sol itself. My sons are its best hope and I make this record in the hope that they may read it and know me and why I became their champion and betrayer of my beloved Euroforce and I suppose Earth Prime.

Gazing out across the frost-encrusted gardens I see the bright sun climbing higher into the sky, too soon it will reach its zenith and I will watch for the last time its descent to the end of my final day. I do not want my final hours to feel so cold and stark so I make my way back into my apartments and move to the west balcony. On the west balcony I can enjoy the heat of the jungle gardens within the vast arboretum my balcony overlooks. The expansive plexi glass panels that are the walls of this fine tropical microcosm encompass all of the balconies and windows of the west wall. Exotic alien and Earth plants mix with those exotic plants brought back from Sol. The exotic centrepiece, are three Ironwood trees, a gift from the Elvin council of New Paris. A light force field around the balconies and windows repulse the insects but allows the heat and the sweet smells to waft through and into the apartment.

I can walk those gardens and all of the many corridors of this exquisite French palace. The tracking device inserted in my right calf prevents me from leaving the Estate. Should I attempt to leave, the device would render me unconscious and unable to move.

I drop off my furs and kick off my slippers, the thick wool carpet that covers the floor feels soft and warm against my bare feet.

Beyond the distant expanse of the plexi-glass walls of the arboretum, I spy the waters of the English Channel. There, hovering a few hundred feet above the sea, I can see the distant profile of one of the great floating cities of this world. These great cities are the children of those ocean going mechanised islands, they can float over sea or land. Defying gravity with the aid of another of those ancient technology discoveries, they replaced the floating cities of the sea, fitted with antigravity generators, on invisible wings of gravity repulsion; they lift themselves out of the sea to take to the air.

Even without binoculars, I can make out the three Mayan pyramids that mark it the Brazilian city of Teotihuacan. The Brazilians hold the contract for state executions and Teotihuacan city travels the world providing the service so that no countries need execute anyone on their native soil, it is all very civilized. The city also acts as a city of exile where those whose punishment falls lower than that of execution and it is a place where they can suffer their exile and be able to live and work in reasonable comfort.

The sun rising from the east above the mountains, kisses the tall aluminium towers and copper capped pyramids casting rays of gold and silver from that majestic city. From the coast of Saint-Malo, tiny metallic dots skip across the ocean, like a swarm of metal pond hoppers they move out to pull that mighty city to the docking pylons that will give access from Teotihuacan onto European soil.

I stand behind one of my plexi windows and touch the lower right hand corner. The window lights up with control icons and I am able to use the screen to zoom in on Teotihuacan City. Scanning the far city, my display shows detail of the buildings, their names and function. I move my screen to focus on the second highest pyramid where I can see the sobering sight of the people there, preparing the site of my execution. My panel tells me the weather will be bright, warm and sunny tomorrow and I suppose it will be a good day to die. I always liked pyramids, right up until today I liked pyramids. On that copper-topped replica of that Mayan pyramid, with my ever-faithful comrades, I will see my final moments, my final request to die in my native state of Ireland denied by the English officers of the Euroforce courts martial.

On my desk surface, I idly examine the electronic files that contain the scanned paper copies of files that document my life's achievements and conquests; those precious copies returned to Sol at the behest of the Nisse emperor, King Kennet. All except for my life journal, the one my beautiful princess began for me and the one in which I will write my final words.

The journal, the documents gently glowing at me from the surface of my desk, tell my story, my entire life laid out on the desk before me, the story of a soldier, a prince, a rogue, a hero. Some call me a fool and some a messiah and yet to others, I am nothing other than a traitor. Here is the story I need to tell you, a story I need to tell to my sons and my people; a story I hope will save countless lives.

Chapter 1

"Trolls don't do Kung Fu!" That's the line my Drill Sergeant would drum into us time and time again, along with his many other military mantras, each one proved their worth every single time; every single time until this time.

We had to work hard and to a tight deadline. All through the hot day, sweltering under the forest roof and into the chill of the night, my squad chopped, sawed, and cut underbrush. At least the elvin kept the bugs at bay. Every time a bug would fly from the underbrush, an elvin barrier spell would immolate the insect, a sharp crack and a blue spark the insect turned to ashes. Large or small, they looked like faerie lightening. The odd time they would catch a bat, a bird or an Asrais, when that happened it would be a large blue strike and a crack almost like a rifle shot.

By the false dawn, our work done, exhausted and cramping in the cold we retired to our bivis and bedded down for some well-earned sleep.

Epona the larger moon sunk beneath the horizon and the smaller darker moon Hekata following his legendary love lay low in the sky. At the end of our shift, elvin sappers lowered and extinguished the light globes that floated between the Ironwood trees like disembodied spirits.

All was impregnable darkness beneath the forest canopy almost two hundred feet above us. This was a young forest; some of the trees in older forests stood a massive five hundred feet tall and bigger than a human house in girth. Those monster Ironwood trees could contain whole families of elvin, nymphs, sprites and other assorted wood dwelling fae. In some places, where the trees were large enough and the fae there free thinking liberals, these fae shared the trees between families of the various races.

The monsters came for us just before true dawn, in the final hours of that chill spring night. We posted our sentries and slung our indestructible Decamole bivis. Our green maggot army issue enviropads lay on the ground within the bivouacs. We had to work all day and most of the night clearing the trees and the undergrowth for the drop boxes. Those lucky enough to pull a patrol got to miss all the chopping and hand sawing, the cutting and hauling.

My squad laboured long and hard for a full hot summer day and through the cold night. We fell behind victims of heat and the forest insects until the elvin sappers turned up. We had no choice but to work through the night. The drop boxes would be here tomorrow 08h00 and we could not to afford to miss our delivery slot. If we did, there would be no other drop slot for two weeks and that meant two weeks of eating field rations, crapping in insect infested bushes and living in our cramped bivouacs. Our only blessing, our green maggot enviropads. When we climbed into these pads, we would benefit from the internal sonic shower, which would clean our bodies and our wrinkle free uniforms. We could set the temperature within to a comfortable air-conditioned level and our expelled oxygen when needed could be re-circulated for an indefinite period of time.

Our preparation work was complete before the dawn and Major Morgan dismissed us to catch some well-earned shuteye before the drop boxes arrived, and another set of work began to put them together. I pulled my maggot around my cold aching body, my feet at last out of my boots. I set the bag's heater to a comfortable 20 degrees, I could feel my toes, numb with the cold, begin to warm up. The tingle of the sonic shower both cleansed me and massaged my aching muscles.

"Stand to! Stand to!" an unseen sentry yelled. Soldiers stumbled from their little fabric caves. Adrenaline of the alarm pushed the exhaustion out of my body. I scrambled from my maggot and grabbed my boots, unplugging them from the maggot as I began to stand. There were shouts of "East! East! ... Incoming from the east!" It could only mean an attack, troll jaeger vagt, gnome militaar or the terrifying goblin horde.

'Where the hell is east?' I thought, trying to get my bearings as I scrambled from my bivouac. Still crouched I ducked out of my bivouac and at the same time, ensured I could slip my sword from its scabbard. My foot still tingling with pins and needles, caught in the folds of the maggot hood and I went down to my knees. A trollish yari shot past my head and embedded itself in the tree beside me. If I had not tripped, that spear would have been through my chest.

Troll jaeger vagt I realised, I had mixed feelings on that discovery. Trollish jaeger vagt were big and scary but I was glad we would not have to contend with the gnomish or goblin dream weaving. The maddening illusions they cast in the mind during an attack or the skin dancing where they would possess the bodies of their enemy, seeing out of their eyes and the stronger ones controlling their victims from afar. Those fiendish red-eyed gnomes and black-eyed goblins could cause havoc and serious damage even before their first physical strike.

Following the flung yari, a hulking shadow came crashing out of the trees, it loomed before me just to my left. I had no time to do anything other than draw my weapon. In one swift movement, I regained my footing I stood barefoot with my katana in my hand. This was not looking good for me. I could not run about the forest floor barefoot like a bloody nymphan, so my actions against this Troll would be extremely restrictive.

The troll took a fighting stance; its short javelin like spear held high. It screamed its raging battle cry and I brought up my katana in a desperate, feeble effort to defend against his thrust. A smaller troll, perhaps a youth and inexperienced in battle, crashed out of the bushes and slammed into the big troll's back knocking my would-be attacker off balance.

Seizing the happy accident, I cut down hard and fast on the beasts flailing right arm and took it cleanly at the elbow. The troll froze in shock to see the clean-cut stump begin to spurt its thick dark blood. The smaller troll disappeared back into the trees without stopping, bent on its own savage mission.

My monstrous assailant went down to its knees huddling the bloody arm to its chest. I sidestepped, spun, and took the top of its head off with my second blow. It was a bone-jarring wrench. The monomolecular blade cut all the way through the troll's thick armoured carapace but the blow sent a stinging shock up my arm. I meant to go for its neck, but with us both moving in the dark, I missed my mark and the arm-wrenching strike nearly lost me my weapon. I jabbed the blade into the ground and flexed my tingling left hand. I watched for that second beast to show itself again but it was gone without a trace and lost in the forest shadows.

There was no more doubt where east was. The magic the monsters used to conceal their approach shattered and the noise of the attack burst upon the camp from the left. I crouched down and pushed on my high-leg combat boots, the black fabric hugging my lower calves formed a breathable waterproof seal around my legs.

My katana, although a two-handed sword, I preferred to use one-handed in my left, with a 12" magnum tanto in my right. Since my basic training, I had found a distinct advantage in being left-handed when it came to close-quarter combat with the regular army issue katana. I spent many years building arm strength to wield the sword with one hand, and being left-handed, it gave me the opportunity of becoming Regimental Sword Champion of the 4th Parachute Regiment the Dragon Riders.

My boots secure, I had my bearings and I moved quickly into the fray. I spotted corporal Burgess, pinned against one of the huge trees, a spear through his shoulder; and a troll, hands on the shaft and foot against the corporal's chest, was about to wrench it out to finish him off. The beast's attention focused on his bloody work; I came up unnoticed behind and plunged my katana into its left major heart. I needed to move quickly, there would be some fight left in the filthy beast, its right minor heart would keep him going for some time yet.

I used the handle of my embedded sword to assist my leap onto its powerful wide back, all muscle and rough ridgelines; I reached around its neck, tanto in hand. The troll, not the cleverest denizen of Sol, released the spear and extended its long arms over its head to grab at me with its claw like, three fingered hands. It pulled me around to its front to get at me. I was relying on the beasts' predicable reaction; my blade sliced deep across its throat as it heaved me over its shoulder. I rolled away when I hit the ground to avoid those razor sharp talons. The brute clutched at its throat, gurgling out its last few breaths, through the gaping bloody wound, my tanto left in its wake.

Staggering back, the monster toppled backwards into the dense ferns. I scrambled after it to retrieve my katana still embedded in its thick rough hide. A twist to open the wound and my long blade slid out with a sickening slurp! I wiped the red-black blood from the length of the blade on the suede tunic the filthy brute wore.

I pushed myself back to Corporal Burgess. He braced himself against the tree to take the weight of his body off the ground.

"How bad is it, Colour?" He panted between words.

"A big hole, but it doesn't look like it's poisoned or enchanted." I studied the wound closer as I fetched up the heat-sealed packet that held the pain-killing pen-ejector. I ripped the top off with my teeth to get at the contents inside.

"Not too much blood, Bob." I reassured him. "I suppose you're gonna live."

I pushed the fine needle into his shoulder and the point buckled sideways. I looked up at Bob's face to see his wooden expression staring lifelessly back. Now, when I say wooden, I mean wooden. The spear was enchanted and it turned Corporal Bob Burgess into the same substance it had touched after passing through his body.

A bloody tree! I had no time to lament; the attack was still in full execution. The fighting was hard and bloody amongst the thick trunks and dense underbrush, and it was fortunate for us we had that Elvin detachment with us. It was a mistake of our strength that cost the Trolls a conclusive victory; we would not be their morning barbeque. The Trolls swung through the massive tree trunks like great roaring apes, launching themselves off one trunk to land on another, their talon-like nails on hands and feet gripped the wood to support their enormous bulk. The beasts jabbed down at us with their Yari. We had no angor or mulluk mounted cavalry with us, without the Elvin, we would have been sorely out matched. The Elvin had fought trolls for countless thousands of years interspersed with peaceful coexistence, sometimes only a loose alliance, and other decades a firm and strong friendship, they were as fickle as humans were.

The Elvin, although slight of build, were able to move through the trees above the Trolls and force them down to our level with their long thin adamantine swords and enchanted arrows. Even so, we still had an uneven match against the beasts. Within these massive trees, these huge lumbering beasts would have quite literally had us for breakfast. Out in the open we fared better. With the Elvin, forcing the brutes down, we could dart in and slash at the beasts while they harried them from the trees above.

I cut, moved, and cut again, slashing an arm here or a neck there. It was a frantic melee, dodging spears and parrying their heavy battle-axes. I almost severed the leg of our company commander as I lashed out with an undercut to take a troll's leg, the Troll spun out of the way, I made my cut and my blade met air. I managed to twist the blade to strike my OC's thigh with the flat side. Major Morgan glanced down at his thigh and then up at me with a look of relief.

"Evening, Colour Sergeant!" He said in his upper class London accent, as if we had just met on a stroll through Hyde Park.

"Sir." I replied, nodding my head slightly. More spear thrusts and we moved apart in the heat of battle.

* * *

My tanto slid off a troll's nose guard and sank into its right eye. There was some resistance, but I pushed on into its brain, the bulk of the monster crashed down, a dead weight, and I was suddenly aware of the absence of the sound of battle. The heavy shadows retreated through the trees springing easily from trunk to trunk. While I would not say we won the battle, we did not lose it either, we held our ground.

Major Morgan yelled at me, "Colour, take your brick, see if you can take down a live one!"

"Charlie 34 Bravo, Charlie 34 Charlie to me!" I shouted and both platoons rallied.

"My brick… that way!" I pointed after a pair of trolls. Separated from the pack, they swung away through the trees. "Charlie 34 Charlie! Go right and flank these bastards!"

We set off after the rapidly retreating pair, swinging from branch to branch like deadly giant baboons. I hoped we could keep pace with them; they headed towards the edge of the forest and the treeless savannahs beyond. At least I hoped so.

Now trolls are good for monkey travelling between the trees, and they can march a steady pace for miles, but the way they use their knuckled fist on the ground to supplement the short gait of their stubbly legs, they cannot sustain a run of more than a few hundred yards, unless it is a battle charge.

In a battle charge they are wound up into frenzy by their Battle Priests, this mad frenzy of blood lust can sustain their charge up to half a mile. I have seen trolls run themselves to death in such battle frenzy. I knew that so long as these monsters did not swing back into the war party, we had them. I followed this particular pair because as I suspected by their garb and satchels they wore, they were their pack's signallers, the dispatch riders of their freaking, crazy army!

They would be making for their tribe's base camp or going to communicate to another tribe and I hoped that whatever particular tribe they were heading for, was very far away. We struggled to keep pace, and I feared we would lose them in the trees. I spotted the two squatting on a thick limb arguing together. I made silent hand signals to put my men in silent hiding.

The big troll was gesturing back towards the main war party and the smaller one pointed out towards the savannahs, I could just make them out through the forest. We squatted in the underbrush awaiting the outcome. Bigger trolls usually got their way by either intimidating the smaller ones or ripping their throats out. I worried we would lose them. I signalled to Corporal Jens Yde, leading the other brick, to take his bowmen and ease between the trolls and the war party. Charlie 34 Charlie moved silently away into the darkness to flank the pair. We had chased and tracked them for over a kilometre in the forest and it was only a few hundred meters to the savannah.

The smaller troll lashed out at the larger troll and for the first time in my years of experience with these beasts, the big troll backed down and raised his hands, palms up, in submission. Both trolls swung away towards the forest edge and hope rose in my mind that the twelve of us would be an even match for these two out on the grasslands. This odd pair leapt from the forest edge and made off in their apelike gate, using one arm and knuckled fist to assist their stubby legs in their strange lumbering run.

We followed them into the savannah while Charlie 34 Charlie was careful to maintain position between them and the general direction of the retreating war party. We lost our advantage of cover and the trolls spotted us as soon as we broke from the trees. We pursued them further into the savannah and away from the main raiding party. Several times either the big troll or the little troll glanced around to see us following. Not before long, they dropped into a forced march and I knew we could catch them.

Charlie 34 Charlie sprinted ahead of them to cut them off. Six men ahead and six behind, the trolls realized their situation, trapped on the ground between our two bricks they had nowhere to run. We were about a kilometre into the savannah in the open and away from the forest cover. We could not rely on elvin or nymph magic to assist us. Twelve men against two trolls was an even match, especially out in the open, I even believed we had the advantage. The short troll perhaps seven foot tall, was a good ugly head and shoulders shorter than his companion.

"OK lads. Watch their Pig Stickers!" I rallied my men. We had two crossbows in our brick, and another three with Charlie 34 Charlie. They held their repeating crossbows at high port aimed at both trolls. I raised my right arm indicating I wanted the big beast felled first. The big troll saw my signal, and raged defiance as he beat his chest like some demented King Kong. I silently congratulated myself that I had made the right decision.

The big troll hefted his Yari and launched it at the bowmen in Charlie 34 Charlie. Its target, Trooper Jake Henson, aimed his crossbow at the smaller troll; he did not see the flying troll Yari until it was too late. Corporal Yde, the brick commander, shouted a warning and the bowman raised his head only to see the spear come down and through his neck, it impaled him backwards at 45 degrees to the ground. Trooper Henson body slid back down the shaft as his legs gave way.

Chapter 2

Two arrows sprouted from the trolls back, and two more from his chest; the bowmen cocked the loading handles of their crossbows and another arrow from their magazines dropped into their wells. Corporal Yde scooped up the repeating crossbow out of the dead troopers arms and a third arrow joined the two in the trolls back while another pair of arrows sprouted front and back, the monomolecular point of the arrow heads passed easily through the beast's hard leather battle armour. The beast reared up, screamed a blood chilling battle cry and charged. I stood my ground, my men backed away. I drew my sword as the monster thundered closer. One slip, the slightest hesitation, and I would be dead.

The ground shook as the nine-foot brute pounded towards me. My heart pumped in my chest and I feared it would explode. My eyesight sharpened while my mind fought my brain to choose fight over flight. The rampaging troll wounded and enraged, nine feet of solid muscle, with its battle armour it looked as wide as it was tall and it stampeded directly toward me.

I stood motionless and drew steady breaths, my heart pounding; I could feel the blood coursing through my neck, the pounding echoing in my ears. My Katana I held out to my left, like a matador facing a charging bull. The monster bore down on me, the ground trembling with its charge. At the last possible moment, I side stepped to the right and drew my blade across its waist as the brutes momentum carried it past the spot where I stood. Its battle-axe swung into empty air, its short legs tangled in its own viscera that slopped out from the gaping hole in the monster's stomach. Careering head over heels it tumbled forward and onto its back. The fall forced the arrows in its back all the way into its chest, and I thought it dead on the ground.

"Colour! Second man!" Trooper Emerson shouted and brought his crossbow to bear on the smaller troll. Focused on the big fella; I did not notice the smaller troll had joined the charge. Obscured behind the bulk of its comrade and with all my concentration focused on the previous target, I missed it.

I spun back to face the new threat, expecting the charging bulk of the shorter troll, still a formidable seven foot tall. The men sprinted to my side in an attempt to take this one alive. Instead of taking the usual headlong charge, this one used its long Naginata to pole-vault over our heads. It sailed over us with a surprising grace and broke the neck of Trooper Tomlinson with a well-aimed kick in mid-air. It landed lightly behind us. To be exact, it shuddered the ground, rather than shook it. We turned to follow the beast's vaulting leap and I began to give the order to fire and be damned with it.

Upon its landing, the Troll spun its Naginata and took up a fighting stance like a Shaolin gorilla! The long curved blade, almost as long as my Katana glinted in the morning sun. The unusual stance gave me pause, and I knew I needed to attempt to take the beast alive. It was at this moment that I learned the chant that my old Drill Sergeant would so often repeat. *"Troll's don't do Kung Fu!"* was in fact, so very wrong.

Well, it might have looked like some crazed Shaolin monkey, but this was no Kung Fu movie and we all charged it at once. We moved to quickly overwhelm it and bring the monster down with the weight of our bodies, the troll vaulted on its Naginata, using the length of the pole to launch itself over our heads again. It repeated the lightning kick, which Trooper Emerson managed to avoid. The monster landed lightly outside our scrum, and struck another martial arts stance, the blade of its weapon pointed toward us. Two of the squad, swords in hand, rushed him. Moving only its Naginata spear, and with four rapid, fluid moves, the beast knocked the swords from their hands and flat-sided their heads, knocking them to the ground.

The beasts Naginata was in the classic troll shape, the 30" blade, like a Katana, curved with one razor sharp edge. A man could shave with the edge; nevertheless, they lacked the technology to create the monomolecular edges we could produce on Earth Prime. The shaft, instead of the usual heavy-ridged one, was a shimmering flexible version. With the troll's slighter build, the dimensions looked the same as its larger brethren but now that I had time to weigh the monster up, the Naginata looked proportioned to it, and I could see that it used the weapon differently to other Trolls. That is when I noticed the dull, metallic skull motif on its right shoulder; we were dealing with an officer here, and a high-ranking one at that.

I understood now why the big troll had deferred to this smaller troll. Sometimes bigness could be measured in ways other than weight and height; I just did not think trolls thought that way.

All four bowmen cradled their cocked and ready crossbows with their arrows notched.

"No shooting! The OC wants this one alive." I shouted to ensure no overeager mistakes in the heat of battle.

The bowmen nodded their understanding, but their crossbows remained raised. We fanned out in a wide circle, ready for any opening. The troll commander executed the most graceful series of katas with its battle spear; the point whirred with a buzz, the moves a blur to the naked eye. We knew there would be no opening anytime soon. I was deliberating the next move, when Corporal Jens Yde, the leader of the second brick called over.

"Colour…. may I?" He hefted off his body armour and unbuckled his weapons belt.

"Give it a go, Jenser." I said, understanding his intentions.

The big Swede, Jens Yde, was our Battalion close quarter, unarmed combat champion and instructor. He held more black belts and awards than I believed possible for one man. He was no idle boaster. At 6'1", he came up to the troll's shoulders. He had shocking white hair, cropped military style, and those Swedish bronzed, boyish good looks girls love to fall in love with. He knew it, and often took advantage of his natural good fortune.

Jens moved to face the troll; fists clenched against his chest in the Trollish battle challenge. The commander looked surprised and smiled, if you could call it a smile; it was like how a crocodile smiled, all teeth and flesh-tearing death, just before it pounced. The troll stood upright, planted the shaft end of its Naginata into the ground and clenched its fists against his chest. Then as casually as you like, it raised its long right arm to lean on the shaft of his spear, crossed one leg over the other, it slipped a pocket watch from a breast pocket and checked the time. It closed the watch and slipped it back into its pocket.

"Very well, Corporal…would you not like some of your little friends over there to join you?" The troll asked in a perfect middle-English accent, albeit with a light serpentine lisp over its thick, pointed tongue.

We looked at each other, Jens just as surprised as me.

"No sir… I believe I will do just fine." Jens replied, the troll noticed his north European accent.

"Sind Sie Deutscher?" The troll asked, this time in perfect German.

"No, Swedish… Sir." Jens replied, and glanced at me, as unsure as I was of the confusing troll before us. Jens gave the enemy officer the respect of its high rank, a natural reflex from a seasoned veteran soldier.

"May I know your name, Corporal?" The Troll commander pleasantly enquired still reposed against its deadly spear.

"Jens Yde…. Corporal Jens Yde…4th Parachute Regiment, the Dragon Riders."

"Aha! Dragon Riders! Very worthy opponents indeed!" The troll commander replied with that crocodile smile. "Yde is a Danish name. From Jutland to the east, is it not? The troll commander asked, knowing that its comments and questions astounded us all.

"Why, yes. But I … We, my family, have been Swedes for many years…. Sir."

My men and I had only ever heard trolls speaking their own language. Mostly shouts and swearing in the heat of battle, or telling us to go to hell or do unrepeatable stuff with our mulluk mounts, in their deep guttural dialect, most of it sounded very much like angry Klingon.

"Well. We really must get on…" The troll commander added. It stood to full height and un-strapped its weapons halter which he let fall to the ground with its heavy battle-axe and long skinning knife.

"Corporal Jens Yde. I speak your name and salute you at the time of your death. May your flesh feed many." The troll stated formally and struck its chest with its right fist.

"And your name, Sir?" Jens asked pulling on a pair of padded leather martial arts gloves, which he wore when he battled without weapons.

"Commander Uffe Jægerblod, of the 10th Legion." The troll replied with pride.

"Well, Commander Uffe Jægerblod of the 10th Legion… You are under arrest!" Jens saluted British Army style and smiled every bit as deadly as the troll.

The troll commander laughed deep and loud, taking up the praying mantis stance. He left his Naginata buried upright in the ground beside him. Seeing any troll in battle-dress in the praying mantis stance was something I thought I would never behold. It was as impossible as watching a monkey and a kangaroo dance Swan Lake!

Chapter 3

Jens went in hard and fast, the Troll parried and they danced their martial forms, arms and legs striking hard, powerful blows.

Jens went down a few times but well trained, strong and surprisingly agile for his size, he recovered before the Troll could take advantage. More than once the Troll Commander came in for the deathblow, Jens parried, and counter-moved, always just ahead of his monstrous opponent.

The contest was amazing; it was not like the dirty battlefield scraps of fast victories and any cost and by any means available. This battle was more like a rehearsed and gracefully choreographed duel. The fluid moves masked the power behind the blows. I would have enjoyed it more if I had not been worried about the Corporal's life. Jens changed forms quickly, from one style to another, in an attempt to confuse his opponent.

Trolls do not like change, and that was the annoying thing about this Trolls fighting style. Yes, trolls do not do Kung Fu, or any other type of martial arts, other than a particular style of karate called Wado Ryu, my own personal favourite, a deadly form that suited their short legs and long arms. Win Chung Kung Fu would have been just as good, but they had adopted this style called Wado Ryu on Earth Prime, and as I said, trolls do not like change. I suppose that is why they kept menacing and eating settlers from Earth Prime.

The Troll Commander changed from the weird looking praying mantis with elongated arms and barrel-like chest, to the monkey style. It circled Jens using its long arms as an extra pair of legs as an ape would move. The Troll rolled into Jens like a dark craggy bolder, and Jens went down. There was a crack, and Jens' left arm bent in mid-forearm. The Troll took the advantage, rolled forward, and came up with both hands clenched together above its head to deliver the deathblow. It cried a triumph call and I slammed the flat end of its spear into its ugly face.

The Monster stumbled back, long arms flailing. Jens was up, and jumped onto its chest, wrapping his legs around the Troll's waist. His left arm hung limp, he gripped the Troll by its leather tunic. Twice he smashed his forehead into the Troll Commander's face. The first caused no hurt but bloodied Jens' face as it struck the ridges of its wide armoured forehead. The second landed directly between the beasts eyes, the Troll's nose flattened even further with the pop of broken cartilage, and it fell, knocked out cold.

As the Troll fell back, Jens fell on top of it and rolled to the left. He cried out in pain as his own body weight fell on his broken forearm. Jens rolled onto his side, stunned by the pain, and panting deeply. It was not how I would choose to win a fight, but this was not a competition.

By the time the Troll Commander came to, we had its arms bound with Kevlar cuffs behind its back. The Troll was face down and three of my men stood ready, their crossbows aimed squarely at the Commander's back. Jens' left arm was in a sling and we placed the dead soldiers into black plastic body bags, their dog tags we stored in the little transparent pocket near chest location. I stopped my men from making stretchers. I intended to have the troll beast carry the bodies all the way back to camp.

The Troll Commander grunted and spat out a thick clot of blood it had coughed and sniffed into its mouth. The lads tidied its face as best they could while it was still unconscious. It had been known for a soldier to lose a finger, or even a hand, to a trolls multiple canine-fanged mouth.

"Commander Jægerblod...can you stand?" I asked.

It nodded its head and winced with the pain. "I will need assistance, Colour Sergeant." The Commander replied.

Trolls could not right themselves without the use of their arms. A good point to note, on the rare occasion you catch one alive. It took four of us to get it on its feet. We left the big troll where it lay, yards of its guts tangled through its short legs. I cut its throat to end its misery and to ensure there was no more fight left in it. I had thought it dead but I felt one of its hearts and it still pumped.

"Do you want to bury your soldier?" I asked Commander Jægerblod.

"No, leave him, his spirit is gone and it is but an empty shell; he has journeyed to Valhalla and will rest and feast with his wives as a warrior should. However, take his necklace; it belongs to his firstborn now." The Commander spoke with pride and respect. "Go, Legion Skade, and depart with pride. You fought with power and died well." Commander Jægerblod turned to me and added, "His Spirit is gone, he will make a good meal for his men and his flesh shall live on with our people. If we do not eat him, the beasts may take him, the carrion birds or dragons and his flesh shall sustain them until my people take that flesh to live thus the Allfathers circle is complete."

The Troll sounded like it was quoting some sort of bestial scripture. I nodded in understanding and removed the necklace from the dead Troll. The Commander bowed his dark-skinned head, and I put the necklace around its neck to join another three there also, I could see that each was slightly different from the other.

'Troll dog tags.' I thought. The Troll sighed and nodded.

"Have you got a cigarette?" The Commander asked politely and surprisingly softly. I do not smoke, so I beckoned one of my men forward. The Trooper produced a pack of Marlboro and he cautiously offered one up to the Troll's mouth. "It's OK soldier, I don't bite." The Commander smiled that deadly crocodile smile. Trooper Emerson placed the filter end between the Troll's thick lips and touched the end with his lighter.

"Will you remove my bonds?" Commander Jægerblod asked between puffs.

"Will you give me your word?" I asked.

"You have my word, as an officer and a gentleman that I will not attempt to escape your custody until the sun kisses Sol once more." I knew the Troll's word was as binding as its Kevlar cuffs but it did look comical with the cigarette bobbing up and down as it spoke its oath. Until dawn tomorrow, or was it, dusk today? I was not quite sure which but for the meantime, it would do for me. I indicated to Private Emerson to release him and it flexed its muscled arms. Commander Jægerblod took the cigarette between his fat fingers, and exhaled his smoke into the air.

"Well, then." It asked, "What now?"

* * *

"You will carry the body bags, and we go back to our camp."

"It will be my honour to carry your fallen comrades back to your soldiers." The Commander said. It picked up the bodies and slung them over its heavy broad shoulder without the slightest sign of effort.

"OK guys, open patrol formation, bowmen at the rear. You can smoke on the march."

The two squads fell in together and we moved off. I walked beside Commander Jægerblod, two of my men in front of us, the rest behind. The Trooper behind the Troll Commander carried its battle spear. The Para behind me carried his weapons harness.

We walked together; I could not help noticing that the Troll's hair cut in a Mohican style had a red tinge to it in the sun. All trolls have I encountered, which was not many, have coal black hair. Commander Jægerblod's skin was lighter than other troll's with a dark copper hew. I could not help but wonder if the Troll was a Mix, something most trolls reject.

Trolls are for the most part solitary beasts. They are well suited to herding goats and grall in the mountains and vast lonely places. The Mix trolls stayed isolated but they did trade with the other races. Sometimes they engaged others like the Imperial Elvin race to communicate with their trollish purebloods. MixTrolls are the untouchables, ignored and even killed by their fellow pureblood Trolls. The Mix form loose groups and settlements as outcasts. When born to a pureblood family, such Mix children taken by their mothers on the night of their birth, they are handed over to the nearest Mix troll settlement; this is one of the rare communications pureblood trolls make with their Mix cousins.

The pureblood mother turned out with the baby and the rest of her children cannot return with the Mix child. Some of the mothers choose to stay with the child especially if the child is her first. A Mix troll takes that pureblood mother to wife and at their first union; she becomes an outcast Mix troll herself. How a Mix child is conceived in a pureblood camp is a mystery we have yet been unable to discover. Perhaps an occasional rape from a Mix troll encounter but even that did not explain the regular occurrences of these children in a pureblood troll tribe.

"Forgive me for asking, Commander Jægerblod, but I could not help noticing that you do not look like the other trolls we have encountered. Are you a Mix troll?" I needed to ask to satisfy my own curiosity. Commander Jægerblod coughed over its Marlboro.

"Oh, no, no, no...I am no Mix!" It laughed in reply, its tone seemed to carry a hint of affront.

"Please forgive my insensitive question. I meant no insult." I replied in a formal troll apology to avoid the Troll Commander from feeling obliged to tear out my throat.

"None taken...." Commander Jægerblod puffed on the cigarette, popped it into his mouth, and ate the remainder. "Hmm...nice cigarettes."

I caught the hint in his remark.

"Hey, Dave, give me a packet of your smokes!" I called to Trooper Emerson, the Para that offered up the first one

Dave was one of the bowmen and a crack shot with the repeating crossbow as well as the conventional pulse and solid slug weapons back on Earth Prime. He came trotting up from the rear of the patrol, packet in hand.

"Ya takin' up smoking again Colour?" Dave smiled and spoke in his native Glaswegian accent as he proffered the packet of cigarettes.

"Ye'll be replacing them I hope!" He added.

"Why? You want the money now. What are you going to do? Buy an ice-cream?" I asked looking around at the grassland to one side and the heavy forest of tall ironwood trees on the other.

"Well maybe there'll be a couple of wee nymphs in there to sell me one." He thumbed over his shoulder at the dense forest behind him.

"Back in line!" I dismissed him with a laugh, he knew I would pay him when we got back to barracks and I would not be surprised if Dave did find an ice-cream parlour run by wood nymphs in this crazy world.

My patrol once came across a beautiful ornate wagon drawn by a snow-white team of four mulluks the size of shire ponies and with the bulk of massive bulls. Their shaggy white fur hung almost to the forest floor. A massive black and red lacquered coach on a rather sophisticated suspension system, its wheels were taller than my six foot height. It turned out to be a mobile bakery shop with solid fuel ovens and an enchanted refrigeration cabinet. The dwarves inside were selling their famous fresh baked breads and pastries to an orderly queue of elves, wood nymphs, dwarves and other assorted faerie creatures thrown in, some of which I could not recognise as they were either Mix or from a race I had yet to encounter.

I had believed that our patrol was on a forest road in the middle of nowhere until one of the woodelves pointed out that we were really in a quite large elvin forest town called Eldermeer. A gesture from the woodelf and I could clearly see the lights and building structures; either sung out of the massive ironwood trees or cleverly built into a hillside or natural mound in the gently undulating countryside.

My eyes were drawn to a doorway and little vegetable garden beside a home in a grass-covered mound; it reminded me of that famous first line from an ancient classical story, one of the many, my grandmother would read to us brothers when she was not reading her own faerie stories about her own mother.

"In a hole in the ground there lived a hobbit."

The woman of the house came around the mound from the back. She carried an armful of rhubarb-like vegetables in one hand and a wicked looking paring knife in the other. She wore a brilliant white blouse with puffed sleeves, over which she wore a snug fitting black bodice. A long apron of light blue tied over a longer full red checked skirt that stopped about six inches from the ground to show off her dainty green-skinned bare feet. She wore a yellow headscarf with her auburn hair flowing down to the middle of her narrow back and over her shoulders to fall over her ample breasts. The woman looked to be in her mid-twenties, but I knew that she might be as old as three hundred years. She was a wood nymph. I could see why human men were so attracted to these women, a hobbit she was not; but a perfectly petite five-foot of green-skinned desirable womanly beauty she was.

Chapter 4

"With my compliments Sir" I said handing the pack of cigarettes into his enormous three-fingered hand. One of those fingers was opposable; not exactly a thumb but an opposable finger all the same. Each of those fingers topped with a black talon-like fingernail, too often I witnessed trollish fingers like those gut and flay a man like a set of steak knives.

"Why thank you, Colour Sergeant. Such unwarranted kindness... May I know your name?"

I glanced at Jens, his arm slung in an olive drab-filed dressing.

"Oh, no!" The Troll laughed. "I just want the honour of knowing the name of the soldier who shows such kindness to his prisoner." The Commander smiled as he unwrapped the plastic cover from the cigarette pack. It surprised me just how dextrous a three-fingered troll could be.

"OK then" I smiled back. "I am Colour Sergeant Raine... Jon Raine."

"Jon Wayne!" The Troll laughed and pretended to draw a pistol like a Wild West gunslinger.

"No Jon Raine. R. A. I. N. E." I spelt out my last name. It was not the first nor I supposed the last time I would have to explain my name, it was cool as a kid but it became rather tedious as a grown man, especially in the Euroforce with a bunch of men that seem never to grow up.

"Oh... Jon Raine" He said again rolling the R in his almost perfect Middle English accent, with that slight sibilant lisp.

"I am sure you get teased quite a lot by your fellow soldiers." Jægerblod smiled that deadly fang-toothed smile, yet now it seemed to have familiar warmth to it.

I must admit the Troll's open and friendly attitude and its deft use of our language impressed me. His clear polished accent just did not fit his thick trollish features and ape-like body.

We walked for a time along the line that separated the forest from the savannah. The forest would give us cover but it held so many dangers and traps that our preference was the open land where we could make faster time and with our whereabouts now known, we need not force ourselves into the forest cover before we needed it. Our faerie tales of Earth Prime told many times of the dangers of wandering off the path and into the woods. Those tales on Sol were very appropriate and their warnings all too real indeed.

"Commander Jægerblod ..." I began

"Oh, please call me Uffe."

I shook my head and smiled, still amazed by the monster's accent and I could not match, in my mind, his voice to the ape like fighting machine that strode so easily beside me even though he carried both bodies.

"OK, Uffe... and please call me Jon."

"Jon." Uffe nodded rather formally.

"So forgive me... Uffe but if not a Mix troll then why do you look rather different from the other trolls, and ... well... the Kung Fu?" I asked.

"Well Jon, I am definitely no Mix. I am a little different because my tribe is from the north. I am from a land you call Denmark. I am a pure blood and actually a second cousin to our King." The Troll said with some pride. He impressed me once again and I could understand why he, as a member of the Danish troll royal family and, I supposed, a minor royal himself, held such a high rank.

"So Uffe, why is a Danish Troll so far south?" I asked.

"Now, Jon that would be telling wouldn't it." Uffe replied waggling both fingers in which he held the unlit cigarette.

Uffe put the cigarette between his lips and touched the end with his fingertip. The cigarette end glowed red and he drew in and puffed out the smoke with a satisfying sigh. I had seen such demonstrations of magic from other denizens of this world but never from a brutish troll, never before had they shown any signs that they could perform any type of magic. Only two forms of magic were associated with trolls, the first the Yari and second Trollgates. Of the trolls we encountered in the countries of Lugon, Alfheim, Catalan, Vanaheim, Temair and the Province of Denmark, we know on Earth Prime as Scotland; we only ever saw them use those two forms of magic. The Yari was not even their magic but dwarfen constructed and enchanted. Trolls traded with the dwarfen precious stones and metals for the Yaris and most of their other metal weapons. UFE intelligence believed them to be the only sentient race upon Sol without natural access to magic. As for the Trollgates, we did not know how they managed to create Trollgates and if by the use of magic, it was the only magic we thought they possessed. Uffe's demonstration, behaviour and demeanour rapidly changed my mind about these brutish trolls. This would give me a lot of kudos with the intelligence boys. I was always aiming for an intelligence job.

"Now that was impressive." I remarked.

"Oh it is such a small thing, well within my small ability. I am a keen student of magic; in fact, I am a student of many subjects. I love magic and the study of peoples and their various ways, the races of my world and the people of yours."

"I must say that I have never seen trollish magic."

"It is saxicoline magic, the magic of rocks and earth and not too common among those tribes of the south. They have forgotten the old ways." Uffe lamented.

"Are you here to act as a shaman or a battlepriest then?" I asked.

"I could say yes but that would not be the truth, so I will say nothing. I do however act as a doctor amongst the tribes here."

"A doctor?" I asked "How so? Do you employ herbs or are you some sort of surgeon?"

"No. I sing the Solsong."

"I'm sorry Comman ... Uffe... I have never heard of the Solsong. Is it like how the elvin sing the trees and the wood?"

"It is closely related to the elvin song." The troll carefully considered his thoughts. "All magic is related to all other magic. The glue holds our world together. The Solsong is the song of growth and rebirth."

We walked on for a short while in the hot sun, now well above the horizon our long cold night of work in the forest, almost forgotten in the memory of the rude and violent raid in the early hours of the morning.

Uffe suddenly stopped and turned to me. "Shall I demonstrate the Solsong, Jon?" He asked as if suddenly remembering our recent conversation. I looked askance, suspicious of the offer.

"You have my word, do you not?" He stated.

I did have his word to which I knew bound him as surely as the Kevlar cuffs once did. I had a sudden thought.

"Just to be clear Commander, you did mean dawn tomorrow morning and not dawn this morning or dusk today?" As I spoke the question, the men about me drew their swords in sudden doubt. The bowmen turned their loaded weapons towards the troll.

"Please gentlemen, I did mean the sunrise tomorrow. All troll pledges end at dawn. You should know that." Uffe scolded as he gestured with his powerful overlong arms for the men to lower their weapons. I nodded and gestured with open palm down, the sign to the rest of the patrol to lower their arms.

"Just checking Commander." I apologised.

"Come, let me demonstrate." The Troll Commander said as he gently laid down both body bags.

A couple of strides and Uffe moved over to a small group of flowering Dogrose plants.

"How very appropriate." He commented cryptically and gestured for me to come closer. I made the sign with my fist for the patrol to take cover and with my hand flat; I signed the bowmen to take cover within the tree line but to watch the Troll.

"Watch." Uffe spoke as he squatted next to the small bush. He touched his black talon-like fingernail into the mouth of one of the flowers then into another to pollinate it. Cupping his leathery hands around the flower, the size of a rose but tiny in those big claw like hands, Uffe began to hum from deep within his throat almost like a growl. Throwing his head back, the deep growling hum became a varying clear note, in a deep rich baritone. The flower's seed-sack grew full and became ripe. Uffe gently eased the seeds from the ovaries into his hands and motioned to my water bottle. I slipped the bottle out and poured a little into his cupped hand. As he continued his Solsong, he dropped the seeds into the pooled water in his broad hand and then cupped his other hand over the top, he held it there for a moment before he uncovered them again, the seeds had sprouted their first tiny primitive roots and leaves.

Uffe pushed his fingers into the ground and placed the seeds into the indentations, gently pressing the soil around the planted sprouts leaving the primary leaves exposed. He placed his hands palms down on the ground either side of the shoots, his song became deeper, stronger. I could feel the tingle of magic in the air; it made the fine hairs on my bare forearms stand on end like static electricity wafting over them.

Through the sensation of the hairs on my arms, I could feel the magic gather towards Uffe. More leaves appeared and like a time delay film. The six plants sprouted branches and in a few moments, there appeared another six flowering Dogrose bushes almost identical to the original parent plant. I had witnessed this type of magic used by the elvin builders when they sung and shaped their habitats into the massive Ironwood trees that dwarfed our own Redwoods of Earth Prime. Even though these were small flower bushes, it was no less amazing.

"That was truly outstanding Uffe!" I said as I touched the leaves and flowers, they certainly felt like the real thing.

"It was of little import." Uffe replied.

"Well I think it was important to these flowers!" I commented as I examined the fully-grown bushes. "So how does this power act as a medical resource to the trolls?" I asked, thinking that they force-grew medical plants and herbs.

"So let me demonstrate something a little more impressive." Uffe suggested. "My opponent in combat, Jens Yde I believe?"

I called Jens over from the trees where he was checking the bowmen's positions.

"Jenser, I think the Commander wants to treat your injury."

Walking back from the tree line, Jens looked doubtful. "I suppose it can't hurt to try ... can it?" he asked in second thought.

I looked to Uffe.

"I cannot promise there will be no discomfort but it will be less pain than you are in right now." Uffe advised, acting the caring and compassionate monster.

"Your call, Jenser." I said leaving the decision up to him, it was, after all, his arm.

Jens hunkered down and between the both of them; they eased the broken arm out of the sling into Uffe's hands. Uffe handled Jens arm so gently with hands I knew could gut and disembowel a man without the need of a weapon.

Jens looked up at me; I nodded my support, my hand casually rested on the handle of my tanto. I noticed that Jens did the same with his good arm. Uffe noticed too, he gently shook his head. I felt a little embarrassed, like a scolded child; I could see that Jens sensed the same.

"I should not do this, as you defeated me without honour." Uffe commented. We could see that it was a gentle tease. The troll laughed softly and it sounded like a cornered cat hissing before it strikes.

Jens moved back slightly, not sure what would happen.

"Maybe next time, Sir." Jens replied.

"Yes, I will look forward to killing you with honour. You will make a fine meal!"

I could see that Jens tensed. He wanted to pull his arm away. I would not blame him if he did.

"Settle, Corporal Jens Yde. Today is not your day to die." Uffe stated flatly and went back to his rhythmic humming. Jens looked up at my face and I saw something I had never seen before. Fear on Jens Yde's face.

Uffe leaned his head back and continued that Solsong. It felt stronger this time, the long savannah grasses waved around us; moving as if in a gentle breeze yet the air around us remained still. Again, I could feel the tingle of magic in the air, only much stronger now. I noticed the savannah grasses move as if blown towards us, forming a perfect circle of flattened grasses. The image of crop circles came to mind.

Between Uffe's deep musical humming, he said. "Yes, crop circles."

I did not realise I had spoken out loud, as a matter of fact I was sure I had not spoken at all... almost!

Jens shivered as if standing under a cold shower and I saw unusual movement under the flesh of his arm, his bones moved and the muscles realigned themselves. Uffe stood from his squatting position and Jens followed him to his feet. Uffe took both of Jens hands into his own and said.

"Now let us even those arms up." Every bit the caring doctor, I smiled thinking of the Troll Commander as a Euro Health Service doctor in a GP surgery scaring the shit out of his patients.

Uffe took a deep breath, his head rolled back and he began that song again, this time a different pitch, a different tune. Jens' arms flexed as the muscles moved of their own volition, we all watched fascinated, the muscles in his upper arms growing like inflating balloons. His upper arms grew in girth by at least four inches while his forearms grew in proportion to match his upper arms. The veins in Jens arms bulged and we saw the blood within visibly pump through them. Jens chest expanded as if he took a deep breath but there was no intake of air and I knew that his upper body muscles expanded as well.

Uffe let Jens hands go.

"Now I think you may stand a fair chance in combat Corporal Jens Yde. I will look forward to our contest." Uffe smiled if you could call it a smile. Jens flexed his muscles and winced a little.

"They will be a little sore for a couple of days. What is it you humans say? No pain no gain!" Uffe laughed, this time his laugh sounded like a battle roar and I wondered if their battle roars were actually troll laughter.

Jens nodded startled thanks, flexed his arms again and smiled broadly.

Denny, one of the troopers called out.

"Hey, Commander! Could you do that for me?" He pointed to his groin.

"I'm sorry little man but even the strongest magic has certain limits." Uffe replied in jest. The remark gained a nudge in Denny's ribs from the others and laughs all around. I had to frown, I was the Colour Sergeant and the Patrol Commander but I must admit, I was laughing inside.

Jens struck a muscled pose and said.

"Look, Colour ...I'll be back!" he laughed in an Austrian accent, imitating an action hero from the old 2D movies we often watched together.

Jens drew his katana and went through one of the practice katas. Our katas are a series of choreographed moves that enable us to practice our martial arts either alone or in formation. I could see from his confident fluid movements the extra muscle mass was not restricting his actions in any way, Jens smiled as he appreciated the new found strength in his new pumped arms and chest.

When finished, he sheathed his katana with the ease and familiarity of a master swordsman.

"Bravo!" Uffe called and politely clapped his claw-like hands. "Shall we continue our walk?" He asked, as if out on a Sunday afternoon stroll. The troll had already shouldered both body bags. I made a series of hand gestures and my men fell into open patrol formation once more. At a forced march we set out to make it back to the main party, I reckoned it would take us about 20 to 30 minutes at the pace I set.

Commander Jægerblod did not seem to mind the hard pace even though he was carrying both bodies. I could see the target balloon through the trees and the red smoke from the main camp. The balloon was a call for air support for a 'Casevac' of the casualties of the attack in the early hours. Air support would fly in reinforcements and supplies and take out the wounded. The Drop Boxes we worked all night to prepare for came with the first of the support dragons.

Chapter 5

With a deep whooshing, like the ripping apart of the air, the sound of the support dragons' wings came over the trees, even though we could not yet see the massive beast. The trees were too dense for a clear view; we knew that Air Support had come in forest side. A shadow fell upon us blocking the sun; the support dragon swooped around and came over from the trees to catch the thermals of warm rising air from the savannah around us. No matter how many times I saw a support dragon, I could not feel anything but awe at the sheer physical size and the fact that it flew at all.

The support dragon arched over the savannah and leaned to the side to come around, we could see the pilot cabin strapped forward of the front pair of wings, it was a field grey and emblazoned with RAF roundel insignia. The cabin looked like one of those elephant platforms seen on elephants in India, only this one could hold twenty men with ease. The dragon was fully inflated, it carried a full load, and its bulk dwarfed a zeppelin balloon. The burden it held under its red and green striped belly by its four claws was a massive grey metal container with a set of doors that opened onto a ramp, the container as big as an old airliner fuselage. The dragon effortlessly clutched it by the great handles at each corner. On the ramp stood soldiers in their Drop Suits, they made ready to jump down through the trees below them.

The front observers seated at the nape of the dragons long neck signalled down to ask if I required support, they spotted the troll with us. I signalled back an "All Clear" and the behemoth of the sky sailed over us. We could feel the down thrust and hear the deafening whooshing from both pairs of massive wings, reaching out like a giant bat. The wings membranes blocked the sun as it passed over us once more and we could see the mesh of veins through the backlit wings.

Although the dragon had an altitude of around 250 feet, it looked uncomfortably close to us; this beast was the largest of the giants of the sky. On this world, they acted as our heavy cruiser and air support ships. The pilot ordered the dragon to descend to treetop level. We knew this from a bellowing roar from the dragon. It raised its head and expelled the buoyancy gasses from its stomachs and out through its mouth. With a sharp snap of its jaws, it caused a piezoelectric spark that ignited the gasses rushing at high pressure, out of its throat. The flames burst into the air in wide licks; we could feel the heat from our position on the ground. This flame, or 'Dragons Breath', as the Nats called it was the hottest flame known in this world and nothing, as far as we knew, could withstand its penetrating power. Nats was military slang, short for natives, small and annoying; we used the word to describe Sol's residents when we could not determine to which fae race they belonged. The dragons breath shot from the dragon's diamond shaped head atop its long sinuous neck; the forward observer could wield this discharge as a weapon using cables to direct the dragon to narrow or widen the flame burst as was necessary. When the required amount of gasses were expelled the pilot achieved whatever altitude was required, the excess skin along the sides of the dragon would naturally fold into creases. The dragon would lose its bulbous shape for a sleeker profile. Both pairs of wings allowed for an almost vertical take-off and landing, the beast could manipulate its wings in a circular motion to sustain a fixed position in the air. One of the notable oddities about the pilots was that they were all women, the support dragons all insisted on it.

  We were nearing our main camp and Paras were dropping in standard formation from the back of the cargo hold. The support dragon belched more flaming buoyancy, and then levelled off at about 200 feet, almost touching the top of the tree canopy. The trees in our immediate area were relatively young at around four hundred years old; they had not reached their full height of 500 feet or more. The Paras crashed through the trees in their drop suits, armoured exoskeletons; their antigravity units slowed their descent, on Sol they were not as efficient as they were in our own universe but we were grateful that they worked at all.

Our descent suits were used for all drops, from low level like this one, to atmospheric re-entry from orbital troop ships in our own universe. On Sol, physics did not work in quite the same way. Here it was possible to use conscious thought to manipulate physical objects, and through this use, with what the Nats called magic, they could by various degrees of expertise, and natural ability, perform various feats impossible in our universe.

Our standard issue drop suits were only thirty percent effective; instead of lightly touching down, we would hit the ground with a bone jarring crash. The REME boys back on Earth Prime came up with a solution for the drop suits that utilized the old style Para roll from the days of parachutes and air resistant descent. They programmed the Drop Suits to make such a roll when they hit the ground and depending on whether we were in combat mode or not, the suits would roll out onto our feet with weapons drawn if the situation warranted it.

Once, during early development of the drop protocols, one of the Paras in the team rolled out and a glitch in the program caused the soldier to wipe out a complete section of combat simbots before he could take manual control of the suit.

The soldiers jumped out of the cargo hold and crashed through the tree branches without harm. We could hear the snapping of branches as the armoured drop suits ripped through the canopy even from as far away as we were.

We entered the forest as the last of the wounded ascended on stretchers, hoisted up by the aircrew using a clever device that used the power of the beating dragon wings to winch the ropes up. One aircrew would sit in the harness beside the stretcher to control the assent to the Support Dragon above.

The patrol broke formation on my command to assist with the dropped supplies. All supplies were stored in the standard Drop Boxes, which could be slotted together to form a more permanent set of buildings for this forward outpost. This area we prepared to be established as a permanent forward military outpost.

I walked into camp beside Commander Jægerblod to locate and report to our OC C Company, Major Morgan. I found him in the main command tent. The Major came out of the tent when he spotted the troll, head and shoulders above all the other personnel. I came to attention and saluted. The Major returned the salute and stared at the troll.

"I said one brick, Colour." Major Morgan commented as he walked around Commander Jægerblod.

"Sir... against two trolls!" I protested, knowing that I had detailed the second squad without Major Morgan's specific orders.

"Good call, Colour. I would have charged you if you hadn't brought back a live one, even if it is a baby." He said as he continued to study the prisoner.

"Yes sir, I mean no sir. This one's fully grown." I explained.

"Indeed." The Major replied as he noticed the skull insignia on the Commander's right shoulder.

I handed the Major the diplomatic pouch Uffe carried when we captured him. The Major gave it a cursory glance. It was sealed and we had no authority to open it.

"I want an elvin open order for that pouch." He demanded and handed the pouch to Lance Corporal Mills.

"Sir!" Lance Corporal Mills snapped his reply and hurried off to make the signal.

"Is he a Mix?" Major Morgan asked, Uffe growled.

"No Sir. He's from Denmark."

Major Morgan saluted the troll. "Major Morgan 4th Parachute regiment, the Dragon Riders."

"I see." Commander Jægerblod grunted roughly, as a troll would, he looked up through the trees at the support dragon that shadowed us. The dragon sucked in air, it heaved and pumped its great wings to gain height, the downward push of those leathery wings brushed the treetop canopy, it slowly moved away and dappled sunlight fell on our camp once more.

Commander Jægerblod stood taller and struck his chest to return the salute. "Commander Uffe Jægerblod ..." He replied. Major Morgan waited.

"Commander of the 10th Legion." I volunteered.

"10th Legion? ... There are no more than eight trollish legions," The Major stated, both to the Troll Commander and to me.

Commander Jægerblod glanced at me sidelong and cold, I guessed he was upset and disappointed, I had volunteered information that I think he did not want divulged. He had stated his command to me in the heat of combat and now it was something I believed he did not want to disclose.

Major Morgan snapped the skull insignia from the Commander's shoulder. Jægerblod reacted by reflex, he stepped away and raised his arms in defence. Corporal Will Hallsworth moved between them.

"Stand still you filthy animal!" he shouted and swung a roundhouse kick at Jægerblod's head. The commander smoothly blocked the kick, his arm shot out and his talon like fingers circled the Corporal's neck.

"No Commander! Release!" I shouted and started forward to intervene.

"Back off, Colour. He is my prisoner!" the Major ordered.

"No!" I shouted. I could see Jægerblod's next move. The troll smiled all teeth and tusks, his word fulfilled; he was no longer in my custody. I heard the sickening crack in the Corporal's neck, his head jerked violently sideways. Commander Jægerblod dropped the lifeless body to the ground.

Swords flashed with metallic scrapes, drawn from the surrounding soldiers' scabbards, my sword was in my hand. Commander Jægerblod froze; the hub of a wheel of deadly blades; he knew it and stood as motionless as a statue; right arm still extended, the two body bags on his left shoulder.

"He had given me his word Sir!" I protested. The Major understood all too late.

"I see." He replied almost in apology. "Kill the beast." The major ordered and turned his back. The men moved to make the kill.

"No!" I shouted. Why I shouted that, I never quite worked out. "Please Major, a moment."

Major Morgan turned to me. "Thirty seconds. Speak."

"Sir, with all due respect, this is no ordinary troll." I started.

"You're damn right it is no ordinary troll. It just murdered one of my corporals!"

"Sir. The troll is from Denmark, we have never yet encountered a troll form Denmark." I tried to reason with the OC.

"I met a troll from Denmark once. It was in a museum square in the city of Vejen, it was made of stone and that was close enough for me." Major Morgan growled, now he sounded like a troll.

"Sir this one is a high-ranking officer and carrying a diplomatic pouch. We need to at least interrogate it." I hoped my rant had reached the angry Major's reasoning.

The Major stood there for a moment deciding whether to execute the troll or give heed to my request.

"I see..." The major replied. I knew I had gotten through to him. Another day and he would have killed Uffe himself.

Two field medics removed Corporal Will Hallsworths body for exit interview. Major Morgan ordered the other two bodies removed for interview as well. Commander Jægerblod laid the bodies to the ground with a surprising gentle respect. We who surrounded him, eased a little with his demonstration of reverence.

"Will you give me your oath word Commander?" The Major asked. The commander offered no reply.

"Jægerblod?" Major Morgan demanded, almost a shout. I could see he was considering the execution still. Uffe raised his chin in trollish defiance.

"I see." Morgan sighed. "So... It is the 10th Legion is it?"

"Yes... I am a commander of the 10th Legion." Jægerblod replied in the guttural accent of the common troll.

"Sir! The commander speaks the King's Catholic English with ease." I spoke out, not as guilty as I had felt when I revealed his military identity. I had to think of something, anything that would keep Uffe alive for the next few moments. We were not yet officially at war with the trollish nations but we may as well have been and he was the enemy after all.

"What is the location and strength of this 10th Legion?" Morgan demanded. The commander made no reply.

"He's a Danish troll Sir." I repeated my statement.

Uffe did not look at me this time, I think he understood my situation and I was sure that if it had been reversed and I was his prisoner he would be half way through eating me by now.

"So... From the north ... and the strength of your Legion?" Morgan asked again.

"Very strong." The Commander grunted.

"No, I mean the number of men in your Legion?"

Jægerblod was silent for a moment. I thought he would refuse to reply again.

The eight trollish legions varied in size. I did not know if a legion was a loose description for all the soldiers in a given clan or if there was, a fixed number and some were under or over strength. For the most part, we estimated the largest legion to be just over three thousand strong and the smallest numbered between seven and eight hundred.

"Five hundred." The Commander grunted.

The Captain laughed. "No wonder we haven't heard of the 10th Legion." The rest of the soldiers laughed as well.

"Thousand." The Commander continued.

"Five thousand?" The Major asked as he sobered to the Commanders claim.

"No." Uffe replied softly and we all relaxed.

"Five hundred thousand." He finished.

There was silence in the group of soldiers that surrounded the troll; everyone had heard Uffe's guttural reply.

"And the 9th Legion?" The Major asked almost reflectively.

"They outnumber us two to one." Commander Jægerblod spoke softly but still in that thick trollish brogue.

One and a half million trolls!" The Major whispered incredulous. Commander Jægerblod simply nodded. Major Morgan turned to me and spoke.

"He's your prisoner, Colour Raine."

Uffe nodded agreement and the men lowered their weapons.

"Take him to DQ12. How long is his word for Colour?"

"Until dawn, Sir." I replied.

"OK. No restraints necessary until dawn but I want the guard doubled around DQ12. In addition, I want that damn diplomatic pouch opened, now! There is another drop in an hour and I will signal for an Intelligence Cell and Psy Signals to attend. That will be all, Colour." Major Morgan dismissed us. We saluted each other, including Uffe with that trollish strike of his closed fist to his chest.

Chapter 6

"Commander Jægerblod, the Colour Sergeant will show you to your quarters." The Major nodded to the troll and disappeared back into the command tent.

Uffe was safe, at least for the next few hours, I thought with quiet relief. I had to catch myself. Why should I care what happens to him? The Troll Commander and I made our way across camp and I knew that the Major had gone back into the tent to make ready to interview the three dead soldiers. Their spirits still tied to their physical bodies they would give us valuable local intelligence before their full release in a few hours' time.

The spooky spirit thing was one of those revelations that shook the religions of Earth Prime and those of the belief that death was the final moment and no life existed beyond. It had been only a few months after the first government sponsored expeditions that they found empirical evidence of necromancy as the sorcerers of old Earth Prime like to call it. Now you could not talk to your long dead granny or great uncle, but communication with what they called earth bound spirits was possible using shamans of various kinds. Most of them were fraudsters and carnival hustlers even here on Sol; the whole thing was dismissed quickly as local superstition while various governmental shadow organisations set up secret research centres on Sol. It stayed that way until a French government official of some note and reputation made the revelation public that he, with some mediumistic talent, had been able to speak to the recent dead. The French state government attempted to smother the revelation and keep it secret, they did everything including threatening the life of the French ambassador to keep it secret.

Ambassador Kouchner took sanctuary with the Elvin government and supported by the British and Austrian state governments, he came out with his world-shaking evidence.

Most of the facts we already knew, woven amongst the folklore and legends of most Earth Prime cultures.

Such as the spirit will hang around the body for a few hours and sometimes up to a few days, depending on the type of death, the weather conditions, and whether or not the local people or the local fauna ate the cadaver. Sometimes the astral umbilical cord would not break but fix itself to some physical object or person, tying the spirit to that person, place or object. For some spirits the ties of unfinished business were so strong that it would cause the un-tethered spirit to remain earth bound until it felt that the business was either complete or over time became so diminished in importance to allow the spirit to move on.

There were rare occasions where the released spirit became earthbound and would remain around for years or even millennia. Such a spirit, usually one with some magical ability, would increase in power and ability, becoming something of a minor deity. With its increased power, the spirit would be able to strengthen its earthbound ties and eventually affect the physical world. Some that usually came from higher cast families or royal blood would obtain followers and believers and this in turn would strengthen its earthbound ties. With increased power, the spirit would be able to possess the bodies of its followers and even the weak spirited non-believers.

Still, it was not a perfect science yet and we had a long way to go before our necromancers would be as good as the local fae shamans, wizards and necromancers. The Celtic corners of Britain and the Irish states produced quite a number of talented necromancers who found themselves drafted into the military and schooled in the Psy Signals Academy of New Exeter, a large settlement city, built up around one of the larger British portals.

We had two of these Psy Signals Corps "Ghost Whisperers" attached to C Company of the 4th Parachute regiment; the first was an ignorant individual. In his late twenties, he was French. Now the French are quite dapper dressers, but this person shamed the French nation, he was a tubby, lazy bag of lard, I could not stand the sight of him. Lieutenant Jaquette wore the honorary rank of lieutenant and he insisted on wearing the unearned wings and parachute badge of the Dragon Riders. The fool would insist on being saluted by all subordinate ranks even in the field in full view of the enemy and would report anyone who would fail to do so. This pompous bag of lard, who was Lieutenant Jaquette, was treated by everyone in the Regiment with the contempt he deserved.

Now the other "Ghost Whisperer", as we like to call them, was the complete opposite; she was a tall brown-haired woman, slim but buxom with a stunningly beautiful face, full lips and flawless skin, she had vivid green eyes and a way of looking at you that seemed to pierce right into your very soul. Lieutenant Amanda Stewart's ample breasts and wide shoulders tapered down to a narrow back and a flat well defined stomach, which eased out to what the dwarfen called child bearing hips. She had long shapely legs unfortunately usually hidden under issue denims and high leg combat boots; however, Amanda made even the dowdy issue uniform look sexy. She wore the beret of the 4th Parachute Regiment but she wore the badge of the Royal Corps of Signals, as that was the mother corps of the New Exeter Academy. Amanda was equal in beauty and elegance to the most attractive fae, elf or nymph. Her natural good nature made her very popular in the elvin military clubs and lesser courts of the local nobility. Lieutenant Amanda Stewart was our Ghost Whisperer, she had been a law student in her final year in Leeds University when she tested positive for necromancy.

I walked with my humongous prisoner through the busy camp, everyone that came into sight stopped what they were doing and stared at the troll strolling with its escort through their midst.

"Good morning and how do you do?" Uffe threw greetings out in his flawless English. Nobody thought to pick his or her jaw off the floor to answer him.

"Am I not saying it right?" Uffe whispered to me.

"No, Commander, you are doing just fine." I replied with a wry smile. In spite of myself, I could not help but like this seven-foot killing machine.

On our journey to DQ12, we spotted Amanda walking the other way; she had just crawled out of her bivi tent in green vest, combats and high leg boots. Like the rest of us, except for Lieutenant Jaquette, Lieutenant Stewart pulled her weight cutting and pulling brush through the hot day and the cold night.

She shook back her long auburn hair and reached her arms over her head to tie it back in a ponytail. Her breasts strained against her vest and her eyes went wide at the sight of the troll casually strolling along beside me.

I saluted her.

"'Morning Ma'am." I smiled; I could not help but glance down at her perfectly proportioned body. My eyes were not the only eyes that noticed the Lieutenant's obvious charms.

Lieutenant Stewart smiled back at me but Commander Jægerblod's lusty animal growl wiped that smile off her face.

"Colour." She nodded in formal greeting and pulled on her beret as she quickened her pace away from us. Amanda glanced over her shoulder to see us looking after her and she broke in to a trot, eager to distance herself from Uffe's trollish attentions.

Commander Jægerblod and I glanced at each other and laughed.

"Is that your woman?" He asked.

"I wish!" I replied. Long ago, almost in another life, I once made overtures as had nearly every other officer and enlisted man, but all felt the sting of her rejection. Some bad-minded individuals circulated the rumours that Amanda was lesbian, which attracted the attentions of a few elvin women and wood nymphs. Some of the female service personnel around various camps tried their luck but they were also rebutted which led to Lieutenant Stewart earning the nickname of the Ice Queen, it was rather an unfortunate name as it did not match her warm and open personality.

"Will you not take her? Is she sick?" Uffe inquired.

"No Uffe, she is an officer and I am not. It is strictly forbidden." I replied with the only simple explanation that came to mind. We continued to walk across the camp towards DQ12.

"Who is going to know between her sheets?" Uffe commented a question to me or a comment to himself, I did not know, I answered it anyway.

"I would." I replied, although in spite of myself I did not know why I had responded with that answer, as it was a blatant and transparent lie.

"Very honourable, Jon." Uffe said. "I have learned some very interesting things as your prisoner. I will consider deeply your treatment of me and the kindness and respect you have shown me this day." The comment made me feel a little better about my reply. Honourable? ... Well I suppose so, at times I could be a real Saint Teresa of Calcutta.

"Tell me Jon. If we trolls are the barbaric ones then why do you let your women fight as the elvin do? We do not let our women fight." Uffe pointed out.

I have never thought about it. It had been many generations ago that women did not have equal standing in the armed forces but it was so long ago that it is all but forgotten now.

"They are our equals. Everyone that joins the Euroforce is a volunteer and when they join they are expected to perform the same as men." I replied to Uffe's question.

"How barbaric." Uffe commented almost to himself.

The guards detailed to DQ12 gathered themselves from their resting places in the shadows of the trees near the armoured door to the Box. I was pleased to see that they were alert, in separate positions and had their crossbows ported and arrows notched. They hefted their weapons, clearly unsure of the seven-foot tall troll casually walking towards them; their reactions sated by my presence beside the massive beast.

"Peter... Bobby..." I hailed as we approached.

"Colour?" Peter replied, clearly unsure as to how to react within killing distance of a troll, other than to kill it.

"Lads, let me introduce Commander Jægerblod of the 10th Legion."

The soldiers stood a little taller, their training demanded respect for a senior officer yet their fingers never left their triggers.

"Sir!" Bobby greeted the troll, acknowledging Jægerblod's senior rank albeit grudgingly.

"Commander Jægerblod will be Major Morgan's guest and my prisoner until the Int Cell takes him tomorrow. They'll be bringing the Provost and you make sure the Commander is suitably restrained when you hand him over."

"Yes Colour! This way ... Umm... Sir." Peter ordered and motioned to the secure Melentum door of DQ12.

Peter drew back the sturdy bolts top and bottom, undid the secure clasp in the centre and swung the door outwards.

Chapter 7

The inside of DQ12 was surprisingly spacious. All Drop Boxes measured 4 meters each way and although called a Box, this DQ12 was actually two Boxes slotted together so it went back eight meters. To one side was a set of three 10-foot bunk beds, long enough for the tallest troll and a full 1.5 meters wide. The back Box contained a toilet, shower, a mini kitchen and a small fold away writing desk. On the opposite wall to the bunk beds, there was a wall mounted fold up table. The top two beds could be folded away to allow the bottom bunk to be used as a seat to sit on when using the table. The Boxes had a potbellied stove in one corner for heat and an air conditioner that worked very well on Sol and much appreciated in the heat of these summer days.

"He's a bit small for a troll." Peter remarked from the doorway as Uffe inspected his temporary accommodation.

"A very nice cave, Colour Sergeant." Uffe commented in his Middle English accent, Peter and Bobby shared the same astounded look as those in the camp through which we had just wandered. Uffe regarded them with the side of his eye and I could see that he was amused at their reaction.

"I am a Jotunn from Jotunheimr far to the north east. You may call me a troll as we have the same First Mother. I am considered rather tall by my people, if somewhat slight of build." Uffe explained, his bulk filling the rear box.

"A very fine cave indeed." Uffe remarked as he tried the hot water taps and switched on and off the lights repeatedly with a self-satisfied grunt of pleasure.

The drop boxes were manufactured for the military by a company in a city called Exeter in the Euro State of England. Their main business used to be building modular student accommodation for universities until the economic war of 2102 that unified Europe, and our special relationship with the USA came to an irrevocable end. The UFE gained the technology to economically put man into space. Not only was the technology economic it was reusable and the Eurostella crafts became the first space faring crafts of the United Federation of Europe. The technology was a gift from our new allies in the New Soviet Block. The UFE were so grateful that they allowed the New Soviet Block entry into the Eurovision Song Contests.

The company applied their building techniques on the first UFE civil mining colonies on the moon, quickly followed by the Martian colonies, and further to Ganymede. After the first failed terra-forming efforts of Venus, they built an orbital factory near the moon of Earth Prime; they were able to use the vast metallurgic resources to manufacture the buildings for Venus. One of their finest developments was Melentum; an alloy whose composite substances, mined from the moon and smelted in zero gravity of space, together formed a substance lighter and stronger than steel or any of the advanced plastics known to man. They benefited from these weightless manufacturing techniques of space and they invested heavily in acquiring two fully articulated Candarm's, the Canadian arm famously used on the first primitive American space shuttles. After great success with the rich mineral deposits found on the Moon, better and more specialised habitats were launched towards Venus where they became the first cities of that planet. Their Research and Development team had come up with some fantastic designs, and their armoured drop cubes found great success on Sol as military and civilian accommodation that could withstand the fiercest of trollish or dinosaur attack.

A new large permanent portal formed just outside Exeter from which they supplied all the British, Canadian and Soviet interests in the Europa provinces of Sol.

The logistics to supply Europa from Avalon the army easily achieved, the stretch of fresh water sea that separated Avalon from Europa was a shallow 0.3km channel of water that separated New Dover from Nouveau Calais; a sturdy wide wooden bridge built by the elvin spanned that narrow stretch of sea. A multi-million euro project to span the Europa Channel with a concrete and metal suspension bridge had been underway now for the past 15 years and the completion neared its end.

The Irish were extremely put out when they found that their landmass they named Temair, was attached to England at the Cornish and Yorkshire coasts. The landmass bordered a massive freshwater lake named Avon. None of the other landmasses was that much different except of course for Australia.

I left Commander Jægerblod in the capable hands of the guards after watching them bolt the door shut securing the seal to DQ12. I strolled through the camp and I was always impressed at the speed at which the REME lads transformed the hitherto makeshift bivi camp into a permanent fortress. Elvin engineers were singing the biggest standing trees into elegant living accommodation and storerooms, while our own engineers assembled and linked drop boxes into offices and barracks. Our own squads that toiled yesterday and last night to prepare the ground got customary first preference and they quickly evacuated their present bivouacs into their allocated drop box barracks.

I debriefed with my men under Company Sergeant Major Collis. We had a prayer for our fallen comrades. There were few unbelievers now after the revelations of life after death. Lieutenant Stewart relayed their last reports to us, as was military custom so that we would be the first to hear our friends and brothers last reports.

Jake Henson

Jake was the lance corporal bowman who had taken the lance in the neck. His report was the strangest report of all three of the recent dead. At first, he gave the usual intelligence he had gathered as a disembodied spirit, locations of trollish and gnomish forces and locations of any interesting mineral deposits and if there were any adverse or unfamiliar magics being manipulated in the region. When the light formed for Jake to take him away from the physical world, he gave a running commentary of his journey through the tunnel of light. Usually communication ends as the spirit enters the tunnel, but for Jake, he was able to sustain communications all the way through that journey.

Only five times in our histories in Sol did this happen and Jake would go down in those history books as the sixth such account.

The communications sustained through the tunnel of light only occurred between people of the closest spiritual bond, soul mates. All recorded cases were between a male spirit and a female living subject usually the spirit's wife, mother or daughter. The female had to be Psy positive with advanced and fully developed ability.

I later learned that Jake and Lieutenant Stewart regularly shared a sleeping bag and did so the night before the troll attack. So much for the lesbian Ice Queen, unknown to her she bore his child when she read his report, she read it professionally yet we noticed and chose to ignore the hint of sadness and a stifled sob here and there, which she vainly attempted to disguise with a cough. I kept record of that account, as it was such a rarity and something I felt I would investigate... sometime.

After the usual local intelligence report, it went something like this:

"... Tell dad I love him and I know that the hardest thing a father can do is bury his own son. Tell him I am going on an extended mission and one day I promise to report back to him.

I see the light... The light is forming now ... Are you still receiving? Over."

"Yes. Over."

"I am moving into the light ... walking ... walking ... no ground below but I can feel solid footing. A tunnel ... I am in a tunnel ... I am walking but I feel that I am moving forward with great speed. ... Sensations, something like orbital acceleration but no G force. Receiving. Over."

"Yes! Over."

"Holy crap, you're still receiving, Amanda! Over."

"Yes... Yes clear, go on Jake. Over."

"The light before me is dissipating; I am nearing the end of the tunnel. People… many people ... Mum? I can see my mother! She is standing with others. I ... I think they are my family. She is standing beside two men. Everyone is in white; the men who are standing with my mother seem to be wearing white hats of sorts, they are round but made of linen or cotton. There are squares of green tied about their waists, the colour stands in vivid contrast to the bright white clothing.

"I need to move before two other men, one is a big guy, as big as a troll, maybe taller but white hair and bronze skin, very powerful, big powerful arms. He looks like a bloody Greek god. The other is normal A1 north European male, looks like a dwarf beside the big guy also white hair, very white hair. Receiving. Over."

"Yes ... Yes receiving Jake. Go on. Over."

"Well I'll be damned! On the other hand, maybe not! I'm gonna be famous after all! I have to move to stand before the smaller guy. Over."

"How do you know that, Jake? Has anyone spoken to you at all? Over"

"No, no-one is speaking. I don't know how I know, I just know. He is extending his hand, reaching out to shake hands. Friendly, he is smiling; no aggression ... There is a door behind him. No wait, not a door, gates, tall solid gates. I try to shake hands … I cannot... Don't know why ... I am trying to shake hands but I cannot. I know I must, but something is preventing me from doing so. I am confused, a little frightened. The man and the big guy are smiling, I feel reassured. The big guy points to my family. I know I must go to them, to my mother and the other people, some wear the green, and others do not. Mum has her arms out, she is laughing, others are laughing to. They are happy to see me. Happy… laughing. Receiving. Over"

"Yes. Over."

"Receiving? Over."

"Yes Jake. All clear, go on. Over."
"Oh my God! I can remember now. It is all becoming clear. The veil is lifting…Over."
"What do you mean? Over.
"Are you receiving me? Over."
"Yes. Clear, go on. Over."
"No reply ... I have no reply ... I am ending transmission ... I love ..."
End of report.

* * *

Jens located our drop box accommodations and I had a much appreciated shit, shower and shave. Our company was still under active duty so I carried my swords strapped to a fresh clean uniform. On Sol, I carried both my blades off duty as well but that was my prerogative.

Back in my room I flaked out for a few hours to catch up on some well-earned sleep, my alarm went off at17h00. I found the new sergeant's mess. For the first time in three weeks, I had a properly cooked meal. Steak and two veg, one of which I knew was peas; the other looked like lime green carrots. There were potatoes and gravy, followed by jam sponge and custard, it tasted like a banquet compared to the freeze-dried ration muck they gave us to eat on patrol. I did however like the boiled sweets and the English chocolate that came in the 24-hour ration packs.

I drew a mug of freshly ground coffee and went out to the junior rank's mess next door where Jens and a few of the men were having a smoke.

"Colour." Jens greeted me.

"Jens ... lads." I greeted them. They all began to stand or move away from the walls they leaned against an automatic mark of discipline and respect for my rank.

"At ease, lads." I motioned them back and they relaxed back into their easy postures.

"So what did you think of Jake's exit report then, Colour?" Dave asked.

"Strange that." I reflected.

"D'ya think Jake was shagging the Lieutenant?" Dave asked with a laugh.

"Not for me to say... Stranger things have happened."

"The Ice Queen has melted!" Jens laughed and we all joined in exchanging experiences and memories of our dead, but not forgotten, friends and comrades.

"Colour. I have something to show you." Jens said in his deep Swedish accent. "This way." We all walked over to the newly laid out practice square. Jens had a word with the Range Master in charge of the square.

Every camp and barracks on Sol had a square like this one. Here we would practice our martial arts once the construction was completed. The Range Master and Jens went to the weapons lockers and Jens returned with the troll commander's naginata spear.

"Colour, the weapon is well balanced." Jens said as he spun the long shaft with his many years of disciplined practice and his newly acquired muscular physique, not that he was in any way skinny before. I would not like to face Jens in battle and I was very glad he was on not only my side but one of my closest friends as well.

"There is more." Jens moved towards the practice dummies. Man thick shafts of wood embedded in the ground; they would take the hardest sword thrust from our regular blunted training weapons. The use of our combat weapons was forbidden, the monomolecular weapons we used could, with a practiced cut, cleave the practice dummy in two.

Jens swept the naginata at one of the dummies, the blade passed right through, the top half spinning into the air. As it returned, Jens cut that in two as well.

"A monomolecular blade edge!" I exclaimed. It was the other major breakthrough for us, with a Zero gravity manufacturing process. The edge found quite by accident when a length of Melentum shot out of an electromagnetic forming press and an unfortunate foundry worker tried to catch it. The find made the foundry worker so rich he could afford one of the new robotic hands indistinguishable from his human hand but with an array of handy snap on gadgets.

Jens stopped and nodded. I walked over to him and examined Uffe's naginata, it was a monomolecular blade edge and by default, it had to have come from Earth Prime. I studied the weapons blade and soon found the Sheffield Melentum mark on the blade close to the ebony shaft.

"You know what this means Jenser." I said with worry.

"Yes, our armour will not prove as effective against such blades. However this is the only one we have come across." Jens tried to be positive.

"Yeah, true enough but what if the 9th and 10th legions all have these blades?"

"We'd be screwed." Jens remarked rather matter-of-factly.

"Yeah we'd be royally screwed. We had better make Major Morgan aware of this." I said, as I hefted the weapon to feel its weight and balance. It was a damn fine weapon.

"Already told him. I thought he needed to know before the last drop so he could send word back."

"Well done that man." I congratulated Corporal Yde who should really be a sergeant by now.

We walked off to join the rest of the guys and we talked over the implications of the monomolecular troll naginata. After the talk and another smoke, Jens and the men bid me farewell and made for the junior ranks club and a well-earned beer or three.

I went back into the mess and asked one of the cookhouse assistants for one of their big serving pots. When the soldier dug one out and handed it over, I picked up four large rare steaks and heaped raw potatoes from the vegetable bins into the pot. I also filled my coffee mug again.

"Hey, Jon! Planning a barbeque?" The Cook Sergeant called over from the burnished metal cooking stoves. The Cook Sergeant knew exactly what I was doing, otherwise I would not have been allowed into the cookhouse kitchen.

"For our little guest in DQ12." I explained.

The Cook Sergeant beckoned me over and walked to a steel bin. He lifted the lid and used a set of long tongs to heap raw liver, hearts and kidneys into the pot I held out, two thick tongues followed them from another bin. I had to put the lid on quickly, I may be battle hardened but the sight of this offal made me ready to heave. The Cookhouse Sergeant gave me the thumbs up and I am sure he was glad for one less chore he had to deal with. With the steaks, the potatoes, and offal inside and the lid firmly on, I balanced my precious coffee mug on top. I made my way out of the cookhouse and over to DQ12. The junior ranks club was on the way, so I balanced my way in to scrounge a couple of packets of cigarettes from behind the bar for our honoured troll guest.

"International relations, Corporal." I explained to the club steward. "And I am sure the trollish nation will fully reimburse you. You'll just have to go and ask!"

"Yes I can see it now ... Yes, Troll king fellow, that's 40 Euros for two packets of Marlborough and please stop eating my leg!" He laughed as he put the cigarettes into my breast pocket. "You have them Colour, on the house, international relations and all!"

The guys in the club laughed; glad they were not delivering the food to the troll. The sun was lowering in the sky by the time I arrived at DQ12. Every camp had a DQ12 even if they had less than 12 drop boxes. DQ12 was the name given to the local nick for prisoners both military and civilian and like now, the enemy. As I approached, I noticed that the CSM had doubled the guard on the prisoner, at the behest of Major Morgan. He was not there when I brought the troll in but I am sure he must have heard of Corporal Will Hallsworths unfortunate demise. Now that brownnosing little crawler needed demising.

I had to relinquish my weapons before entering DQ12. The Lance Corporal in charge of the guard locked them away into the weapons box. One of the other guards unlocked the Melentum door and I nodded my thanks before entering with the pot of steak, offal and potatoes and my mug of steaming coffee balanced on top.

Chapter 8

The door slammed shut and the bolts rasped closed, it was a sound I had the misfortune of hearing many times before. I do not think I could ever get used to that rasping sound of metal against metal scraping my freedom away. Uffe was at the back of DQ12, he had just poured fresh coffee into a large green plastic mug, the image of my own.

"Ah lunchtime!" he smiled. "Coffee?" he raised his own mug and offered the half-empty glass coffee jug.

"I just got a fresh one from my mess." I said as I put the pot down.

"Want some sugar or milk for that coffee?" He asked.

"Just milk please."

Uffe took the carton from the cool box embedded in the wall and handed it to me. "Semi-skimmed, healthier for the cholesterol."

"Cholesterol wasn't something I thought trolls cared about." I commented, topping up my coffee with the offered up milk.

"One must look after one's self." Uffe replied. "Do you really think we are savages?"

"Well actually, yes I do ... No offence, Sir!" I replied, realising I had just insulted a troll in a locked room and I was in here with him.

"Oh, big scary monster wants to eat you all up!" He growled as he leaned right over me, his tusked and horned face inches from mine. I leaned back in alarm wishing I had at least one of my weapons at hand. Uffe leaned back and laughed aloud, it sounded like a trollish battle cry.

"Do you think your weapons would do you any good here in this confined space?"

One of the guards banged with the handle of his sword on the window in the door.

"All right in there?" He shouted.

"Yes, all right." I called back, unsure if it was the correct reply. "... Isn't it?" I asked the troll.

Uffe laughed softly. "Don't worry Jon; I am not going to bite your head off. Well, not yet any way!" and he laughed again and turned his attentions to the food.

"Aha! Cow meat, and earth apples, my favourites ... Do you know cow meat Jon. Tastes just like wood nymph." Uffe commented excitedly.

I had no reply to the ghoulish remark and I just sipped at my coffee. Uffe used his fingernail to dice the meat, the inch long talon slid through the thick steak like the sharpest of carving knives. I shuddered to think that he had six of these at hand, one on the end of each of his fingers. Uffe noticed my concern.

"Do not worry Jon; did I not give you my word?"

I nodded in acceptance of his statement. "Uffe, may I ask you some questions?"

"Ha! So the interrogation begins ... Are you the good cop? I see no bad cop." He laughed and leaned in to me. "The elvin convention Jon; name, rank and legion only." Uffe wagged a deadly finger and popped a morsel of raw steak into his fanged mouth followed by a whole liver, which he slurped down all in one piece.

"No ... no, nothing like that ... Well I suppose it could be taken as ..."

"Jon you're babbling again, get to it man." Uffe cut me off.

I had a list of questions as long as a troll's arm, both of them. So long, I did not know where to start.

"The Kung Fu." I said before I knew I had said it. "Trolls don't do Kung Fu." I added.

"And who told you that?" Uffe asked lifting a potato and biting into it like an apple.

I felt rather foolish and I did not know if I should explain.

"Jon ... Jon! Don't let your mind be a garbage can for someone else's rubbish." Uffe said shaking his massive head.

That statement shocked me to the core; Uffe said it exactly as my Grandma Linda used to admonish us.

"A fine woman, your Grandmother."

"Commander Jægerblod! You're mind reaming me!" I exclaimed, and moved to the door intent on calling the guard. No one had any idea that trolls could mind ream, this troll was obviously very different.

"Hush now, Jon. No need for that." Uffe motioned me back to my chair.

I stood undecided for a moment; I knew I should summon the guard and alert the Elvin Psy Corps to the mind ream.

"No need, Jon. They already know." Uffe said and pointed to the window.

"Will you stop doing that?" I complained and moved again to the door to look out of the window. Across the clearing, I spotted two elvin officers in Euroforce uniforms with their distinctive yellow shoulder flashes of the Psy Corps, standing in the cover of a copse of trees. They were staring intently in the direction of DQ12.

"They have blocked me again." Uffe added. "It's like a game of chess. I make a move and they counter it. I only get glimpses and strong images.

"You loved your Grandmother very much did you not? I am sorry she is gone. It seems she had a very happy life and I got the feeling that she loved your Grandfather very much. You are named after him are you not?"

"You got all that in a moment?" I asked, taking my seat again.

"And a little bit more. I gathered when we passed the Lieutenant Kvinder that she is one of your goals?"

I could feel my face redden. "You don't need to be a mind reamer to spot that one!" I said.

"Kvinder, is that what you call your women?" I asked hearing the strange word for the first time.

"Kvinder means more than just woman. It is a respectful address like calling her a lady." Uffe explained.

"That goal is shared by nearly every man in the regiment and a few of the women as well!"

"Well, keep up with that one Jon. I believe you will soon be successful in that quarter." Uffe smiled and popped the rest of the potato into his mouth.

"You mind reamed her!"

"Yes, it was she that alerted the Elvin Psy Corps. That's why she trotted away."

"And you think I've got a chance there?" I asked; my interest aroused.

"Most certainly, especially now that her heart is broken for the loss of her present love, she needs a shoulder to cry on and a bed to share soon. I think I did you a favour in a roundabout way." Uffe replied and picked up a couple of the cubes of steak. He offered me one.

"No thank you, I have just eaten." I explained. Uffe looked truly disappointed.

"Oh go on then, I reckon I can find room for a bit more steak." I reconsidered, hoping to find some common ground. Uffe flipped his hand over and dropped the cube of meat into the middle of his palm. The meat browned up and began to sizzle. In a few seconds the meat was well done. I lifted the meat and had to juggle it between my fingers, as it was so hot. I touched the palm of Uffe's hand and it was normal skin temperature for a troll, kind of cool and clammy. I bit into the meat and it melted in my mouth like fine braised steak.

"You gotta teach me that trick!" I said as I chewed.

Uffe smiled that deadly fanged smile again. This time I felt no menace facing those rows of shark-toothed canines.

"The Kung Fu, Uffe ... Aha! Kung Fu Uffe!" I laughed and Uffe laughed with me.

"I mean how ... where did you learn Kung Fu? I am sure you know that all trolls use only one form of karate and that is Wado Ryu yet you are very well versed in Praying Mantis, Monkey Style and the naginata, now that was impressive!"

"You know your martial arts well Jon, are you a student beyond the army training?"

"Yes, my family practice bushido and I have been a student of the arts since I was a child. I have practiced Shotokan and Wado Ryu but I prefer Wado Ryu. And you Uffe?"

Uffe took a cigarette out of his pocket and that reminded me of the packets I had in my breast pocket. I took the packets out and offered them to Uffe.

"Ah! Another small kindness from Colour Sergeant Jon Raine." He laughed and made that gunslinger move again.

"Alright Jon, for your kindness I will give you a little trollish history lesson." He lit his cigarette from the tip of his finger and I made a mental note of another question I wanted to ask.

"Are you sitting comfortably?" He asked and I nodded my head. "Then I will begin."

I had a very strong image of my Grandma Linda. It was exactly what she said before she would read to my brothers and me when we were infants. I so loved her faerie stories and I really missed her.

Uffe was staring at me as if he were remembering as well. He came out of his reflection, slurped another liver, and began.

"Back before... well before the invasion, we would get strays coming from your world into ours, most would go mad but some would excel and successfully integrate into our societies. We knew about your world and the violence you perpetrated on one another. We were very worried that the sickness of war and violence as you had on your world might infect the races of Sol. We might have had come to our world such violence and barbarism as you perpetrate upon each other. We did not want to see that mindless violence in our world. To avoid it we thought to ensure that our peoples were protected from your barbarism. We knew that if the gnomes and certain factions of dwarfen and troll were exposed to the human lust of war and violence that we would have an infection we could not control or get rid of.

"The Nations decided that we would watch those that fell into our world. We would mind ream them and if we found those strays acceptable and peaceable, we would allow and indeed assist them to settle and live amongst us. Over time, some would find their way back into your so-called Earth Prime and stories of Sol would find their way into your myths and legends. When an organised force came across, especially a military band, we would set upon them and wipe them out before they had a chance to establish a foothold in our world to steal our lands and subjugate our peoples.

"The elvin races were above the use of such base violence and so it fell to the troll, dwarfen and unfortunately goblin and gnomish nations to be the war givers. Now the elvin will fight and fight well but they have strict rules and guidelines and the best and most sure way to win a war is to strike first and strike with overwhelming force. Elves found that they could not bring themselves to slaughter a weaker race even if that weaker race threatened their own civilization.

We trolls, dwarves, goblins, gnomes and mercenary units from the fae of wood elf, sylvan, faune, satyr, the minatons, the centarean and others that wished to stand and fight for Sol, did our jobs well, but the gnomes took delight in torturing your fellow human invaders.

They would torture not just physically but mentally, entering human dreams and giving such terrors previously forbidden by the Common Law of the First Twelve. However, war sometimes brings strange bedfellows, I may sadly say that at times past even the trollish, and dwarfen armies would use such tactics. Yes, I am truly shamed that my people should have done such things but it is better that a few should perish than many nations fall. Those acts are written in the runes of the stone of the past and can only be changed by the most powerful of sorcerers."

"You can change the past?" I asked.

"You want the 'Kung Fu' story or the 'I can change the past' story? You are only getting one tonight." Uffe scolded with a wagging talon, upset that I had interrupted his flow. All I could think of was my Grandma Linda scolding our constant infant questioning in exactly the same way. I noted another question and nodded for him to go on.

There came from the east a band of men in robes of priests with shaven heads of the like we had never seen before. They were four hundred strong and such a sizeable force we could not ignore. The first to make contact were the eastern goblins that lived in the underground burrows of the Great Plains. They are a most warlike people and very different from the industrious goblins of the Southern Lands. Without warning, eastern goblins sent a war party of four thousand regular troops to strike and destroy this perceived threat. It was the first time eastern goblins encountered such a sizeable force from Earth Prime; and fuelled with the stories of warlike barbarism, they did not wait to question the intent of this band of Earth Prime men. They set upon them with a terrible vengeance, the goblins outnumbered the hairless priests ten to one and they were wiped out to almost the last man."

"So the goblins massacred them?" I asked, shocked even the goblins should undertake such a mass killing.

"No Jon, the goblins were massacred." Uffe replied quietly.

"Four thousand goblins... killed?" I exclaimed under my breath.

"Four thousand two hundred and six all told." Uffe added. "The battle commenced with the usual volley of war arrows. The priests simply stood there and plucked from the air the arrows that rained down on them. Their pike men charged the orange ranks; the goblins thundered towards them head on. The orange robed priests carried no visible weapons; they carried no shields. The goblins expected to smash into their ranks and break the lines arrayed before them; instead, the priests flowed through the charge like mists through the forest. The priests, unarmed, took the pikes from the goblin soldiers and turned their own weapons against them. The priests flowed and danced their fighting style against the brute force of the goblin horde. The result was annihilation of the goblin pike men with only minor injuries to the priests.

When the cavalry charged their beasts, seasoned war mulluks galloped to the lines of orange robed priests, their paws churning the savannah beneath them to mud. At the point of engagement the mulluks simply refused, they stopped so suddenly that many of the mounted cavalry soldiers vaulted over their saddles and fell under their own milling beasts, many died then. The orange robed priests took to the mulluk mounts and transformed instantly into a precisely controlled cavalry unit. Those goblins that remained mounted had no defence against the pike armed, mounted priests who spun and whirled their pikes in such a strange and deadly manner that the goblin cavalry still trying to control their refusing mounts gave little or no resistance, they swiftly fell to the last brave soldier. These mulluk mounts were well trained over many years to refuse anyone but their own masters, even other goblins in the very same unit could not mount each other's mulluk, or if they did, it was with the utmost difficulty. Seldom other than a Beastmaster could ride another's mount, yet these priests took control of empty mounts in an instant.

The result on the goblins was bloody carnage in a scale never seen before. Brave goblin support teams of cooks and victuallers, wheelwrights and blacksmiths formed into their assault units, every eastern goblin, and a warrior before anything else. They formed up and attacked these men in robes of priests; they fell like wheat under the harvester's blade. Only a few of the goblins survived to warn their people of the men they called 'The death that walks as priests'.

Of the support goblins that fell to the fierce fighting, with every man fighting to his death, a few were surrounded, overwhelmed and disarmed. These eleven goblin warriors were brought to two of their fallen brothers. At first the goblins were horrified, the signs the priests made, they thought the hairless priests wanted them to eat their fallen as we trolls do after every battle but as they tried to explain that they were not trolls they realized that the priests were indicating that they should perform their burial rights on the dead dwarves. The eleven survivors built two burial pyres while the priests watched and after lighting them and allowing the goblins to finish their ceremony, the priests secured the men, broke up into groups and built burial pyres for the thousands of the dead they had just slain. They had to burn several goblin warriors per each pyre, each of the pyres a replica of the two built by the eleven surviving prisoners.

When all blazed alight, the eleven prisoners were given back their weapons and each was given a mount from the remaining beasts of the goblin cavalry. To the utter amazement of the goblins, their mounts were as docile as milking nurse dragons. The priests parted and allowed the survivors to leave. As they rode away, they looked back to see the priests lined up silently watching them, and behind the lines of priests the darkening skies of dusk were glowing red, orange and black with the fires of the burning pyres and the oily black smoke from the burning bodies.

Within a week, 'The death that walked as priests,' visited the first dwarf citadel. Gondafell's only defences were its high walls and four thousand city guards; mostly retired soldiers and part time servicemen from the city dwellers and farmers that lived and worked there."

I remained silent awaiting the account of the battle of the fall of Gondafell.

Chapter 9

"Another coffee?" Uffe asked with a smile. I looked down to see that my mug was empty.

"Yes please." I offered the empty mug and Uffe filled it from the brewed coffee jug kept warm on the coffee makers hotplate.

"So Uffe, what happened to Gondafell?"

"Nothing." Said the Troll

"Nothing?" I asked as I sipped my coffee.

"Not a thing. The death that walked as priests came to the eastern gate, while the dwarfen lined the walls with their bows and spears. Ten of the orange robed priests walked forward and laid flowers at the foot of the gates like maidens to a wedding; then just walked away. The dwarfen waited tense and at the ready for several hours for the attack. They thought the flowers were some sort of offering to the priest's war gods on the eve of the battle. The dwarfen watched the priests walk around the city and disappear over the horizon to the west. They waited a full day and no attack came. They sent out their scouts to find their enemy, only to have their scouts return with the tame mulluks and to report that they found the orange robed army simply walking away to the west. Their citadel of Gondafell and all the people inside were spared."

"However, during the time when the priests approached Gondafell, the dwarfen sent emissaries to their old enemies the goblin nations to the south with which they had a loose peace pact. They entreated the goblins to come to their aid, the goblins being those that were easily turned to conflict and angered at their previous defeat, found the request one that they could not resist. They sent a powerful force of many thousands against the priests. Tracking them down, they found the group on the plains of Edenssell. On the first night, the goblins managed to capture two of the forward scouts, but again with a great loss of life on the part of the goblins. Through the night, the goblins attacked. They assaulted the sleeping priests with their dream weaving but found only high walls and void, no thoughts could they glean or shape, no dreams could they invade.

"The goblins had never fought a foe with such resistance to their dream weaving; their only recourse was to attack physically. From the false dawn, they crucified their two prisoners. The goblins aim was to awake the priests with the screams of the tortured, crucified priests, yet even with the application of branding irons and the stripping of their flesh not once did the priests cry out. They beat the bodies and peeled their skin yet the priests hung upon their roughhewn wooden racks, their faces placid and serene.

"The goblins jumped back when the hanging bloody priests began their soft chanting as the sun kissed Sol on the distant horizon. The chanting filtered across the grasslands to the ears of the monks already awake and ready for the battle to come. Aware of the surrounding numbers of goblins the priests took defensive positions. They began the same strange musical chant, which seemed to comfort the tortured and crucified priests. Again faced with such numbers the priests arrayed themselves against the goblins with that same enigmatic calm.

"From the lines of the orange robed priests emerged two individuals. They calmly walked from their lines to approach the racks where the battered bodies of the tortured priests hung. The goblin archers let fly with a deadly volley of war shafts. The priests knocked aside the arrows that would have felled them and stepped through the rest that landed in the ground to surround them, like a knee-high forest of bamboo. At fifty paces from the hanging men, they extended their arms and metal stars flew from their hands to embed in the hearts of their brethren.

"They killed their own kind, a concept so barbaric and alien to the goblins that they just could not comprehend it. In the stunned silence that followed, the two priests turned their backs and walked back to their own ranks. A roar went up from the ranks of goblins and they charged the orange robed priests in the sure and certain knowledge that they would quickly overwhelm their foe by sheer weight of numbers and brute force of arms. At the end of the war charge, two hundred goblins fled in terror and watched from a distance as the priests burnt their dead and prayed to their gods. The surviving goblins could do nothing but stand and watch as the priests formed up into their caravan and moved off to the North West.

"By the time the death that walked as priests reached the lands of the trollish nations, the rumours and legends that preceded such an army of yellow faced demons had already reached us. Against the death that walked as priests, there was no defence against their strange and unusual battle magic. By the time they arrived at our borders we had heard of their baby stealing, changing water into blood, the taking of women and slaves to sacrifice to their own demon gods, and the vile desecration of our temples and holy places. Some said that these demons were here to murder our Gods and our First Council of Twelve.

"We took all of our warriors and met them in the valley of Sonogram; we counted four hundred thousand trollish warriors. Even the God killers could not stand against us."

"You speak as if you were there." I interrupted.

"Indeed I was there. It was but eleven hundred years ago."

"Seven hundred years! How old are you Uffe?"

"I am eighteen hundred and thirty years old last month." Uffe announced proudly. I could see that the announcement of the troll's age was something of pride for him.

"No way!" I exclaimed.

"Way!" Uffe replied, he lit another cigarette and helped himself to another mug of coffee from the pot I had made while I listened to his tale.

"We faced the demons and watched them for a long time. They built their little huts, ate their plants like the nisse do. They prayed to their gods, all before the might of our trollish nations.

"They had no slaves, no women, no babies and I began to doubt the stories of the demon priests without souls. My father Ullrick, who was in command of the war party, led a number of trollish officers out from our masses. I was his first son from his chief Kvinder, thus I was included in the party that walked under the dragon skull of peace. Two old priests came out to meet us. They carried strange implements we feared to be weapons or magical devices. They neared to twenty paces and sat on the grass.

"One plucked at his device while the other raised his to his mouth. There came from their devices a strange and peaceful sound, some of our battle priests bravely made wards against their magic. The sounds continued but caused no harm. We thought of our families and our homelands. We knew that these monks were casting a spell of peace such as the elvin do. We squatted and listened to their music, some swayed to the rhythm of the melody. When they finished they stood and smiled. We trolls stood and gazed down at these small yellow men in their orange robes, little men we heard to be such powerful warriors, how could these little men threaten our Gods?

"My father called forward with his two finest warriors. I was one of those warriors." Uffe puffed up his chest and thrust his tusks into the air. "My father made the silent language to indicate that we should surrender our war spears. Trolls came to us with practice staffs of Ravenwood we carried on our war mulluks. Two of my father's trolls threw two such staffs at the feet of the old priests, and father indicated as best he could for them to return to their ranks and send forth their best warriors. We stepped forward into a combat stance, the other troll officers stepped back leaving only father at our side. The old monks lay down their musical instruments and picked up the staffs. Father pointed again to their ranks then to us, inviting them to bring forward their finest.

"The priests stood there smiling serenely, leaning on their newly acquired staffs. Father shrugged in frustration and using our silent hand signals, he indicated that we should go forward and beat the old priests back to their lines. It was with great reluctance that we stepped forward, disappointed that we should be humiliated to have to beat such frail and elderly men. As we moved forward, the other priests clapped politely as if we entered a combat arena.

"We moved at them only half-heartedly and swung our weapons to begin their beatings. The old priests spun their staffs in their hands and ours were on the ground.

"What magic was this?" I thought, and bent to pick up my weapon. The old priest rapped me sharply on my head and pushed my staff away.

"I looked to my father who stared back both puzzled and angry. He lifted his left hand, three fingers splayed wide, he gestured for us to use full force and defeat these old men. We moved as one to grab at these old priests but found ourselves on the ground, the priests standing over us laughing like kindly old men. We rolled onto our feet and moved away to take up unarmed battle stances with one fist on the ground. We had been disarmed in our challenge so we were forbidden to take up other weapons. We lumbered about the old men looking for an opening. The priests began, as I thought, to mimic us, I later found out that they were using Monkey style Kung Fu.

"They rolled into us, a blow from a foot to my knee felled me and as I fell, a blow to my kidney sent me rolling in severe pain to the ground. My warrior brother fared no better, the other priest had touched him on the neck and under his arm to render him paralysed. He toppled over and spasmed on the ground trying to regain control of his body, a wet patch on his pants showed that he had lost control of his waters. My father roared with laughter at our misfortune.

"Now that is the power in battle I want!" He exclaimed between his laughter. The ranks of orange robed priests laughed and cheered and the trollish armies gave a great cheer for a match won in pride. Thus came to our land a Shaolin Kung Fu monastery.

"For the right to remain and live peacefully we required of the Shaolin monks that our warriors would be trained in their martial arts. They required of us the Oath that we would never use Kung Fu as the aggressors in any war. After a great trollish debate, we gave the oath as a nation. Some of our warriors became monks and live to this day in the monastery. Your human life times are but a short while to us and even the youngest of these priests grew old and passed into their heavens. Now there are only Danish Troll Shaolin Kung Fu monks on Sol."

"The skill you displayed is phenomenal. It would take many years of dedicated training to do what you do. How long did you study with the monks?" I asked.

"I was there in the monastery but for three years and no more." Uffe replied as he lit his tenth cigarette. I was glad of the air conditioning unit that hummed away in the ceiling.

"When it comes to the art of war you need only show a troll warrior once, once is enough. After those years, I had to leave due to duties and obligations I had to my people, so I studied with the trollish cadre in the city in which I had to reside. The art of combat has always been one of my great passions."

"You are well versed in English. I have heard you speak German as well, so how is it that you have such command of our languages?"

"I have crossed many times into your world. Your Earth Prime as you call it fascinates me and I enjoy seeing how your peoples deal with your lots in life. You lack the knowledge of the old ones. You do not have the strength of the trolls or the ogre. You cannot run or jump like the elvin nor do you have the endurance of the dwarfen, yet you survive; and your races have reached great heights albeit on the backs of slaves and the sacrifice of many of your people. You slaughter one another for the sake of a piece of land or for trinkets of gold or a few gemstones, yet you are capable of such great love and sacrifice. You are an enigma to us.

"Your lives are but a few generations and you breed so many even though most of you practice such uncivilised habits such as mating with a single female. Of these latter days, you have mastered the strange magic of technology and I have seen you conquer the heavens. Why the Gods do not bless civilised people like us with this technology I do not know.

"I have journeyed in the marvels of your technology, trains, trucks and I have even flown in an air-o-plane." Uffe laughed at the memory.

"I convinced an American in Utah that I was the ancient named Cain and he took me in his crop duster high over his lands. Such a sight I have never seen the equal. Now I wish to visit the moon and maybe some of the settled planets before…" Uffe cut himself off. I felt that he had said something he did not want me to hear. He stirred uncomfortably and I got the feeling that he wanted to move away from that line of conversation. I was hungry for more information as revelations of the true sophistication of the recluse northern trollish nations unfolded a little within Uffe's stories.

"So Uffe how many languages do you speak?" I asked hoping he would take up the conversation again. Uffe stood a little taller his pride swelling his chest.

"I speak twelve earthen tongues and thirty Sollen tongues. In my travels I searched out a powerful sorcerer, one of the First Council of the Twelve."

"You have met a Titan?" I asked in disbelief.

"I have" Uffe replied and made the sign of the hammer in the air before him.

"The ancient blessed me with the gift of tongues. I have but to hear and study a little and I am able to master a language with ease. In your world I use the internet to download cracked versions of language courses, movies and television shows from all over your Earth Prime."

Uffe went on to recite line after line of movie clips mimicking the actors and actresses voices perfectly. Like a Trellian songbird, he could mimic every possible voice he had heard, male or female, bass to soprano. Uffe's talent for mimicking was about the most amazing thing I had seen him do so far. I pictured myself with a stage show of trolls reciting Shakespeare or some classic play like the Merry Widow or Rocky, recalling movie pieces and demonstrating their martial arts. I could see myself as the new world's Buffalo Bill with two legged buffalos that could sing and perform like tame bears in an old European circus.

"Have I lost you Jon?" Uffe interrupted my imaginings.

"Oh I'm sorry Uffe." I replied refocusing back into the real world. I glanced at my watch; it glowed 20h03 hours. "It is getting late Commander Jægerblod and I have a patrol tomorrow." I excused myself as I stood to leave.

"Of course. You are right Jon. I really must be going myself. A long busy day ahead you know."

The troll warrior's comment rang alarm bells in the back of my mind. At the time, I thought it an odd statement but I was not sure of the meaning behind the words and I dismissed it as a lack of clear understanding. I reasoned he meant sleep and his impending interrogation and forced mind reaming. I moved to the door and pressed the attention button. The amber light lit up the darkness outside.

"Ah, Colour Sergeant." Uffe spoke behind me. I turned and he offered me back my mug and pot.

"My apologies Jon but it is a technicality." He added with a deadly fanged smile. I looked askance but he bade me go on.

"It was a pleasure to speak with you Jon. I am sure I will make a troll of you yet. Good night and I look forward to our next meeting."

"Good night Commander Jægerblod." I donned my beret and saluted. Uffe stood tall and struck his right fist to his chest to return the salutation. I did the same and Uffe replied with a fair imitation of a British Army salute. We laughed and I demonstrated how a British Officer raises a sloppy salute. We were both laughing when the door opened and pair of puzzled guards stood watching us salute each other. They held the door open, I waved farewell to my new pig ugly friend, and I stepped out of the secured door.

Outside I retrieved my weapons and headed for the briefing room. An hour or so of debriefing from my visit with

Commander Jægerblod then a review of the planning for the patrol tomorrow before I would see my bed that night. I was really looking forward to resting between clean sheets, a warm duvet and a real mattress under my weary bones.

Chapter 10

The admin clerk led me into the officers briefing room; there I found Lieutenant Stewart and two elvin Psy Corps officers. Every time I got up close to elves I could not help but think 'Skinny Vulcan's!' and in the case of these two individuals, Romulans came to mind. As I entered, they were politely laughing at some shared amusement. I stood to attention in the doorway as military decorum dictated and Lieutenant Stewart bade me enter.

I walked up to the desk and saluted the officers. Major L'Acendal the senior officer returned the salute. These officers saluted without headgear, an American trait I could never get used to.

"Take a seat Colour Sergeant Jon Raine." Lieutenant Stewart invited me to the table. I noticed the other elvin officer raise one of those Mr Spock eyebrows at my name. I did not bother to explain.

"You know Major L'Acendal." Lieutenant Stewart began the introductions, and this is Captain Risenn." The Mr Spock eyebrow guy politely nodded. They wore camouflaged Euroforce DPM camouflage lightweights and their blue NATO berets lay on the table before them, the yellow shoulder flashes indicating their membership of their respective elvin Psy Corps. These elvin wore our uniform as they were attached to the Euroforce on 'Operation Changeling' that allowed the exchange of military for up to two years. Some of the elvin exchange soldiers found themselves attached to one of our Off World deployments and I knew from experience that they were either petrified, or having the time of their lives. There was also a set of exchange astronomers that postulated that the two worlds belonged in the same universe but in different places and they were trying to locate the positions of the two worlds in relation to each other.

The three officers before me were sitting behind a long desk; the major in the middle with Amanda sitting to his left and Risenn to his right.

"So, Colour Sergeant." Major L'Acendal began. "Can I offer you a beverage?"

"No, Sir I am fine."

"Perhaps a sweet then?" He indicated the crystal bowl of Jelly Babies. The sweets bowl was an ever-present item when the sweet-toothed elvin were present. I picked a black and a green one. Green sweets were my father's favourite and black were mine. To the elvin, one was impolite and three considered the height of greed, to refuse was a downright insult. I did consider taking four just to get that eyebrow going again.

"So Colour Sergeant Raine what were your initial impressions of Commander Jægerblod?" The Major began the mind reaming interrogation. I felt some pressure in my frontal lobes with the three of them jointly reaming my subconscious. I knew I was in for a monster of a headache in the morning.

I began as briefed for these types of interviews by speaking those impressions that immediately came to mind. It did not matter that my words made no logical sense other than to clarify the images in my mind. I could see that the Lieutenant and the elvin Psy Corps officers were concentrating intently on my words. They were reaming my thoughts in all aspects and depths, seeing my mental pictures and somehow leapfrogging through my mind and into the trolls. It felt like ogres playing rugby in my head. I did not exactly know how this mind stuff worked, but I knew from experience that they saw with my mind's eye, and even those thoughts and images I believed I forgot.

One of my instructors once explained that our minds record every single moment of our lives and it was just a matter of technique to recall those images and memories. A memory was like a path in the woods, every time you pass along that memory it becomes clearer and better fixed in your mind. All memories leave a trail but some need an expert tracker to follow them. The Psy Signal Corps or the elvin Psy Corps were those mind trackers and they could extract all kinds of hidden thoughts, even those you thought you never had. There was also a sort of complementary recording, like an empathic unconscious ESP, where normal blokes like me will unknowingly receive and record mental images from another. It was far from perfect and a bit of a black art to sort out the real images from the imaginary.

I did not really speak a lot but the officers were furiously scribbling in shorthand or something very like it as I related that which I could recall.

There were some urgent whispers and Captain Risenn left the room in a hurry. Lieutenant Stewart noticed my hesitation and urged me to continue. When I had exhausted those points I thought important, the major encouraged me to sit at ease and reflect on the meeting. I did as instructed, but my mind wandered a bit and the point Commander Jægerblod made about Lieutenant Stewart and I, welled up as a memory. I immediately thought of Jake and Amanda, Lieutenant Stewart looked up, a little embarrassed, and exchanged a glance with the elvin major. Her tryst with the dead Private Henson was now official knowledge and I think Lieutenant Stewart wanted to keep it out of the records. I shuffled uncomfortably and the Lieutenant gave me a pointed stare. I shrugged my shoulders in apology and from then on, I could not shake the lewd mental images of Lieutenant Stewart and I doing that which comes naturally. Every time I tried to suppress the thought, it would resurface again. It was like trying to stop giggling when faced with a funny thought in an important meeting. At one point Major L'Acendal laughed softly and Lieutenant Stewart promptly closed the interview.

"I think that will be all for now Colour Sergeant Raine." She said.

I stood and came to attention and the Major dismissed me with an American salute, and I thought that these elvin have been watching far too much TV.

"Sorry Ma'am." I offered

"That's quite alright." The lieutenant replied with a warm suggestive smile and I knew I was on to a sure thing. 'Thanks very much Commander Jægerblod' I thought. Both officers sat upright with worried frowns on their faces and I knew that they had reamed something important from my mind.

"I must get this image to intelligence central immediately." The Major spoke in grave tones and shuffled his papers into his brown leather attaché case.

I was about to ask what when the sounds of frantic shouting came from outside. The shouts drew my attention to the mounting alarm.

"Stand to! Stand to! Prisoner escaped!"

I could hear running boots on the hard packed earth outside and the shouts of the guard turning out.

I drew my katana and we rushed out of the office block, both officers held their swords drawn at high guard, the major with his thin elvin rapier and Lieutenant Stewart's katana the mirror of mine. The major waved us a hasty farewell and left us to rush, I supposed, to the intelligence cell offices. Lieutenant Stewart and I trotted over to DQ12 watching all the while for anything suspicious in the failing light of the evening. I was sure we could spot a seven-foot troll in our camp on a clear evening. The camp was alive with armed soldiers; everyone knew their duties. There was the efficient chaos of squads of soldiers locking down the camp and its perimeter.

The engineers and the support staff let the Paras get on with the business they knew best; however, they all stopped work to stand where they were, swords at the ready. A number of officers and NCO's were calling off directions and orders, no one was going to get more than a few yards in this Black Alpha alert state, especially not even a seven foot Troll no matter how high a rank he was.

At DQ12, military police in red armbands with white "MP" lettering, stopped us. Lieutenant Stewart exchanged a few words and they let us through their inner perimeter. Major Morgan was coming out of the access door to DQ12.

"Lieutenant Stewart, Colour Raine, take a look at this." He said and closed the door. He indicated that we should look into the only window to DQ12. We peered in and there was Commander Jægerblod pouring coffee from the percolator then moving over to take a seat by the folded down table. We looked at each other, then at the Major.

"Look again!" he said.

We looked and Commander Jægerblod rose from his chair, he walked idly around drinking his coffee. Again, we looked at the Major.

"The percolator, man!" The Major barked.

The glass jug was full; it should have been nearly empty with the size of the troll's mug.

We watched the Commander exactly repeat the motions of pouring the coffee and taking his seat by the desk. In every detail an exact repeat of his previous actions.

The Major opened the door and DQ12 was empty. I examined the inside of the door to see a clever combination of Sol sorcery and Earth Prime technology. Magic paper was blue-tacked over the door window.

"How did ...?" I began.

Trooper Stephenson noticed the coffee jug and decided against orders to check inside. The trooper in question stood there with a self-satisfied smile on his face.

Lieutenant Stewart made a hasty mind ream of the soldier.

"That's how he escaped. He walked right past the guards and through the open door."

The smug smile fell from Trooper Stephenson's face.

"Ma'am I swear, I did not see..." Stephenson began to protest.

"No you did not see." Amanda interrupted. "The troll commander hid his physical form from you with a spell of concealment, rather like the one used in the attack last night. He simply hung from the ceiling and when you opened the door and came in he slipped out." Lieutenant Stewart ignored the embarrassed trooper and turned to Major Morgan.

"Sir, with that spell of concealment, unless a Psy Corp officer, a wizard or a witch is looking directly at Jægerblod, there is no way anyone else will see him. I believe the spell is chameleon in nature and the Commander will be able to make himself look like anybody he so chooses."

"Seal the perimeter; no one is to leave the compound." The Major ordered and one of the guards ran off to relay the orders and intelligence to the Guard Commander.

"Lieutenant there is a note on the writing desk." added the Major.

We entered DQ12 and there on the desk sat an A4 size page of fine parchment, a silver tipped feather quill and a large bottle of dark ink, beside them was a rolling blotter none of which were present in DQ12 before the Commander took up residence there. We knew the implements to be the preferred writing implements of those trolls we were familiar with, yes surprising as it may sound, most trolls could read and write. Commander Jægerblod had been thoroughly searched by the guards; there was no way on either earths the writing implements should have been there. Lieutenant Stewart pointed to the parchment, and in neat stylised roman italics, there was a short note. The few words were the most worrying words I had ever read. They sent a chill down my spine and made the hairs on the back of my neck stand on end. The note was signed by Uffe Jægerblod.

It read:

"We Are Coming"
Ard Commander Uffe Jægerblod.
The 10th Legion.

Chapter 11

Lieutenant Stewart and I walked back from DQ12 towards the main offices.

"Ard Commander!" I said again almost to myself.

"Yes, Ard Commander of the 10th Legion." Lieutenant Stewart replied. "We missed it completely. I can see now why the General was projecting those lewd mental images; they were a shield for his deeper thoughts."

"Is that what you saw just when the alarm went off then Ma'am?" I asked the Lieutenant.

"Jon, please call me Amanda in private." Lieutenant Stewart said. Allowing me to call her by her first name was an unwritten rule allowed within military protocol and it meant that I could become more familiar with Amanda.

"Yes Jon, we missed it and both the Elvin Psy Corps officers and I are going to have to explain that to HQ."

"Will it go badly Amanda?"

"Well, we won't be welcomed with open arms and a medal for losing the supreme commander of this 10th Legion." Amanda had a worried look on her face; she could not afford to lose rank while she was still within her probationary period.

"Jon I need to tell you about the images we saw just at the end of the interview."

I realised that the worried frown was not for the pending carpeting she was about to receive, but the other images that seemed to be the worrying factor.

"So what were the images Amanda?"

"The Captain rushed out when he saw the troll in their courts. When their King Ullrick entered the throne room, all bowed down except for this Uffe Jægerblod. Any other time even within their tribal chiefs assemblies, such an action would cost the troll his head, and he would be served as the main course for the next banquet. This Ard Commander however, stood tall with impunity. We have never seen such a situation before; it puts this troll in the highest regard second only to their

King himself. We knew then that we had an important troll indeed."

"And now we know he commands the 10th Legion." I added.

"Yes correct, and that is the problem." Amanda replied. "The last images we had from you were a vision of many thousands of trolls and other fae swarming over the northern plains and sweeping down to New Paris annihilating every human settlement in their path."

"Thousands of trolls! ... And fae ... Fae with trolls." I exclaimed. I knew that we had such a hard fight with a few hundred scattered and disorganised trolls. What would such numbers of troll warriors do to our settlements?

"The majority of the fae marching with the trolls were Nisse." Amanda said.

"Nisse? The northern elves? I have heard whispers and rumours. What kind of people are they?" I asked.

"We know precious little about these nisse. Like these northern trolls, they have been reserved, refusing all diplomatic contact with humans. The first three ambassadors sent to the northern trollish nations were returned immediately, escorted across their border by nisse guard. The next two we sent the trolls just ate. They and the nisse have very little communication with us. The elvin Psy Corps officers thought the images very important. I felt the fear rise in their minds." Amanda commented as we approached the main offices.

"Elves with trolls, its unprecedented is it not?" I asked.

"In our lifetime it is indeed unprecedented, but not in theirs. One other aspect of this vision alarmed us and the elvin in particular." Amanda replied as we stopped before the admin block. I waited in expectation for her explanation.

Amanda took a breath to steady herself; she looked shaken when she thought of these images.

"At the head of this moving sea of warriors rode three people. Uffe Jægerblod and the nisse commander Princess Erika Nisse, between them rode a human. His black skin denoted him as a mated nisse or elvin, yet he was a human and at the head of this northern fae army."

"Did you recognise him?"

"No, his face was obscured with powerful shields and we could only discern his black skin but we know of him."

"How?" I asked.

"There is a Sollen legend shared and agreed by all of the faeian races. When a great evil has befallen the races of Sol, a leader, a deliverer, will appear. They will know him, as he will take the nisse princess royal as his wife. He will be of no races and of all races and all will bend the knee to acknowledge him as their saviour. The nisse call him the Black Messiah, he has other names amongst the other fae. We need to find this man and deal with him before this event happens. Hundreds of thousands of human lives are at stake." Amanda said, she looked at me and I could see she had more news to tell me. "The note Jon, it was for you." She added. "Specifically for you."

"A warning ...? How do you know?" I asked before I realised I was talking to a talented Ghost Whisperer with Psy abilities that surpassed even the elvin.

"I think I would like to explore the implications of that note Jon. Can I make an appointment say tomorrow night? How about dinner in my quarters?" She asked folding back the collar of my combat jacket. Two junior NCO's stepped out of the admin block at that moment and I knew that before I got back to my room the news of me bedding Lieutenant Stewart would be through the entire camp. The NCO's passed us smiling.

"Afternoon Ma'am... Colour" They said as they passed, both saluting Amanda. Amanda returned the salute with a smile and I stared hard at those two corporals.

Amanda stepped close to me, so close I could feel her sweet breath on my face. "So dinner then, tomorrow night?" She asked looking up at me with her magnetic brown eyes.

"Yes Ma'am ... Amanda." I corrected myself. "It's a date then?" I added.

Amanda smiled that alluring smile and replied softly. "Well I suppose it is, Colour Sergeant Jon Raine."

Should I kiss her now? I was as nervous as a schoolboy, if I kissed her and word got back to the senior officers one or both of us would be posted to different assignments. "What the hell." I thought. I took Amanda by her waist and pulled her close to me. We kissed for a moment that seemed like an eternity but was too short by far.

"Do you think those two corporals will gossip?" Amanda asked. She must have reamed my thoughts.

"Like bees to honey I'm afraid." I apologised.

"Well if we are going to suffer from the gossip, we might as well give them something to gossip about." Amanda suggested. I raised my eyebrows in pleasant surprise.

"How about a coffee then?" Amanda asked.

"Yes I could do with a coffee after all of that." I smiled. Amanda and I stepped off to her accommodation block.

I did not know how tonight would go but tomorrow night was one date I was definitely not going to miss.

* * *

I never made that date. Mid-morning the following day I returned from my patrol to find my bunk cleared, my burgen packed and waiting. Standing by it were two elvin Intelligence Cell Officers. My immediate thought was of the kiss yesterday afternoon. After the kiss, we went to Amanda's room. We were careful; I did not think that the senior officers knew it would happen so fast. The Int Cell Officers took me to the newly cleared landing pad and a support dragon came over the trees to hover above the pad.

For loads like us, it was easier and more convenient to winch us up to the cargo hold held beneath the support dragon than to go through a landing sequence. We were winched up by the dragons' aircrew our destination was HQ.

The flight took almost the rest of the day and although sad and disappointed that I would not see Amanda that evening, I was glad to be back in the air once again. The payload area contained a few other passengers strapped into jump seats along the walls, a number of Paras in their Drop Suits; they looked like an Ironman convention. There were some support staff from other established bases hitching a ride back to HQ. None of them were pleased that they had been diverted to our remote outpost to pick us up.

"You owe me several beers!" Company Sergeant Major Dixon grunted from his seat facing me on the other wall. CSM (Dixie) Dixon was an old friend and we had seen a lot of action together; first in Afghanistan then Ganymede. I was one of his corporals when we quashed the Martian miner's rebellion of 2189. Dixie recommended me for promotion to Sergeant then. He was a small man with dark receding hair, he had the heart and the roar of a battle dragon and his slight frame gave many an unfortunate solider the idea that they could push him around. He had spent four years in the SAS before they returned him to the regiment, no one ever found out just why that had happened. The record was sealed, none of the Admin clerks knew, and they knew everything. One thing we did know about Dixie's RTU was that it was not a voluntary "Return to Unit" order.

"Not my fault Dixie!" I called back knowing he would make a large alcoholic hole in my paycheque.

"What's this all about, the Int boys and all that? I heard you bagged yourself a high up beastie boy." CSM Dixon asked.

"Yeah, disappeared from right under our noses, from DQ12 no less." I said as I shifted position to take the jump seat beside him. The Int Cell officers had moved down the payload bay to speak to another elvin officer they seemed to know.

"Those guys were waiting for me after I got back off Stagg." I nodded to the Intelligence officers further down the bay. "I hope they don't have in mind what they had planned for the troll!" I added.

"You're still armed aren't you?" CSM Dixon grabbed the hilt of my katana. I did feel marginally comforted that they had not relieved me of my weapons and I was not on a charge, at least I hoped so.

"The Int boys have been tight lipped about this request." I said.

"Have you done anything wrong? Killed anybody you shouldn't have?" Dixie whispered. I knew Dixie was joking but the thoughts of what I was doing with Amanda yesterday afternoon in her room came to mind. Dixie caught my hesitation.

"What have you done?" He asked.

"You know Lieutenant Stewart?" I asked.

"You didn't. Not with the Ice Queen." Dixie laughed and I knew I should not have told him.

* * *

At HQ, we took the easy way down. The support dragon deflated with great roaring licks of fiery dragon's breath to allow us to touch down on the landing pad. The support dragon remained on top of their under slung payload platform. The dragons on the landing pad usually perched upon their payloads and waited for one or two others to arrive before they crawled off to their crew quarters. The aircrew hoisted up the rear door and deployed the ramp. As we walked down the ramp, the ground crew were in place to unload the various cargos from the massive payload container. My Int Cell escorts flanked me either side and I waved farewell to Dixie and the other soldiers as we made our way off the airfield.

We walked towards the arrivals block; it was strange to hear these massive beasts speak to one another, over our heads, in booming God-like voices. Our dragons spoke English to each other as they considered it polite in our company, however as I was taught and indeed experienced, these dragons seemed to be able to converse in any known language.

The airfield was a strange mixture of RAF airmen and officers busy about their various duties and the flapping and roaring of their winged charges that looked like an invasion of pre-historic flying monsters. There was the noticeable absence of the usual kind of powered aircraft you would expect to see in such a vista. The helicopters, the VTOL ships and war craft, the Mark 18 Eurojet fighters, were all absent. Above us, and ringing the airfield, we could see the old style barrage balloons once used in World War II. Floating, tethered to Kevlar cables to protect the HQ complex from airborne attack, not only from the faerie insurgents on their winged dragon mounts but also from the wild predatory versions of the winged beasts of Sol. This world had not seen the ancient cataclysm that had put an end to the age of the dinosaurs of Earth Prime.

Our air defence batteries were giant crossbows that each had a three-man crew, two archers and a striker. The archers would load and fire the arrows. Within each arrow shaft at the end just behind the metal point was a charge of a magical potion that exploded when the striker spoke the magical word to ignite the charge. Each potion had a different ignition word and the striker had to read the word before the arrow left the crossbow. Some efficient Strikers knew the next dozen or so ignition words so that the Archers could load and fire in rapid succession.

The strangest of all were our own airborne strength. Great dragons to carry aloft our troops and equipment, they could carry up to two hundred men in full battle armour or four full carriages and teams of pulling stock of mulluks; these were the closest things we had to horses on Sol. They were as varied as Earth Prime horses, from the dwarf mulluk to the massive breeds used as farming beasts of burden, and as dependable as our own lumbering oxen. As with horses in our world there were the well groomed, fast running breeds. These faster mulluks served as mounts for our heavy cavalry, two heavy cavalry could match a troll on the field of battle. Although they were generally shaped like horses, they had coats like woolly mammoths and long prehensile snouts like an anteater with boar-like upward growing tusks, which they used to dig into the earth to forage for their food. Those tusks I had seen many times used bull-like to gorge the enemy and toss them, dwarfen, goblin and even trolls into the air.

The light cavalry used two legged reptiles called angors. The size of a pony with sleek dark fur, they moved with the grace of a leopard. Those mounts could run, as long and as fast as an ostrich, they were extremely intelligent and very deadly. It was only with the use of specialised magic and long patience that our beastmasters could tame one of these beasts and bring it under enough control to use effectively. Angors were also used as guard dogs; you knew never to approach one without its charge or a beastmaster with you. Over the years, there had been many hands, arms, legs, and even complete bodies lost to their multiple rows of razor sharp shark like teeth.

One beastmaster, usually quite safe with their magical endowments of control; had suddenly gone AWOL. The authorities thought he had gone native; many here do disappear into the vast stretches of unchartered land never to be heard of again. They would either settle into life as a native or end up as a ready meal for any amount of man-eating plants, animals and people of this earth, especially the trolls. Trolls are quite fond of lightly roasted humans, cooked until the juices run clear. The trolls often said that humans tasted much like grall, pigs to you and me.

For three days we had searched for the beastmaster. Upon the third day one of the angors, a pregnant female, had been sick and another beastmaster found the missing person's hand in the regurgitated contents of the female's stomach. The corralled pack had torn him to pieces and eaten every bit of him, clothes, boots everything. So without a handler or beastmaster and even when muzzled, you just did not approach one if you had no business to do so.

Our air force consisted of fighters mounted on flying beasts, Pteranodons or Petinosauri. Pterodactyls proved far too difficult to tame even by the most talented beast masters. On

Sol, jet engines, propeller powered craft and other such powered aircraft just could not produce enough power to weight ratio to take off. The physics here, so I have been told, was different and different rules of magic enforced solutions without technology.

Yes, some technology worked here but to attempt to develop more than 24 volts on Sol for any sustained time was impossible. The scientists compared it to the law of light speed back in our universe. The critical theoretical value was 23.7 volts. The highest anyone was practically able to produce was 23.2 volts. We did have a lot of equipment that ran from batteries but one other unfortunate inconvenience was that batteries never kept their charge and no amount of sunlight or magical coaxing could push a battery charge for more than 96 hours.

Chapter 12

My new room was a single man room in the sergeant's mess, it was one of the larger ones usually only allocated to warrant officers and it was rare to get such a big room, although I would not be ringing up the mess manager to complain. The room had a shower, toilet and double bed, a two-seat settee with a couple of armchairs around an ornate black lacquered coffee table all sung in the elvin style. In the corner was a rather battered and used writing table; a remnant from the old days of army furniture and at odds with the other fine sung furniture.

I dropped my kit and tried the bed. As I lay down, in my mind, I could feel myself falling further down into the world of dreams. I knew this effect was caused by the enchantment of an elvin bed. I felt like kicking off my boots and sleeping for a week. Better still, I thought as I stretched back on the soft mattress with my body seemingly floating away, when Lieutenant Stewart got some leave I would show her the beautiful furniture in my room, especially the elvin bed. I smiled to myself; I may need to sleep for a week after that. I felt myself drifting off into a sleepy magically enhanced fantasy with Amanda Stewart when there was a crash, and Dixie stood there framed in the doorway where the door used to be.

"Ever heard of knocking, Sir?" I complained.

"Why? What were you doing you didn't want me to see." Dixie laughed.

He gave a low whistle of appreciation for the room and its contents.

"Is that an elvin bed?" He asked.

"Huh, Yeah." I replied shrugging myself out of the enchanted slumber.

"You wanna see the shit room they gave me!" he said. "Get yer lazy ass out of that pit and get down to the bar with me, you've got some beers to buy me." Dixie pointed out; he was never one to hold his words back. I swung myself out of the bed and we made our way down the back stairs and into the bar.

Jens was waiting there for us so that we could sign him in. The corporal was a regular visitor to the sergeant's mess. He had passed his promotion exams and waited for an opening and the pleasure of the Commanding Officer to obtain that third stripe, it was well overdue.

"Got an earlier transport." He explained, as he saw the surprised look on my face.

"You got any idea what's going on?" I asked as we pushed through the western style swing doors into the bar. It was busy but there were plenty of spare tables. I ordered two pints of Carlsberg Special and a synthahol with a few snacks. We still had good old pints in the mess instead of the European litre measure. That was on the orders of the Regimental Sergeant Major, he was an old West Country real ale drinker and his word was law in the Sergeant's mess. I passed the barman my mess card and he swiped for the credits.

We grabbed one of the larger tables as we expected other NCO's to join our company for "sandbag" stories from the frontline.

"We are on CQP for some Nat guests." Jens started to explain, he used the derogatory army slang for the indigenous people of Sol.

"Close Quarter Protection? What guests?" Dixie asked.

"Well I'm sure you'll get briefed sir, I'm supposed to keep it to a 'need to know' basis."

"So they call us back off the frontline instead of giving the duty to those HQ boys or the Black Hawk security guys." I cut in.

"Well every bugger is gonna know around here!" Dixie laughed, "Go on Jenser spill the beans."

"Well apparently we all got requested." Jens went on.

"Requested... by whom?" I asked. It was not unusual for bodyguard duties to be detailed within the regiment and I liked them, I got to see how the officers wined and dined; particularly if they had general officers or civilian dignitaries; but to pull soldiers off forward patrol was practically unheard of and strictly against military protocol. There were plenty of brown nosing bodies around HQ who would jump at the chance to do the easy number, and rub shoulders with the local dignitaries and the occasional royal.

"You know that troll commander, Uffe Jægerblod, the one you let escape, Jon." Jens smiled.

"I didn't bloody let him..." The two men laughed in interruption at my protest and I knew they had me hooked on Jens' iniquitous fishing pole.

"Well." Jens went on. "He's no ordinary commander; he's the Ard Commander of this 10th Legion. The top dog! He pulled off his other three skulls before we got to him, the sneaky bastard."

"So we bagged the big fish. I knew that!" I protested.

"Yeah, well, I bet Amanda didn't tell you he's some royal fella as well, right from the troll Kings court!" Jens added.

"Lieutenant Stewart to you, Corporal Yde." I scolded. "And as a matter of fact she did tell me."

"Ooooh! Aren't we sensitive today Colour!" Dixie laughed.

"What's that on your shoulder?" he asked.

"Where?" I tried to look where Jens was pointing.

"Na it's nothing. I just thought it was some ice melting all over you." The pair burst out laughing again.

"Hey Dixie, the Colour here smacked this troll up side the back of his head with his own spear. He could have killed him!" Jens laughed pointing at me irreverently with his thumb.

"Yes Jenser, I do recall he was murdering you to death with his bare hands." I said coolly as I leaned back in my chair and took a long cold drink of my much-appreciated pint.

"So what's the detail then?" Dixie asked; he was six years my senior and I had first met him when he was my instructor corporal and I was a new Para recruit. If I ever needed a second father, he would be the one. Dixie had been the mixed martial arts champion for eight straight years until Jens had arrived and literally knocked him off his undefeated pedestal.

Jens continued to explain. "This Ard Commander Uffe Jægerblod has requested us."

"God he's only just escaped last night!" I exclaimed.

"Yes, tell me about it! He's now leading a joint troll military and nisse government envoy for talks with our own lot. Ricky the office clerk tells me there are fifteen trolls and twenty nisse dignitaries and all of their staff. Their lead ambassador is this fairy princess of the Seelie Court called Princess Erika Nisse who is also commander of their armies."

"You mean like supreme commander? Like Field Marshal L'Rundel?" I asked. I had never met Field Marshal L'Rundel but I had heard him address the Joint Land Forces once. He was the top ranking elvin officer and one of King L'Rundel's cousins and close advisors.

"It has been said that she outranks him." Jens added.

A young elvin officer of the general staff appeared at our table, we had not heard or seen him approach, most had the ability to move around unnoticed, and they were mostly secretive little men. This elvin looked different from his comrades, instead of the upward pointing ears; they were even larger and swept back. His eyebrows extended to his hairline and he wore a neat Van Dyke beard. I knew without ever seeing one before that this was a nisse.

"Sergeants... Corporal." The Lieutenant addressed us rather formally. We were in our mess so we had no obligation to stand up; we all did in polite respect for his commission even though it looked like he should not be out of school. The young man took a step back in mild surprise and spoke again.

"Gentlemen... I am Lieutenant Sareal on Princess Erika Nisse's personal staff." He stated with pride.

"How did you get in here sir?" Dixie asked. All guests, especially one that was armed and from another force would be held in a secure corral and not permitted onto the base proper unless vetted or escorted.

"I was dispatched by Ard Commander Uffe Jægerblod's request." Lieutenant Sareal replied flatly, he knew the intent of

Dixie's question but his obtuse reply indicated his unspoken intent not to explain how he managed to get past the guards both natural and supernatural.

"Sir." I interrupted. Dixie opened his mouth to further challenge but I butted in to save embarrassment on both sides.

"Sir, may I respectfully request you state your business?" I asked. I used the formal address required to give to an elvin officer wearing the purple sash of an official diplomatic messenger; even if he was a nisse, it was close enough.

Lieutenant Sareal reached to his leather messenger pouch, a diplomatic bag, properly badged and strapped to his unusually plain and unadorned weapons belt. Diplomatic messengers were usually from high houses and the young officers purchased the most expensive jewelled swords and scabbards. Usually they wore a finely tooled weapons belt with a gaudy ceremonial sword; the scabbard would be bejewelled with precious and semi-precious stones and gold or silver filigree. This messenger's weapons belt was old, scored and pitted, the scabbard plain but well-oiled leather, the sword handle looked well worn, perhaps replaced several times from the markings around the hilt. This sword had seen many battles maybe an old family heirloom. Our hands went to our daggers; Lieutenant Sareal froze.

"Gentlemen, with your permission." He said smoothly. "May I deliver you this message contained within?" He asked, watching our hands. A classic mistake by such an inexperienced officer; he should have been watching our eyes. A fighter's eyes will give away his intent to strike a fraction before his hands or feet move, a technique that saved my life on many occasions.

"Jon, Dixie." Jens nodded for us to follow his eyes. The Lieutenants left breast displayed amongst other diplomatic and campaign flashes, and almost hidden, the small blue and yellow flash of the New France Campaign. The Nisse Emperor Kings elite group of imperial guards, the SkyggenNisse, fought this famous campaign. The Elvin King and his Supreme Court magician had endowed them before the battle almost ninety-five years ago. Since that Campaign only a few Nisse have been given the endowment. SkyggenNisse could move at blinding speed, many times faster than a normal elvin or nisse and with the strength of ten; a single elvin had considerable strength under normal circumstances.

The Lieutenant looked no more than nineteen years old, but with this blue and yellow flash, I put the true age of this young Nisse to be more than one hundred and twenty years old. The hair on the nape of my neck stood on end, the three of us made no more than an even match for this seemingly junior officer. He glanced up to our eyes as he saw that we had noticed his campaign decorations. I realised the age and experience reflected in his dark brown eyes. His eyes had been lowered, not through inexperience, but to disguise his vast combat experience. We were looking into the eyes of a killing machine, a SkyggenNisse and not those of a young inexperienced staff lieutenant as I had first thought. I was grateful no one had drawn his weapon.

Dixie being the senior soldier nodded his acceptance and we all relaxed our stances. Lieutenant Sareal produced a black silk package from his diplomatic pouch and placed it on the table; he opened the cloth and smoothed it flat with respectful care around its contents, careful not to touch the crystal contained within. The crystal was a smooth ball, a little larger than a tennis ball with a flattened bottom and as clear as glass. The nisse indicated that we should take our seats again.

"Colour Sergeant Raine, if you would care to touch the crystal." He requested. I hesitated, unsure if I should or not.

"Colour Sergeant, the crystal is keyed only to you, any other touch would erase the device and the message contained within. There would be an uncomfortable shock. I assure you Colour Sergeant that you will feel nothing and there is no danger to you or any one of your company." The diplomatic messenger explained. "Please." He added politely and indicated to the crystal with his outstretched hand.

I leaned forward and touched the globe.

Chapter 13

The room about us dimmed and it lost its vibrancy of colour. I knew this to be an enchanted privacy shield. To all others in the room, unless they stepped past the ward they would only see us sitting there looking at the crystal but see or hear nothing else. This type of enchantment came in differing strengths and variations; from this type of passive ward to a full strength shield that would make us all disappear, and passing the shield would either melt the flesh from your bones or immolate you depending on race and combination of the ward.

The boundary of the ward was marked on the ground by the illusion of white petal daisies that showed the edge of such a faerie ring. Although I had never witnessed it myself, some of the faerie rings had the ability to transform a person stepping across the border into any type of animal or insect. This forced transformation could at times be a permanent change and the only way the Psy Signal Corps had found to reverse such a change was to bring the affected person back through a portal to Earth Prime where the most powerful permanent spell would dissipate in a few days. Most of these permanent transformed humans died in the process, the change was long and painful, all of those so far that changed into an insect without lungs, died. The unfortunate individuals who changed into insects found that the transforming body could not sustain both systems while the change took place; the remaining survival rate was less than twenty percent.

On the other hand, one of the more amusing aspects of this type of curse was that any person so changed could not increase or decrease in physical mass, this resulted in the unfortunate individual being transformed into a fifteen stone bug, spider, mini dragon or elephant.

I read a report once of a human beastmaster accidentally transformed into a small Pegasus. He refused to make the journey back through the portal. The beastmaster remained very happily as a native with a herd of beautiful and obedient female

Pegasi who adore him. He remained loyal to the Euroforce and his herd of devoted wives currently act as reconnaissance scouts up on the northern border between Alfheim and Lugon.

* * *

The area above the crystal misted into a mini storm cloud with flashes of blue lightning within the rolling angry darkness. From the centre, the cloud lightened and spread outwards stabilising the storm into a settled lighter cloud. Ard Commander Uffe Jægerblod's face and shoulders seemed to grow within the confines of the cloud as if the fabric of the cloud itself sculpted his bust.

"Colour Sergeant Raine and friends." Uffe looked about as if seeing Jens and Dixie. We had been told that these crystals contained only recordings and could not act as two-way communications.

"Sir, you can see us... hear us?" I asked

"No Jon." Uffe laughed showing his rows of deadly fangs. Dixie leaned into me and whispered. "Dude! You captured that!"

"Way!" I nodded.

Uffe continued. "We have made some improvements to the crystals and the enchantment engages this reply to your question. It is still very limited and this is only a beta test release." Uffe looked again at Jens and Dixie. "The crystal detects others by you and adjusts accordingly. I did the upgrade personally. Nice piece of kit don't you agree." Uffe announced with pride. I was about to agree in spite of Uffe's explanation but caught myself before I spoke.

"Jon, first I wish to apologise to you for the ruse of appearing to be a lower ranking officer and second for appearing to escape under your custody. I did not break my oath bond nor shame you in this, as Major Morgan claimed my custody when I took the life of that rude corporal." Dixie glanced at me and I indicated that I would explain that later.

"When he gave me back into your custody, that required a new oath, thus my oath word was honoured and my escape made possible. As I said to you before, it is only a technicality." He smiled that deadly smile again.

"Apology accepted and understood." I replied.

"Aha! Good... good!" Uffe's image exclaimed with a hearty laugh, a laugh that sounded worryingly like their trollish battle roars. His expression became serious and his head leaned forward in a comparative manner. We all leaned back through instinct alone.

"Jon. There is trouble... I cannot explain in full as the intelligence we have is circumstantial and the sources are unreliable. Nevertheless tomorrow night at the officers' ball in honour of Princess Erika Nisse there is to be an attempt on the Princess Royal's life." Uffe let the startling news settle upon us before he continued.

"We have long known of Baron Mikal Nisse's designs on the Seeley throne. The Baron is a RiNisse, a royal by right of blood. We know he has a circle of friends and allies who believe he has an ancient claim to the throne. Princess Erika, as first daughter to Emperor King Kennet and First Captain of the nisse host, stands between Baron Mikal Nisse and Emperor King Kennet. It is our belief that tomorrow evening at the first official engagement between your people and the Nisse Nation, Princess Erika will be assassinated and the blame placed with NATO, the Euroforce and more specifically the Dragon Riders.

I tell you this tale as you and your friends here will act as Princess Erika's personal guard and escort at the ball. You three and two others of your special detachment will be permitted close proximity privileges. You will be permitted to touch the Princess without the usual forfeit of your lives and I guarantee no automatic executions will be required no matter what your actions. Please be aware gentlemen, that Princess Erika believes her SkyggenNisse, RiNisse Guard and personal staff sufficient for her personal safety, she resists and resents this arrangement.

The princess is aware of this unusual threat and the steps we take to combat them. Because of this, the Princess has reluctantly agreed to your privilege. This high privilege is only ever extended to a few of her closest assistants and SkyggenNisse. Never before has another race been given such a boon, not even a race of Sol. You may think her SkyggenNisse extremely formidable and able to meet this challenge. I would agree but there is suspicion that Barron Mikal's allies may infiltrate them and the RiNisse Guard. I have chosen you three based on my personal screeings and those of my king's court sorcerers hence the nature of our meetings." Uffe explained.

"Commander, do you mean this has all been prearranged? Your capture and all?" Jens asked.

Uffe's image looked at Jens and then to Dixie.

"Yes Corporal Jens Yde that is so." Ard Commander Jægerblod replied and added. "CSM Dixon may I recall your famous running skirmish in the Iron Woods of Jurançon?"

"Yes I remember it very well. Two years ago my company was ambushed by a troll force of over one hundred beasts." Uffe coughed in interruption. "Apologies, over one hundred troll Jaeger Vagt, a sortie from the mountains to the south. We ran a running battle for nine days and lost nearly a third of my troop. The overall count was three hundred men dead, and fifty Jaeger Vagt." As Dixie recalled the battle, his own storm cloud reflected in his countenance.

"Yes, a fine battle and some very fine barbecues." Uffe remarked. Dixie tensed ready to spring to his feet, his anger red in his face.

"No CSM Dixon, please... I mean no disrespect! Your men fought valiantly and I salute both the living and the dead as heroes. Their songs are still sung by our tribes at our camp fires."

Dixie relaxed a little at the high trollish honour of which Uffe spoke.

"Do you remember the battle where you lost your sword in the forest clearing? A veteran troll with a missing right horn surprised and disarmed you in his attack?"

"Yes I do. I was backed against a large boulder and the troll's spear was inches from my chest." Dixie further explained.

"And on the death thrust another troll knocked his spear aloft and flipped your katana back into your hand. Remember that CSM Dixon?"

A sudden realisation and recognition flashed across Dixie's shocked face.

"It was you sir. It was you!"

"Yes CSM Dixon, I was that soldier!" Uffe replied with his hearty laugh.

"And you Jens Yde of Sweden. The brave one to stand against one such as me." Uffe looked at Jens. Jens nodded with a self-satisfied smile; we could see Dixie was jealous.

"Your family would summer in Tyresta Park, South East of Stockholm would they not?"

Jens nodded in reply; we were all interested in where this was going.

"And when you were 11 years old, did you not wander into the woods as the sun kissed Sol and you became lost?"

"I did. I would never forget that experience." Jens said. "I wandered about for hours as the night approached and in the darkness I became completely lost. In the shadows of the undergrowth, something big and black moved towards me. Like a bear or a monster, it huffed and growled. I ran for my life too frightened to even look back. The monster almost got me several times and I had to change direction as it pursued me. Remarkably I ended up back at the camp scared witless but safe and sound."

"Can you remember what you were shouting as you ran into the camp Jens Yde of Sweden." Uffe asked.

Jens was silent for a moment then the light of realisation lit up his eyes.

"Yes... Yes I do. I remember now. I was shouting Troll! Troll! The Troll is after me! It was you Sir, wasn't it? You were the monster in the forest." Jens said, finally realising what Uffe was getting at.

"Yes I was that troll." Uffe Smiled.

"And it was no accident that I ran back to the camp was it?" Jens smiled.

Uffe grinned back.

"And you Jon." Uffe looked towards me.

"You were the troll in the forest that ran into that other troll that was going to spear me during the attack."

"Yes, but more than that, Jon. I have known your family for many years. Your Great Grandmother had a story of the troll that lived in her cupboard. You know that story Jon?"

"I do. I know it very well. She called him her troll prince. She told stories of how he would take her through her cupboard and into his kingdom where he presented her before his father the King. It was an upside world to her, where those that looked like monsters were good and those that looked fair were bad. My Grandmother took her mother's stories and published them as a set of novels; she became a famous fantasy writer... That was you wasn't it Uffe?"

Uffe nodded with a sad smile on his face.

"Yes she was a fine woman."

"You were the troll that lived in her cupboard." I asked astounded at the revelation.

"Yes I was that troll." Uffe smiled and even his rows of fanged shaped teeth could not put the usual menace to the sad and melancholy shadow that sat upon his face.

"And the stories my grandmother wrote, the ones that made her a famous writer. They were all true... real experiences? About her Mother?" I asked.

"Your Grandmother Linda found your Great Grandmothers journals and thought them fantasy musings of her mother's imagination. They were your Great Grandmothers diaries, not faerie stories as the world believed. They were accounts of your Great Grandmothers adventures with me." Uffe replied.

"Uffe. Were you the monster under my bed?" I asked
Uffe Nodded.

"And the monster under my bed?" Asked Dixie

"And..." Jens began but Uffe prompted his question with a nod.

"You have been grooming us for something, haven't you?" Dixie asked in suspicion of Uffe's motives.

"A troll's plans are long in the making and to live as long as a troll you have to be very patient. Very patient indeed."

"This is part of it isn't it? This CQP detail we are taking on." I asked the cloud head of Uffe Jægerblod.

"I must stress that you must be careful tomorrow night. Barron Mikal is a RiNisse, a minor royal. Nisse are very clever and sophisticated fae, they are highly evolved and very experienced magicians as well as the fiercest fighters' trolls have ever eaten. They have the most experienced non gnomish Snigmorder on Sol." Uffe Warned.

"What's a Snigmorder?" Was Dixie's worried question.

"Assassins." Jens explained.

"Correct." Uffe nodded and continued his impromptu lecture. "Baron Mikal belongs to the Unseelie Court and he wants the Emperors throne and title, to rule the Seelie Court. He wants the UnSeelie Court back in power, not just for half the year as it was of old but also for the whole year long, just as the Seelie Court rule now. The Unseelie Court of dark fae have a long time grudge, eight hundred years ago the Seelie Court refused to give up their rule at the end of their summer semester. They have ruled all year long since then and the Unseelie Court have thus far been unable to wrest control from the Emperor Kings Seelie Court.

This assignment more than any other you men have undertaken, will be the most dangerous you have ever performed. Do not be distracted by the pretty uniforms and polite dignified company, there will be real and deadly monsters at this ball and most of them will look like Prince Charming." Uffe warned us with a seriousness that left us no doubt to the veracity of his warning.

"OK sir, we understand and will take great care with our duties. I will immediately inform ..." I made to detail our plans.

"No! This communication must not go beyond this company here now." Uffe hastily interrupted.

"Ard Commander Jægerblod, with all due respect, we cannot agree to that." Dixie responded. "We have a duty to report all acts of aggression. We cannot..."

"CSM Dixon, you all owe me your lives. I want to assure you that I have communicated this threat to your General Staff and they are aware of the highest confidentiality of this matter. Your forces are officially informed and protocol requires that the safety of the princess will fall on Euroforce shoulders and will be their sole responsibility. Should harm befall her, your General Carson has a recorded message from my King, King Ullrick and his Royal Highness Emperor King Kennet himself. When you go to your briefing, you will be informed accordingly and I ask you only keep this communication in confidence until then. If you are not satisfied after the briefing is over then you are free to make whatever report you feel necessary. Can we at least agree on that?"

Jens and I looked to Dixie, as he was the senior soldier; it was up to him to make this decision.

"Sir, with all due respect, you are asking us to trust a troll officer. This is an unprecedented scenario and we are not commissioned officers." Dixie took a moment to seriously consider Uffe's request. "However I see no reason to delay making our report until after our briefing." Dixie paused to further consider Uffe's demand and added. "I see it like this. I will be able to comply with our military duties and obligations by verbalising the intent to file a full report after the briefing unless ordered to do otherwise by a ranking officer. What say you men?"

Jens and I nodded our assent. My experience of trolls was of many battles, skirmishes and sorties plus two conversations with this Ard Commander Jægerblod. Against all common sense and rationality obtained through long years of experience of the trollish nations, I felt that I could trust this man... Man. There, I had said it to myself. I saw the troll as a man and not as a brutish animalistic enemy. Did I even consider this troll an enemy? Was it the fight with Jens? Was it his amazing use of Kung Fu? Was it the long walk back to camp or the conversation that evening in DQ12? I did not know. With this man, my image of these trollish brutes changed. Did my attitude change just for him and his tribe or was it for the entire trollish nation?

Dixie closed the deal with our temporary obligation of secrecy.

"I am pleased you could find a way to proceed. Now I have no need to execute you!" Uffe laughed and his image winked out. The cloud disappeared and the room snapped back to normal as the ward and its border of daises disappeared.

We sprang to our feet in an attempt to anticipate any threat. With the faerie ring, disappearing and our flourish of drawn steel, other armed NCO's in the mess drew weapons to support us in whatever threat we faced. None came.

"Anything? Jon? Jenser?" Dixie asked scanning the room, his katana before him.

"Nothing." I reported.

"Nothing ... not even Lieutenant Sareal!" Jenser added quietly.

Blades flashed around the room as fellow NCO's seeing no attack began to sheath their weapons.

"Hey Jon, just how good do you think he was?" Dixie asked.

"Maybe we find out tomorrow." I replied pushing my katana back into my scabbard.

"Anyone see the elvin officer leave?" Dixie called out. No one replied.

"Sir! He has signed out!" The club steward called from the doorway.

"How did he do that?" Jens exclaimed.

The steward shrugged his shoulders.

Chapter 14

After a long well deserved sleep in my elvin bed, I spent the morning jogging and exercising with the other men called in for this CQP detail. In the afternoon we had Captain Dennison's brief. Captain Dennison was our liaison for the royal visit and he was well versed in nisse history and customs. He received an endowment of tongues and he was fluent in nisse language and script.

In the afternoon, our CQP troop of thirty Paras gathered in our ready room. Captain Dennison carried out the usual security briefing and handed the meeting over to Lieutenant Sareal to brief us on the finer points of royal protocol for the following night. Every one of the thirty Paras detailed off for this CQP duty was a seasoned battle veteran. We could ill afford any lack of experience on this detail.

"Men!" In closing, Captain Dennison began. "Anyone here not fully conversant with the wing protocol of the royal household?"

Most of the NCO's raised their hands in a spontaneous group lie. It was rumoured that the 3D holovid of the wing protocol was the most erotic movie you could watch legally and we were going to see it free.

"In a moment Lieutenant Sareal will run through the wing protocol. Anyone the least unsure had better take advantage of this opportunity. Do not become distracted by the elvin and the nisse in the show, learn from it. That will be all, men." We all stood as the Captain moved to the door and left the briefing room.

In Lieutenant Sareal's lecture of the elvin wing protocol, he played the demonstrations in high definition 3D and it did prove the rumours true.

After the lecture and 3D video show, Lieutenant Sareal asked if there were any questions. No one raised a hand; most of us were stunned at the sexual intensity of the holovid. All of us were of the same rank for the evening but we all stood as Sareal left the room an automatic reaction from veteran soldiers.

The thirty strong squad had about twenty minutes to wait for the transport. We used the time to have a last coffee and run to the bathroom.

"Do you think these pig stickers really work?" Jens asked fingering his black leather holster, the weapon loose and ready for a quick draw.

"Do you want me to shoot you and see Corporal?" Dixie asked.

"Just asking, Sir." Jens replied somewhat offended.

"Well the chickens didn't stand a chance." I added to lighten the mood. I drew a cup of coffee from the Urn. Dixie drew his weapon and weighed the solid weight of it in his hand.

"Magic ray guns! What will they come up with next?" Dixie laughed.

"Well at least they made them look like proper field issue side arms rather than those weird girlie weapons they demonstrated in the holovids." I added drawing my own sidearm.

This was the first time I saw a Scorpion pistol, they were rarer than sorcerer's sand due to a sourcing problem with the payload. Physically the weapons were easy enough to manufacture but the ammunition was a bitch to get hold of. We each had a full complement of thirty rounds and there were plans to develop weapons with up to seventy rounds each. The bigger rifles and machineguns would hold hundreds of rounds. The manufacturing difficulty holding back the mass issue of the weapons lay with the poison used in the slug.

The slug was approximately the size and weight of a household sewing needle and made of toughened absorbent plastic that held the poison. The slug had a monomolecular point and would, if needed, penetrate any armour used in Sol. This poison was proving very difficult for our scientists to reproduce artificially. A rare New Spanish scorpion produced it naturally. Less than an inch long, its venom caused instant body paralysis immediately followed by death, it worked on everything and there was no cure and no time to administer one even if one was developed.

The delivery system within the pistol, modelled after the old Browning 9 mm, was a twofold system. First the poison needle was embedded into its round which was a slimmer version of a standard ballistic .22calibre shell. The load consisted of compressed gas. The round would not eject as if a normal spent round. It was held in a chain within the magazine that moved one position with the firing of the weapon to present a new round in the firing position within the alignment chamber. The magazines would be loaded in the standard way. When the weapon was fired, the round would be expelled along the barrel and at exit, the really interesting stuff would begin.

Each weapon had a micro portal that flashed open as the needle accelerated up the barrel. The portal allowed the needle to enter into some sort of special space that allowed the payload to travel in a straight line until the needle struck living tissue in our space. At this point, the needle would somehow move back into our physical world so that it could embed itself in that living tissue. It used its microscopic barbs to slow its velocity. The barbs also held the droplets of poison.

A poison round fired at a target at any distance, the delivery looked instantaneous. The payload, the scientists told us, would go on forever until stopped by a living body. Now, some of these scientific types argued that as the universe was shaped like a donut due to the law of multidimensional space, the needle if unhampered would simply travel in a straight line before arriving back at its original location. The time it took to travel this unbelievable distance would be about one hour. They were able to come up with this time calculation as some of the rounds turned up back at the same place approximately an hour after been fired. The first time it happened, an unfortunate lab assistant cleaning the firing range proved the theory when she stopped the bullet in her thigh.

During tests, the dart only reappeared five times in twenty experiments. The other fifteen shots they believed, encountered living flesh during its journey circumnavigating the Sollen universe. That meant that the rest of the deadly needles killed fifteen something's during their journey around the universe. I could imagine some unbelievably exotic creature in some far off galaxy just falling down dead in the street. It worried me to think of what mayhem these Scorpion pistols would cause when they became more widely used.

To gauge the effectiveness of the poison, Earth Prime scientists tested it on every living thing it could possibly strike, including five subjects of every race, including humans. We were told that the five humans were volunteers, either terminally ill or severely disabled. In UFE law, such unfortunates had the right to assisted suicide. The law was called the Dignitas Act. The government approached some test subjects. The ones that signed up to be shot were given, in whatever time they had left, the very best treatment and living arrangements either world could offer and their spouses or near relatives were given generous pensions and benefits that afforded them the luxury of never having to worry about money again. We were not given any details about the sentient subjects of Sol and we did not ask. All we were told was that the tests were an absolute success.

Now we had side arms of a sort, and soon we would be able to soldier as the Gods intended.

"Dixie, what do you think our chances are against SkyggenNisse, Jaeger Vagt or gnome Militaar and the like?" Jens asked, examining his scorpion pistol, we dubbed them scorpion after the source of the venom.

"Maybe two against one and on an even playing field we might stand a chance." Dixie reflected.

"About right I think." I added. "So long as they don't get a hold of these scorpions."

Jens' eyebrows rose in alarm as he realized the implications of one of the weapons getting into the hands of such master assassins.

Like me, most of the men in the room had spent the last nine months in battledress. However, this night we were to be paraded in Number One best blues. We were all to have the local rank of lieutenant for this guard detail and our uniforms were adorned with the two pips of that rank on each shoulder. Our knee-high boots we polished to a high gloss finish our dark blue tunics immaculate adorned with our individual campaign and battle medals. Some of the least decorated men in the detail wore more than five of these battle and campaign flashes. Others drew appreciative glances and comments as we battle hardened veterans preened ourselves and each other like a group of giddy nymph feather dancers.

As one, we all rejected wearing the NATO blue beret for our own burgundy Para berets with the winged badge and hackle of the dragon riders. Our breeches were tan coloured riding jodhpurs as worn by the cavalry regiments, and adopted by the regiment with the addition of the Para burgundy stripe down the outside of the leg. For the first time, I wore the leather 'Sam Brown' belt of an officer to which was attached my katana, tanto and scorpion pistol, a few of the men swaggered about like courtier officers out of the history vids to the cat calls and rude remarks only found in the enlisted men's barrack room. It was unusual for us to have the local rank of lieutenant but this was an unusual CQP duty.

Para guards in battledress opened the double doors, they stood to attention as Captain Dennison and Lieutenant Sareal strode back in, both dressed in parade uniform minus the scorpion pistols. Sareal wore his long thin foil of the elvin, and I supposed nisse officer caste, I could tell it was the same sword he had worn in the Sergeants Mess. The hilt and circular guard handle were plain and functional, the leather bound handle well worn; his sword was not that of a ceremonial court fop but a weapon as deadly as any of our own katanas. Those that made the mistake of thinking otherwise would pay the price in blood. Sareal glanced at our pistol pouches with a puzzled frown; I could see that he had no knowledge of the scorpions. As they entered, some of us stood, others hesitated as their inbred discipline conflicted with our new, if temporary, officer status.

"At ease gentlemen! At last a cadre of officers that can fight!" Captain Dennison laughed. We all laughed in jest, every enlisted man complained of pampered officers but we all knew from our individual battle experience that our own officers could and would fight alongside the best of us. Captain Dennison remained standing as we returned to our seats. A few stood at the back of the room joined by Lieutenant Sareal.

"Men! We have a rare and privileged service and assignment to perform tonight. You all know your respective roles. Lieutenants Dixon, Raine, Yde, Jameson and Brownlee will act as last line to the Princess's person. Her personal guard have been briefed and to be candid men, there remains some resistance to this unique arrangement. Do not forget men that these RiNisse guard are seasoned veterans including without doubt the Jaeger Vagt assigned to Ard Commander Jægerblod." Captain Dennison indicated Lieutenant Sareal and continued. "Lieutenant Sareal informs us that there are SkyggenNisse among the RiNisse guard. Treat them with due respect, notwithstanding, and I make this very clear. This company present in this room have full authority to act in complete control of all situations and the personal safety of the princess and the general officers are in your hands this evening.

"You have all been handpicked, and I know that you have all served with each other down through the years. You may not all be bosom pals but I know you have respect for each other's experience and professionalism as I certainly do.

"Those with specific duties, attend them closely, take your lead from those assigned to the princess, as they must at all times have direct access and physical contact with their subject. You other men will, with full authority and by whatever means necessary, perform and carry out your duties. Gentlemen, lethal force is authorized. That will be all." The captain closed his address. We remained in stunned silence for a few moments. I could only remember two situations where lethal force orders had been issued, both times all hell had broken loose.

As soldiers, we were used to using force and indeed lethal force as the situation warranted it, but a Lethal Force Order was different. No matter what we did in the execution of our duties, no action or investigation would be undertaken against us. It was an uncommon order and rarely issued and only after a great deal of consideration and situation analysis. To give such an order to a group of Paras was almost unheard of. Still there it was and the guys in the room would without hesitation deal death in an instant, I myself was just as handy with my scorpion and trusty katana.

We filed out of the room into the corridor.

"Princess' personal guard this way please." Lieutenant Sareal called through the bustle of passing men. He indicated a side door and the five of us moved through it and into an office as large as our ready room. Behind a large highly polished oak desk on an elvin sung ogre armchair, sat Ard Commander Uffe Jægerblod. The only items on the desk were a dwarfen made silver serving tray upon which sat two crystal decanters and five matching sherry glasses. The decanters held liquids of different shades of yellow.

Jameson and Brownlee hesitated at the doorway seeing the bulk of the troll lounging resplendent in his trollish robes of office. Gold and silver thread sown through his cloak that was draped off a chest piece of gem encrusted gleaming gold. Uffe was adorned with enough gemstones and precious metal to ransom a king.

"Ah gentlemen, the princess' escort!" Uffe rose from the richly upholstered ogre chair sung from a single piece of wood that looked like walnut. The chair could comfortably sit two adult men. Uffe stepped around the polished oak desk and lifted one of the crystal decanters; he poured three glasses from one and two more from the other decanter.

As if a demonic waiter from the deepest level of Hades, Uffe passed out the glasses from the tray serving a glass to each of the men. Uffe could see us looking askance as he gave particular glasses to each of us.

"Mister Yde and Mister Brownlee get the other glasses because they are not blood group O positive." Uffe explained as if we should understand.

"What's in here?" Dixie asked, examining the contents of his sherry glass.

"You have in there an enchanted elixir developed by our finest trollish magicians. We created it in response to the SkyggenNisse endowment that enhances their abilities. The original elixir was developed to put our Jaeger Vagt on an even playing field. It will give you the abilities of our Jaeger Vagt. By taking this elixir you will be as empowered as the SkyggenNisse."

"Cool!" exclaimed Brownlee and downed his glass in one gulp.

"Why not give this to the whole crew?" Dixie asked, putting the glass to his lips.

"It is very rare and difficult to produce; this strain developed for humans is only in its experimental stage. We do not know if it will kill you. A lot of blood, sweat and tears went into that!"

Brownlee retched as Dixie moved the glass away from his mouth and wiped his lips.

"Uffe, when you say a lot of blood sweat and tears, do you really mean ...?" I began to ask. Uffe nodded as we fell silent looking at the glasses Uffe had served to us.

The troll studied Brownlee for a few silent moments.

"There now, I knew it would work!" He smiled. "Well gentlemen if it were to kill Sergeant, oh sorry, I mean Lieutenant Brownlee, then he would be dead now." Uffe added. He looked rather proud of himself. Brownlee's face was ashen; he took a seat seemingly unsteady on his feet.

"It will pass in a moment." Uffe assured him with his deadly fanged smile that did little to comfort the shaken man.

I looked at Dixie and he looked at me.

"Senior soldier?" I suggested and raised my glass in salute. Dixie regarded the glass again and downed his shot with one gulp.

"Quite nice." He remarked smacking his lips. I took mine slowly to savour it in my mouth before swallowing, it tasted like goats piss! I grimaced and forced it down.

"Goats piss! Bloody goats piss!" I coughed. Dixie laughed.

"Yes Lieutenant Raine, one of the main ingredients." Uffe replied. He nodded seriously as if explaining a creation of an exotic cocktail. The others hesitated and Uffe urged them to drink up. My head started to spin as if I had just drank a full bottle of fine Bushmills whiskey. I put my hand on the desk to steady myself as I felt I would topple over. As the head spinning passed, I could see that the men had suffered a similar fate. Jens, who was a teetotaller and only drank synthahol, fell to the ground and was on one knee steadying himself before rising.

"This small amount of elixir will remain in your systems for nearly two weeks depending on your own metabolic and body absorption rates." Uffe explained his voice seemed to grate upon my ears with this enhanced hearing.

"Please take a few minutes to orientate yourselves before re-joining your party. The rest of the men will be waiting for you by the coaches outside."

Colours, smells and sounds assailed my body and it took me a few moments to separate and process all the new information. I could discern hues and colours that before I could not see.

"Gods this is like smoking the biggest joint in the world and downing a full bottle of Viagra at the same time!" Brownlee exclaimed with a wide smile.

"I had noticed that." Dixie replied as he shifted uncomfortably in his tight riding breeches. I felt no less comfortable myself.

"Watch this!" Jens called and drew his pistol; it was out in an instant, back in his holster and back out again. Although quicker than the human eye, our enhanced vision could see the complete movement.

"That was cool!" Brownlee said and repeated Jens' quick draw action.

"If you think that is impressive, watch this." Dixie said. He took the decanter and pulled it along a pane of glass in a sideboard door. The pointed nodule on the decanter body etched the glass in the door.

"That guys, is a diamond decanter!" Dixie held the container up to the light. I examined the glass still in my hand and touched it to my teeth.

"This as well!" I added.

"Yes gentlemen, just as the elvin sing wood; we trolls sing the stone and precious gems." Uffe held up the silver tray. "This and my rather ornate robes are sung by the dwarfen people."

"So what do nymphs do?" Brownlee asked.

"With your new found vigour, I am sure you will find out lad!" Uffe laughed. "But not before you fulfil tonight's duties I hope." Uffe slapped Brownlee's back. I noticed that Brownlee did not recoil as much as an ordinary human would after such a powerful if friendly blow.

"OK men ... to work!" Dixie, the ever-dutiful Company Sergeant Major called us to order.

Lieutenant Sareal led us out of the building to the three royal elvin coaches each with a team of six snow-white pegasi all resplendent their snow-white wings tucked swan like upon their backs. Their great, feathered wings flexing through their silver studded harnesses. The coaches were something straight out of an H.C.Anderson faerie tale and I felt a little embarrassed as the Lieutenant showed us to the middle one. While the front and back coaches were ornate in the extreme, our coach was a massive jewel encrusted golden pumpkin. I had never before seen an elvin royal coach let alone a nisse one. We had been briefed that the coaches were magically enhanced, and could perform some amazing feats. They would be ideal protection to get the Princess to the officers' mess and after that, hundreds of Euroforce military would surround her.

"So Cinderella shall go to the ball!" Dixie remarked to hide his own embarrassment behind his soldierly bravado.

"Seems like it." I answered, inspecting the gold leaf Celtic designs of the pumpkin shaped transport, the thing was enormous and four grown men could sit abreast inside. I noticed that two of the troopers sat upon the footman's seat to the rear and another two sat, one each side of the nisse driver in front. The wheels of the carriage stood six foot high. Between the front and back wheels there ran a footboard on which stood one of the CQP guard, each side of the coach. Uffe halted us before we made to climb into the coach.

"You will be riding inside with the princess when we pick her up. I will be in the last coach with my staff. There will be two ladies riding attendance with the princess and another five in each of the coaches.

May you die in glory with your sword sheathed in your enemy's bloody chest." Uffe placed his massive claw-like hand on my shoulder. His trollish farewell did little to dispel the discomforting thought that this would not be the usual highbrow "meet and greet" dinner and dance everyone expected.

Lieutenant Davies opened the heavy coach door and pulled down the three folding steps.

"Ladies. If you please?" He gestured to the open carriage doorway.

"You'll be pulling the dirtiest duties for the rest of the month, Corporal." Dixie snarled in a fair impression of Uffe's trollish growl.

"Mister Davies if you please, Lieutenant." Davies smirked back; I could see he was going to enjoy his moment no matter what the cost.

"That Lethal Force Order may just include you, Mister Davies." I laughed as I climbed in after the growling CSM.

Chapter 15

The hot humid day had begun to cool as the sun; an amber furnace, kissed Sol to the east. I ran my fingers between my high buttoned collar and my freshly shaven neck. My newly enhanced senses caused even this minor discomfort to increase tenfold.

Our squad stood lined up outside the elvin embassy. A tall-spiralled palace of graceful lines and a fantasy like elegance. The entire structure sung from Ironwood in modular form, and fused together with enchanted elvin magical seals once assembled. This embassy stood in various places for the past one thousand years; it took twelve powerful nisse sorcerers in a magic circle to transport the nisse palace from one place to another.

Usually three weeks before the royal palace was due to arrive, dwarfen sappers and nisse engineers would turn up and create a massive concrete like surface for the wooden palace to sit upon. The gardens that would surround the palace were planted and sung to maturity. For those three weeks, the place has an air of carnival about it, while the village or city prepares to host the royal family. When completed the palace appears out of magical mists and an official royal ball is held that evening in and around the grounds. Local nisse commoner, dignitaries, and lower ranking officers and officials are invited to see and meet the princess and at times the Emperor King Kennet himself.

The palace is said to be a miniature image of the nisse Emperor King's personal palace; this miniature replica stands taller than Big Ben and twice as large as Buckingham Palace. We stood fifteen each side of the open tall double doors that led to the colossal reception hall, we could have driven the faerie coaches right into the cavernous room.

Inside, the RiNisse guard continued our lines on through the great hall and up the main stairway that gradually swept up and to the right and on to the upper floors.

A deep resinous gong rang out; the sound seemed to penetrate right through our bodies. A servant announced.

"Princess Erika Nisse, heir to the Nisse throne, Captain of the Nisse Hosts and most fair daughter to the Emperor King Kennet. All hail Princess Erika Nisse"

Upon the announcement, Dixie and I stepped forward as briefed and turned inward, and then with the rest of the men we were to bow at the waist to show deference and respect to the royal princess. This was going to be a difficult night.

We stepped out in unison and turned as one to face the entourage that descended the wide sweeping staircase. Although still some distance from us, we could easily make out all the detail of the descending procession. The strikingly beautiful and exotic elvin faces, nisse faces I had to correct myself, should have been indistinct at such a distance but I could clearly see the colour of the eyes of each nisse that approached us. The sight that assailed our eyes was breath taking, in both beauty and majesty.

The Princess Royal walked to the front and centre of a V shaped procession, her Hofdame which we would call her Ladies-in-Waiting each walking gracefully behind the princess then each other in a carefully choreographed court ranking system. Each Hofdame wore an elaborate ball gown of various elvin, nisse and human designs, a few wore Versace and I recognised other human styled gowns I could not identify, but I could see that there were expensive designer creations amongst these royal Hofdame each as elaborate as the other yet carefully chosen to avoid outshining the princess's gown.

The dress colours ranged in every pastel shade one could imagine. Arrayed behind the backs of each vision of beauty fluttered large gossamer butterfly wings, each set of wings mimicked the hue and colour of the Hofdame's individual dress. The effect was enough to raise the interests of any red-blooded man, troll, ogre or any other race, male or female, that could comprehend such beauty.

My eye caught the dark shapes of the SkyggenNisse flanking the Princess Royal and dotted amongst the procession as if they politely escorted the procession of unbelievable beauty. Formal and precise I could see their poise, like coiled springs they had that deadly grace of the killing machines of which their reputation told.

    Within one hundred metres of Dixie and I, as we watched mesmerized by the enchanted winged fairies, the SkyggenNisse streaked forward from their charges to form two lines before us. They faced us tapering out to match the V shape procession led by the Princess. Dixie and I startled and stepped back slightly at the speed the SkyggenNisse moved. They had the delicate pointed features and swept back ears of the nisse but none would mistake the look of death dealers in the glint of their dark, emotionless eyes.

    Hands on sword hilts, they stood to attention. I looked upon these SkyggenNisse and thanked the Gods that we did not to have to face them in battle. My eyes glided back to the princess drawn as if by magnets. I felt as if my heart stopped beating; her perfect porcelain like face would shadow the beauty of Aphrodite herself. Golden blonde hair held up in elvin fashion, fell in a wave of lustre over her bare right shoulder; she wore a high crafted gold and silver tiara upon her golden locks woven into the perfect tresses of her hair. The finely crafted tiara was fashioned in the shape of a holy, ivy and mistletoe leaves and woven together to form a wreath around her head. At the front of the delicate tiara, there stood a diamond the size of a goose egg and within I could see an image of the world on which we stood. This was the priceless royal diamond of the HausNisse. It was not just an image or clever engraving; it was a live moving image of the world. I could see the clouds move over the surface of this image of Sol.

    Her eyes turned to me and with every fibre of my body, every part of my soul I wanted that woman for my own. Her large eyes were ice blue with a passion that blazed within, she glanced into my eyes and for that eternal second her butterfly wings flashed an instant of pale blue that shimmered from the root of the wings to the furthermost tips before returning to the pale yellow that complemented her floor length wedding cake dress. I heard a gentle giggling and a few exchanged whispers from the nisse Hofdame, and the princess's wings flashed the dark red hue of displeasure. The Hofdame fell into obedient silence, the SkyggenNisse captain that stood before me raised an eyebrow, he may as well have screamed.

"Stop ogling my Princess! You bloody human scum!" Dixie began to bow as etiquette demanded; I stood transfixed, etiquette momentarily forgotten in the presence of this goddess. Dixie stopped and drew my attention with a slight "Phist!"

I came to myself and joined him in the formal bow.

"My escorts tonight?" The princess spoke in a dismissively royal manner.

"Your highness." Dixie replied and bowed slightly again.

"Well gentlemen, lead on!" She added and added her yellow gloved hand to stifle a feigned yawn of royal boredom, the Hofdame giggled again. Her disinterested command was that of one who was used to immediate obedience. We fell in beside her; Dixie shot me a glance as if to say 'We have a right one here.' I certainly agreed she radiated that royal 'battiness' that we were briefed about. I could not fathom how this spoiled little brat could be the commander-in-chief of the nisse armies; Princess Erika was more suited to strutting along the fashion shops of Rodeo Drive, Los Angeles than leading an army on the fields of battle.

I wore only my right white dress glove as I stood to her left, I was to take her hand over mine to escort her to the coach and six, whilst Dixie took the right side, our sword arms to the outside and free of any obstruction. Brownlee and Jameson walked before us and Jens Yde took up the rear, right behind the Princess and beside the stoic SkyggenNisse captain.

My gloved arm raised, the princess's dainty gloved hand rested on mine. We were warned never to touch the bare skin of a female elvin or nisse. I heard a ripple of giggling again and a few quiet whispers. I had not seen but Jens told me later that the princesses wings had shimmered light blue again. Beside the princess, I had to battle against the urge to seize her in my arms and kiss her passionately. I knew this urge to be caused by the pheromones the female nisse excreted, on humans, they had a mesmerising affect and without doubt, they had that present effect on me.

Erika Nisse may have been a spoiled brat but she was the most devastatingly beautiful spoiled brat I had ever encountered. I could see the eyes of my men follow her as they watched her parade by their formed lines. I knew that this woman was well out of my league but walking beside her with her warm hand upon mine I felt that in all the worlds, this was the most right I had ever felt, for the first time in my military career I envied being an officer. After this duty I, like the rest of the men paraded each side of us, would resume our ranks and our normal duties as NCO's, sleeping in the mud and dirt and fighting in the blood and fear of battle.

We reached the carriage and one of the men released the steps up to the doorway. Two of the princess' Hofdame came forward to arrange her voluminous skirts so that she could step up. I noticed that the massive fairy wings had shrunk to the size of a normal butterfly on her back. One of the Hofdame, her dress covered in delicately embroidered butterflies stepped behind the Princess, she removed from the Princess's bare back the butterfly that owned the wings, the butterfly transformed into a crystalline cocoon in the flat of her hand. It was then that I noticed that all of the Hofdame's backs were bare. The butterfly-lady slipped the cocoon into an individual compartment within her green velvet purse lined with yellow silk.

At all times the Princesses' hand never left my own, now minus her wings and with the two other Hofdame supporting her skirts she stepped up into the coach, she squeezed my hand slightly to steady herself.

Her touch ran through me like a hot iron. 'Damn these enhanced senses!' I thought 'If it's going to do this every time I get close to this woman, I'm gonna be in big trouble before the night is out.'

Princess Erika took her seat in the coach in the centre of the leather-upholstered bench. I stepped in to take my place to her left, passing before her to get to my station. We were to stand within the coach until it left the courtyard. As I glanced down, she glanced up and our eyes met, she sat in a sea of pale yellow silk and satin skirts, the tight bodice of her dress barely covering her pert breasts, her golden tresses cascading over her bare shoulders almost shone in the relative darkness of the coach interior. I wanted to take her in my arms and kiss her passionately. The princess's eyebrows rose and her full lips curved upwards. My face flushed red with embarrassment. I coughed and turned away, I had forgotten that these nisse were mostly empathic and I hoped she had not seen the images that had flashed through my mind. If she had not noticed then I would stand a fair chance of keeping my head firmly attached to my shoulders. I looked out the coach window forcing myself to my duties only to notice that the pane of glass was sheet diamond.

"Well nothing is gonna get through that." I whispered and that led me to think of my scorpion, I shivered at the thought of the implications of such a weapon introduced by us into this world. The princess gave a stifled gasp and I knew she had noticed my thoughts.

Two of the Hofdame, one of them the lady with the butterfly dress, took their positions on the opposite equally luxurious upholstered bench. Brownlee, with a pleased smirk, stood between the two beauties, he would be seated between the Hofdame when the coach left the courtyard. Brownlee noticed the princess looking at him and at least he had the common sense to drop his eyes and wipe the idiot grin from his face.

The skirts of the ball gowns took up all the legroom and no matter how ravishing they were, they would be in the way in a combat situation. I made a mental note of the voluminous skirts, not something I had ever needed to take notice of before. As I took in this rather attractive problem, I noticed a flash of thigh; the skirts of the Hofdame opposite were slashed up the right side showing a slim attractively tanned leg. I glanced at the princess and the butterfly-lady and their skirts were similarly cut, the copious amounts of skirts and underskirts hiding the fact. The princess moved in her seat and her skirts shifted to show her left leg. My high-buttoned collar felt uncomfortable again. The princess smiled up at me, she had also noticed the flash of thigh and had moved intentionally so as not to be out done. All sets of eyes were looking at me; I felt my face grow a darker crimson. I coughed and grunted and made my eyes look back out the diamond window vowing not to look back inside the coach unless absolutely 0necessary.

A shout to the Pegasus from above and the coach jostled forward. The procession passed through the courtyard and rolled to the front gates. The gate guards pulled the doors open wide. Although I have witnessed similar coaches using their magical warping effect to pass through any opening, no matter how narrow or low the opening may be, there is nothing to prevent the feeling of imminent destruction when cantering in a massive coach towards a small narrow gateway. We cantered towards the gates building up speed; our middle coach was about fifty per cent wider than the gates and two feet taller than the arch over the gateway. I flinched expecting the crash or the shouts from above as the metal archway swept the soldiers off the roof. It did not happen; without slowing, we were through and clear. I wondered what would happen if two coaches passed each other in one of the many narrow city streets.

Once outside the courtyard, Dixie and I were able to take our seats. Up top at the rear and front rode two pairs of our men with loaded war crossbows, they were heavier versions of those we carried on patrol. One of the steel-topped arrows from such a weapon would pierce the heaviest of armour and I had seen such an arrow go clean through an armoured troll and pin him to a tree, they were also armed with scorpion pistols. With them on each carriage roof sat two elvin bowmen, their lighter steel compound bows were of an Earth Prime construction and although lighter than their normal bows, they were deadly accurate. Their arrows, obsidian black with white fletches, were magically endowed to find the target the elvin bowman was aiming at. An experienced archer could guide the arrow around obstacles by moving his sight as the arrow flew to its target. The elvin bowmen recognised that we carried firearm holsters attached to our Sam Browns; I hoped they thought the holsters ceremonial but I knew that as soon as the princess could, she would relay the images she had reamed from my mind. I thought the bowmen would be nisse and I gave thought to where the SkyggenNisse might be. I glanced up at the rooftops to see the SkyggenNisse leap from rooftop to rooftop easily keeping up with the cantering Pegasus.

 I took my seat, the Princess's frothy yellow satin skirts spilling over my right leg in the confined space between us, the flesh of her slender leg showed through the thigh high split in her skirts, her modesty preserved by some sort of mid-thigh underskirt. Her bare leg brushed against my tight riding breeches and the touch of her thigh burned into my very soul.

 'Damn these enhanced senses.' I thought again not daring to look down. I tried to maintain some semblance of professional decorum but my peripheral endowed vision took in the princess's bare shoulders and delicate bare back to betray me. I could smell her scent and my mind fought my pheromone induced baser thoughts. 'Stay focused Jon, stay professional.' I repeated the mantra over and over in my mind; I was there for work not pleasure. Brownlee had that idiot grin again and I dared not look across the princess at Dixie.

 I was relieved that after a short uneventful journey through the narrow winding streets of Metz City we reached the officer's mess.

 The carriage door opened. I took a moment to scan the small courtyard between our carriages and the entrance to the Officers Mess. Our men were in place and Lieutenant Simmons unfolded the carriage steps. The CQP team were not lined up as they were in the princesses' safe palace grounds; they dispersed out to seek vantage points and scanned all around for anything that may prove a threat.

Lieutenant Simmons in the CQP team signalled 'Safe to debus' and I moved to step out of the carriage. The princess's hand took my forearm and I turned to look at her, alert to some request or concern. The heat of her ice blue eyes burned into mine and I felt as if I was falling into them.

"Very professional." Princess Erika smiled with a knowing glint in her eye.

"Gods! How much did she hear me think?" I thought, her Hofdame laughed lightly at my embarrassment. I stepped out of the coach and the butterfly-lady followed. I offered my hand to assist her stepping down and again a graceful slender leg extended out from the pale blue and white silken folds of her wide skirts. The butterfly-lady smiled seductively seeing my eyes travel over her shapely legs and up her slender body. I harrumphed awkwardly knowing these women were teasing us with their bodies like adolescent cheerleaders.

I knew this night was going to be a difficult evening in more ways than I had expected; I was dreading it, yet excited and looking forward to the engagement. The second nisse Hofdame stepped out leaving only the princess inside. Dixie and Brownlee had exited the other side and stepped around the carriage checking the immediate area and the regular army guard that were deployed the other side of the carriages.

I awaited the pleasure of the princess as she paused to give time for her Hofdame to array themselves between the carriages and the entrance to the officer's mess. They arrayed themselves with the precision and efficiency of a European Federal Royal guards unit. Princess Erika slid forward to stand, and both her legs exposed to mid-thigh, her eyes on me; I knew she did it deliberately. She took my arm to step down with the grace and style of a Russian ballet dancer. The two Hofdame fussed over her skirts and the butterfly-lady reached behind the Princess. In her hand was the same butterfly she had removed from the Princess's back, it had transformed back from the crystalline cocoon, which was the state it travelled in the butterfly lady's bag.

"Lady Sommerfugl." Erika nodded to the butterfly-lady.

At the princess bidding, Lady Sommerfugl placed the small butterfly on to the Princess's back between her shoulder blades. The strange flattened butterfly legs seemed to effortlessly slide under her skin as it eased itself against her spine. At once, with a powerful whoosh like a parachute opening, the wings of the butterfly shot out to full size, they fluttered and morphed through a range of pastel colours to settle to a matching yellow to complement the royal dress. As the wings settled, the other Hofdame wings spread like multi-coloured umbrellas, in a strict ranking structure from the high Hofdame to the lower Hofdame to the Maids-In-Waiting. With the flapping, fluttering, and changing colours, it was a fantastic display of delicate faerie power.

Arm on mine Princess Erika and I proceeded in a stately walk through her arrayed Hofdame with our men standing behind the exotic winged nisse. Halfway to the entrance the Princess's wings reduced in size from the large stately size to a small set of dainty more manageable wings, slightly wider than her shoulders, they reached down to the arch of her delicate narrow back. The other Hofdame followed the example of their princess and the display brought such colour and majesty that can only be experienced and never described.

The holovid explained how the nisse could adjust these wings to the size and colour as circumstances required or protocol demanded the colouration was used both in long-range communications and as a sophisticated court language. A little like the fan language used in the Earth Prime palace courts of the sixteenth and seventeenth centuries. I had picked none of that up in the briefing. I was too enchanted by the erotic nubile nisse and elvin Hofdame that provided the instructional display.

Chapter 16

The entrance hall to the officer's mess was ablaze with candles glowing from wall mounted silver and crystal candlesticks. A massive ornate chandelier suspended from the ceiling glowed with hundreds of bright gnawer wax candles and a large enchanted elvin glow globe floating within the structure of the chandelier to augment the candlelight.

Around the room near the ceiling, other smaller floating, glow globes dispelled any lack of light in the high vaulted ceiling. These were not like the functional high intensity orbs we used in the forests, these smaller globes gently swirled with a multitude of soft colours giving texture and life to the normal illumination. The smaller faerie lights shifted through the colours of the rainbow, although a natural phenomenon, the elvin wizards that created the effect timed the ignition and position of the faerie lights to cause pretty geometric patterns.

All the officers, men, guests and fae checked their various weapons to the officer's armoury, adjacent to the cloakroom. No weapons other than the princess's guards were allowed into the ballroom proper. The troll Jaeger Vagt refused to surrender their weapons to human soldiers but they came to an agreed arrangement where they surrendered them to the elvin guard on duty in the front hall, even this they did with growls and huffs of resentment.

Two SkyggenNisse and two troll Jaeger Vagt remained fully armed in the hall along with over twenty armed Paras dressed in number two green uniform, they also wore scorpion pistols and katana attached to their regimental staple belts, I think all the scorpion pistols manufactured so far, were issued that night. The Paras were there as a counter to the armed Jaeger Vagt and SkyggenNisse as the armoury would remain open and accessible for the evening on the insistence of the troll diplomatic party.

Ard Commander Jægerblod, his guards and assistants entered the ballroom before us. It looked like an invasion of a biker gang to a royal garden party. Within the ballroom I could easily pick out the trollish Kvinder, the title trolls gave to their females. I had expected a smaller version of the ugly males but with breasts; and I expected them to be ridiculously attired in similar gowns to the elvin and human females. I could not have been more mistaken. The Kvinde were as tall as the males, dark copper skinned but lighter than their males. They were clad in long tight fitting leather dresses with high batwing collars reaching above their heads and framing their faces. The skirts were either full or pencil like with splits up the front and back. Their proportions, although heavy, somehow gave the impression of slender powerful arrogant grace to match even that of the princess herself.

The Kvinde had small gold and silver tipped stubs of horns from the sides of their foreheads and cheekbones where the males had larger thicker horns. Their teeth were fanged although smaller and I noticed glints of gold and silver decorations on them. Given their trollish countenance, their faces were strongly beautiful; erotic in a strange dominatrix leather clad way. I am embarrassed to say that I thought, given the choice, I do not think I would toss one of them out of my enviropad on a cold winter's night, my face flushed at the thought in spite of myself.

Tinkling bells washed over the ballroom and silence fell amongst the beings within, an elvin courtier positioned by the door struck his black lacquered staff thrice on the ground. I could have said he banged his stick three times on the floor but the "thrice" seemed to fit the grandeur of the occasion.

"Princess Erika Nisse, heir to the nisse throne, Captain of the Nisse Hosts and most fair daughter to the Emperor King Kennet and party. All hail Princess Erika Nisse." He announced in that high musical chant reserved for royal announcements and magical incantations.

All eyes turned towards us as we entered. A light polite clapping rippled around the room amid nods of acceptance from the Princess, the usual collapsing and prostration on the floor dispensed with this night.

Princess Erika's butterfly wings flashed out to full size and all the elvin and nisse Hofdame, both in the room and behind us, immediately followed her display; this was received by many gasps and another ripple of polite clapping from around the room. The room was now officially a royal court for the night. The Kvinde flashed blue-black bat wings in imitation of the elvin women. The flexing of those membranes with curved gold and silver worked talon fingers, only enhanced the erotic sexuality that oozed from the trollish Kvinde, like Unseelie demon succubae amongst the faerie princesses.

The trollish compliment was received by appreciative clapping from all fae in attendance. The male trolls made a sort of huffing noise rather like a bull snorting. The Princess curtsied in thanks to the Kvinde standing beside Uffe Jægerblod, she in turn bowed deeply to the Princess; troll Kvinde did not curtsy. We turned to descend three more steps to arrive at the floor of the ballroom. I felt proud and yet embarrassed to be at the centre of attention, the princess royal accepted the attention as a right.

"Uncomfortable, Lieutenant Raine?" The Princess Erika whispered as she nodded to various dignitaries.

"Somewhat, Ma'am." I replied. 'Keep it simple Jon, don't complicate things, mind on the job, mind on the job' I thought.

"Yes young man, keep your mind on the job and I will protect you." She smiled words from under her breath.

'By all the Gods; she's done it again with that mind reaming stuff.' I thought, trying to guard my thoughts as trained by the Psy Signal Corps. 'Bloody young man indeed, I must be ten years her senior, spoilt little stuck up brat!" I mused, angered and annoyed at her arrogance and assumed superiority.

"Mr Raine... Regard the ribbons upon my breast." She whispered. I was too scared to look.

"I not only command the SkyggenNisse, Sir" She turned her beautiful elfin face up to mine. "I am a SkyggenNisse."

"Gods! That would make her over one hundred years old." I thought.

"I am one hundred and sixteen years old, if you must know Sir." Her face still inclined up towards mine. I could feel her intense ice blue eyes burn into the side of my face.

"What is a brat Mr Raine?" she added.

"Umm ... well, a spoiled little child, Ma'am." I cringed in reply.

"I see... and what am I stuck up with, Mr Raine?" She added.

To my great relief we arrived before the Commanding Officer of the Metz City Joint Military Base, Commander Jægerblod and a few of the civilian dignitaries.

"Gentlemen." The Princess greeted them as they all bowed respectfully. Dixie and I took up positions slightly behind and to each side of the Princess, her butterfly wings now at the smaller more practical size. Dixie cast me a glance, a rueful grin on his face; he was certainly enjoying my discomfort. Princess Erika glanced around and heeled me to her side like a lapdog. I reluctantly moved forward to stand beside her. Uffe and the two elvin dignitaries, and two male nisse nobles raised eyebrows at the Princess beckoning me forward. Although, at the time I felt offended and humiliated to be treated that way, I did not realise that, by motioning me forward to her side, she was actually making an unprecedented statement. Only the Emperor King, her husband or most privileged of the high nobility and only with specific permission, was allowed to take the position at the side of the Princess.

Princess Erika exchanged pleasantries with Uffe and the other men. Every now and then Uffe would glance at me and I felt as if I could discern some sort of pleasure bordering on satisfaction, I thought it was my imagination.

The Princess took my arm and I escorted her around the ballroom. She mingled with the representatives from the various races, executing her royal duties with a pleasant grace I began to recognise as I quietly reassessed this ancient teenaged brat

SkyggenNisse. I could see that she, at all times, was aware of Dixie and my positions, and adjusted her path and position with the expertise of a professional soldier, she was always in a place where either Dixie or I were less than a sword's length from her person. She made our escort duties so easy we had time and flexibility to give our charge the attention she needed to assure her safety, rather than negotiating the crowds. Every time our eyes met, the surrounding nisse Hofdame would whisper conspiratively under their collective breaths.

"What's with the sniggering, Dixie?" I asked when I got the opportunity to whisper to my friend.

"Notice the blue flashes on the Princess' wings when she glances at you?" He whispered back. I nodded as we scanned the crowd.

"So?" I replied under my breath, "The Hofdame's wings are doing the same."

"You weren't listening to the court wing briefing were you?"

"Yes... OK no, I wasn't." I said.

"Means she wants it, my friend." He stated flatly.

"Wants what?" I realised Dixie's meaning as I uttered the words. My face flared again and the Princess turned a secret knowing glance towards me. I am sure my face was as red as the General Carson's sash.

I caught a slight eye movement and nod of the Princess's head, she ordered the conductor to begin the music.

Elvin bells twinkled and the pompous looking elf with the black staff tapped it thrice more.

"Your Highness, Excellences, Lords, Ladies and Gentlemen. Please take your partners for the first waltz."

The Princess beckoned me to her and Dixie and I were at her side in an instant, alert for any situation except the one that occurred.

"Mr Raine, shall we?" She asked, indicating the dance floor.

I hesitated, looking to Dixie for salvation. He had the ever-present Lady Sommerfugl on his arm.

"I'm er ... not very good at this Ma'am ... I mean ..." I stammered, no more words came out.

"Come, come Sir... who is going to complain?" She remarked with a smile and moved forward. I stepped out, Princess in arm and Dixie followed closely with Lady Sommerfugl. I wished for all my heart that I faced a troll battle charge; at least I would know what I was bloody doing!

We took position, the Princess took a loop on her finger from the hem of her skirt and the petticoats flashed a frothy white under her pale yellow silks. I took her hand in mine and placed my other hand around her slender waist to the small of her naked back, keeping the distance decorum and etiquette demanded. The Princess took a half step forward and pressed her royal body against mine to the scandalous gasps that rippled around the ballroom at the sight of the blue faerie wings. Her firm breasts pressed against my lower ribs her head just topping my shoulders. I could have encompassed her entire waist with both my hands.

The orchestra began and we glided over the floor. The princess' wings remained a constant pale blue shimmer much to the aghast of the SkyggenNisse and RiNisse officers watching attentively from the crowd.

Beside us, Dixie and Lady Sommerfugl kept a shadow to our waltz, Dixie the brutish Colour Sergeant Major by day was a natural graceful ballroom dancer and every bit the picture of a gentleman officer. I smiled a wicked smile; I could not wait to tell the men.

"Mr Dixon and Lady Sommerfugl look a natural couple do they not?" The Princess asked.

"Well they seem to command the dance floor alright." I replied.

"Sir, I command the dance floor!" The Princess retorted with a smile. I could see it was a gentle jest but the truth was self-evident, not only did she officially command the floor by virtue of her rank and status; she commanded the floor by beauty, grace and charm. The bratty teenager vanished and I found myself dancing with a true princess.

We danced the second waltz before Princess Erika indicated that we should stop and engage with the party again.

"Shall we get a drink?" She sparkled like a girl at her high school prom.

In another time, in another world, we could have been high school sweethearts on our first date.

"How cute!" The Princess commented and I wondered if I would ever get used to this mind thing.

At the punch bowl, I served the Princess and Lady Sommerfugl with Turrel, an amber coloured extract from the sugary stalk of the Perry fruit plant. It was common to the local area and fermented into an elvin delicacy. Dixie and I took iced lemon water, which tasted wonderful to our enhanced palettes.

Ard Commander Jægerblod loomed to our side.

"Princess Erika! Are you enjoying the party?" He asked, filling his plate with English mushroom vol-au-vents.

"Why yes indeed Uffe." She smiled almost with a sweet innocence.

"I hope your escorts will allow some of us old men the pleasure of a royal waltz." Uffe smiled his deadly shark toothed grin, taking Dixie and I in with a polite yet deadly glance.

"I am sure Ard Commander I can find room on my dance card for an old friend of my father."

Uffe nodded with polite respect and daintily popped one of those vol-au-vents into his cavernous maw.

The dancing continued yet the Princess danced with no one but me. Every time someone came close to cut in, one of the Hofdame would split away from her dance partner to engage and whisk away the approaching lady or gentleman. One human junior cavalry officer managed to get to us and tapped my shoulder to cut in.

"May I, Sir?" He asked in his cut glass Oxford accent.

"You may not, Sir." The Princess replied and we waltzed away. The Princess's wings flashed the ruddy hue of angry red and the SkyggenNisse officers moved one-step closer on instinct alone. A senior cavalry officer ushered the startled young officer away and politely tore him a new ass.

Now I do not think myself a prude or a homophobic, the archaic outlawing of homosexuality abolished in the British Army many decades ago, and it is one of those things the present liberal royal government would like to quietly forget. Yet to see two of the troll officers waltzing together sure took a little adjustment on my part. I only just got used to the sight when one of the famous ferocious warrior SkyggenNisse cut in and danced off in what could only be described as some homoerotic version of Beauty and the Beast!

Well, worlds turn and people must live their lives how they are happiest or why live at all, I reflected. My eyes followed the unusual sight to fix in turn on Lieutenant Stewart. Amanda was dressed in her number one dress uniform which for our Para regiments were the exact same as the male. The only exception was the Al Qaeda Regiments who were strictly Shi'a or Sunni Muslim and not so long ago our bitterest enemy. Although our uniform was unisex, Amanda filled it like no man and only a few women could. Her uniform jodhpurs looked sprayed on. She gave me a cold hard stare with those big brown eyes then turned to engage her puzzled companion in conversation. I considered it was going to be quite a challenge to show Amanda Stewart my new room and the elvin sung bed after tonight. I felt disappointed and relieved to return my attention to the Princess as she mingled with some UFE Army officers. Princess Erika, always alert, noticed the exchange of looks.

"Have I spoiled a liaison Sir?" She asked.

"Well no Ma'am, she is an officer and I am an enlisted man ..." I began to explain British military etiquette. She waved the explanation away with a royal hand.

"And since when has a few badges and social status stood between the heart's true desires? Who will know your rank or status between the sheets of your elvin Bed?" She asked with that flashing smile seemingly oblivious to the history of Earth Prime. I did not know if she were talking about Lieutenant Stewart or herself. I felt that uncomfortable collar again.

"Princess, have you been talking to Ard Commander Jægerblod?" I sighed.

"Not of late Lieutenant." She replied with a wry smile. "Should I be talking to him?" She added.

Thankfully, bells tinkled and the elf rapped his black staff thrice again.

The people began to clear the floor and the music changed to an eerie harp like melody. Over our heads leapt wood nymph dancers, they mimicked the tight bodice ball gowns of the nisse and elvin Hofdame present, their skirts were different, gossamer they reached to mid-thigh, to my pleasant surprise the skirts they wore were practically transparent. Their double sets of very real wings enhanced their leaps and they alighted lightly upon the dance floor. The music swirled and the wood nymphs twirled and moved to the flow of the music. I had heard of the wood nymph faerie dance but I had never experienced it, all the lithesome grace and beauty these creatures used to dance would arouse the passions of even the most reluctant of men. My eye caught the unlikely nisse, troll couple I watched dance the waltz before; even they seemed to be enchanted by the erotic dancing of the nubile wood nymphs.

The dancers looked very much like the elvin but for their rounded ears and their stunning hair and skin colour. They were the forest colours of brown, green, yellow, red and ochre, not just their hair but their skin as well. No two were alike, yet they somehow looked alike. The display was as dazzling as the elvin or nisse butterfly wings. I noticed that Dixie carried away with the ball had his arm around Lady Sommerfugl's waist; he was in for one hard time with the guys when we got back to base.

The wood nymphs danced and cavorted to the swelling crescendos of the music. Two of the nymphs broke from the dance and glided over to Princess Erika, their dainty feet inches above the floor. They took her hands and pulled her gently towards their fellow dancers, as they did, Princess Erika's wings expanded and fluttered to take her weight just as the wood nymphs did with their real wings. At the same time, Lady Sommerfugl reached for the Princess's waist. When Erika moved forward the skirt of the ball gown remained in the Lady Sommerfugl's hand. To my relief and excited disappointment, Erika wore a yellow gossamer skirt similar to the wood nymphs outfits. A rustle of silk and satin rippled around the room as nisse and elvin ball gown skirts unwrapped and fell to the ground, all of the elvin and nisse Hofdame defrocked to display a myriad of long shapely legs in their short flared transparent skirts.

The trollish Kvinde, not to be upstaged, defrocked as well. With the flap of soft leather skirts they unwrapped as if they were capes, most were lined with red or blue silk and with a flourish of scarlet, blue and black, they were cast aside leaving the women looking all the more like leather clad warrior vixen. Most of the Kvinde wore short black flared leather or satin skirts whilst the rest went skirtless in only their leather body suits, their powerful dark skinned legs were an eroticist's dreams come true. I was extremely pleased, as were all the men, that they felt that the Kvinder should mimic the elvin women. It was a singularly delightful trick.

The Princess, led by the wood nymphs, stepped into their dancing sisters. There was a shimmer of colour and to the delightful clapping of the crowd the Princess's pale yellow spread through the nymphs dresses until all were identical. The dancers performed a vertical aerial wheel each following the others in a reverse barrel roll, the Princess amongst them. They swirled, leapt and spun to the music in a perfect choreographed formation, the Princess only distinguished by her bronzed skin and single pair of wings. My heart pounded in my chest as the music grew intense, filling the expanse of the room, as did the exotic dancers. The finale was a crescendo of music in which all the dancers leapt high in the air above our heads spinning around us. As gravity gently took over they fluttered down like falling apple blossom petals, the Princess landing lightly beside me, her chest heaved as she drew breath.

"Well Sir, how did you like our show?" Erika asked between breaths.

"I... I mean ... Oh yes, very nice. Very nice indeed." Again, words failed to form in my mouth although my brain had lots to say. If I was going to make this officer thing work, I was going to have to learn to speak proper.

The crowd was still clapping when the Princess signalled the conductor to continue. He bowed slightly and a quartet of singers took to the bandstand. One male singer stepped forward in a classical Earth Prime suit and tie, he struck a pose and the band began to play a classical number by the twentieth century composer Elvis Presley.

The band played "Jailhouse Rock" Princess Erika pulled me out onto the dance floor once more. The crowd invaded the floor with us, laughing and jiving to the beat. This was my kind of music, our briefing told us that the Princess and her Hofdame could dance any dance known to the races. All formal etiquette abandoned, elves jived with humans, humans with trolls and the Princess had all the right moves. I swung her around and she spun and twirled; all the time her sensual laughter filled my heart and my mind with its own sweet music. I do not know how long we danced but when we broke from the still dancing throng, I forgot the prime reason why I had been present here in the first place. Dixie shadowed us along with Lady Sommerfugl and their presence quickly reminded me of the serious nature of our attendance.

We made our way to the royal seats; a cluster of senior officers to the right caught the Princesses eye, she glanced at me and I could see she had a look of concerned caution, the same look reflected on the faces of the officers, Ard-Commander Uffe Jægerblod amongst them.

"Princess." The Commander addressed the Princess in hushed tones. "Three perimeter guards have been found dead. The base is on high alert."

There was a noise of argument and violent scuffle from the entrance hall, the distinctive ring of the clash of blades. Dixie, Brownlee and the others formed a ring of steel around the Princess. Uffe indicated for me to go to the hall.

"Settle that, Lieutenant and report back on the situation." He ordered as if he was a senior Euroforce officer. His troll Jaeger Vagt took positions in an outer ring just beyond my men; the trolls produced hidden blades from their clothing, some as long as a full-length human sword. At a glance, I noticed the blades were Obsidian blades magically hardened to that of steel and undetectable by any of our technology. For the first time in my life, I was grateful to see so many armed trolls. I moved away from the defending group towards the sounds of the affray.

"Heads up! Incoming!" A human soldier shouted a warning. A lance of energy streaked from the doorway directly at me. I moved to avoid the beam of blue death; as I ducked out of the way it seem as if everything slowed, I turned to watch the beam sear past me and into the chest of a Jaeger Vagt. It burned through his chest before striking the wall behind him. More blue streaks crashed through the windows while two more flashed from the same doorway. One streak of energy headed directly for my chest. If I stepped away, another being would die. I drew my sword and with the flat of the mirrored blade, I deflected the bolt upwards towards the ceiling. I hoped no one stood on the floor above the lance of energy. To me the energy bolts travelled slowly and they incinerated everything and anyone in their way. In those few moments, while most of the people moved so slowly I could see the SkyggenNisse, some troll Jaeger Vagt, and my men move in my time.

My scorpion was clear of its holster and I spotted a dark shadow moving quickly along the edge of the room near the royal seats. I fired a double tap at the shadow. It tumbled and fell.

"Jon!" I heard the shout and turned to see the Princess there just two yards from me, moving in my time, she leapt and her wings shot out to a size larger than I had ever seen before. The beautiful princess sailed through the air, massive faerie wings outstretched about her perfect form. Her slender legs wrapped around my waist, her arms around my neck, her wings enfolded me as a magical blast crashed through the room. Her lips pressed hard against mine as we fell back under her forward momentum.

A moment that lasted an eternity and all was cold, too cold to be death.

Chapter 17

The brigantine, a two-mast vessel, square rigged on the foremast, with fore-and-aft sails on the mainmast. The Amazon was a typical Bluenose softwood vessel of about 220 tons, built in Spencer's Island. The Amazon sailed the trade routes and later became the Mary Celeste. The brigantine, shown above, is rigged with two staysails set between the masts. 99 feet long, 25 feet wide. There is a legend on Sol that says you can get anything on the Amazon.

* * *

I found myself in freezing water, I opened my eyes and all was murky grey. The cold shock wracked through my body and I gasped in reflex. I lost my precious katana in the shock of the freezing water but I managed to hold on to the scorpion. The Princess gave me breath into my mouth, her full lips sealed upon mine. In my shock all I could think was that, I was disappointed that it was not a real kiss after all.

I took in her sweet air, as I had no time to gasp my own it tasted like wild barley and my mind saw fields of colourful wild flowers. The cold tightened around my chest like steel bands. The water in my mouth was not salty and I believed we were in a lake or something similar. We broke the surface and I gasped in the fresh clean air. The waves were high, maybe eight to ten feet, and rain fell like iced needles against my face as I drew back to take in more air. Not concerned how I got there, my main and immediate concern was to survive and preserve the Princess's life. In the rolling waters, I managed to holster my weapon and fasten down the pouch flap. I could feel the cold rapidly invading my body and no matter what idea I could hope to come up with, I could not see any way out of our situation. The fresh water lake seemed to be massive; we could see no visible land to strike out for, even if we could sustain our strength and consciousness in this ice-cold water. The waves swelled powerfully around us and I knew we could not make any headway other than to go where the waves took us. I could see no way out. The cold permeated my body and I could feel myself shutting down. I felt the cold gradually leave me and I knew hypothermia was beginning to set in.

The waves went still and I saw it settle as if a still pond surrounded by a raging sea only yards from us.

"Hang on Jon. The Klaubautermann comes." Erika shouted over the rage of the crashing waves.

The water around us warmed and I felt embarrassment, I feared I had lost control of my bodily functions. The water continued to warm and a thick fog gathered faster that I had ever experience before. Before the mists enveloped us, I saw the raging waves break against an invisible wall just a few dozen yards from us. The rain stopped and I could see that some invisible barrier was deflecting it the icy droplets running along the invisible curved surface.

"What's happening, Princess?" I asked as I treaded the calm waters. The warming water brought feeling back to my body. Painful tingling in my arms and legs brought the good news that I would not lose any of them to the cold. The fog was so thick that I could not see any more of the invisible wall that separated us from the storm.

Erika treaded water before me and I noticed that she gazed upward over my right shoulder.

"The Klaubautermann." She whispered in awe.

I turned in the water and out of the thick fog. Looming over us was a ship I could only describe as a pirate ship, straight out of the old 2D action adventure videos I watched as a child. Above us on the decks I could see men looking over at us, some were lowering a heavy rope net while others swung a wooden boom with a rope slung bosons chair. Sailors scrambled over the sides and down the netting. One of those sailors on deck slung a large orange flotation ring tied to a long rope, into the water between Erika and I; we pushed to it and clung to the floating ring. It was a welcome rest for our limbs, a welcome break from the constant treading of water.

The sailors at the end of the line pulled us towards the arms of their fellow shipmates now in the water and clinging to the rope nets. When we got to them, they slipped the bosons chair over our heads and we pulled it under the water and under our bottoms. One of the sailors on the netting shouted up success, there was an order called from the deck above and we were hoisted clear of the sea. More shouts of command and grunts of effort and we were level with the deck of the ship. The sailors on the rope netting nimbly scrabbled back up to the deck with the ease and speed of mountain trolls.

The sailors hauled the chair in and gently lowered us to our feet. The bosons chair fell away and I collapsed, my legs unable to take my weight. Erika caught me and with a show of surprising strength, she lowered me with care to the wooden deck. Two sailors wrapped me in thick warm blankets while another draped a blanket around Erika's shoulders. With the thick blankets around me, the warmth returned to my body. I looked around to see the storm lashing against the invisible barrier.

"Where did all the fog go?" I asked the sailor nearest me.

"The fog be still there lad." He replied. "It be all round us." He explained.

"It's as clear as day." I said, not able to see any kind of fog at all.

"Ah no, soldier fella. It be still here." The sailor replied. He certainly sounded and smelt like a pirate. "It be a one way fog. Ye can only see the fog from one way... from out there." He pointed off towards the storm raging against the bubble like protective cover.

"Like a cloaking shield?" I asked.

"Aye, like a cloak of ghostly mist; to hide the comings and the goings of the Klaubautermann." The sailor waved his hands about and wiggled his fingers magically.

A door in the wooden wall between the upper deck and that on which we sat opened, and what I could only describe as a pirate captain stepped out of a doorway from under the fore deck. The captain was dressed as the classic pirate with a black three-cornered hat, a brown leather frock coat and high black leather boots. Around his waist, he wore a thick leather belt with an elaborate buckle shaped like a tree. Attached to the belt he wore a cutlass and a brace of pistols. To my surprise, I recognised the pistols as a pair of chrome plated Magnum revolvers. From beneath the leather sleeves, his snow-white shirt had cuffs of fine lace that matched the extravagant frill down the front of his shirt. He swaggered with the arrogance and confidence of a man without equal. This pirate sea captain strode over to us carrying two large steaming mugs.

"Coffee, anyone?" He asked, with an arrogant yet friendly smile.

The pirate captain offered the mugs and I took the handle of the hot steaming beverage, only to find it was a large Starbucks Coffee mug.

"I bought those fair and square." He offered too quickly for it to ring true.

The coffee was a frothy cappuccino with a generous sprinkling of chocolate powder.

"Did I get it right?" The pirate captain asked as he watched me inspect the coffee.

"Now, if this was Belgian chocolate ..." I put the coffee to my lips. "Oh yes, this is exactly how I like it. But how did you know?"

"Jon. May I present the Klaubautermann?" Erika announced, now sitting on an upturned wooden bucket. The Klaubautermann swept off his three cornered hat, showed a leg, and bowed with the grace and arrogance of a French Nobleman. He extended his hand to me, I took it and he pulled me to my feet. I swayed a little; I was still unsteady on my legs. At that moment, the ship lurched heavily to the right. The captain kept me from falling. A gush of spray shot into the air from the other side of the ship.

"There, now." The Klaubautermann spoke as he steadied me and returned his hat to his head. "Shall we go inside? I can see you both could do with a clean-up and one of my fine meals inside you." He said, as he dismissively inspected my torn and soiled clothing. "And we must be getting away from here." He added as he glanced over to the waterspout now beginning to fall back down. Erika stood, accepting his offer, we followed the swaggering Klaubautermann across the deck and to the door, and we had seen him emerge from. As we walked the short distance across the deck, the Klaubautermann kept looking around as if wary of some danger unknown to us.

We arrived at the door and the Captain reached for the door handle. There was a rumbling and scraping from below. The ship heaved again. It felt as if something immense rubbed up against the bottom of the ship's hull.

The Klaubautermann stood by the door and bowed again to offer us entry to the corridor within. Out in the water there arose a mountainous head of a sea monster. It looked nothing like any sea monster I had ever read about, a green rearing head and swaying tentacles. Its head held three eyes on both sides and a wide mouth of multiple rows of sharp teeth, each easily as long as a full-grown man. The monster moved its massive head from side to side as if it was looking for something. I was in no doubt as to what that something was. It roared and the ship shook under my feet from the force of it.

"We must be away from here before our friend finds us." The Klaubautermann spoke with a laugh but I could see the monster worried him. "Welcome to my humble abode." He added. "Please stop when you enter." He added, as he held the door open. We stepped over the raised threshold. I expected a narrow wooden corridor leading to the captains quarters with perhaps several other wooden doors. Facing us was a door not made of wood; I could not identify what material it was made. To either side a corridor ran into the far distance with no end in sight. Every four meters or so there was a door the image of the one facing us. The doors and walls looked like a fabricated substance maybe plastic with the strength and rigidity of concrete. All flush with silver handles the doors bore no signs or symbols on them. The roof that gave bright light like the midday sun gave its light from its very surface; the entire seamless roof glowed down upon the long corridor with its steady artificial sunlight.

    I am no sailor but I had estimated the width of the ship to be between twenty-five and thirty feet, the length somewhere near 100 feet. The corridor however stretched away into a small dot in the distance. I looked to the corridor then behind me at the still open door. I was unsure if I was more frightened of the monster outside or the ship inside. The Klaubautermann smiled as he entered, shutting the door behind him. The inside of the door was an exact match to all the others.

    "I see you have noticed a little difference between my ship and others you may have experienced Jon. It does take a lot of getting used to. My little ship is much larger on the inside than it seems from the outside." He said.

    I went to open the door again and the Klaubautermann placed his hand upon mine to gently stay my action.

    "Please Lieutenant Raine you do not want to open that door right now." He cautioned.

    "Because of the monster?"

    "No, much worse than that. If you open that door now you would succumb to the madness of looking into nothing. Not the space between the stars, no, no blackness, and no light, no darkness, nothing, just nothing. There is just nothing beyond the ship right now; we sail to another place and away from the danger our previous place holds."

    I did not understand him but I did not argue with him either. I took my hand from the door handle.

    "What about your crew? Should you not get them inside as well?" I asked worried for the men that plucked us from certain death from the cold sea and that monster.

"They will manage well enough, now, that's a fine fellow." The captain smiled as he lifted my hand from the door handle and touched golden ornate scrollwork on the modern wall, I was sure the scrollwork was not there a moment ago.

The floor, or the walls, began to move. I was not sure which, as we did not feel the inertia, we should have felt if it was the floor that moved, and we were in a normal world. The walls and doors moved with ever-increasing speed until the doors seemed to fly by us.

"Where do all the doors lead?" I asked, I noticed that we passed corridors branching out each side and they seemed to reach out to the far distance with no end in sight. The corridors seemed to be endless and the doors without number. We turned into one of those corridors in a wink of an eye then in a few seconds, another turn. We felt no inertia while we did those instant right-angled turns.

"Each door leads to a different world, some lead to the same world but at different times and places. Others lead to worlds that would steal your mind and leave you mad." He stated with a dramatic flourish of his lace-covered hands. "Sometimes a door will lead to one place then later to another place entirely. I know at all times, every place, each world and every door leads to." He smiled a self-satisfied smile.

"How is that possible?" I asked in spite of myself, I felt a bit woozy with the doors shooting past at incredible speed.

"Because behind every door is the Klaubautermann!" He replied.

"Yes." I replied waiting for something more I might understand.

"And I am the Klaubautermann." He said simply, too simply for my liking.

As fast as we were moving we suddenly stopped dead. Inertia should have caused us to shoot forward like rockets. We did not, we stopped with no sense of forward inertia at all, it made my head swim, and I was a veteran of hundreds of atmospheric re-entry falls and light speed hyperspace jumps.

Nothing could have prepared me for this kind of impossible travel.

We stood before two red lacquered doors, the large handles and Chinese dragons that adorned them shone with the lustre of pure gold and the beasts eyes inlaid with precious stones. I touched the golden carvings to feel the smoothness of the dragon's scales.

"Do you like the doors? They are Ming Dynasty." The Klaubautermann declared with pride. "I don't often get the chance to show them off." He added in false modesty.

"That is fantastic workmanship. Where do you get such talented artisans?" I asked as I stepped back to inspect the entirety of both doors again.

"Ming Dynasty." The Klaubautermann repeated, and opened one of the doors to bid us enter.

Chapter 18

The room inside was no less impressive. It was a high ceilinged room, with curving walls. On the opposite wall a large sheet of transparent material curved to meet the walls on either side. The view through this massive window was of the most beautiful garden I have ever seen. It looked as if it was high summer and everywhere there were brilliant coloured flowers. I knew my enhanced senses were making the flowers radiance so much more intense. It was then that I noticed the oddity. Every tree not only bore flowers, they were also heavy with fruit.

"That is a fantastic garden. Is that a plexi glass video screen?" I asked impressed with the creative intelligence and artistry that went into this video creation.

"No. That is a garden out there." The Klaubautermann replied. "Come, let me show you."

We stepped down the five deep carpeted steps to the centre well of the room, I thought to be about the size of a basketball court. In the middle of the well sat a long polished oak dining table that could seat twenty-four people, eleven seats each side and two large ornate oak carved dining chairs each end. As we walked across this incredible room to the windows, The Princess and I gazed around to take in the decor.

Around the room, up on the raised floor that ran the perimeter, sat many fine old and modern seats and settees of various colours and designs. Along the walls stood an extensive library, row upon row of books sat on multiple shelves all the way to the ceiling. Dotted along the walls between the shelves were doors leading, I supposed, to other rooms and corridors. Above the doors were displayed suits of fighting armour and weapons of various origins. I recognised the medieval suits of metal armour and two complete suits of samurai bushido armour from the United Nippon Chinese Nation. Some of the suits I did not recognise; they were of strange irregular sizes, not for human or fae or troll for that matter, some had four arms. Two of the suits caught my eye, they seemed to be made of some translucent material, one glowed a dark shade of red while the other glowed green. The swords displayed beside them were of the shape of a katana with the long curved blade yet the material of the blades was the same translucent substance as the armour. The glass armour and swords fascinated me and I wondered if they were real or just for decoration. It crossed my mind to ask the Klaubautermann if he would spare a replacement sword for the one I lost and sorely missed.

"I see you are taken by the Zaemlan Armour. They are great sword masters, as great as Sol's blademasters, a worthy ally to have at your side and a dangerous enemy to have at your back." The Klaubautermann said with a cautioning tone.

We climbed the five steps at the other side of the room to stand at the great window that curved above and before us, the fantastic garden beyond.

"Who? The Zaemlans or the blademasters?" I asked.

"Well both, I suppose." The captain replied.

I looked through the windows to see the vast array of plants and animals like a botanical garden zoo. I could see to the far horizon under a clear blue sky.

"And this garden is on your ship?" I asked amazed.

"No Jon, that Garden is far too big to be contained on a simple little vessel like mine." The Klaubautermann said in mock humility. He held out his arms to the window. "That, my dear Lieutenant, is Eden."

"Yes, it is truly stunning; it would be how I would picture Eden." I declared.

The Klaubautermann smiled again. "Lieutenant Raine I have not made myself clear. Please forgive me. That is the Garden of Eden." He repeated with a flourish of his lace-cuffed arms.

Erika took a startled breath.

"You mean... The first garden; the once home of Mother Lilith?" She whispered.

"The Same... Watch." The Klaubautermann replied and stepped to the window. He pushed a pad on the low wall below the wide curved window and it swept to the side and disappeared into the wall.

The captain leaned over the now curved balcony and held up his glove covered hand. A small colourful bird flew down from a tree and alighted there.

"This small thing, this delicate bird, is as old as the worlds of Sol and Earth. Nothing ages or changes in Eden. There is no end to life, there is no death and there is no birth." The Klaubautermann spoke in a saddened whisper. I did not know where to start; words failed me. Erika brought some structure to the exchange. The Princess walked forward to take the small bird on her finger.

"I cannot believe this small thing is so old." She stroked the bird lightly on its ruffled chest.

"Princess, please lean out of the window. The bird is forbidden to leave the garden and will surely die if it remains on my vessel. He has forbidden all things of Eden from boarding my ship."

"Who's He?" I asked in wonder that there was someone more powerful than the Klaubautermann.

"He is the Allfather, He who created the Garden." The Klaubautermann explained. "He doesn't half hold a grudge does he not?" He added.

"You mean God?" I asked in disbelief. The Klaubautermann nodded.

"Yes. Father Adam and Mother Eve, the first human parents, they walked this garden before time began." The Klaubautermann breathed in a lung full of garden air and savoured it like a fine wine.

"The Klaubautermann tended the Garden." Erika explained.

"So you were here after Adam and Eve?" I asked.

"No, when the Garden was created I was created to tend the Garden. I am the first fae the Allfather ever created in this universe. I was there with Adam and Eve. However, before Eve there was Lilith, she was black of skin and the fairest of women.

She so loved the Garden and her husband Adam, and I so loved her. I knew she would be ever faithful to her husband and I had to tend the garden, I loved and watched them, the woman I loved and the man I despised; enjoy their lives and each other.

When Allfather made Lilith, he made her not from pure dust like Adam but from the dark clay from the lowlands by the great sea that filled almost all of the earth. Lilith was dark and beautiful, she loved Adam but she sought to stand equal with Adam and not as the Allfather intended, a helpmeet and servant for the man Adam. She loved Father Adam but she would not remain subject to him but sought to be Adam's equal. Adam tried to force Lilith to submission but she called on the true and magical name of God, rose into the air, and disappeared forever from her world. Lilith chose banishment rather that submission.

"It angered me that she should be cast away like that, and I was angered against the Allfather. I waited and tended my perfect Garden. I waited until the Allfather came to walk the Garden in the cool of the evening. I stood before him and declared my love for Lilith and my anger that she should be cast away from the world. He listened carefully to my words. In my defiance I used the sacred name of the Allfather."

"What did he do?" I could not contain myself.

"He cast me out." The Klaubautermann replied. "I was cast out before the first humans Adam and Eve, and let me tell you, they would never have fallen while I tended the Garden. All the time I tended that garden I would not let the Serpent within the borders of that wonderful place.

"The Allfather did not banish me to be with my love Lilith, knowing all things he knew how much I loved her and he was angered against me. He cursed me with a most grievous curse and yet the greatest blessing I could have.

"Banished from my precious garden never to enter that place again, I was forbidden to stand upon the Earth evermore. Forbidden to touch anything from my Garden ever again, hence the gloves. Not just this Earth but also any Earth. I could never be with Lilith ever again. More than that, He cursed me to be in all times from the beginning to the end to know all things that happen upon the worlds I move between. To always, know the beginning and end of all things, even the end of my own existence. I am to live until the end of this universe, then oblivion; I will no longer exist. Neither in body, nor in spirit."

I was speechless, and Erika sobbed quietly by the window.

"Well that's enough about me for now." The Klaubautermann finished with a dismissive laugh. "How about you kids? You really do need to freshen up and get some of my fine cuisine into you. Princess, Lieutenant Raine, first let me see to your comforts." He added as he inspected my tattered clothing.

"Your Highness" He beckoned the princess to one of the doors in the wall. "Please avail yourselves of these private chambers. Through there you will find a hot bath and a selection of clothing for your pleasure, my lady."

The Klaubautermann looked to me then at the princess. "I see you look quite fair your highness?" The Klaubautermann commented as if it were a question rather than a compliment. Erika flushed in embarrassment and unusually remained silent as if chastised. I did not understand the exchange of words and I felt too tired to ask.

"I am sure you will feel much better after you clean up and partake of a little something to eat." He added almost sympathetically. "Will you be bathing together?" he inquired with a salacious smile.

My face burned as red as it did at the ball.

"Ah no, we are not ..." I began but the Klaubautermann interrupted.

"Not to worry. Please forgive my insensitive inquiry. Please, this way." The Klaubautermann indicated another door further along the wall. "Please feel free to freshen up and choose whatever clothing you would like."

I entered through the door he indicated and found myself in an equally impressive bedroom. Impressed again by the size

167

and decor of this elaborate room I looked about to see the furnishings. It was comfortably furnished by a large four-poster bed that was as wide as it was long. I could feel from the draw of the bed that it was elvin sung. The matching writing desk and ornate chairs wrought from dark oak and polished to a high sheen. I walked over to inspect them and I was surprised to find an uplink terminal slate sitting upon the desk.

The room displayed many glass shelves of crystal and glass ornaments and pieces of art that sparkled from the light of the glowing roof. I wondered how all the objects stayed in one place and in one piece as we were on a sea bound ship; surely, they would have moved and fallen as the ship moved with the motion of the seas beneath it. It was then that I realised that I had no sensation of movement, neither up nor down as ships move, or in any other direction for that matter. I may as well have been in a brick building. My immediate idea was to use the uplink slate to communicate with any of my own forces. I lifted the lid and the screen winked on.

I sat down in the high-backed chair. The furniture bore the joins and lines that told of joinery and wood machining rather than the elvin sung wooden furniture, which for the most part they sung out of one solid piece of wood. The slate screen displayed a login and password dialogue box over a background of a coat-of-arms, above the crest were the words 'Klaubautermannn.net'. I tried a few passwords but I am no computer expert and any idea I had to communicate with my people quickly died with my failure to gain access to the slate. I quickly gave up that attempt and turned my attention back to the room and particularly the bathroom entrance.

I went to the bathroom stripping off my tunic shirt, boots and pants. I stopped in the doorway when I saw that the bathroom, as large as the bedroom, contained two female elvin. They were tall for elvin the tops of their heads came up to my shoulder; they both had waist long straight black hair. They bore a vague resemblance to the Klaubautermann; they could have been his sisters or cousins. The tops of their pointed elvin ears poked through the tresses of their hair. One held a large white bath towel, which she was hanging on a golden towel rack, I had no doubts that the towel rack was of pure gold. The other elvin noticed me standing in the doorway and curtsied in the elvin custom.

"Welcome Lieutenant Raine, would you like to bath or shower?" I stood for a moment allowing myself to look over these two raven-haired beauties. Both were identically dressed in short beaded skirts of strings of tiny precious stones over a tight fitting body suit high cut over their shapely legs and as is the custom of the elvin and nisse, the suits were backless.

The one that had racked the towel moved to a glass door and slid it across to show a tiled wet room, with cascading warm water that poured from multiple showerheads in the ceiling and walls. The steam filled the room but did not move across the threshold of the open door, for a moment I thought that there was a second glass door, until the girl stepped through to test the water. The other girl moved over to a large bathtub big enough for six or seven people, as she stepped in, the water began to bubble around her slender legs. The sight of these two scantily clad elvin beauties beckoning me and my almost nakedness left me both excited and embarrassed. I hesitated for a moment then walked to the shower. The girl in the shower laughed sexily and pointed to my army issue boxer shorts.

"You will not need those, Lieutenant." She said. The second girl stepped out of the bathtub and was by my side.

I stepped out of my shorts naked, embarrassed and excited; I walked into the showering room. The girl inside began to soap my chest and shoulders while the one outside stepped in and slid the door closed behind her. She began to caress my shoulders and back.

I stood there enjoying their touch and I could not but help notice that both girls hair remained dry even though hot water poured over their bodies, their long black hair swayed around them as if cast in a light breeze.

The shower was an elvin delight I had experienced rarely, once I spent an entire month's salary for an experience that paled in comparison to that which I presently enjoyed. Standing in the shower with these two attentive ravishing women, all those unanswered questions and puzzles in my mind disappeared. I found myself in a place I did not know or even begin to understand. I let myself go to the pleasure and enchantment of one of the finest elvin showers I had ever experienced.

After thirty fantastic minutes, I left the shower to dress, thoroughly clean and quite exhausted, yet somehow refreshed and invigorated. Both the elvin beauties followed me out to the bathroom. They drew warm towels from the golden rack and dried me from head to foot. I was fascinated to see that they and their clothes remained completely dry. When they finished they took me back into the bedroom where they guided me to a hidden walk-in wardrobe. The sides were lined with various evening attire, some I recognised as black or dark blue tuxedos, others had a style and cut I had never seen before. Flicking through the garments I noticed mid rack, a blue military dress uniform just like the one I had been wearing, mine however had been torn in the blast and soiled with my time in the sea.

I took out the jacket to look at it. I saw that it was decorated with the insignia of a Lieutenant of the Parachute Regiment the Dragon Riders. The set of medals on the left breast was an exact image of the array I had been wearing. I was impressed with the attempt to provide such a close copy when I noticed a small imperfection in the lining of the jacket. This was my jacket. I could not fathom how they could clean and repair my clothes so quickly. I walked out of the wardrobe, jacket in hand to look at my torn and shredded one on the floor where I had left it. I looked again at the jacket in my hand and I was sure this was exactly the same jacket as that which lay in shreds on the floor.

I suddenly remembered Erika and the Klaubautermann waiting for me in the next room. I struggled to dress quickly and the girls helped me even though they thought it quite amusing to see me flap around in such a panic. I stepped quickly to the door, all the while the girls fussed about my uniform to ensure it was a perfect fit. I lifted my right boot to see the small nick I had made to identify them from all the other boots in the regiment. I looked over at the soiled and damaged boots I had been wearing when I entered the room. I shook my head in confusion.

One of the girls presented me with my Sam Browne. I immediately saw that the scabbards were empty. While I had lost my katana in the freezing waters, my tanto should have been in the scabbard.

"Where is my tanto?" I demanded.

"We are sorry Jon, but the Klaubautermann took it." The girls spoke in unison and with what seemed genuine regret. I checked my holster and the Scorpion remained inside. I had no idea where the blade would be, I had no the time to search for it so I returned to the main room, comforted at least that I had my pistol and I was not completely defenceless.

Chapter 19

I stepped through the doorway adjusting my Sam Browne; the Klaubautermann sat at the head of the great table. He held a large cigar in one hand and a black diary like book in the other; it seemed to have his interest. Erika walked from one display to another touching those she could reach. She had donned a white silk dress that hugged her figure all the way down to mid-calf where it flared out over many layers of white frothy lace.

Her shoulders and back were bare in the elvin style but her arms were covered in matching long evening gloves that were fingerless and attached to her middle fingers by diamond-encrusted rings that allowed the palms of her hands and her fingers to be free. My heart raced at the sight of her anew and in spite of myself, I became conflicted with embarrassment and guilt as I recalled that which I had been doing only a few minutes ago, with the two raven-haired elvin beauties in the shower.

Erika turned and scowled at me and I hoped to hell that she was not mind reaming me.

"At last the wayward Lieutenant returns." She spoke, as she stepped down the carpeted stairs to join the Klaubautermann at the dining table. A vision of blonde elegant beauty her anger only complemented her loveliness.

"Can we eat now?" she asked of the Klaubautermann. I sensed that the Klaubautermann had abstained from dining until I had arrived.

The pirate captain put down his book and lifted a delicate crystal bell from the table. It rang with a clear sweet chime.

"Please be seated." He indicated the chairs either side of him; he stood to move behind the chair to seat the princess as she arrived, and I took the chair facing her. From one of the doors on the opposite side of the room three servants emerged, two waitresses carried plates, while the waiter carried a large soup tureen. One of the waitresses was the girl that stepped into the bath; she caught my eye and winked with a smile as she placed a plate in front of the Princess. The Klaubautermann noticed the sly wink.

"A good shower?" He asked with a wry smile.

"Yeah, it was OK." I replied, somewhat embarrassed, and I hoped that Erika failed to notice the exchange and find out what I had been doing just a few minutes ago.

"What's that book you are reading?" I asked, trying to change the conversation.

"It's your journal." He explained. "I took it from your cell just after they collected you for your execution."

"What?" I exclaimed; my hand went for my sword only to find an empty scabbard. I drew my scorpion.

The Klaubautermann raised his hand and laughed.

"No no... Be still. There is no present threat to your person right now. Your execution is many years away."

I looked to Erika, but I could not read any reaction from her serene face, except perhaps a shadow of worried expectation, she hid it well.

The Klaubautermann slid the journal across the table and I picked it up to leaf through the pages.

"This is not my handwriting and I can see it is a language I do not understand. It... It looks elvin."

"It is nisse. Go further along Jon to about the middle of the book." Instructed the Klaubautermann.

I flipped through the pages, selected approximately the middle of the book, and examined the pages once more.

"It looks like my handwriting but the language and... and well I don't remember writing this."

"That is because you have not written it yet." The Klaubautermann explained as if I should understand.

"The beginning is in the hand of the Princess." He bowed his head to Erika. "And when you master the nisse tongue you will write in the book yourself."

"But what does it say?" I asked.

"Pass it to Princess Erika. She understands nisse."

I duly slid the book across the highly polished table and Erika caught it before it fell off the edge. Erika thumbed the pages with a puzzled frown on her face.

"I cannot read this." She said. "The pages are blank!" She added, and held up the book for us to see. It was as she said; all the pages had no writing on them.

"What kind of trick is this?" I demanded. The Klaubautermann laughed.

"Of course there is nothing on those pages. You haven't begun to write in it yet. Please accept the journal as a present and a memento of your time aboard the Amazon with the Klaubautermann."

Erika and I sat in stunned silence. None of this made any sense to me and I could see from Erika's expression that she felt the same.

"Please write in the last page." The Klaubautermann requested of Erika.

She wrote in the book and held it up to show us. I could not read the nisse words but Erika said it was her name and titles. Written in the most beautiful script, it was almost a work of art.

"Close and open the book again." The Klaubautermann instructed.

Erika did as bidden; she closed the book and opened it again.

"It's gone! The writing is gone!" She declared and lifted the book up to show us.

"Now your highness, please turn to the front page."

She did so and her writing was on that first page.

"That is amazing." I gasped with a smile.

"More than that Lieutenant, the book never runs out. It is a life Journal and will only be complete at the end of your life. Every time you fill the pages more blank pages appear at the end."

The Klaubautermann stood and walked over to one of the bookshelves.

"Now, I took the liberty to make a copy and I have had some of your Journal published. It makes a damn fine read, lots of intrigue and exciting danger." The Klaubautermann wiggled his fingers at us. Each one had a jewelled ring.

"Now where is that book?" He commented as he searched the shelves. "I think I left it... Ah yes, here it is." He smiled as he selected a hardback book from the shelf and returned to the table. He handed the book to me with the cover open at the fly page.

"Would you be so kind as to sign my copy for me?" He asked and took a gold pen from one of his many pockets.

The book looked like any other normal book; its darkly coloured dustsheet had a picture of a statue of Uffe Jægerblod in a crouching fighting stance on the front, a couple of Asrais in the background and a pair of Kobolds sitting in the foreground. The title read "Trolls Don't Do kung Fu."

I tried to open the pages but anything I tried failed to open any more than the fly page. The rest of the pages were tightly sealed.

"Why can't I open this?" I asked.

"One of the rules you must abide by my friend. You may not have a clear view of what is to befall you in the years to come." The Klaubautermann explained, almost in an apology.

"So you are some sort of time traveller?" I asked as I tried to make sense of my confusion.

"No Jon, the Klaubautermann is not a time traveller." Erika explained. "He sails the seas of all the worlds at all times, in all times." Erika seemed to understand the Klaubautermann's curse more than I did.

'Yeah, that explains everything that does.' I thought in dejection.

"Now let us not get too downhearted!" The ever-smiling Klaubautermann chipped in.

"Let's look to the future!" He added in a flourish as he stood.

"But you said we shouldn't ..." I began.

"Ah, yes but I am the Klaubautermann." The Klaubautermann replied.

"This is getting to be like a bad faerie tale." I growled.

The servants cleared away the soup dishes and we were served something that looked like a four-legged chicken.

"Aha! All the world is a faerie tale and we are just players in it." The Klaubautermann declared with another dramatic flourish, which was getting right on my nerves.

"Is it not a Shakespearean quote that goes
'All the world's a stage,
And all the men and women merely players;
They have their exits and their entrances,
And one man in his time plays many parts,
His acts being seven ages...'"

"No, no, no, nothing like that at all! I just made it up!" The Klaubautermann cut in with a tone of sincere affront.

Erika shook her head at me as if to say to take him under sufferance.

I slurped down some of what I hoped was mushroom soup.

"I have presents!" The Klaubautermann lifted a box over from a side stand by his chair. I was sure the side stand and box were not there just a moment before. He laid the square box on the table. The box was made of wood and it looked like a black lacquered box about twelve inches in dimensions.

"First some things thought lost and returned this day." He dipped his arm into the box and drew out my tanto; I could not see how it fitted in the box at all. The length of the tanto looked longer than even the diagonal space in the wooden box. He slid the blade across the table towards me. I picked it up and replaced it into its scabbard. The Klaubautermann rolled up his sleeve and again he dipped his arm into the box. This time he reached right in, his arm going in up to his shoulder and he withdrew my katana; all three foot of it! The sword glistened wet and the Klaubautermann flicked the water off the blade, twirled it quite professionally and tossed it to me handle first. I caught it out of the air and the handle was still wet and freezing from lying at the sea bottom for the past hour. The Klaubautermann wiped the water from his arm with a white Egyptian cotton table napkin then rolled his sleeve back down again.

"I expect you will need these." The Klaubautermann pulled another box from the first. He slid it across the table to me. I opened the lid to see what looked like about two hundred rounds of the scorpion ammunition and three more magazines for the pistol.

"How did you get these?" I asked.

"I'm the Klau..."

"Don't tell me. You are the Klaubautermann." I said. I felt that eventually I was beginning to understand what he was saying. The Klaubautermann smiled.

"You will want to dry the hilt and oil that blade before the air gets to it." The Klaubautermann indicated a bookshelf with a small under cupboard. "You will find the things you need in there."

"And for Princess Erika." He produced a rather ornate but sturdy slim dagger in a black leather sheath with straps to tie around an arm or leg.

Erika examined the dagger by slipping it out of its leather sheath. The blade was highly polished and glinted in the sunlight from the garden; double edged like a commando dagger tapering into a wicked point at the end. Yes, it was a fine knife for a princess.

"Sir. Is this the dagger of Diana?" Erika asked in awe.

The Klaubautermann smiled at the Princess. "No, that I could not manage; but it is a fair approximation, a sister to the original and with all of Diana's dagger's functionality. There are now but two in all of the known universe."

"I do not know how to thank you Sir." Erika beamed and strapped the knife to her thigh.

While I enjoyed watching Erika strap the dagger to her leg, I did not think it would be much use in a pitched battle, unless it exploded or shot a death ray from its handle. The weapon looked about 12 inches long with about 5" of that being the ornate white bone handle, carved with an intricate pattern that reminded me of a complex Celtic knot. Such a weapon in the hands of an assassin or worse still, an angry Princess would be a very deadly weapon but it would have limited use in a pitched battle. I would have to find Erika something more substantial in case we had to fight before we reached safety.

While the Klaubautermann grew in my estimation, I knew there was much more to him than we would understand. Somehow, I did not think that getting back home was going to be very easy.

Again, the Klaubautermann reached into his magic box, produced two soft fabric packets, and placed them on the table before him. He indicated the packets and said, "I would like the both of you to select one of these."

We did as requested. "On the centre of each packet there is a small patch. Please peel off the patch. When you have done so, touch your tongue to the black side of the patch. Now replace the patch, black side down, on the packet again."

We did as requested, and when the patches were fitted back on, the packets quivered like a couple of blobs of blue-black ink.

"These packets contain chameleon suits." The Klaubautermann explained. "Please change into them, you may use your rooms if you should desire."

"I'll just change here." I said.

"I have no reason to hide my body." Erika added.

"Ha! Nisse." The Klaubautermann smiled.

I stripped to my waist then unfolded the chameleon suit from the packet. The packet cover was actually a hood to a long poncho like garment. The sides were sealed leaving hand holes where they met the top edge. Erika put her poncho over her head and when it was on, she slipped out of her dress.

"Please remove your pants and all undergarments, shoes and any other clothing." The Klaubautermann asked of us.

"I wear no other clothing." Erika said as she slipped out of her high-heeled court shoes. I raised an eyebrow in pleasant surprise and Erika frowned at me.

With hesitation, I removed my pants, undershorts boots and socks. Erika and I stood naked wearing only these shapeless poncho garments. I felt so foolish.

The Klaubautermann raised his arm to indicate two full-length dressing mirrors that were not there just a moment before. I was getting used to the furniture's surprise appearances.

We stepped over to the mirrors and stood before each one.

"Now picture in your head the type of clothing you would like to wear right now. Look into the mirror and picture yourself clearly wearing the clothes you prefer."

I did as he asked and was startled to see the poncho ripple like oil and spread itself all over my body. I could feel the flowing fabric push under my feet and I reacted by lifting each foot in turn. I now stood in a dark blue Armani tuxedo with a black bowtie and white silk shirt. I looked to Erika and a similar transformation had taken place. She stood in a short, shimmering green dress that hugged her attractive upper body and flared out in a skirt that reached to mid-thigh. On her feet, she wore green high-heeled pumps.

"How did the fabric detach and make the shoes?" I asked admiring her shapely attire. Erika twisted a leg to show me the back of her calf. A line ran down her leg from under her skirt to her shoes below, it looked like a line from a sheer seamed stocking and I guessed it was how the gown kept attached to the shoes below.

I stared at Erika. "Now, that is rather good." I smiled and looked back into my mirror to appreciate the transformation of my ugly poncho.

"Now think of another type of garment. Think clearly now, will yourself to wear it." Said the Klaubautermann.

My dinner suit changed into my camouflaged battledress and high leg combat boots. Erika's gown morphed into what I could only describe as a brilliant white elaborate wedding dress that ran to the floor.

Erika admired herself in the mirror. "This is my naming dress. I was given my official royal title and military rank in this dress." She said and swooshed around holding out her skirts.

"I could not imagine many generals dressing like that." I commented and added. "Maybe on the other hand I could!" We both laughed at the bizarre idea. We morphed several times more and with every change, Erika was an ever-startling vision of royal beauty.

"After you have finished dress up I can show you some other more practical application of the clothes." The captain suggested.

"I cannot think of anything more practical as this but please lead on captain." Erika said as she admired herself in the mirror.

"OK, Princess Erika, walk over to that wall and stand before the bookshelf." He nodded to a bookshelf not far away.

Erika walked over to the indicated spot; she had morphed back into her green metallic dress.

"Now wish yourself invisible." The Klaubautermann said.

The green dress shimmered and melted all over Erika's body covering her head to toe, even her face, and she winked out of view.

"Erika!" I called to her, startled that she should disappear so quickly and completely from view.

"Fear not, I am here, Jon." A disembodied voice replied from where she had disappeared.

The Klaubautermann raised his hand for silence. "Now move one step to the side."

Erika stepped to the side, for a moment I saw Erika's form made out of books shimmer as she stepped to the side. When she stopped, the shimmering stopped and she disappeared again.

"Yes, the only weakness is the moment the chameleon suit takes to adapt to your background as you move against it. If you move too quickly you will be seen, move slowly and it is not so apparent. Princess, try stepping back again only this time move slowly."

After a moment, Erika said. "OK I am back again." This time I did not see a thing.

"That's amazing! Erika can you see us?" I asked. It was always a problem in stealth technology. Many ideas failed because the user behind the stealth technology needed to see through the shield.

"I can see you clearly. It is as if I am wearing a sheer veil before my face. There is a lessening of colour but still clear visibility." She explained.

"Princess. Concentrate on Jon's eyes. Wish to see them clearly in your mind."

"My goodness!" Erika exclaimed.

"What is it?" I asked.

"I have focused into your eyes as if I was standing next to you. I can look at anything and it becomes close when I wish it, like a farseer."

"Like a telescope?" I asked.

"Yes, like your telescopes."

"Princess, please think of yourself as a shadow." The Klaubautermann instructed and Erika winked back into view as a black silhouette, as if her body form was cut out of reality with nothing to replace it. To me it looked more worrying than her completely disappearing.

"Come to the window and look upon the Garden." The Klaubautermann lifted his hand to point to the windows. The black shape moved to the windows like void in human form.

"Look into the Garden and see how you can view far and near."

"It is amazing!" Erika said almost to herself. "I can see the smallest detail on a leaf or petal clear across the valley to the ridgeline of the far mountains. How is this possible?"

"In the same way the chameleon garment can change shape and colour it can also bend light to allow light from behind to bend around the body and on as if in a straight line. The bending of light can also make things faraway look so very near and those small things naked to the eye can be seen clearly." Explained the Klaubautermann.

"What kind of magic is this?" I asked.

"It is the magic of technology for your world's far future. I give these presents to you as this is the only way I can help you."

"Sir, you have the power to return us to our very homes. Why do you not help us thus?" Erika pleaded.

The Klaubautermann looked pained "I am sorry Princess; I cannot, for it is not how this game is to play itself out."

"This is our lives and it is not a game." I interrupted with anger.

"I wish it were not so but I cannot help you in this way. You are to return to Sol by your own means, to continue the journey you undertook when you captured Ard Commander Uffe Jægerblod."

I stared angrily at the Klaubautermann. "I should have known he would pop up in this somewhere."

"More than you would know Lieutenant." Came the Klaubautermann's cryptic reply.

"I can shelter you this night, but you are to be put off in the morning."

"And what of these Chameleon suits. How are they supposed to operate in Sol?"

"Quite well, actually. They are nanotechnology and they need but a few hours exposure to the sun to continue to recharge and work correctly. Their charge will hold for no more than 48 hours but they will function correctly, as they need very little to operate.

"You keyed your respective suits to your own DNA when you touched your tongues to the label and attached it to the package. They will always work for you and only you. If the suits are taken from you, they will not work for anyone else. The label works once only and cannot be used again." He explained.

"Well at least we are thankful for these gifts." I sighed.

"Children you will need to rest, you may not have the opportunity for some time. Use it well." The Klaubautermann sounded very sincere; he showed us to our rooms again and bade us good night.

I looked longingly at Erika entering her room and just before she closed the door, she gave me the same longing look I gave to her. I felt my legs wanting to move to her, I could see myself walk up to her and take her in my arms. I hesitated for a moment in my own world of turmoil and confusion. I failed to seize the opportunity and she closed the door.

'Carpe bloody Diem' I whispered to myself, I knew I missed a very special opportunity that I did not think I would have again. I entered my own room and closed the door behind me. When I turned, the two servants that had showered me were kneeling on the emperor sized elvin bed and a wide smile broke upon my face.

Chapter 20

I awoke in the bottom of an open boat. Erika slept close by, she wore her chameleon suit as did I and they seemed to be a barrier to the freezing temperatures around us. I knew it was cold because my face was exposed and I could feel the tingling numbness upon the skin of my cheeks and forehead. I sat up to look around to see that we were surrounded by thick sea fog; I could not see much further than the rowboat in which we lay. When I sat up, the movement wakened Erika. She sat up beside me. I felt refreshed with my sleep in the elvin bed even after the company of the Klaubautermann's cabin crew.

Looking around I sighed, "Looks like our welcome on the Klaubautermann's ship ran out."

"It would seem so." Erika replied.

I noticed a note pinned with my tanto to the boat's wooden seat, it read.

Row south and all will become clear.
My Fondest Regards.
Till we meet again. (As I recall, we had a good time then as well.)
The Klaubautermann.

Beside the note was a compass.

"I suppose we have no option but to row." I said.

Erika moved to take the seat in front of me but she stumbled. I had not seen the Princess take a wrong step since I met her.

"Are you OK, Princess?" I asked, as she took the board seat in front of me. "I do not feel well, perhaps the food last night." She suggested. We both took up the oars. 'Well at least she is prepared to literally pull her own weight.' I thought tenderly.

We rowed for almost half an hour without speaking other than for me to call to Erika that we were moving to the right or the left to bring us back on course. I tried using the words Port and Starboard but I was not sure which was which and Erika had never heard the words before so we stuck with right and left.

The fog began to burn off with the warmth of the rising sun and we came out of the shroud to immediately spot land.

"Land!" I called to Erika and she turned to look. I noticed that the lines around her eyes were slightly more pronounced than usual, but I thought that was because of the glare of the sun upon the water and in our eyes. There seemed to be a hint of tiredness around her eyes and in her posture, she looked a little slumped as if the tiredness was taking its toll.

Within a few more minutes, we were in clear air just about a half a mile off shore and making for the beach. I could tell from the sea spray that this was salty sea. Sol's seas were fresh water. The sun climbed steadily higher in the sky. I felt it warm upon my face, I realised by the size and position of the sun rising from the east that we were not on Sol and I hoped we were on Earth Prime and not some other world of the many that the Klaubautermann hinted at back on the Amazon.

The sun that burned the morning mists away blazed its warmth down upon us both. I lifted my left arm to shield my eyes; my right held the handles of both oars. I wished I had a peaked cap to shield my eyes. As soon as I pictured the cap on my head, the material of the chameleon suit climbed to my head and formed the cap.

"What is that code? Is it some sort of distress signal?" Erika asked over her shoulder. I took off my baseball cap to look at it. It was red with the lettering 'I (heart shape) NY'. The cap had a thin thread that ran from the cap to my dark green shirt.

"Yes, princess it is a distress signal. If anyone sees it they are obliged to render assistance." I said, with a straight face. Erika formed the same cap on her head, red with the 'I (Heart Shape) NY' blazoned across the front. I smirked to myself knowing that Erika would immediately realise the joke. Erika made no response; it was as if she could not see the comical mental picture in my head. I thought of Amanda Stewart, nothing. I thought of Amanda Stewart in an Elvin bed, still nothing. I thought of the scorpion pistol and again no reaction whatsoever.

"Princess, what am I thinking right now?" I asked to confirm my suspicions.

"You are thinking how attractive my back is." She replied without turning her head.

"Other than that?" I asked. Erika was silent for a moment. She turned her head and looked at me. "Jon, we have a problem." She looked as if she was in her thirties, an extremely attractive thirties but older nevertheless.

"This is Earth Prime and nisse magic does not work the same here." Erika pointed to shore and the forest beyond. "I need the trees; I need to get there now, Jon." The desperate urgency of her words spurred me to action. I took hold of the oars and pulled with all my might. It looked about half a mile to shore and there was a side current. I reckoned that anywhere along the bank was good enough for us, so long as we reached the trees beyond. Erika did not take up her oars again; instead, she curled up into a foetal ball in the bottom of the boat. She looked so vulnerable, so helpless, my heart broke for her.

"Princess, is there anything I can do?" I asked.

"Keep pulling on the oars and get me to those trees. I need the trees. If I am unconscious before we arrive, strip me naked and hold me against a tree."

"What?" I exclaimed.

"Just do it, Jon. My life depends on it. My magic is dissipating and the magic is what keeps me young. I am using up more magic than I should because we are on salt water. I need to replenish the dwindling magic with another force otherwise I return to the trees that gave me life."

"You will die." I asked, shocked at the revelation.

"Yes I will die as you call it. I will be no more Erika Nisse daughter princess to the Emperor King."

I rowed with all my might and the boat picked up speed but I feared we were not moving fast enough. There was a tail wind and I wished we had a sail to aid us.

My clothes melted from my back leaving me as naked as the day I was born only a lot colder in the freezing wind and sea spray.

Tendrils from the black inky blob that was my chameleon suit reached out and touched the princess's clothes, they melted away leaving a frail naked beautiful middle-aged woman to shiver at the bottom of the boat. I had no time, or desire, to appreciate the happenstance of being in a boat with Erika and her sexually magnetic nakedness. There were streaks of grey in her blonde hair.

Both chameleon suits oozed to the front of the boat like an octopus out of water. In an instant, a large black parachute-like sail exploded open in front of the boat with thin tendrils from each corner attached to the stem. The rowboat leapt forward and I had to brace myself to avoid falling backwards over the plank I sat on. Four more thin tendrils reached for me, each pair, left and right, merged making a pair of handles for me to grip. I found that I could control the Para-wing sail thing from my sitting position as the boat lurched forward with increasing speed towards the shore. With the wind behind us and the boat gaining speed, the effect of the icy wind lessened and I felt a little warmer albeit I was still freezing cold.

"Outstanding!" I laughed, ignoring the bitter breeze that caressed the exposed skin of my back. I knew I would be on that shore and back in my suit before the hypothermia set in.

I was freezing and just about in control of the Para-wing when the boat hit solid bottom. I did not know where we were but I could still see the forest edging the sand of the beach about 100 yards away.

The black mass that was the Para-wing oozed back to surround our bodies with comforting warmth. I took but a moment to allow for the pain and uncontrolled shaking my body underwent as the warmth seeped back in. Erika was a frail grey-haired old woman in the bottom of the boat and even the warmth of her chameleon suit failed to raise her from her unconscious state.

I picked her up and with my precious cargo, I jumped out of the boat and onto the beach to run for the trees. No princess was going to die on my watch, especially not this one.

As I ran up the beach, I looked to my left and right along the shoreline. To my right was a manufactured bridge in the distance, spanning the water between two landmasses. Given the scale of the steel and concrete construction, I estimated it to be more than half a kilometre long. It was definitely of human construction, which reaffirmed Erika's statement that we were on Earth Prime. I got to one of the trees that edged the forest. They were Earth Prime sized trees and not the massive ironwood trees of Sol.

I stripped Erika as requested and held the wrinkled old woman against the tree. I hoped that no forest walker would happen by to see this perverse looking scenario. The needles of the tree turned brown and fell about my shoulders. I looked up into the branches and all of the evergreen needles of this fir tree were brown and falling as if in a great drought. The rest of the trees remained a healthy green. Erika took a deep breath and her body seemed to fill out, the wrinkles receded and her body grew young again.

I held the princess I knew before; her grey hair darkened to a rich nut brown and her skin tone shifted to a deep golden tan. The princess opened her eyes and looked up at me. The ice blue eyes were gone and green eyes peered at me in their stead.

"How do you feel, Princess?" I asked

"Erika, please ..." She asked. "Let's dispense with formalities and protocols for now."

"I would be delighted your ... hum! Erika."

"I had hoped we were in the lands of the nisse," She said "but I know we are not... The land looks familiar..." She gazed around and spotted the faraway bridge. "No wait. I know that bridge. Jon, I believe we are in Denmark. That bridge spans

Lillebelt and connects the city of Fredericia with the island of Frunen.

"Denmark, Eh?" I commented.

"Jon, we need to get back to Sol." Erika strained to speak, she sounded worried. I still supported Erika in my arms and now that she had grown young again, it was not such an effort to continue to do so.

"I need to get away from the water and into the trees."

"Yes, but first I need to contact..."

"No! We need to get back now!" Erika cut me off. She looked around shading her eyes from the sun. Her chameleon suit oozed back up her legs and covered her body again. The red I (Heart) NY cap appeared on her head once more.

"If I do not get back or find some sustaining life force, I will drain all of these trees of their life force and after that I will surely die."

"How? Why?" I exclaimed, age seemed to creep back into her eyes again, even though she was still a vision of beauty. She pulled her dark brown hair back and tied it up into a ponytail that fell from the crown of her head to the middle of her back. Her posture was not as vigorous as before. I reluctantly released my supporting hold from Erika's waist.

Two elderly forest walkers happened by.

My suit changed almost by reflex into a Danish officer's number two uniform. Erika morphed into a very becoming yellow flowered, halter necked summer dress

"Godmorgen." They greeted us in Danish.

We smiled back and Erika gave a friendly wave. They walked on along the path between the forest and the sea.

"The new hair colour is very becoming but you are still not looking well Erika, I know only of the portal in Hanover, Germany and that is more than an hour away, if we are where we think we are. I don't even think we would get permission to travel through right away."

"There are other ways; as with the fae bomb that took us to that other world." Erika replied. "I need a tree." She added.

"A tree?" I asked, and as I stretched out my arms to show our surroundings, I added. "Any type of tree? We are in a forest after all."

"An oak tree, Jon." Erika pointed into the forest. "That way."

We made our way deeper into the forest and away from the beach. It was a tall old established forest by Earth Prime standards but it would have been dwarfed by Sol's colossal forests.

"We need to get deeper into the trees Jon, away from the sea." Erika said and stumbled against me. I caught her and checked her fall with my body.

"Are you alright Princess?" I eased her back to her feet; she looked a little older and I feared she would quickly return to the old decrepit woman she had been a few moments ago.

"I grow old because my magic wanes fast here on your earth. I used nearly all my resources in the boat. Fae are not very good around salt, it is a poison to us, and it makes the change more rapid. I found relief with the fir tree, I have fed of its life force and it has sustained me and made me young again. This life force is of your Earth and will sustain me longer than my Sol magic, but it is not my family tree, my father tree that hatched me.

"I can repeat this feeding from the fir trees but it is only temporary and I will kill all of the trees in the forest then die myself shortly after. If I die like this, in your world, I will never be able to go back to my own world. If I die here I will cease to exist, there will be no life ever after for me. For me on your earth there is only oblivion." She gasped between strained breaths. "I need an oak tree, Jon."

"So you are a vegetarian vampire then?" I quipped without thinking.

"You would call me a demon?" Erika asked offended.

I tried to hide my stupid comment. "I didn't mean it like that. We have Vampire bats here on Earth Prime and they aren't demons."

"We also have vampire bats on Sol and they are demons. They can take the form of a nisse, elvin or troll; they kill with a bite and feed on the blood of their victims."

"Vampires like Dracula?"

"You know the house of Dracul?" Erika asked "And you would call me such a demon." She pushed my hands away.

"Ok already, I said I was sorry." I complained.

"No you did not." Erika shot back.

"An oak tree." I murmured. Erika struggled to maintain her balance.

"Take it steady Erika." I cautioned as I grabbed her waist to hold her up once more.

"I can feel the weight of my years upon my body. I can feel saxicoline magic here." Erika said and perked up as her bare skin touched another fir tree.

"Yes! We are indeed on Earth Prime, near Fredericia to the east of the land." Erika stated in sudden realisation. "I feel the memory of the flora within this forest, it gives me some vitality. The saxicoline magic is strong here. There are trolls in this land and a troll gate is near."

We passed a white sign with the word "Brandmateriel" printed upon it.

"Yes, certainly Denmark." I said recognising the Danish word. "Saxicoline magic is troll magic is it not?" I asked when I saw that Erika seemed to be able to support herself. Her face looked a little younger yet it still reflected the age of her years.

"Trollish magic is the magic of the rocks."

"How can you feel troll magic when you say magic cannot exist on Earth Prime?" I asked.

"I did not say it cannot exist here, I said it was different. Magic is both simple and complex. There are different tolerances in different areas for different magic's. In this Denmark of your earth trolls have a strong presence. The veil here is very thin which makes Denmark a magical place, here troll magic exists, not as strong as on Sol but it exists nonetheless."

"You think trolls have a hand in this?" I asked.

"I don't know. The style of attack was goblin. That shadow you killed was a gnomish Snigmorder, although I sensed the bomb was elvin in nature."

"Gnome assassins?"

"They are Snigmorder, a secret and highly efficient team of killers." Erika warned. "And this Euroforce army knows far less than it thinks." She added. "Its own arrogance and reliance on technology weakens the warriors within."

"I think we do okay." I replied quickly defending my military colleagues.

"My love." Erika smiled and put her still trembling hand to my face. "You need not defend your world's Euroforce. Your path takes a different turning now."

I felt a rising worry with Erika's comment.

"Worry not about the trees Jon, they are not dead, they are my brothers and sisters, they will live yet for many years to come. They have but infused me with some of their years and this will sustain me for a while. I cannot use this magic but I will live."

I think she missed the subject of the worry rising in my mind and took it for concern for the trees. She looked relieved and I smiled and swept the needles from her shoulders.

"The trees have told me of the oak tree I seek, it is in that direction." Erika pointed deep into the forest.

Chapter 21

We followed rabbit and deer tracks and natural partings between the underbrush to zigzag through the forest floor in the general direction of the oak tree Erika was looking for.

Each time we passed a tree, Erika would reach out to touch it and glide her hand in a caress across its rough bark, each time she did this she took some vitality from whatever tree she touched. Each little addition built upon her and by the time we reached the oak tree Erika looked almost as youthful as I had first seen her, yet still different with darker hair and skin.

She walked to the tree and put her arms around a low upward curving branch. Her chameleon dress took on the colour of the bark and her skin darkened a shade to a deep brown tan. The most startling effect was her hair, her tresses and ponytail changed from the dark brown to lustrous burnt ochre that glinted in the dappled sunlight. The new growth leaves on the branches took on the many shades of red and gold that autumn brings, and they began to fall around us. First only a few leaves fell, then in a downward fall that filled the air, and obscured everything around us. From the surrounding forest, I could tell it was early spring here on Earth Prime even though it was high summer on Sol. Erika kissed the branch she hugged.

"I give my humble thanks to you Father Oak. I thank you for your life giving energy. Health to your forest and strength to your branches, may the Emperor's blessing be upon you and your posterity, and may the spirit of the Nisse dwell with you as long as the nisse live."

Erika moved away from the branch when the leaves stopped falling. She caressed it like a familiar friend.

"I have taken sustenance from Father Oak, Jon." She said, walking toward me through the rustle of leaves.

Her bright eyes sparkled dark brown and her burnt ochre hair shone in the dappled forest light; with the fallen leaves about her hair and shoulders she looked so very like the wild wood nymphs of the Sollen forests.

"Jon I beg a service from you." She added as she sidled up to me, her face upturned and pleading; her eyes held mine in their dark green embrace as hypnotising as her ice blue eyes had been before.

"Yes, Erika. I need to find a way to get to ..." I began planning.

"No Jon. I have need of you." She interrupted laying her hand on my chest. My heart leapt within and I had an uncontrollable urge to take her in my arms.

"Erika we need ..." I held her waist trying to find reason and fight the urges of my passion.

"Jon, I have taken the essence of the oak, it is my father tree, the tree from which I hatched. When I take the essence, it is a powerful stimulant. I need your human life within me or I will soon lose control and return to the earth."

"You want to bite me and feed on my blood?" I asked as I stepped back. Erika laughed.

"No my love, I need you inside me." She looked down at my groin.

"You mean us? I mean you want us to..."

Erika ended my words by kissing me full on the lips, her passion hot. She pulled me close. There was no mistaking it, her passion overwhelmed me and in spite of myself, I wrapped my arms tight around her lithe body. I felt her hot form against mine and I was deeply lost in her green eyes.

Erika laid back upon the fallen leaves, her chameleon skin taking on their earthy tones she almost disappeared before my eyes.

I knelt beside her and before I could pull off my chameleon suit Erika pulled me down upon her. I could feel the fabric slip between us as it reformed into one large sack like garment, much like a large green dappled sleeping bag. There was nothing between us.

"Take me Jon; take me under the shadow of Father Oak. Give me life on the bed Father Oak has provided. I am yours." She spread her arms wide as if reclining on the softest of beds. I obliged the Princess in every way she desired. We spent an hour in glorious oneness in our magic sleeping bag amongst the leaves on the forest floor. Several times, we had to remain motionless as passers-by stopped to remark on the state of the tall oak tree. Most of them, I did not understand as they spoke Danish, some I understood, as they were German.

The leaves completely covered us and the bag took on their colours and patterns, we lay still and unseen until they passed on. The chameleon bag would conceal not only our naked bodies but our scent as well. The intensity of lying beside her delicious body and remaining still was too much for me to bear and my passion burned like a wild fire within me, I took the Princess several times again.

I am not a man of innocence, I have known a few women in my life, some were whores, the military camp followers, duly certified and regularly medically inspected and the arrangement reduced the rampant new sexually transmitted diseases that flared up in the years after the portals were discovered. In that hour with Erika, I found the true love of a woman, I lay beside her naked and exhausted; the brittle leaves felt like the softest feather bed. I knew then that I loved her from the moment I beheld her on the palace stairway. I felt so fulfilled yet melancholy; I knew she was beyond my possession, our lives so different, I knew that when we returned to safety, if we returned to safety, I would lose her.

I understood her need for me but her need was just that, a need, a need I understood and found ultimate pleasure in fulfilling.

I lifted my arm before me; my skin was a dark bronzed brown as if I had spent months under the desert sun. I looked down at my body and it was entirely the same colour.

I jumped up to my feet. "What the hell have you done to me?" I shouted.

"The colour suits you." Erika smiled. She stood and caressed my chest and stomach.

I pushed her hands away. "Turn me back you bloody Lillin witch!" I growled.

"I cannot Jon, the change is permanent." She spoke sadly yet she seemed somehow pleased. "See the branch that forks into three, high in the oak tree." She pointed to her Father Oak.

"I, I see it but what ..." I started to speak.

"Focus on the branch."

"Will it turn me back?"

"No."

"Then why ..."

"Please Jon, just for a moment."

I decided to humour her and focused on the forked branch.

"Leap onto the branch, Jon." Erika requested flatly.

"What? It's like fifty feet in the air!" I exclaimed with a dismissive laugh.

"Believe me Jon. Focus and jump!"

I thought I would humour her just once more so I focused and leapt. I shot up into the air as I had seen the Elvin do, only my arms and legs wind milled in the air out of control. I headed for the forked branch, missed it completely and fell fifty feet to the ground where I landed with a hard thud in thick bramble bushes.

I stood up and checked my naked body. I remained unhurt among the brambles.

"In the name of the Gods, did you see that?"

Erika leaned over and grabbed the sack that was our love nest. With a swirl, her part of it detached and wrapped itself around her and shaped into the stylish yellow and white short summer dress she had worn before, it enhanced her dark tanned skin. She turned to me and stood there with her arms crossed in a self-satisfied pose.

"Still want me to change you back?" She asked.

"Well, I will consider it." I replied and pushed through the thorny brambles. They tore at my stomach, thighs and arms yet they remained unscathed. My skin would not rupture under the assault of the sharp thorns. I felt them against my skin but I felt no pain. In truth, I should have been ripped to shreds in the heavy undergrowth, yet I forced my way through the thick vines as if I was strolling through long grass. I walked to Erika examining my arms and body, nowhere was there any mark, yet I had survived a fifty foot drop and forced my way, naked, out of the thick thorny vines of the bramble bushes.

I picked up my chameleon suit and it wrapped around my body to form a functional jumpsuit of mottled greens and browns.

"Jon, wish your feet free of the covering." Erika asked

I obliged wondering what other surprise she had in store.

Erika took me by the hand. She led me in a walk that rapidly turned into a trot.

"Run Jon, run with me." She laughed.

I ran with this Goddess, we ran through the trees. Branches would whip at our faces and bodies yet we felt no pain nor did they leave any mark. Ever faster, we sped like dark streaks through the trees, to us it was clear and safe, we could easily anticipate any obstacle, leap and vault any hurdle. We laughed and tagged each other, sometimes Erika would nudge me into a tree trunk and I would strike it so hard that it should have shattered my bones. I would bounce off and laugh, only to speed up to catch her as she ran off. I caught her by the waist and carried her while I ran through the trees. We headed for a large silver birch and before I could dodge it, Erika nimbly swung out of my arms and onto my back.

"Up Jon, to the tree and up!" she gasped into my ear. I followed her direction, although I had more care due to the previous fifty-foot leap I missed so badly. I made to climb and found that I needed no hand or foot hold. Like a troll, I climbed the trunk and was up near the pinnacle in moments. We remained there to scan the treetops. Every bird call, every movement by wind or fauna we could hear and see with clear clarity. I could see shades of colour I had never seen before. I heard calls and noises that should have been beyond my capacity to hear.

"This is fantastic Erika. I feel like a superman, like a god."

"This is my gift to you for the service you have rendered me." Erika whispered into my ear.

"I get to make love to the most beautiful woman in all the worlds and I get a supercharge makeover for the effort!" I laughed.

"So shall I change you back, Jon?" Erika laughed.

"Can you do that?" I asked worried now that she could.

"No Jon... As I said, it is permanent there is no changing back." Erika assured me. "See the tree between the tall firs." Erika pointed over my shoulder.

"I see it." I replied. Erika climbed up my back to stand upon my shoulders. She leapt and flew gracefully across the four hundred yard distance to the tree. I leapt after her and as I landed, she leapt to another. We followed each other from tree to tree like a pair of giant squirrels at play, every leap and dash impossible for a normal human.

I spotted Erika in a tall elm, I leapt to catch her, and she did not leap. I took her by the waist to leap again.

"Wait Jon, I feel a doorway nearby." She whispered.

"A doorway? You mean a portal back to Sol?" I asked trying to force my mind back to my duty.

"Erika, there is a Danish Signals barracks in Fredericia. I know they have a Psy Signal Corps somewhere there. We could request help." I suggested.

"No time." She dismissed the idea. "I need to get back now Jon. My power can be sustained within these woods but I would need to take the energy from the trees and eventually all the trees would die. My power drains faster here as magic is weak in your world and I will not be able to venture far beyond this forest. We are too close to the sea and this is trollish country. The nisse are not in this forest and I am remote, they do not know where I am. We need that troll doorway. It is close by." She pointed through the trees to a farmhouse and out buildings. "There Jon, it is there." She exclaimed with sudden realisation. She jumped down from the tree and strode towards the farm buildings. I followed her.

Between the farm buildings and us stood the Father Oak under which we made our love. We stopped to retrieve our weapons. The Chameleon suit formed a Sam Brown Belt with scabbards and pouch for my weapons. Erika strapped to her thigh the ornate knife the Klaubautermann had given her. It looked quite sexy in a James Bond type of way. Properly dressed we could almost pass for normal people at a distance.

"Let us proceed." Erika said and strode off through the forest. I took a moment to look around to appreciate the place where I first found true happiness, I wished a silent wish that we could remain here and play together between the trees forever. It was not to be and I paced off after the love I could never keep forever.

We stepped on to a wide well-worn forest path. It was a firebreak and ran arrow straight in both directions. Erika turned left towards the farmhouse that lay at the end of the path. Framed in overhanging foliage the path led straight to the front gate of the small front garden.

"There Jon, that way, that is a troll safe house. I can feel the saxicoline magic; it is strong in that direction."

We walked the forest path in the heat of the midday sun. The path was warm with pools of strong warm light where the trees allowed the sun to shine through. I heard no forest noises; all was still, too still.

Erika stopped. She looked like a delicate fawn sensing danger.

"Jon, there are others that hunt us here in this forest. They are from Sol."

I did not ask how or why she knew; I just accepted her words as fact now.

"Where are they?" I asked, I remained calm and I cleared my scorpion from my holster.

"In the trees, look to the shadows but not directly. See the shadows as you saw them in the ballroom."

I scanned the shadows in the direction she furtively indicated. Shadows moved, more than shadows, something was there, several maybe more than six; they circled, seeking us like a wolf pack.

"Snigmorder." Erika whispered her body tight for fight or flight. "I cannot fight them all, I am too weak."

"Don't worry Erika, I am here with you." I assured her.

She looked at me as if I was a child, as if I did not know what I had said, the look completely unnerved me and I was a seasoned soldier.

"Fight? Like a magic fight?" I asked now unsure of myself.

"Yes... No... Maybe but not now." Erika ducked down and squatted by a tree.

"Get down!" She whispered. I hunkered down to join her. Hoods moved over our heads. We did not wish them but the action seemed to be an automatic function of the suits given that we had a great desire not to be seen. The suits bent light around us and we completely disappeared.

We waited only a few moments but it felt like forever. Two shadows moved through the trees towards us. I peered towards them trying to make sense of the shadows. They seemed to slip away from my eyes.

"Do not try to look at them. Look away and regard them with the side of your eye as you would do if you were hunting at night." Erika whispered, her lips close to my ear, I barely heard her. I did as she said and I could make out the shadows a little easier yet still they were difficult to focus on.

I peered beyond the two closest shadows to see many more spread out behind them through the trees; I counted at least ten more shadows. The two nearest us stalked closer, they were feet away from us. I could hear their breathing, their heartbeats. They stalked ever closer and I feared they would physically fall right over us. We held our breaths and feared to move at all. The two Snigmorder stopped sensing something close, but seeing and hearing nothing, they raised their noses to the air to sniff our sent. Somehow, the chameleon suit masked even that and we watched them creep past. I was amazed and grateful that they had not sensed us in any way.

When they were far enough away Erika put her lips close to my ear again and whispered. "To the doorway, Jon. We must make it to the doorway."

I aimed my Scorpion and dropped both shadows. With my enhanced senses, I could see the needle streak through the air. The mini portal at the end of the barrel did not open in this world. The weapon was still deadly; the rounds had armour piercing monomolecular points. The poison would find its mark, as deadly in this world as it is on Sol. We moved slowly and silently in the cover of the heavy undergrowth.

An arrow whistled past my ear like a dark emissary of death. Now I was sure I did not know what Erika meant when she looked at me before. We broke cover and ran our goal, the troll safe house. The shadows closed in fast and took form as they passed through the dappled sunlight. Three appeared before us cutting off our path to the trollish doorway.

"Gnome Snigmorder." Erika hissed.

Chapter 22

Squat and powerful, the gnomes long arms all held short fat blades that circled their fists. I aimed from the hip and dropped two more instantly; the third darted behind a tree. I fired again; the needle like dart hit the tree trunk. I heard the sharp scrape of the needle imbedding itself in the tree. No warping magic, the needle stayed in this physical world, the enchantment of the weapon too weak to trigger the warping effect.

A short ebony arrow sprouted from Erika's right thigh and she went down. The arrow came too fast for the chameleon suit to react and the arrow tore through the fabric and into Erika's leg. I rushed to her side, she grunted in pain. Two shadows darted in from the side to make a quick kill. I did not know the exact number of assailants, but by now, I had spotted ten different shadows. I fired again while drawing my katana. 'A good day to die' I thought. 'And it will be an expensive day in blood for those short ass little monsters.'

Both Snigmorder held those short fat blades in each hand. The right gnome swerved as I shot and my needles missed their mark.

'Those little shits learn real fast' I thought. They were on us; my sword came up to engage in a battle I knew I would lose. Outnumbered over ten to one, with a wounded charge to protect I could see no way out of this one. A trollish Yari streaked out of the trees as if launched from a ballista; the gnomes shot violently to the left. Both Snigmorder skewered by the same Yari, the point embedded in a tree, only one set of feet struggled clear of the ground the other pair hung limply. One Assassin dead the other pinned between the tree and his dead comrade, he squirmed in pain and shuddered in death throws, his final seconds only moments away. He was beyond help and no further threat to us. There was no way the Yari would be enchanted on Earth Prime but the spear did its bloody job nevertheless.

"Where the hell did that spear come from?" I whispered but I knew not to dwell on the unexpected in mid battle.

Another Snigmorder rushed me from the trees. He was unaware that I was more than human and the mistake cost him his life. I took his head with one fluid cut of my katana, the blade as deadly in our world as it is in Sol. The others retreated into the safety of the shadows. I had only moments before they regrouped and once more pressed their attack. Still unsure of the numbers of Snigmorder and with their enhanced speed they were able to dodge the scorpion needles in mid-flight. I had been lucky to get four of them but the surprise was over and my luck seemed to evaporate like mist in the morning sun. These gnomes were professional killers and it was victory or death for them.

The arrow stemmed the flow of blood from Erika's thigh and the chameleon suit sealed around the shaft and tightened which also helped to stem the blood flow. I broke off most of the arrow shaft so as not to cause any further internal injury, I left enough to work with if I ever got the chance to attempt to remove it from her leg; I feared it might have severed an artery. I lifted her unceremoniously across my shoulder and I gave silent thanks that she was so light, and I was endowed with this newfound strength. I sprinted off towards the troll safe house. Into a gravel courtyard, I ran and spotted a car park to my right. A few cars parked up there and I knew that given a few moments, and if I was lucky, I could hotwire one. The Fredericia Psy Signal Corps came to mind again, and with a car, I could be there in minutes and get medical help for the Princess in my charge.

The Gods were with us, a grey haired distinguished looking man stepped out of his parked car. As I sprinted to him, I noticed the German plates.

"Schlüssel!" I shouted demanding his keys, my scorpion pointed at the man's face. His eyes wide with shock, confronted by a crazed solider dressed in strange shifting colours armed with a sword and a pistol, carrying a beautiful woman with a crossbow shaft in her leg, the man froze in confusion.

"Gib mir deine Autoschlüssel!" I demanded his keys again. He raised his hands; the keys in the fingers of his right hand. I threw my katana in through the open door and grabbed the keys out of his hand. I bundled Erika into the passenger seat. The man stepped forward seemingly seeing an opportunity, maybe he was an old soldier, I did not know. I spun around, my weapon again to his head.

"Stop, jetzt wieder!" I demanded him to move back. My German was far from perfect but I knew he got the message. He retreated a few steps, his hands in the air again. I keyed the ignition and shut the driver door. A short black arrow whistled from the woods and embedded in the front driver's side wing, a second cracked the windscreen but deflected upward and away.

"Euroforce! Colour Sergeant Jon Raine!" I shouted towards the stunned German, hoping he would understand. My suit flashed into a normal Euroforce combat uniform.

"John Wayne?" he called back in question.

I did not have time to explain. I rammed the gearstick into reverse and spun the car around. Into first and the car shot forward. I headed for the exit.

"The doors, Jon. There!" Erika pointed towards a large set of red painted wooden doors in the sidewall of the farmhouse barn. Erika saw me hesitate.

"Please Jon. Trust me. The doors... Drive... Drive!" she pleaded through her pain. We shot past the doors, more arrows thudded into the car. I was determined to get as much distance between us and our hunters.

"Jon." Erika whispered, pleaded and on her word, I changed my mind. Against all I knew was logic I swerved back into danger, spun the car around and back into the car park to aim it in a suicide run at a pair of heavy red wooden barn doors.

I sped up one avenue around a tree-covered island and back down the way we had come. The tyres screeched their protests against the tarmac as I used the handbrake to line the car up towards those tall doors. They looked extremely solid to me just then but I trusted Erika's words. I floored the accelerator, the tyres spun on the asphalt.

A shadow flashed. A thud on the roof. A long thin blade pierced the roof and skewered Erika through the shoulder and into the seat. She screamed in pain. The chameleon suit sent tendrils up the thin blade to stop it penetrating deeper into Erika's shoulder, although a painful twelve inches had already gone in.

"Doors, Jon … Doors!" she yelled. The engine screamed and the car shot forward in a suicide run towards our target. I was sure this was the end.

The doors loomed large; impossibly large, we headed to our deaths. I braced for the collision, comforted in the knowledge that the collision would kill the shadow on the roof as well. The doors came fast, too fast. I closed my eyes; my knuckles were white with tension as I gripped the steering wheel; my arms locked for impact. There was a bone-jarring thud, the air bags exploded in our faces to ease the impact and we were through the doors. The car spun a few 360-degree horizontal circles. Everything was a flashing spinning confusion. The shadow thrown from the roof, it lay on the short grass in Sol's early morning sun, and it was clearly one of the Snigmorder. Drawing my shorter tanto, I sliced into my airbag to deflate it then sliced the passenger bag to free a shocked and wounded nisse princess. Apparently, nisse princesses did not know about air bags. I hand braked the car around and floored the accelerator again. There was a double bump as the wheels hit the gnome prone on the ground. I braked hard and Erika gave a stifled scream as the inertia shifted the blade in her shoulder. I reversed back, hard over the gnome. The double thud again, I knew that gnome was not getting up. Four more rushed through the doorway, a mirror image of the one we entered, set within a doppelganger farmhouse in the middle of Sollen grassland. One of the gnomes, still running, let loose an arrow that thudded into the car's rear door.

"Move, Jon! Drive!" Erika screamed, her own blood splattered her neck and face and oozed over her dark chameleon suit.

"The blade Erika, I have to..."

"No Jon move, drive now or we are dead!" She pleaded. I pushed the gear stick and sped away over the dead gnome again; the live ones gave chase but rapidly fell behind.

I reckoned about fifteen to twenty minutes of drive time before the car was useless, enough to put some serious distance between us and those shadows that hunted us. I looked across to Erika desperately trying to guess how far I could drive before I needed to attempt to save her. She still had the arrow shaft in her thigh and with the neck wound, I knew she was bleeding fast and her chances of survival, if any, were very slim.

I concentrated on the way ahead and slid onto a well-worn wagon track thankful I was not driving at speed towards a cliff edge.

The tendrils of Erika's chameleon suit clasped the thin blade that skewered Erika by her shoulder to the seat and eased that thin blade back out of her body. I winced at the pain she must have suffered, the blade inched upwards and slowly withdrew from her shoulder. When pushed up far enough the wind resistance tore it out of the roof and away. I glanced to her shoulder expecting spurts of blood and readied to stop to put pressure on the vicious puncture. The blood stopped surging out of the tear in her flesh. Erika passed her hand over the wound to wipe the blood away and to my complete astonishment, there was no wound. The chameleon suit quickly covered the tear and in a moment, it looked as if nothing had pierced either her shoulder or the fabric of the suit.

I had seen Elvin healers do some remarkable things, almost miracles in themselves; but to heal such a deep wound so rapidly I had never seen the like in all my years in Sol. Erika turned her attention to the arrow in her thigh. She placed her thumb on the broken shaft end and began to push it through to the other side. The barbs in the arrowhead made it impossible to withdraw the arrow out the way it came in. Erika pressed steadily on the broken arrow shaft and forced the tip on through her flesh to the other side. Every bump in the dirt road caused her to whimper in pain. Slowly the arrow pushed through and she must have suffered unimaginable pain while the arrowhead passed through the rest of her leg. I imagined the horrific tearing inside her thigh as the head passed through her flesh. The arrow tip broke skin and Erika pulled it and the rest of the broken ebony shaft through her leg. She wiped the blood away from her thigh, and as with her shoulder, there was no wound. Erika gave a deep relieving gasp as the last of the pain left her body.

"Neat trick Eh?" She smiled her girlish smile again as if the mind wrenching pain and torture she had just put herself through had never happened.

"Ah, Yeah!" I said my mouth still open in shock. "You'll have to show me that sometime." I added.

"Do you think about twenty minutes of carriage time?" Erika asked as if she considered a jaunt in the countryside.

"Maybe ten, perhaps fifteen at best."

"Then turn the car around."

"What? Back there?"

"Yes, back to the doorway, the portal, as you call it."

"But Erika they will ..."

"I know what they will do. They will come after us. They will never stop. For them it is victory or death. They have harassed the Royal Person and there is only but one punishment for such a rude act. I have no RiNisse guard here to do their duty so it is up to me and I suppose you to hold the honour of the house nisse and my Father the Emperor King"

"But there are at least ten of them, maybe more."

"I see, Lieutenant Raine." She had reinstated the formality I had feared. "If you think you are not up to it then we can always go on and I will have my SkyggenNisse hunt them down later... As long as they don't get us first" She finished with folded arms and an angry teenaged huff.

I braked to a stop and shot her an angry stare.

"Well, if you are going to drive like a Mormon I had better belt up." She reached behind her shoulder, pulled the seatbelt across her breasts, and clicked it home.

"I think you meant moron." I laughed.

"Did I?" She replied in a huff. We had stopped, and Erika... Princess Erika sat in a huff, her arms crossed and pointedly forcing herself to stare out the front windscreen.

"Well then, I suppose you need to drive on then." She commented in her arrogant childish manner, I had hated it since the first time she used it.

"OK, Princess. It's your funeral." I said through my teeth; and in another moment of madness, I swung the car around to head back the way we came.

"Now, that's more like it." She smiled. I sped off back again on another suicide mission thinking about how in the seven Hells I got myself into this mess.

Erika slipped the small ornate dagger from the scabbard on her thigh. The gleaming blade was about six or seven inches long and gleamed lustrous silver that could only be Adamantine steel, the white ornate bone handle about five inches long.

"Is that all you got Princess?" I sneered dismissively. I knew she was a SkyggenNisse but really, us against ten or more Snigmorder. She would need a better weapon than an envelope knife.

"It's enough. It is the sister of the dagger of Diana." She replied gently as if explaining to a child, I almost believed her.

"Here, take this." I drew the eighteen inches of the blade of my tanto.

"No Jon, you need to start trusting your princess."

I sheathed the tanto as I drove. 'My princess?' I thought. 'Does she think she is queen of the whole bloody world?'

Chapter 23

The squad of eleven Snigmorder raced across the savannah in a steady pursuit pace when we first spotted them; gnomes with their long legs and short bodies were great runners and could cover many miles of territory in a single day. I knew they could keep that pace up for days on end. Their path changed and they turned towards us through the long savannah grass, I knew they had spotted us. They knew we had no bows or crossbows, and I was sure they did not fully comprehend my scorpion pistol and how it worked in Sol. They however, were armed with their crossbows; I believed they thought they had the advantage.

"I could stop and take them out from here with my pistol." I suggested as we sped towards our pursuers.

"I want to get up close." Erika used a tone that gave me no doubt as to why she wanted to get close to these Snigmorder.

"Princess, I have your safety to think about." I protested.

"If I was only reliant on you Mr Raine, I would be dead now."

I could not fault her argument so I added. "We would be safe from this distance."

"They have laid harm to the Royal Person and for that insult I want to see the reds of their eyes when I put them to the blade."

I resolved that we would have to engage and kill them all if we were to survive the fight. Leaving just one gnome alive would leave us with an ever-present shadow with a duty of revenge to seek us out.

Out in the grasslands with no shadows to hide them, their strange camouflage could not work; they did not slide away from our vision. There was nowhere to set a trap and they were not expecting us to return. They thought they had the upper hand and headed straight for us. The eleven Snigmorder rapidly closed the distance between us. I sped in their direction and we closed in on them. I could see that we had a fight on our hands.

They spread out; I knew it was in anticipation of my scorpion. I closed the distance faster than they would have guessed. Two to the left of us were close enough for us to have a go. I hit the first full on, he ricocheted high into the air and the other spun away like a rag doll as I clipped him with the wing of the car. We hand braked and spun the car to swat a third before he could jump away. I stopped the car, grabbed my katana from the rear seat and was out and running. The clipped gnome was on his knees, fat semi-circular blades in his hands; I took his head as I passed him by. Their crossbows were of no use close range as we could avoid their flight in normal time. The gnome Snigmorder could match our strength and speed. I heard the zing of a sword drawn from a scabbard and Erika held a long wicked blade in her hand. I realised she held three feet of magical Mythral steel and not Adamantine steel as I thought before. That was something about which I needed to ask her. The other gnomes had converged on us quicker than I would have liked. I went down in a crush of bodies, blades rung out as we clashed together. They thought to take me first by weight of arms, and five Snigmorder converged on me while three went for Erika.

    I spotted Erika dancing around the three gnomes before my attention was forced to my immediate assailants attack. They hoped to bring me down and flay me with sheer weight of numbers. One short flat blade caught my right forearm and blood sprang from the wound, pain jabbed up my arm. My chameleon sleeve moved down to close the wound and hold it fast. The Snigmorder saw it and hesitated in disbelief. I took the advantage and stabbed him in the throat. Another gnome came in for a quick kill, I parried his thrusts as I went to my knees, he raised his arms in a double bladed hammer blow, a move that was almost impossible to foil but left him dangerously exposed. I sent my long katana up through his chin and into his brain. I withdrew my blade just in time to parry another gnome's blade with my tanto. I turned again and a Snigmorder was there, he thrust his blade into my unguarded stomach. When the blade met the chameleon suit, it stopped as if I wore Kevlar armour. The gnome pressed hard against the resistance but the blade did not pierce the suit. I stabbed the surprised gnome through the eye with my tanto and battled on with the others. Erika still danced blades with the other three. I kicked off the other two gnomes and took one head while they scrambled to regroup. I stabbed the other in the stomach with my katana and drew my tanto across his neck. He still had fight in him. He lunged, another cut to my upper arm, deep and vicious. I willed my chameleon suit to cover my arm and hold the wound together. I spun and deflected the gnome's blade away; in my spin, I launched a roundhouse kick to his head and he went down. In that same moment I saw Erika in the air, for a second I thought she was injured and thrown away in the gnomes attack. I was wrong. I dashed to Erika's side, and as I reached her, I saw that her flight was actually a somersault; she twisted in the air like a gymnast. Her long thin blade ripped one of the gnomes from groin to sternum, his viscera spilled to the ground as he watched in amazed horror; he went down screaming as if he felt every inch of the tear that ended his life. The scream gave pause to the remaining gnomes' attack. The last two Snigmorder divided to attack each of us separately. It was a fierce close quarter exchange of cuts and thrusts, parries and lunges. At one moment, I feared we would succumb to the last two assassins but Erika was a superbly expert swordswoman and I could see the decades of experience in her moves.

    Erika slipped and tumbled on slick red blood and she went down on one knee. Her opponent seized the opportunity and raced in to finish her off. His blades held up to give the killing blows, he found himself impaled on Erika's slim blade extended backwards under her arm, the stumble a feint; she drew the gnome to his death. She twisted the weapon, withdrew and stepped away, the gnome stood for a moment in stunned silence, he took one-step forward and fell face forward to the grass.

    The final Snigmorder realized he was out numbered and out classed. He disengaged and ran as fast as he could. I drew my pistol to aim at the retreating gnome; I could not leave him alive.

"He is mine!" Erika demanded and hefted her sword like a javelin, the handle grew long and fletches appeared at the end. She launched the weapon at the fleeing gnome and caught him in the middle of his back. He fell lifeless into the long grass. Erika reached out her hand and the javelin twisted out of the Snigmorder's body and flew back into Erika's hand. By the time Erika caught the weapon it was a thin elvin like sword again.

The Princess replaced the three-foot blade back into her six-inch scabbard and clipped the white bone handle back into place at her thigh.

"Neat little weapon there, Princess." I smiled; I did not want her to know what I thought of the weapon before the fight.

Far to the horizon, twelve more dark images raced across the savannah. We had the sun to our backs so I knew they had not seen us yet. Hoods formed over our heads and veils came across our faces. Our eyes zoomed into the dots on the far horizon. A backup squad of Snigmorder raced to support the first squad and take up the fight.

"Twelve against two." I whispered.

"Scorpion?" Erika suggested.

"Sure you do not wish to battle hand to hand this time again?" I commented as I drew my pistol.

"I would but they have not as yet been rude to the Royal Person and I want to see this scorpion of yours."

I aimed at the faraway shapes brought near by the magnification of our veils. Augmented by my enhanced vision I could see every detail of the unit of assassins running in formation. I fired the first round and one of the central gnomes fell at the next pace. I followed with six more aimed shots and six more gnomes fell. I had no need to compensate for distance or wind strength. As soon as the projectile left my weapon, it was in its target. The remaining five stopped and circled defensively, they had no concept of the scorpion pistol and they tensed for another invisible attack; two more shots and two more fell. The last three Snigmorder dropped their weapons and knelt on one knee, their right arms across their chests, fists on hearts; they raised their left arms aloft in supplication of mercy to their invisible enemy.

In wartime, my next shots would have been murder. This was not wartime, I had a Princess to protect and I was under a "Lethal Force Order". I almost considered dropping my weapon to my side in response to their request for mercy. I did not. I fired and three pleading gnomes slumped to the ground. I felt bad, dirty, I was a soldier not an assassin but I knew that they would give no quarter and we could not risk prisoners in our situation.

We sprinted to the motor and sped away leaving the dead gnomes to the carrion birds and flying reptiles that had already begun to circle. They would be a highflying flag to our enemies if we did not clear away from there in the next few moments.

"More will come after us." Erika said flatly.

"If we get enough distance we will be able to stay ahead of them at least until we can get some help." I said and floored the accelerator for as much speed and distance as we could before the engine died.

Five minutes later the car spluttered and began to slow. As soon as it hit thirty miles per hour, the electric motor kicked in.

"Of course! An old Toyota Primus!" I laughed. The vehicle had a dual system and as the internal combustion engine gave in to the crazy physics of Sol, the electric motor took over.

"An electric motor, Erika!" I laughed. "If we keep it steady we may get another hour to an hour and a half."

"Princess Erika." She reminded me pouting her full wide lips.

I do not know how or why but the electric engine lasted the best part of four hours. We took advantage of every downward gradient to free wheel. It grew hot in the car without the use of the air-conditioning, the strong summer sun blazed in a clear azure sky, only the odd lonely cloud moved lazily in the hot breeze. We kept the windows down, our suits kept us at a comfortable temperature but we did not want to over tax them in a sealed glass case with the summer Sollen sun burning hot high in the sky. We made just over fifty miles in the unending grasslands; enough I believed to show any more gnome Snigmorder a clean pair of heels.

Away from the chaos and the fighting, I had time to gather my thoughts and begin to formulate a plan.

"Princess... damn it! Erika." I began.

"Just Princess Erika will do." Erika cut in.

"Listen, Princess." I used the term as disrespectfully as Han Solo. "We are in the middle of nowhere and until we get to what you call civilisation, it's just going to be Erika. Okay? Okay!" I demanded.

"Okay." She reluctantly agreed in her high school sweet sixteen huff, as if she had just bestowed me some great honour.

I glanced sidewise at her and her chameleon suit was again the yellow and white summer dress she had on before. Her bare shoulders, breasts, face and legs all caked in blood and I was sure I was not so different.

As a ghoulish bloodied couple, we drove on under the burning sun, on into the grassland peppered with eclectic patterns of tended farm fields.

The car started to slow and I knew we had only a few moments of power left to us.

"Over there, go that way." Erika pointed to our left.

"Why, what's there?" I peered over the expanse of wilderness grassland to our right.

"See how the grass darkens? That is a river or a stream. We could do with cleaning up." Erika almost sounded reasonable.

"I think we should make the glass go up before we lose the rest of this 'elecktrick' power." She added, straining with the unfamiliar word as I turned the car towards the darkened vegetation.

"Come the night you may need the shelter of this carriage."

I silently agreed, embarrassed that I had not thought that far ahead. The car finally gave out only a few yards from a deep flowing river. It was about 10 yards wide and the water was so clear we could see all the way to the bottom. Someone or something had made a set of stepping stone boulders a little down river and the leeward side of the rocks gave rise to some still water pools that looked mostly chest deep.

Erika began to strip and I coughed uncomfortably and began, reluctantly, to turn my back.

"Come, now Lieutenant Raine. I thought we were to dispense with etiquette for a while. You will not behold anything you have not beheld before." She gave a throaty laugh and her short dress dropped to her feet only to form the dark grey poncho of a discarded chameleon suit.

Now I like to think myself a real man of the world but faced with her perfectly petite body, I did not know where to put myself.

Erika was extremely comfortable with herself and I did not know if this sort of behaviour was usual for her and her kind or if she was teasing me. She moved through the long ferns to the still pool behind one of the larger steppingstones. I watched her move with grace and regal dignity as naked as the day of her birth, I knew then, just as I had when I had first beheld her, that I loved her as much as I loved my own life.

I knew she needed me when she drew the life force from her Father Oak but she was not human and her needs and wants differed from that of a young human girl. Older than my great grandmother and so beyond my reach, all I could do was watch her and hope that we would have some more time together before we reached organised help. How I resented that help at that moment.

I wanted Erika so much it made my heart ache to know that she would resume her royal position and I would go back to being just a grunt again in the mud and blood and fear of conflict but that was the future and not now. Now I had her to myself, dark and sultry, Erika seemed to be in her own element and at ease with her surroundings. I pulled off my own suit and it morphed into a grey poncho the image of Erika's. I picked up her poncho to bring them closer to the rock pool in which we chose to bathe.

With both chameleon suits in hand, I stepped across the rocks to follow Erika into the pool. I could see that she still wore that fascinating knife strapped to her right thigh. The water would have no effect on the bone handle and the Mythral steel blade. So distracted by Erika's perfect body and her dagger strapped to her perfect thigh, I slipped on a slick moss covered rock and tumbled down into the water.

Reaching out to gain a handhold, I lost both ponchos into the swirling, fast flowing water. In the swift current, they moved rapidly down river. My head came out of the water to see Erika dive into the current to follow the rapidly retreating garments. I wasted no time in following her downstream. I knew from the experience on the boat that she had a problem with water and I knew that if I conserved my energy while getting to her I would be able to pull her against the bank further downstream and perhaps recover the suits as well.

Erika caught up with the clothes and I could see her, head and shoulders above the water a hundred yards down river, right in the middle of the swift current. I knew that with her slight frame the strong current would carry her quickly away. Without further thought for my own safety and angry that I had caused this situation, I struck out after her. I swam with the current and allowed it to carry me to her and conserve my energy. My plan was to get to her with the strength and ability to pull her to shore. It looked like a good plan to me.

Erika began to move against the current, she rose out of the water almost to her waist, and was somehow propelled against the fast moving current; she left behind her a wake as if she were a small motorboat. I saw that the chameleon suit formed around her body and she held only my own suit. She sped against the current and towards me as fast as I moved towards her and we came together in swirls of white foam, the water forced from its natural path. My chameleon suit formed around me and I willed it into a body wetsuit, the armoured type the surfers used on Eran347. We twisted around each other in the swirls and eddies. Erika hooked her arm through mine and we locked ourselves together as she pulled me backwards against the flow. I felt as if a steel line from a powerful tractor pulled me upstream and I could not work out where the power was coming from. The water pushed over my shoulders and under my back, sometimes pushing me up, and then forcing me under. I felt Erika push me to one side and we were in the still pool once more.

"Wow what a ride!" I laughed gaining my feet. "How the hell did you do that?"

"You should not underestimate a nisse princess. I asked you to trust your princess, Jon. We are more resourceful than we look Lieutenant." Erika replied and dipped her head under the water. When she came up, she changed the chameleon suit into a very becoming yellow one-piece bathing suit; it showed off her dark skin very well.

"The nisse have many secrets even from our elvin cousins. We are of earth, water, fire and air and my father's empire spans all the elements in all the lands, not only our own but of the entire world."

"But you wanted to get away from the sea back on Earth Prime."

"Yes, your sea contains salt and salt is poisonous to us. Were you not told not to spill salt? Moreover, if you did spill salt, did you to throw a pinch over your shoulder to blind the mischievous imp behind you? Fresh water holds no threat to me."

I thought about what she said and asked; "So if they are secret, why tell me?"

"Because I am your princess and you are my charming prince."

I took Erika by the waist; we stood in waist deep water behind the big rock. This time I spoke softly.

"Again Erika, I am a Euroforce soldier and not one of your subjects and as much as I would wish it to be so, you are not my princess, Princess!"

"Oh Jon, Jon my love, the Gods give you two ears, they do this to tell you to listen twice as much as you speak!" She laughed, and put her arms around my shoulders. She looked up into my eyes and I found myself drowning again in the deep dark green pools of her gaze.

"My love! You said 'My love'. That's the second time you said that." I stammered, not quite believing the words from her mouth. She changed again from the arrogant high school prom queen to an elegant caring beauty. She held my eyes like irresistible magnets. Erika laid the palm of her hand on my chest.

"Your heart beats fast, Jon are you that out of shape?" She smiled up at me.

"I don't think it is the swim that's doing this." I replied.

"Feel my heart Jon." Erika invited and took my hand to place it on her right breast. My own heart hammered like an anvil and Erika smiled such an inviting smile that I had to pull her close and kiss her deeply.

I enfolded her in my arms as she reached around my back, her nails pressing against my back. I ran my hands down her small caramel coloured back and down to her firm rounded bottom, I pulled her firmly against me. We kissed long and deep exploring each other's mouths with our tongues. If felt so good and so natural, I knew it had to be so wrong.

We parted our lips to get air and Erika laid her cheek upon my chest.

"Jon when you took me under the arms of Father Oak, we became one. I am truly your princess. I am yours to possess Jon, and you will be mine if you would just say the words your heart wishes you to say. Accept the offering of my body, my spirit and my love."

I held her away a little.

"If you are serious Erika... Really serious; then I am yours." I spoke not daring to hope.

In the pool we stood where it was only waist deep and I went to one knee and took her hand in mine.

"Princess Erika Nisse, I am yours if you will be mine." As soon as I spoke the words, our hands darkened to ebony. A tingling sensation began in my hands and I felt a sensation of hot power travel up my arms and fill my chest, with it came the ebony colour, the heat spread over my body and the ebony blackness spread within. Erika threw her head back as she felt the same power flow through her; she looked as if she were in the throes of ecstasy. I felt the coldness of the stream disappear and even though the water was more than a little cold, I felt no chill at all.

The princess and I were ebony black; our hair so black it shimmered with blue highlights. Filled with the searing heat of raw magic. Erika's eyes turned from dark green to rich brown, the whites now startling against her black skin, I presumed the same transformation happened to me.

"What's just happened?" I asked in amazement as I scanned my own body, now as black as Erika's own skin.

"We are wed my love." She ran her hand softly across my face. "When you took me, you gave me your seed and now that we are joined and given ourselves to each other, our life forces have joined and we have taken of the life force of Sol to bind our spirits together forever. Now we are one my love. Jon, I am with child."

"Are you saying that you are pregnant?"

"It was to be with child or death for me. And I think I could not find a better man to save me and father the next heir to the throne of the Nisse Empire."

I moved though the pool to sit on the big rock before my knees gave way.

"Jon my love, I am so sorry. You are displeased?"

"No, no Erika it's not that! I am... yes, I am pleased. It is such a shock. We have only just met and I... Well I... Well it's my father." I replied still looking at my black skin.

"Your Father?" Erika looked puzzled. "How is your father involved in this?"

"Princess, my father told me never to get a princess pregnant on our first date and never the daughter of a King, with an entire army at his disposal." I stated very seriously.

"How did your father..." Erika began. I laughed and she realized the joke. I beat my legs to splash her and a spout of water hit me in the middle of my back to knock me off my rock perch and into the pool beside Erika. I stood up spitting water and coughing some water out of my lungs.

"It is an honour and privilege to wear the black skin of a wedded nisse." Erika said and came to me to hug me. I reached out to touch her and she guided my hand to her taught flat stomach.

"In there? My baby?" I asked.

"Yes, feel with your heart and your mind. Feel the life within me."

I closed my eyes and concentrated. I could feel Erika so warm and vibrant, and yes, I could feel a different life force, small and so delicate yet so strong and full of growth and potential.

"That's your son, Jon."

"You know that?" I asked, wondering if the prophecy had given notice of the sex of my first-born.

Erika nodded and smiled. "Yes, my love. When a nisse maiden is taken under her birth tree, it is always a son. Your son, our son."

"My love?" I repeated Erika's words in disbelief. "My love." I said again this time from my heart.

Chapter 24

We slept on a bed of ferns and grasses; there naked in the night air, we enjoyed each other's bodies. I did not feel the chill or the prick of the flora upon which we lay. Neither did we feel the need to make use of our chameleon suits to make the bag we used the first time we were together in the Danish forest of Earth Prime. I understood now, when Erika said that I might need the shelter of the Toyota Primus. She did not mean herself as she could safely bed down anywhere. I was the weaker one and would have needed the shelter if not for this dark transformation. I lay still and asleep as the sun rose above the far horizon to the west. Just like Denmark of Earth Prime, this land was devoid of hills and mountains. The sun's rays fell upon me to flood my body with renewing and invigorating energy.

Erika stretched her lithe body against mine; she lay in my arms beside me. I stroked her luscious black hair, she moved her head to open her dark brown eyes and I stroked her soft ebony cheek. Those dark pools of brown eyes gazed lovingly into mine; I imagined my eyes were the mirror in colour to hers.

"Good morning my love, do you feel how the sun strengthens you?" She yawned; still not fully awake I could see that she too was enjoying the sun's rays.

"Yes I do. I feel great!"

"You are as much a part of this land now as I am. Come Jon, I have so much to teach you."

"Just a moment, Erika. I would like to enjoy this moment." I gazed into her eyes and she closed them and snuggled her cheek into my chest.

"Are my eyes as brown as yours?" I asked the idle question, enjoying the warmth of her body and the rays of the sun.

"No of course not, they are still as blue as they have always been." Erika smiled without opening her eyes.

"Still blue?" I asked. I thought it odd but of no import.

"It is the saxicoline magic in you." She whispered, her eyes still closed and her head resting on my chest.

"The what?" I asked; this time the strange word rung alarm bells in my head.

"You have troll blood in your veins my love; you have troll magic in you. Did Prince Jægerblod not tell you this?" Erika replied, this time she opened her eyes.

I sat up to rise to my feet and Erika did likewise. "Uffe told me nothing of the sort. Prince Jægerblod? " On my feet, I began to ask. "How could I have troll blood in me?" I said and the realisation struck me like an ogre's hammer. "In the name of the Gods! My Great Grandmother and her fantasy stories of her trollish prince that lived in her cupboard. They... He and Great Grandma... Are you telling me that...?" I sat down on a rock while my mind started to put all the facts and information together.

"Uffe?" I whispered. Erika nodded.

"Uffe is my great grandfather? No! It can't be!" I sat in stunned silence. My Grandmother found fame and fortune writing a series of fantasy novels about the troll prince her mother, Annika; fell in love with when she was a young teenage girl.

In her first bloom of womanhood, the troll prince carried her off in the night to his trollish kingdom where in that upside-down world the ugly brutish trolls were good and virtuous and the enemy were the beautiful and powerful nephilim, born of Earth Prime and fled across the gateways to Sol in the days of the Flood. In my Grandmother's books the nephilim were once a great and good race and named themselves of the Allfather and not Adam. However, they looked upon the daughters of Adam and found them fair. They married daughters of men and their seed corrupted in the blood of the fallen Adam. They became the giants of the land, as the children of the nephilim, became the tribal race of ogres.

Corrupted, the nephilim and the ogre fled the cleansing waters of the Allfather on their world and sought refuge with Cain, Lilith and their descendants, the trolls.

"Well yes, and no." Erika reamed my thoughts and corrected them. It was her first lesson on her nisse histories. She went on. "The fae, of which I am one, are the literal descendants of Samael and Lilith. Samael is the Angelic name for Cain and the name he used before he was sent to earth to become the Son of Adam and Eve.

"The Trolls, the Minatons and other races you collectively know as demons and dark Fae, sprang from the union of Cain, as you know him and Naamah. Naamah was Cain's sister wife and their first-born was the first troll, Asmodeus, son of Cain, and brotherfather to all trolls. He carried the mark of Cain upon his head, black as night and as ugly as the beasts he preyed upon. Lilith found the peace with Cain that she never found with his father, Adam, with Cain she lived as an equal partner, Cain had no wish to subjugate her and he treated her as equal. From her loins sprang the fae and the Seelie Court.

"When we find peace and joy, our eternal partner and soul companion, our skin becomes as Lilith and we know we are blessed to know happiness as the ancients know it. We will not give birth in blood and pain as the humans are cursed to do. Our birthing is painless and simple. Almost all of our offspring are born healthy and whole."

"What about the few born ill or disabled?" I asked. Erika though for a long time before answering, I guessed it was a subject she felt strongly about.

"We are born into this world within an egg, that egg is placed in our birthing tree, for me and my house that is the oak. I take my egg and sing to the Father Oak. I will sing the elvin song, Father Oak opens his bosom, and I place the egg therein. There are those that tend the tree and the egg within the tree. They have the ability to sense the child within its father tree. If that child shows any form of imperfection or defect; the

Treewives sing the tree and the egg is absorbed into the father tree to re-join the circle of life." Erika finished. I felt revolted at this abominable act but I did not press the point, I could see and sense that Erika was revolted as well.

We sat on the big rock considering her words. Erika squeezed the water from her hair. She continued her explanation.

"The descendants of Samael or Cain and Lilith became the Seelie Court of fae and those that sprang from the union of Cain and his sister wife Naamah became the Unseelie Court of dark fae or demons as you may prefer. It has remained generally so for millennia but through the ages some races divided and joined the opposing Court. The trolls of Denmark are one such case. Although the trolls formed the Unseelie Court; Danish trolls became members of the Seelie Court and therefore subject themselves to my Father, the Emperor King." Erika said twisting her hair to dry it. As I gazed upon her I realised that she still wore the gilded wreath through her hair only the pinnacle with the large diamond was missing. I realised it was missing from the time she leapt at me in the ballroom.

During my time in Sol, I had never heard of any trollish strife with any tribe of beings that could be known as these nephilim. I knew of them in our early earth histories. If I did not know about this, it would follow that Euroforce Intelligence and thus the Army would not have heard of this history either.

"Erika, you call them Danish trolls and you call your land Denmark. How is it the country is called Denmark on both worlds?"

"We have called our land Denmark for thousands of years before there were humans in your Denmark. They took the name of their land from us and we visited your world through many gateways over many thousands of years. Trolls are the most talented in forming the gateways we call trollgates. Denmark of both our worlds lies very close together and there are many gateways between our worlds here. The veil between the worlds of Earth and Sol is very thin in Denmark." Erika finished and tossed her head to release her hair. The black mane of hair fell about her shoulders glowing with blue highlights in the sun and falling straight and silky smooth as if she had it treated in an upmarket hair salon.

I do not know if I was disappointed or pleased when Erika morphed her attractive one-piece bathing suit into a rather attractive walking outfit of buckskin leather complete with supporting knee high brown soft walking boots that looked like calf leather. Her skirt hid the top of the dagger she wore on her leg but the black sheath showed below the hem of her skirts. The leather overskirt hid folds of white cotton underskirts; and peeking from the dark brown bodice top, Erika's shoulders and neck trimmed in a white under blouse that fell off one shoulder. The white trim was starkly attractive against her ebony skin. The blouse was wide enough to leave exposed the area to which a butterfly would attach to her spine and central nervous system. She moved and I could see that her dagger was easily accessible through a split in her skirts that, to my delight, showed the thigh of her leg.

"Well are you going to change or are you going to sit there covered in multi-coloured rubber all day until the Snigmorder get here?"

I looked down upon the armoured surfing suit. It would be quite out of place travelling the wide savannahs and farmlands. I examined my black arms and hands.

"When the Klaubautermann commented that you looked fair I noticed a questioning glance. Was he asking about this, this change that has happened to us?"

"I believe so. He would have known about it for sure."

I wished my suit to become that functional forest garb I wore before, this time I lightened the camouflage to match that of the light coloured savannah ahead. I took up my katana and tanto, my chameleon suit formed the Sam Browne belt and scabbards for the weapons as it formed the holster for my scorpion. I had the rounds the Klaubautermann gave me on his amazing ship and I thanked him silently for the gift of the ammunition. I checked the pistols action and holstered it once more.

Erika began her morning exercises to loosen her body before the long and arduous walk ahead; I picked a comfortable spot and sat down to watch her. Erika began by performing an exotic form of dance that looked like Yoga, Tai Chi and ballet all rolled into one. After a pleasant few minutes watching her dance through the grass, I decided I had better perform some warm up exercises as well. I fingered the handle of my sword and thought that I might run through a few katas to get the feel of the weight and lines of my weapon now that my body had changed so much.

I picked a clear space and ran through a few cuts, thrusts and blocks, when I felt that I had the weight of the weapon, I took the ready stance and lost myself to the forms and discipline of the set moves. On the final kata, I glistened with the sheen of perspiration. Erika clapped slowly; I looked around to see her sitting on a fallen tree trunk.

"Not bad for a novice." She laughed.

"Novice? And you can do better?" I asked.

Erika stood and walked over to me.

"May I Sir?" She held out her hand for my katana. I handed it to her.

"Okay then Princess; let's see what you can do." I stepped back to give her some space. Erika took a fighting stance with the sword held high and to one side with the end pointing low and forward. The blade spun with a blurring speed that cut the air in a deadly hum. She moved from stance to stance mimicking my moves exactly. It had taken me years of study and practice to master those katas. With a blinding speed that caused the sword to disappear until the move was finished, Erika went through every kata I previously performed. I was astounded that she could control such a long and heavy blade as if it were a small, light knife. Her moves were not only quick they were efficient and economic, just enough to cause the deathblow and nothing more. Erika finished all of the katas I had performed and moved into her own form of sword discipline. She completed all of her own twelve complex katas in the time it took me to complete my eight.

Upon her last stance she looked to me and smiled, her face reflected pride and achievement. I clapped in appreciation.

"Now that was impressive! How did you achieve that?" I asked

"It is like when you moved out of time at the ball. Then, you did it on instinct and out of fear. I used some of that speed to complete the katas with my own will." Erika walked to me and returned my sword with a kiss. She added. "Few, even between the soldiers of the RiNisse and SkyggenNisse can achieve this change using willpower alone. The speed is usually ignited with the release of adrenaline, but if you can feel this in your mind you can ignite it at will."

When we finished our morning exercises we went back to the place where we had slept, Erika collected breakfast when I was first running through my katas. There was a pile of root vegetables, a selection of mushrooms and some strange leafy green stuff. I examined the freshly washed food and felt a bit apprehensive about eating it.

"Shouldn't we attempt to catch a Rabbit or something?"

"No need my love, here try one of these" She offered me one of the large brown spotted mushrooms.

"Aren't they poisonous?" I asked remembering my Sol survival training.

"Only to humans." She said, and took a large bite. "Go on, they are delicious."

I took one of the fungi from her and looked at it.

"I'm human." I commented.

"Not anymore." Erika smiled. "Go on Jon, try it."

"Well if I die I will be very cross." I laughed and bit into the mushroom. It had a crisp slightly peppery flavour; it was as Erika said, delicious.

"Unlike most of the fae we nisse need no meat to survive. We can and do eat meat at times but we can eat anything from the grass on the ground to the bark from the trees."

Erika went to a young tree and neatly sliced through the bark with her blood red fingernails that seemed to be as deadly as a trolls talon fingers. I made a mental note to avoid those particular perfect talons. She passed me the small square of bark.

"Go on eat!" She invited me and offered the bark.

I put it in my mouth and began to chew. It had a flavour and texture like crisp bread.

"This is delicious!" I exclaimed. "If the army knew this they would be able to ..."

"No, Jon, my love, to humans it would taste repulsive. To us nisse... to you, it is food."

"Am I changed that much?" I asked. It worried me to realise that I had changed so much.

"As long as you remain on Sol you will no longer feel the cold, hunger or fear the sun. The forest is your friend and protector. You are nisse."

"What about when I go back?"

"Go back?" Erika asked as she chewed on another piece of bark.

"Yes, when I go back to Earth Prime."

"You want to go back?" Erika spread her arms to show me the land around us.

It was then, standing in that beautiful land, my true love beside me, that the realization hit me so hard it almost knocked me over.

"No Princess, my little princess. I don't want to ever go back." I took her in my arms and kissed her deeply. Our hug lasted for a comfortably long time before we returned to the car.

"We should prepare now, we have a long way to travel." I advised.

"Let's go." Erika said and started walking.

"Erika! We need to check the car for anything that might be useful." I called after her.

"You have your sword and you are nisse. What else do you need?"

"We need as much survival equipment as we can find. A first aid pack maybe?"

Erika stopped to face me. "Jon!" She addressed me as if I were a child. "You are nisse now." She spread her arms again to show the land around us. "We have all the survival equipment we need."

I checked my weapons and looked for the last time at the car. It grated on my mind to have to leave obvious things behind. My survival training screamed at me to collect something, anything useful. I abandoned all logic and began walking to catch up with Erika.

We walked hand in hand for hours.

Eventually Erika broke the comfortable silence. "Jon, you will need to trust me in this. You will need to trust your new found instincts."

"Well, okay, you have proved your word several times but we will need to take some bearings." I suggested.

"This way." Erika pointed towards the northwestern horizon. "The nisse are in that direction heading south. If we walk on this course, we will intercept them. They are four thousand strong."

"How do you know that?" I asked, I thought that maybe as a nisse field marshal, she would be privy to all troop movements; the truth was a startling revelation.

"I can feel them."

"You can?"

"Yes feel deep within your heart, in here." She caressed my chest and I felt her fingers burning against my skin. "Feel deep down inside and look to the horizon."

I concentrated my mind, trying to feel of that which she spoke. I made my mind travel deep within my chest and stared toward the point where the sky met the land.

"Yes, there! I can feel... I can feel... People! Many people, they are moving with one mind, with one intent, an army. I feel worry, fear, and excitement."

"It is part of the nisse army marching south."

"Where are they going?" I asked; amazed at the sense of connection I had with them, like the pull of the earth on falling rain.

"They are going to war, Jon."

"War?"

"Yes Jon, war. And I need to lead them."

"Who are they going to war with?" Hoping the answer was not the answer, which I formed in my mind.

"Humans." Erika confirmed all my fears with a single word.

We walked on hand in hand like teenagers on their first date. Sometimes we would run or play amongst the long savannah grasses. Erika began to teach me her nisse lore. I was in a strange and alien savannah yet I had no care in this world. The unrelenting sun beat down upon our bodies to invigorate us. Hours passed and we walked for mile after mile yet I felt as fresh as when we first started out. The sun travelled its arch and began to set behind us to the east. We walked on; all the while feeling the pull of those nisse, we were closing in on.

Chapter 25

Book of the Beginnings Chapter 4: Verse 23 - 29

23- Yea, He casteth out the Tender of the Garden and he causeth the man who was Adam, who was that First Man, and causeth He him with his helpmeet Eve to tend the garden.

24- In a time that old serpent knowing of the state of Father Adam and the Garden without its Tender, did he creep under and through the Garden to seek out the woman Eve; Adam knowing that old Dragon, would not succumb to the Devils temptations.

25- Eve who was Adams helpmeet and veiled from all worldly things did transgress in her innocence, and did fall to the will of the Serpent, that old Dragon, lo he sorely tempted her saying. 'Has God indeed said, "You shall not eat of every tree of the garden"?' And the woman said to the serpent, 'We may eat the fruit of the trees of the garden; but of the fruit of the tree which is in the midst of the garden, God has said, "You shall not eat it, nor shall you touch it, lest you die."' Then the serpent said unto Eve, 'You will not surely die. For the Gods know that in the day you eat of it your eyes will be opened, and you will be like the Gods, knowing good and evil.' Therefore, when the woman saw that the tree was good for food, that it was pleasant to the eyes, and a tree desirable to make one wise, she took of its fruit and ate. She also gave to her husband with her, and Adam said unto Eve what have you done, you have eaten of that which is forbidden." And Eve was sorely vexed and ashamed and she hid her face from Adam. And Eve spake unto Adam saying. "Adam my husband. I have eaten of the fruit and I will be cast out. I will be alone and you will remain to tend the Garden also alone. And Adam replied saying. "Eve I see that this must be done to bring about my family on Earth." And he ate of the fruit of the tree of Knowledge; to know good from evil and to know the way of the Gods.

26- Lo did the Allfather say, Behold, the man is become as one of us, to know good and evil: and now, lest he put forth his hand, and take also of the tree of life, and eat, and live forever:

27- He cursed Adam and Eve and cast them out of the garden to dwell in the dark and dreary world and becometh Adam, father of all the world of man, and Eve, mother to all men,

28- The Allfather greatly multiplied her conception; in blood and sorrow, Eve would bring forth children and she would be subject to her husband and Adam was commanded to rule over her.

29- And the Allfather did cause to stand at the east of the garden of Eden the Angels, Cherubim, and their Swords of the Flame; which guardeth the way of the tree of life from everyway hither and fore and of all the ways hereunto, that man may not partake of the fruit of the tree of life. Lest they, knowing good from evil, and partaking of the tree of life, become as the Gods. Knowing good from evil and having eternal life that they may war and rebel against the Gods.

* * *

We travelled on foot across the sprawling grasslands, every so often we would find a small copse of trees under which we would rest. We had no real need for the rest or shade from the burning sun but we took the time, in spite of ourselves, to rest and enjoy each other's company. Where we came upon rivers, we would find neat patchwork designs of tended fields along the banks. In the hot summer sun, there were many farmers and their families tending those fields. In some places where the rivers allowed, irrigation channels stretched out either side to bring the precious water to the earth farther out and the patchwork quilts of these fields could stretch out for several miles each side of the river.

Erika did not seem to be in any hurry and so I followed her lead. So wrapped up in just being with her that I almost forgot how we got here and why I was with her in the first place.

We took a route that wandered first South then South West; we seemed not to be in a hurry to go anywhere. The Princess took time to show me the flora and fauna of her world and seeing such sights in their natural surroundings and through the eyes of a nisse, I could not tell if I fell more in love with the land than I was in love with inscrutable Princess Erika Nisse. I was pleased that I did not have to make the choice. I had both of them all to myself.

  During our seemingly endless walks and play, Erika would show me the lore of the nisse, she would show me a plant or a tuber that to humans would prove fatal but to nisse, they were food and medicine. I marvelled at the Princess's knowledge of her lands and the plants and animals that lived here. I kept thinking of her as a sixteen or seventeen-year-old dressed up as a warrior princess and I had to correct myself many times that this young ebony skinned beauty with raven hair was actually one hundred and sixteen years old and her mind contained the knowledge and wisdom that age brought with it.

  When we could, we took to the well-travelled roads of the farming communities. We saw people in the fields toiling in the sun to cultivate their crops. In some places there tended to be more of one race than another. At one point, we passed a couple of trollish and gnome farms and they give us cheery waves, as did the other races we encountered. It unnerved me to see these trolls and gnomes smile at me so widely when, except for Uffe, the only time I saw their teeth was when they attacked us or tried to eat me.

  At each of the crossroads, there was a Wayhut. Wayhuts were dotted all over Sol and it was the responsibility of whoever owned the land to tend to and provide for the up keep of such Wayhuts, they were a travellers rest. A basic shelter from the weather, the inside consisted of a couple of sleeping cots, a stove of some sort as well as basic provisions and fire lighting implements. These Wayhuts are a welcome sight to many a weary and foot worn traveller, they have saved the lives of countless lost fae.

When we stopped at one of these Wayhuts the farmer whose duty it was to tend it, visited us to see to our needs. News of the Princess rippled ahead of us and at every Wayhut, we were given special treatment. It seemed like every nisse farmer and his wife wanted to see the nisse Royal Princess. Erika took all of the attention in good form, her lifetime training allowed her to be patient, kind, considerate and professional at all times; even when I would have easily told our visitors to go away.

Usually the farmer with his wife and children in tow would descend on us for news from afar in exchange for wholesome warm food and some locally brewed Ale or sparkling spring water.

At one point just outside the region controlled by Copperstone village, I had to stop when I spied a bit of neighbourly cooperation that was so bizarre, I just had to stop and stare. A centarean farmer needed to plough his fields for his next tobacco planting. The field needed ploughing and mixing with the potash sitting in mounds at one side of the field. As was the local custom, his neighbouring farmers came to help with this labour intensive work. Now there were some heavy mulluks pulling plough and the farmer's son, a young strong stallion, pulled another with a wood elf tending the plough behind. The most bizarre sight I saw was the old farmer centarean. Too old to pull a plough, a massive troll farmer, standing an easy fifteen foot tall and as broad as a fully grown ogre, was hooked up to pull the plough and the centarean farmer in his straw hat and long farmers coat tended the plough. The troll bent against the harness his long arms supporting his bulk as an extra pair of legs, pulled the plough along. If ever there was the case of putting the cart before the horse this was it. I shivered at the thought of meeting that troll on the field of battle.

All the while, I spent in Sol as a soldier of the Euroforce expedition campaign I had never imagined such a serene and rural beauty as I saw in the fields and farmers faces of these communities through which we travelled.

Our travels paralleled a river Erika called the Rhine. Although called the Rhine on Sol it was nowhere near the Earth Prime Rhine. While Earth Rhine ran through Germany, from Switzerland, to the Rotterdam delta in Holland, the fae named this great river millennia before humans first saw Earth's Rhine. This Rhine named in the first tongue of Sol; Renos meaning raging flow became the Rhine in the dwarfen dialect and thus became the common name used throughout Sol for this river. This Rhine ran from the mountains of Lugon through the elvin country of Alfheim and north to meet the upper sea.

Copperstone village, the nisse colony that controlled this region, was our intended destination. At the outskirts and the isolated outlying farms those nisse tending the fields would stop and turn their faces towards us. The men would bow low and the farmer's wives would curtsy. Where there were children we would see them race off, dispatched by their elders to give to the rest of the community the glorious news of the Royal visit.

We walked past fields of wheat and corn and all of those other arable crops both familiar and unfamiliar the outlying and more remote farms cultivated; we came to fields surrounding the village. Those fields were a checkerboard of vividly coloured flowering plants. Passing by some of the fields that bordered the well-travelled road we could see that the flowers were all of the same species. Like different coloured roses, these plants of the same species were cultivated to bloom in all the colours of the rainbow; there would be a field of yellow beside a field of orange, blues and greens, reds and purples it was a riot of beauty unmatched on any of the worlds.

"I don't think I have ever seen such an array of natural colour like this before." I commented to Erika while we walked between the fields. Erika picked a yellow flower, sniffed its scent and placed it over her right ear.

"Those betrothed or married nisse, wear flowers over their right ears like this. And those that are single wear the flower over their left ear." Erika explained.

"Why so many colours?" I asked.

"The nisse here produce most of the wool used in the finer garments worn by many of the races. They produce many wool fabrics form the thick and warm farmer's garments, to wool so fine it feels like Earthen silk, although these days Earthen silks seem to be the fashion amongst the Nobility. As well as producing those woollen fabrics, they produce the dyes for them from the flowers you see.

Some very useful by-products are the perfumes and dyes made and sold from Copperstone village. These days Copperstone is a village by name alone. The Emperor is about to bestow the title of city upon this village. It is a secret so do not be telling." Erika wagged her finger at me. "Legend says that a girl can steal a man's heart by wearing special perfume produced exclusively in Copperstone." Erika smiled and added. "Maybe I should seek some out."

"You have no need Princess. You have already won my heart." I replied.

"Who says I seek it for you Black Prince." Erika looked away pretending to inspect the fields of flowers. She hunkered down quickly and signalled me to do likewise. I squatted by the Princess, my pistol drawn.

"You will not need that." Erika frowned. I holstered my scorpion.

"See there between the red and the blue flowers." She pointed and I followed her line of sight. Something moved under the flowers.

"What was that?" I whispered, as I watched the little shape flit from shadow to shadow, to keep out of the sunlight and under the flower heads. There were no distinguishing features or colour to the thing. It looked humanoid in shape about a foot long, thin body arms and legs upon an overlarge head. Its eyes were wide and bright as it scanned around, it looked fearful and timid.

"It is an Asrais. They are very rarely seen out in the open. This one looks as if the morning sun caught it. See how it flits from flower to flower. It is trying to reach that yonder span of trees and staying out of the sun. The Asrais can drown in sunlight." Erika whispered.

"Can it hear us?" I asked.

"Have you seen the size of its ears? It can hear your heartbeat from there." Erika said.

"Can we help it?" I asked.

"We cannot even get near it." Erika replied. "To touch one brings great pain to the Asrais and very bad luck to those that touch them." Erika explained.

"Look to the tree line, use the chameleon suit." Erika whispered.

Hoods came over our heads and our eyes zoomed the eight hundred yards to bring the tree line up close. Several of these Asrais perched on branches and plant stalks. They peered out towards the flitting Asrais under the flowers. They made no sound.

"Why do they not call encouragement to the lost one?" I asked.

"They do, we cannot hear it. They mind speak." Erika explained while we watched from our concealment.

The Asrais at the tree line shuddered and drew back in horror. The lost Asrais missed a calculated sprint from one flower to another. The sun caught it and it lay prone on the ground, it looked as if it was in tremendous pain.

I jumped up from my concealment. I willed my chameleon suit to bend the light around me. I looked like a rippling of vision of live seawater as I streaked through the flowers to the Asrais. Careful that no part of my exposed flesh touched the Asrais I scooped it up and shielded it with my arms and chest. A few seconds more and the Asrais and I were within the trees. I could see none of the Asrais that were there before. I looked around to find a dark place where I could lay the unconscious fae. I placed it softly into the shade of the close growing bushes. Even up close, I could not tell if this Asrais was male or female but I had a natural feeling that it was female.

The Asrais lay still but she still breathed. I retreated quickly away knowing her companions would quickly come to give her aid. I trotted over to the roadside where Erika stood.

"I got her out of the sun and into some shade. She looked alive." I explained.

"I should have thought to do that. I forgot we could use the chameleon suits in that way." She said embarrassed.

"It is done now Princess, and if you had not spotted the Asrais in trouble she would be dead now." I smiled to reassure her.

"I have never seen one up close before. Do you think we could have a quick look before the others come?" Erika asked excited at the prospect.

"Come on." I said and we ran back to the bushes where I left the injured Asrais. She was gone.

"They must have come and taken her away." Erika whispered like a child at a faerie story.

"Yes, they must have. Well she will be in safe hands now." I said.

"My hero." Erika hugged my arm and kissed my cheek and I felt as tall as an ogre.

Chapter 26

We walked along a road of packed dirt; well-tended with only the slightest of cart furrows. The flat surface of the well-maintained road made the walk easier and we enjoyed the day, the sights, the smells and each other's company. We felt pleased and proud that for at least one little Asrais our presence in this world had made all the difference.

We came to an avenue of trees their branches sung and shaped to intertwine making a cover above the road ahead. On the first tree to the right was a plaque. On it was what I recognised as nisse script. It looked vaguely elvin but I could not read it. I recognised the blocky characters as nisse.

"What does it say?" I asked touching the beautifully engraved sign.

"It says 'Welcome to Copperstone Village, Peaceful Traveller'."

"Well they are going to have to change that sign soon enough." I commented and after a thought, I added. "Why such a strange address... Peaceful Traveller?"

"It is a welcome and a warning. Non-peaceful Travellers are not welcome here." Erika explained. She turned to me and said. "Jon, draw your sword and run through the avenue of trees."

I looked askance at the Princess.

"Go on Jon, humour me this once." Erika asked with a smile, I could not refuse. I shrugged and did as she asked. I noticed that the avenue led to a circular set of covered hedges. I could not see the far end. I felt a little embarrassed but there was only Erika and I about so I could afford a little foolishness.

I let out a cry like a troll on a frenzied battle charge and ran through the trees fully expecting the branches to come alive, unarm and capture me. I ran to the circular centre and round to the other side, the avenue continued on. I ran on seeing the end far ahead. I was a little surprised to see in the distance, a figure at the mouth of the avenue. I hesitated a moment, I took the figure for a guard of some kind and my defences rose for any surprise attacks. I carefully closed on the figure standing there watching me, when I came close enough I saw that it was Erika. I came to a stop and looked back. I could not see the other end due to the circular path of the hedge.

I ran back around the circular centre only to see Erika standing there waving at me. I repeated the run several times only to find that the avenue constantly turned me back on myself without my knowing. In the end, I gave up and returned to Erika sheathing my katana.

We walked together through the canopy of trees and emerged out the other end. In the distance, we could see the ancient forest of Ironwood trees that were the homes, shops and workplaces of Copperstone village.

"I can see why the Emperor wants to make this a City." I exclaimed astounded at the sheer size of the place.

"It remains a nisse family secret." Erika cautioned with her finger to her lips.

Arm in arm we approached the massive Village, or City as it would shortly be known.

We drew close and their local battalion of LandNisse guard ran towards us. With a body of armed men running at me, my hand automatically went to my katana but Erika rested her hand upon mine.

With a smile, she said. "There is no need for that. They see the Princess Royal without an honour guard or protection; they race to provide us with both. This was a rare and priceless moment these LandNisse guard will treasure for the rest of their lives. They will tell this story to their children for many hundreds of years to some."

I eased my hand off my katana and trusted Erika's words. The first to arrive surrounded us and knelt to one knee. Others followed and dropped to a knee once they joined their comrades.

"Who captains this honour guard?" Erika asked with a regal smile. No one replied.

"Well? The Royal Person waits!" Erika asked with a frown then winked at me. Some of the LandNisse with heads bowed, looked back down the road to glance at a rather rotund battalion captain pounding up the road after his more, fleet of foot, soldiers.

"I shall await the pleasure of the captain of the guard shall I?" Erika commented in light laughter. Nervous laughter and smiles rippled around the soldiers that surrounded us. The Battalion Captain was with us in moments. His face red with exertion, I worried that he might have a heart attack or a stroke right there. Out of breath, he bowed and rested his hands on his knees.

"Your Highness, please forgive my..."

"There is no need for that Captain Commander." I am pleased to see my subjects so loyal to the throne."

"No your Highness... I mean yes your Highness." The Captain panted, completely out of breath. "Forgive me Your Highness, I am not a captain commander I am but a local captain of the village guard."

"Well, first we cannot have a lowly village captain so out of breath that he cannot properly address his Royal Princess." Erika stepped through the kneeling men and stood next to the captain; still bent with hands on knees. She rested her hands upon his shoulder and his lower back, the tubby captain reacted by jerking up straight, his body spasmed and his midriff melted away to show a shadow of the LandNisse guard he once was. There was a ripple of awed exclamations from the kneeling soldiers.

"And finally I cannot have this loyal village insult the Royal Person by sending only a lowly Captain to command my royal guard." Erika spoke in her regal outside voice for all to hear.

"Please your highness, there is no one else." The Captain pleaded.

"Silence!" Erika demanded, like the evil queen from all my faerie stories. There was hush all about her. I felt myself holding my own breath. Erika spoke again. "From this moment on this brave Captain has the royal commission of Captain Commander of the royal host."

A wave of shocked expression rippled through the soldiers around us. I did not know what was going on but I thought that what Erika had just done was rare and special.

The Captain Commander fell to his knees and kissed Erika's hand in gratitude.

"Captain Commander?" Erika smiled. "Can we proceed to your beautiful village?"

"Yes, yes of course Your Highness." The Captain Commander harrumphed through his bushy salt and pepper moustaches. He turned to his men.

"You men there! Into line and form the royal escort of two's!" He bellowed and he reminded me of my old drill sergeant, sergeant Mathews, bushy moustaches and all. His men scrambled off their knees into military order. They formed into a squad mostly behind us, one line of LandNisse each side of us with three rows of four soldier's in front. The Capitan Commander took his position in the row beside the Princess. He nervously held out an arm and the Princess placed her arm on his, again a whisper of exclamation from the LandNisse behind. The Captain Commander stood ramrod straight and puffed out his chest. I knew that it would be a long time before this Captain Commander would wash that arm again.

"Royal Escort!" He commanded. "Will advance at the pleasure of the Royal Princess. Forward March!"

No one moved.

Erika took a step forward and the surrounding soldiers stepped forward in time to Erika's pace. At first, I wondered how the LandNisse guard in front knew what pace the princess was setting before I realised that Erika was their Princess Royal and they could sense her as she could them. For the first time since the battle with the gnome Snigmorder, I felt that I was in a safe place and that shadow of doubt for our personal safety was banished completely as we paraded at the pleasure of the Royal

Princess towards the massive Ironwood trees that were the nisse village of Copperstone.

By the time, we got to the first trees of the village. The several thousand strong nisse community lined the streets and the walkways above, bunting flew in what Erika informed me were her royal house colours of yellow and green, she went to great pains to point out that they are not the green and yellow of nisse Baron Chromal's house colours. Yellow and green flowers fell from the walkways above as Erika waved at the cheering crowds. The proud LandNisse guard in this once in a lifetime opportunity to escort the Royal Person stepped smartly; their chests filled with pride, their families cheering and shouting complements to Erika and the soldiers.

The royal procession halted at the base of a wide hexagonal wooden deck that led down to ground level by five long steps that surrounded the deck on all sides. Silver birch trees held a wooden roof above the wooden deck; it was a clever construction that allowed the roof to be folded back so that the people in the houses and walkways above could see down into the council area. Upon the deck stood the Village council, sheriff and mayor with their families to greet the Royal Princess.

The LandNisse Guard in front of us smartly stepped to either side with military precision that can only be found in constant drill and practice. This formation was only used for royal processions which most rural guard units would never have the opportunity to use. Yet this outlying and very remote nisse village practiced this formation so regularly as to be able to fall into it in a moment's notice. To me that spelt dedication and fierce loyalty to their King.

Erika nodded to the captain commander and dropped her hand from his. She looked at me out of the corner of her eye and I knew I had to do the arm thing now. I raised my arm and as I did so, I wished I were in my formal mess dress. The flash of the change of clothes from forest drab to blue tunic sent ripples of clapping and gasps of awe around the congregated masses. I felt proud of myself that I could impress the impressive nisse this time round. Erika eyed the unexpected change and smiled.

"Very impressive Lieutenant Raine." She whispered. I continued smiling. In a moment Erika was dressed in the yellow silk dress she wore the first time I beheld her. More gasps and claps of appreciation.

One little nisse girl nervously stepped out from the crowd. I spotted her mother's arm gently encouraging her and easing her forward. Wide-eyed and terrified the little girl bravely stepped forward. She clutched a little reed woven basket covered in a green silk cloth with butterflies embroidered in silver and gold thread, slowly, nervously the little girl stepped up to the Princess and awkwardly curtsied. I could see from the embroidered butterflies on her simple shift of a dress that she was the official butterfly attendant for this village. In this remote village, that high court privilege was usually given to a little girl, as there was no hope of such a position ever being officially needed by the Queen or Princess Royal, not in such a remote and unimportant nisse village, at least not until today.

Erika curtsied to the little girl, lower than I had seen her curtsy to anyone before. The curtsy was for equals and the little girl went wide-eyed while the crowd erupted in thunderous roars of acclaim and appreciation.

"Lady Sommerfugl, will you honour me with your kind attention?" Erika asked the little girl in her official title. The shocked girl stood there transfixed. Erika nodded her head to the girl, indicating her back and she curtsied once again. The little Lady Sommerfugl snapped out of her stupor and ran around to Erika's back. I glanced around to see her take a butterfly out of her basket and place it gently on the Princess' back. A thought of Dixie and Lady Serbilan Sommerfugl flashed through my mind and I wished that they were well and unhurt from the explosion. Sadly, I held little hope for my close friends Dixie and Jens and the rest of the guys.

The butterfly eased its legs under Erika's ebony skin and flexed its wings as Erika took over its motor senses. The little

Lady Sommerfugl went up on tiptoes to whisper in the princess's ear.

"It's all done my lady. Did I do okay? Did it hurt?"

Erika still reposed in her curtsy amongst a sea of yellow silk took the little girls hand and led her around to her front. The effort of remaining at curtsy was a tremendous effort of muscle control that looked so natural and effortless when the Princess performed it.

"Well my own Lady Sommerfugl had better watch out, you are most beautiful and skilled, she had better fear for her position." Erika spoke in soft and warm tones to ease the young girl's nerves.

"Oh your highness I would never ever want to take..." Little Lady Sommerfugl exclaimed. Erika silenced her with her finger to the girl's lips. She bent her head conspiratively forward. "And I never felt a thing." She smiled. Lady Sommerfugl beamed a radiant smile back at her princess and with such warmth and affection that I could not help but smile with her.

Erica stood and made a twirling motion with her finger pointing down to have Lady Sommerfugl turn around. Erika reached around, took one of the resting butterflies out of the basket. The Princess looked towards the girl's mother and bowed her head slightly. I believe Erika transmitted her intentions empathically. The girl's mother gasped in shocked surprise and as delicately as any noble lady, she sank into a curtsy. I knew the curtsy was the accepting of the royal intention.

A girl's mother always performs the first placing of a butterfly onto a female nisse back. In an elaborate ceremony equal to Jewish girls Bat Mitzvah or a catholic First Holy Communion. It marked the girl's journey from childhood into youthful responsibility. A female nisse may not be courted, married or presented in any official roles without her wings. Erika requested that honour from her mother. In nisse culture it was one of the greatest honours that could be bestowed on a nisse girl by her Princess Royal, it was every nisse girls dream to be a Hofdame and have her nisse wings presented by the

Princess. I later found out that Princess Erika never performed the ceremony on any girl lest it be seen as favouritism. Erika had no qualms about that here in this remote village with this flame haired little girl.

Erika took the butterfly in her slender fingers and placed it between the girl's shoulder blades. The creature's flat legs slid their way under her skin. She turned the girl back around and held both her arms.

"OK after three." Erika whispered. "One, Two, Three!"

"Princess!" The girl whispered.

"Yes little one." Erika replied.

"Is that one, two, three and go or do we go on three?"

Erika laughed gently.

"In royal company it is always one, two three and go." Erika explained with a smile. "Shall we?" She added. The little girl nodded her head.

"Okay, one, two, three and go!"

Both the wings of the Princess and the Lady Sommerfugl expanded like unfurling parachutes and they rippled through a range of colours to settle on a bright yellow to match the Princess's dress.

Upon the sight of the Princesses unfurling wings, thousands of sets of wings sprang out from the backs of the gathered nisse women. It was a glorious, spontaneous display of colour that rivalled the display of the Hofdame at the ball.

The Little Lady Sommerfugl, the newest Hofdame to Erika's court, wore a green dress and the colours coincidently represented the Princess' royal house colours. Erika motioned the little girl to one side still holding her hand; she kept physical contact with Lady Sommerfugl, as she was too young and inexperienced to control the butterfly wings by herself.

Erika whispered down to the little girl. "Are you nervous?" The little girl nodded. "Well I am nervous too. Will you stay by my side and keep me company and we can be brave together, maybe as brave as the fine soldiers that escort us this day."

The little girl smiled a wide smile and moved into Erika's flowing yellow skirts. Form the side of my eyes I could see that the soldiers were smiling too. Erika could certainly handle an audience and by her actions and attention to the little things, she won the hearts and minds of this village.

"See that one?" Lady Sommerfugl pointed at one of the soldiers in the guard. Erika turned to look at the young soldier, his face went crimson.

"That one?" Erika asked of the girl.

"Yes that one. His name is Carsten and he is my brother." She replied.

"He makes a very handsome soldier." Erika whispered to her tiny escort. I did not know if I should smile or frown.

Erika and I and her new Lady Sommerfugl walked forward together to climb the five steps to the council platform.

At the centre of the dais sat two chairs on a low platform bedecked in yellow and green. Around the two hastily improvised thrones, sat the chairs of the council arranged to face them. Regally we walked up the space between the chairs to the thrones, well Erika regally walked, while we all followed her. Erika allowed the little Lady Sommerfugl to guide her to her temporary throne. The mayor stood and bowed to the Princess then to me. I was a little surprised at that but I played along. The mayor turned to address the people.

"Your Highness, Council Lords, Ladies and Gentlemen. The Princess and her escort are in person and I declare this a Royal Court in..."

Erika lifted her hand to silence the Mayor. "This cannot be a nisse Royal Court as there is missing from the assembly one other royal official."

Chapter 27

Everyone went silent looking around with puzzled faces. There was a push through the crowd and the guard Captain now Captain Commander of the Royal guard eased his way through the crowd to gain the steps of the platform. Across his shoulder, he wore the yellow and green trim for the sash of the Royal guard. It was an actual sash and not a hastily improvised decoration.

As he walked by the mayor, the mayor eyed his new physique. "Captain L'Ussler?" He whispered harshly.

"It is Captain Commander L'Ussler of the Royal guard." The Captain replied proudly.

"What the hell do you think you are doing in that ridiculous get up Captain L'Ussler?" The mayor demanded under his breath. "Have you lost your senses man?"

"Captain Commander. If you will be so kind." Erika interrupted in her royal voice and indicated a position behind the Little Lady Sommerfugl.

The Captain Commander clicked his heals together and bowed formally to the Princess.

"I mustn't keep the Princess Royal waiting. Duties of state and all that." The Captain Commander dismissed the shocked mayor and took his official position beside the princess.

Captain Commander L'Ussler took his place to the right of the princess and behind the Lady Sommerfugl. This position was the most vulnerable point to the Princess Royal's person and Captain Commander L'Ussler proudly covered it his hand leaning on the pommel of his nisse rapier sword.

"Is that an actual sash of the Royal guard, Captain Commander?" Erika asked though smiling closed lips.

"Yes My Lady." The Captain Commander addressed his princess with the title only he was allowed to use in this company. "It is the Sash my Father wore." He added proudly. "My father served the King for two hundred years before retiring to the country for a simple life."

This time Erika spoke openly and turned her head to the Captain Commander behind her. "Ah ha! So that's why the LandNisse guard knew how to deport themselves in front of their princess." She smiled a grateful smile up towards him and a tear of pride fell from the corner of this old soldier's eye.

"In return for the service your father gave mine and for the service you have given to the nisse nation in keeping this outpost safe. I now serve you this day." Erika raised her royal hand and wiped the tear away to the collective gasp of the throng of nisse around the dais.

Now that all was in place the princess nodded to the mayor to continue, the mayor cleared his throat and repeated his pronouncement.

"Your Highness, Council Lords, Captain Commander," The mayor glanced in envy at his old friend who stood smiling behind the princess. "Ladies and Gentlemen. The princess and her escort are in person and I declare this a Royal Court!" A cheer from thousands rose up through the gigantic bows that stretched over them like giant protective arms.

Princess Erika stood and stepped forward to address the crowds. Beside her Little Lady Sommerfugl clasped her hand and pressed herself to her leg. Both their wings fluttered, shimmered and shifted colour in some royal signal to the crowd. Within the crowd, the nisse women gathered with their own wings spread. Their colours shimmered in response to the signal, in a crescendo of marvellous colour. Although not as orderly as the strict decorum of the Hofdames at the ball this spontaneous display came with its own unique beauty that can only be found in the natural world, and I smiled in spite of myself.

"Loyal subjects of his majesty, my father and Emperor King. I bring to you his greetings and best wishes. I bring you his love for his nisse people." Another roar from the crowd and yellow and green buntings shot into the air to gently fall around the people. Most caught in the branches and walkways and provided further festive decoration.

"I come with good news and with bad. First let me announce that your Royal Princess, Erika Nisse is with child." It was obvious by Erika's black skin that she was pregnant; it was no surprise to the gathered throng nisse and assorted fae but they cheered at the announcement nonetheless. A pause to allow the cheering to subside, Erika raised her yellow-gloved hands to calm the crowds.

"This village will always be known for the first official announcement of the life of the future and next Emperor of the nisse people." More cheering ensued and Erika raised her hands again. "Good people I would that you might hear the wishes of my father the Emperor King.

"We stand now at the edge of a great precipice, behind us stands the usurpers of our land and property. Before us, the great void of oblivion. As I look around me I see naught but eager faces, young and old, keen to set forth to retake that which has been taken from us. Our fathers and our ancestors have nurtured and lived on this land. The same land, year upon year. Yet this year we face such a threat as never before seen on Sol. Yet this year we are more prepared, trained, and equipped than ever before. This year we shall retake Sol from those usurpers.

"Throughout my father's kingdom, preparations have surmounted more than any call since first we defeated the gnomes of far Egil. Throughout our kingdom, fathers, mothers, sons and daughters strap on armour long-worn to march beside us. Throughout this kingdom and beyond, all hands have raised and toiled for but one task, one goal, and one unifying goal: to retake Sol from those that come to take and rape our lands, our people.

"As for my own promise to those nisse that follow me, that follow my husband the Black Prince and the Emperor King Kennet, in return we have nothing to offer save blood, toil, tears, sweat and sacrifice and for many the journey with the Ferryman. Nothing save those little things. We have before us a campaign of the most grievous and exacting kind in generations. We have before us many long weeks, months and even years of struggle and hardship before we shall assail and retake or beloved Sol. Many will not return.

"To my people, my father's people I say this. Omit no righteous act that may advance our cause, and put no thoughts above that of Sol, save only the Gods that come above all. Obey your king, your officers and commanders, remember your training and seek to embody the heroes who have gone before us, who venerated the Gods as we do and battled for the safety of our people. Do these things and the Gods will surely smile upon you and we shall retake Sol.

"My beloved subjects, the tide is set, the time has come. To war we march; return with victory, free or not at all.

"He who will lead us in this great struggle stands beside me. No, not the great and brave Captain Commander Waccaar L'Ussler, but my husband the Lord Jon Raine, the Black Messiah. In Copperstone village, nay, I say in Copperstone City," A great collective gasp arouse from the throngs of fae around us. "On this day I have the honour to present to my father's kingdom he who will free our lands, he who will lead us to liberty. My husband the Black Prince, Lord Jon Raine.

"My dear subjects to the Emperor King. There are many fae on Sol. Sincere and faithful fae who are asking themselves this day: How can we sing our trees? How can we give life to our children?

"How can we meet and venerate the Gods with love and with uplifted spirit and heart in a world subject to those that would suck its goodness from its very heart, the very hearts of our people, to leave Sol a world of fighting and suffering and death?

"How can we pause, even for a day, even for this celebration, in our urgent labour of arming a decent royal empire against the enemies that beset it? How can we put the world aside, as nisse put the world aside in peaceful years, to rejoice in the celebration of the Gods?

"These are natural questions in every part of the world resisting this evil thing. Moreover, even as we ask these questions, we know the answer. There is another preparation demanded of this nation beyond and beside the preparation of weapons and materials of war.

"There is demanded also of us the preparation of our hearts; the arming of our hearts. And when we make ready our hearts, we make ready for the ultimate victory that lies ahead. Looking into the days to come, I have set aside a day, this day of rejoicing and celebration and in that proclamation, I say this:

"We have suffered upon our lands and people a war of aggression by powers dominated by arrogant rulers whose selfish purpose is to destroy our treasures, our lives, our institutions. They would thereby take from the freedom-loving peoples of Sol the hard-won liberties gained over many centuries.

"From this day on, my father calls for the courage and the resolution of old and young to help to win a struggle in order that we may preserve all we hold dear. We are confident in our devotion to country, in our love of freedom, in our inheritance of courage. Our strength, as the strength of all fae everywhere, is of greater avail as the Gods uphold us.

"Therefore, I... do hereby appoint this day as a day of celebration and honour of the Black Messiah, it is a day of asking forgiveness for our shortcomings of the past, of consecration to the tasks of the present, of asking the Gods help in days to come.

"We need their guidance that this people may be humble in spirit but strong in the conviction of the right; steadfast to endure sacrifice, and brave to achieve a victory of liberty and peace.

"Our strongest weapon in this war is that conviction of the dignity and brotherhood of the nisse that this day will signify more than any other day or any other symbol.

"Against enemies who preach the principles of hate and practice them, we set our faith in the love of our King and in the hands of the Gods and the Black Messiah. It is in that spirit, and with particular thoughtfulness of those, our sons, daughters and brothers and sisters, who serve in the army of our empire on the land given by the Gods to our Father Cain and Mother Lilith.

Those who serve for us and endure for us we set aside this day for the celebration of life and deliverance. We join with the other nations and fae in a very great cause. Millions of our fellow fae have been engaged in the task of defending good with their lifeblood for months and for years.

    Shall we do no less?
    Shall we fail our King?
    Shall we fail our People?
    Shall we fail the Black Messiah?"

    "Noooooo!" came the collective roar of the crowds

Chapter 28

Night rose as the sun kissed Sol. Stars twinkled in a clear velvet sky. The Nisse tradition is to wait for Epona to rise before they begin the Royal reception. Tonight Hekata, the lesser moon, already in the sky his darker countenance allowed the stars to fill a velvet sky while they waited for the rise of their celestial queen Epona.

The change from day to night brought the early evening breeze upon which we could smell the many different scents from the cultivated flowers the wool spinners of Copperstone used to dye their wools.

A gentle lighting of the far horizon, Epona promised a half moon this night. Above us beach ball sized globes floated amongst the trees bright with enchanted light, each individual globe gently moved from one shade of the spectrum to another until they began again to repeat the sequence. They would continue to do this until the nisse responsible summoned them to the ground and extinguished the enchanted glow. The random changing of colour created incredible patterns which Erika told me occurred naturally; thus out of chaos came these wonderful and breath-taking patterns. Like snowflakes, no two patterns were alike and each display was unique to the beholder.

Erika and I were shown to our seats. I stumbled into one of the pretty nisse villagers as I walked, mesmerised by the light show. Nisse custom dictated that Erika, Captain Commander L'Ussler, and I wore holy boughs on our heads for the feast and celebration. All should wear the holy boughs but there was a severe shortage of holy in Copperstone City.

"I am so sorry." I exclaimed as I caught the nisse maiden before she fell down the steps we walked beside. The holy bough I wore around my head slipped and I caught it in my hand.

"My pleasure." The girl replied, her green eyes gazing into mine, a blue flower over her left ear. In her nisse folk dress of wide skirts, tight black bodice with a white off the shoulder blouse she looked the image of a delectable fairy. I became immediately embarrassed with Erika standing right beside me.

"Making friends already?" Erika asked with a cheeky grin, she mind reamed my embarrassment and played up to it.

"Sorry about that." I blurted my apology and realising I still held the nisse maiden by her narrow waist I quickly let go.

"Thank you, kind sir." The girl curtsied and when she paused at the bottom of the curtsy she looked up at me with her magnetic green eyes and I felt immediately embarrassed again. I just could not get my head around being in a new relationship.

"Your highness" One of the Nisse waiters indicated our seats, another stood behind Erika's lavishly gilded chair. Erika sat in the middle seat at the head of the high U shaped table. Placing my holy wreath on the table I took my seat to her right, Captain Commander Waccaar L'Ussler sat to her left. Seated either side and down both sides of the table sat the nisse village councillors. Each wore a grey gown and coloured cowl. The colour represented the office they filled within the village council.

Above us came the sound of singing. The soft music was vaguely familiar. It was an ancient tune and massed voices sang the haunting lyrics. We gazed up through the overhead branches to see a procession of torch carrying nisse villagers slowly making their way across the nisse sung passageways high up in the canopy of branches above our heads. Although high above us, they were underneath the floating orbs of nisse light. Five thousand strong, each Nisse carried a torch that burned a coloured flame. The torch consisted of a two foot wooden stake on which sat a canister that held oil and a wick from the oil through a hole in the canister lid. Each flame burned a different colour dependant on the dyes added to the oil. The dyes derived from the fields of cultivated flowers surrounding the village or city, as I should call it now.

Looking up at the procession of light I could spy the occasional star, Epona or Hekata peeking through the glowing orbs above. The procession of light wound its way along the

nisse sung passageways from tree to tree descending down to our level like a fantastical glowing snake.

Slowly the possession made its way down to ground level where the torches pooled out as the nisse made their way to the oval shaped tables arranged around a square of polished wooden decking. I immediately guessed this would be the dance floor when the music started. Each of the oval desks was able to seat from ten to twenty nisse at each one and Erika told me that they were seated in strict hierarchy dependant on their function within the village and of course how wealthy, a certain family may be.

While the lights spread out as the nisse walked to their tables, each of the nisse placed their torches on the ground. A pinch of nisse magic and the earth swallowed up a few inches of the stake to leave the torches standing like hundreds of coloured garden candles.

Each table was decorated with flowers, the cups plates and other utensils ranged from gold at our table and the nearest tables on the ground, to silver then steel and finally wood. The wooden utensils were intricately carved; I would have much preferred to eat with them. Erika noticed that Lady Sommerfugl sat with her family at a table with wooden plates, cups and eating utensils. She waved over one of the waiters and whispered in his ear. The waiter smiled and motioned for others to converge on him. He gave them a few hasty orders and the serving staff went to our high table and collected all of the gold cups, plates, knives and spoons. They took them in a regal procession through the surprised nisse seated at the grand tables. They marched to the table of the Lady Sommerfugl where they replaced their wooden tableware with our golden set. They collected up the wooden tableware and proceeded to walk back to our tables and place the ornately designed wooden implements before us. The crowd clapped their appreciation.

Erika stood and all went quiet. "Before all, the Lady Sommerfugl is our newest Hofdame will henceforth eat as a queen in Copperstone City." Roars of support and cheers from those around us. Erika held up her hand to quieten the crowds;

they obeyed immediately. "And what better way for your nisse princess to eat than to eat with wooden implements sung from the trees that give us life." The crowds went wild with their clapping and their cheering. Erika took her seat again.

Chapter 29

When the cheering stopped twelve nisse carried long smooth white poles onto the dance floor. The poles were easily over thirty feet tall. At their predetermined spots, the nisse men and women placed the ends of the poles onto the wooden deck. This time I could sense the use of nisse magic. The surface of the deck where the poles met shimmered and became fluid. The poles sank easily into the ground for about five feet of its length and remained stuck fast when the magic was withdrawn. These thick posts about the diameter of my forearm became fixed freestanding pillars of wood. The twelve men and women began to dance to music performing cartwheels and flips through the air, sometimes using each other to launch themselves into the air to somersault into the arms of another pair of performers, to the applause and appreciative cheers of the audience around them. One acrobat went into a routine of a set of rapid back flips across the floor; he leapt into the air and seemed to execute a forward spinning somersault in gravity defying slow motion. The crowd responded with thunderous applause.

The nisse acrobats took a bow then ran off the platform. At the same time, twelve more nisse in skin-tight white body suits that covered every inch of their bodies including heads and faces, skipped onto the deck. Their suits looked like they were painted on and there were no mistaking men from women among the performers. Ten of them struck a pose while two leapt onto two of the vertical pillars to climb them using only their hands. No other part of their bodies touched the poles while they climbed hand over hand without any outward showing of stress to their bodies. Near the top, they forced their bodies out horizontally until the soles of their feet touched each other's. They put pressure on their feet and let go of the posts with one hand. Both remained suspended horizontally, one hand of each performer holding his respective pole with the other arm raised into the air.

The trick was received with more applause. The remaining nisse performers climbed the poles with ease to carry out a synchronised act that had everyone spellbound. The white suited acrobats finished their act by sliding down the poles upside down using only their legs, their faces stopping only inches from the ground.

More clapping and the acrobats exited replaced by a nisse battle wizard. First, the wizard held up his arms and slowly turned around in a circle. The pillars moved to positions forming a wide circle around him.

Within the standing pillars, the wizard raised his arms and coloured smoke billowed from his wide sleeves. While the smoke swirled about him as if in some way attracted to the wizard, it did not pass beyond the circle of pillars. He weaved his arms as if shaping an imaginary piece of sculpture. The smoke transformed into a giant snake that slithered about the wizard and hissed its forked tongue. Its head came to the very side of the barrier and the beast opened its fanged mouth almost two feet wide. The children before the snake flinched back into the comforting arms of their smiling, laughing parents. The serpents head changed into a trolls head and my hand went to the hilt of my katana at the awful site of this giant snake with a trolls head. To me most trolls look alike but when this troll smoke monster looked around the gathered nisse, its eyes glanced at me and I would bet my very life that Uffe Jægerblod looked at me through those eyes. The troll head cracked a shark toothed grin and the vaporous snake melted into the air to rise in a plume of purple smoke.

The wizard produced more smoke only this time he presented sculptures in the ebony likenesses of Erika and me. The busts smiled at the crowd and the crowd cheered and clapped. I had to admit that I looked quite dashing in the wizards smoke sculpture. The heads turned to each other and kissed. The crowd turned to Erika and me and began to tap their glasses with knives or spoons.

"What are they doing?" I whispered to Erika.

"They want us to mimic the smoke sculpture." Erika replied with a demure smile.

"It would be most rude and unkind to disappoint these fine and honourable people." I said, mimicking Erika's royal mannerism hoping for a favourable response.

"Let's not disappoint them Lord Raine." Erika agreed and leaned into me for that kiss. 'Lord Raine' I liked that, I leaned forward and our lips met. The crowd sent a wild cheer up through the trees to fill the night sky.

We separated after a comfortably long and enjoyable kiss and the smoke sculpture dissipated to rise into the night sky to join the crows cheer. More coloured smoke, the wizard produced further smoke sculptures to entertain the gathered villagers.

A delightful swarm of brightly coloured butterflies began to return to the smoke from which they came when a mighty roar shook the village and I felt the earth vibrate to that bestial growl. For a moment, I thought it part of the act, until I saw nisse men and women jump to their feet, those with swords or axes drew them while others scrambled for their pole arms.

Several green-scaled Tyrannosaurus Rex crashed through the trees to surround the village. A flapping of leather wings and elongated bat like creatures taller than a man and vaguely humanoid in shape, alighted on the tables surrounding us. One female councillor screamed "Dracii" and scrambled backwards in panic to one of the Silver Birches supporting the roof. I drew my scorpion pistol and katana. Two of the Dracii were closing in on the panicked councillor; I took a well-aimed shot at the monsters back. The councillor fell dead to my shot. I stood there in stunned confusion; the dart should have hit the Dracus. The monster turned on me; chaos amongst the villagers, there was no help from that quarter. The Dracus leapt into the air leather wings spread like a demon out of the gates of Hades, it made to leap the space between us.

"Jon. The bough! Take the holly bough." Erika shouted through my fear and confusion. She was right beside me and I did not notice. I reached out on impulse and my fingers touched Erika's hand. She thrust the holly bough into my out-stretched hand. "Place it upon your head." She called to me. Without taking my eyes from the Dracii battling Erika and Waccaar in front of me, I did as bid and placed the wreath back on my head. The Dracii disappeared along with the T Rex, dragons, monsters and misshapen demons that surrounded the villagers.

Three gnome Snigmorder stood before me. Erika and Waccaar L'Ussler wearing wreaths of holly were unaffected by the gnome dream weave attack, stood between them and me, they were pressed hard to keep the gnomes at bay, not a small task given that I was running about trying to defend myself from imaginary monsters.

I got my senses in order just as one of the Snigmorder broke through the Princesses defences to slash his deadly blades at me. I blocked one slash with my upheld blade; his other short fat blade came over the top of my blade to slash at my face. I spun, twisted my blade, and using one of his arms as a fulcrum I sliced through his other to take his arm above his elbow. With the same thrusting movement, I arched back round, my blade doing a figure of eight in the air, I swept down and my monomolecular blade edge took the Snigmorder's other arm mid forearm.

Erika threw her enchanted knife sword at her opponent, a bad move in battle. The knife transformed mid-flight into a javelin that took a Snigmorder in the heart. As the assassin fell, Erika thrust out her hand and the javelin twisted and spun away from the Snigmorder ripping his heart out and flinging it away with the centrifugal force of the spin. The javelin transformed again mid-flight to the Nisse long thin sword, taking the head of the armless gnome before it reached Erika's hand.

Our three Snigmorder dead we pressed the attack on the rest of the assailing force of gnomes. Our assailants, now less three of their men, found themselves hard pressed to keep up the dream weave attack. Their monsters flashed out of existence to leave the seven remaining Snigmorder, each standing in a circle of slaughtered men, women and children. Innocence mercilessly cut down as they tried to defend against the conjured monstrous images while the real monsters tore them to pieces with their razor sharp blades.

Hundreds of blades and pole arms turned on the Snigmorder. I saw one kneel and raise his arm over his head, the universal sign for surrender and mercy. They showed no mercy in their attack and in return, no mercy was shown to them. In moments, all gnomes lay hacked limb from limb.

I tried to get to the closest one before the nisse fell upon him but I could not make the distance in time. The chaotic battle over, the nisse fell into a stunned silence. Erika was on her knees weeping. She held a bloodied child in her arms. The child's left arm was a severed stump and her body lay lifeless in Erika's tender embrace. The bloodstained dress told me from the embroidered butterflies that this was Erika's little Lady Sommerfugl. Unknown to us at the time, her proud mother and brave father lay less than a yard away from the tiny broken body in the circle of slaughtered nisse.

Erika clutched the lifeless girl to her bosom; her grief seemed inconsolable. It was only with the greatest of efforts from several nisse healers and my own small efforts that we managed to prise the little bloodied body from her arms.

One of the healers carried little Lady Sommerfugl in her arms to lie her with her murdered parents. They were only one of many entire families butchered in the confusion of the nightmare Snigmorder attack. Apart from Erika, Captain L'Ussler, and me, only the sentries of the LandNisse guard wore holly boughs this night. We thought the thirty sentries sufficient for our safety. We were wrong. By the morning, most of the city would be equipped with holly boughs but the morning and the rising sun would not bring the dead back.

Captain L'Ussler detailed two wreath-wearing guards to escort us to our apartments, and I led Erika away from the carnage to our rooms high up in the city's Ironwood trees. Another time and we would have taken time to enjoy the romantic peaceful path of the broad nisse sung walkways, sung from the branches of the trees, one branch merged seamlessly with another to make bridges and intersections between the gnarled trunks. The tops of the branches magically flattened and hardened to produce hardwearing roads and passageways. The path we followed wound through the trees with thousands of enchanted fairy globes floating lazily through the forest, each colour changing from one delightful hue to another. After a few minutes of silent walking, we came to the pathway that led to our apartments. The pathway was as broad as ten men and I believed it could support the heaviest of wagons. Waccaar L'Ussler assured me that even though the pathways had no safety rails, there had never been a fall from any. The children played on them and children and adults effortlessly leapt from one path to another. Although I had newfound powers, my human mind and its effect of natural compensation kept me well back from the edges.

Erika saw none of it, maybe she was accustomed to these amazing sights but I felt that she was numb and in a virtual trance due to the trauma of finding her little Lady Sommerfugl hideously slashed across the face and chest. Three quick swipes of a Snigmorder blade ended a life before it was lived.

My arm around her shoulders, her head against my shoulder she sobbed quietly and sought comfort from our embrace, I gently led Erika across the walkway to the door of our apartments. I placed my palm as instructed upon the symbol carved in the door and it glowed a cool blue in a positive response. The magical warding triggered the internal locks and I heard them snick back and release. The door swung quietly inward.

I stepped over the threshold with Erika; I hoped the warding had properly disengaged the immolation shield across the doorway. To step through while the shield was up would render the unwelcome intruder to ashes in the time it took him or her to pass across the shield. We stepped inside and all was well. The two LandNisse guards took up posts outside the door and would respond immediately to any call of alarm.

I eased Erika down onto one of the long plush sofas in the colours of the royal house of nisse. To my surprise, I found a box of Kleenex tissues sitting on the highly polished black coffee table between Erika's sofa and its twin. Leaving Erika with a couple of tissues, I went to the kitchen to pump some water into a glass and brought it back into the lounge. I handed Erika the glass and she drank deeply from it. I removed my holly bough and tossed it onto the coffee table.

"No!" Erika snapped and jumped to her feet. She grabbed up the green crown and pushed it into my hands, I was grateful I had changeling hands; the wreath would have lacerated ordinary human hand.

"Put it back on and don't take it off again until we put up the protection wards." She demanded.

"Okay my love." I replied softly and replaced the wreath back on my head. Erika's delicate silver and gold holly bough remained woven through her hair. I understood now why she wore it, it was not just a fancy nisse tiara, it served a serious function.

"Come darling, sit back down." I ushered Erika down upon the sofa once more.

"How could I?" Erika exclaimed in her sorrow. "This... this attack... These murders are all my fault." She sobbed into her tissue. I sat there beside her; I did not know what to say. I felt as guilty as she did; I too felt that we had brought this attack upon Copperstone city and its happy peaceful population. I held my princess for a time saying nothing. Eventually I knew that I had to break the silence, punctuated by Erika's quiet sobs, every one as cutting as a Snigmorder blade.

"Erika... Listen." I began as I held her in my arms. "We are no strangers to war and death. It is never easy when the Ferryman takes the innocent and when they are children... Well..."

"We shouldn't have come here. We should have passed the village by and never visited this death destruction upon them."

I took Erika's chin in my hand and turned her face to me. "Honestly my love, I feel the same way. But what has happened has happened and we cannot change it. A wise man once told me that only the greatest of magicians can change the past."

Erika looked into my eyes. "I brought this destruction to this lovely village. I did, not you. It is my fault they are dead. Oh Jon, I cannot bear it." Erika broke down and cried into my shoulder once more. So tiny so frail, I kissed her head and stroked her hair of raven black.

"Erika when you spoke this afternoon. When you addressed the city, you spoke of the war that is to come. When you spoke of that war and the toll it will take from the peoples of Sol, I saw everyone, every single person here kneel before you and pledge allegiance to you and your father the Nisse King. They knew that when they did so, they would face death. That death came the very same day and in the very evening of their pledge day. Those simple villagers were as loyal to you as they will be in the months and years to come."

"Jon it does not ease my mind that they pledge fealty this day. That dear sweet child... All of the children. And all of those murdered this night deserved life above all else. No, I cannot go on. I have tried to do my father's will but the burden is too great the price too high. Jon there is something I must tell you."

I picked up Erika's hand and looked earnestly into her eyes. "Wait my love. Before you make any decisions or say anything more, please consider the peoples of Sol, not just the nisse but also all the different races. Think of all who have already lost their lands or will do so because they are in the way. The trolls, dwarfen, centarean, nymph and all those others I cannot even bring to mind right now. Yes and even the elvin. You fight this war for all the fae not just the nisse.

"Look at our own world. We stripped it of nearly all of its natural resources. Then we reached out and took other worlds. We took our wars to those worlds. Now we find another world right on our doorstep and what have we done so far? Strip-mining, pumping oil through the portals. We have relocated tens of thousands of trolls, nymph, and tauraens. We have hunted the great beasts for food and sport and we have denuded millions of acres of forestland. Your forests will go the same way as our Amazon rainforest. Ancient Ironwood trees that have stood for thousands of years giving shelter, homes and places of birth for many Sollen races, those mighty trees now reduced to furniture to grace the lounges and habitats of Earth Prime. What more damage will we humans do if we are not stopped?"

Erika smiled at me. A sad smile but it was a smile. "We humans? Really? You are no more human now than I am."

I absorbed the realisation that Erika was right. I was not human, I was more than that. "I guess you are right. But what am I. A changeling? A half-blood?"

Erika rose to my challenge. "You are Lord Jon Raine, The Black Prince and husband to Princess Erika Nisse, heir to the Nisse throne and father of the next Emperor." Erika raised her pretty chin in regal pride, not haughty pride but the pride of self-respect and loyalty to something greater than herself.

"So I get to fight in this war, only not on the side I reckoned I would be fighting on."

"Jon, there is something I need to tell you."

I put my arm around her shoulders. "Okay tell me."

A tinkling chime echoed around the room as if it came from everywhere at once.

I felt Erika's body tense. "Someone is at the door." She looked worried. I drew my scorpion, this time Erika did not object. Cautiously I walked to the door, my scorpion before me and without opening it, I called out. "Who is it?"

"Tis I Captain L'Ussler; I have someone with me who wishes to speak with the princess."

"Not now Captain. The princess is still too upset for audience." I called through the door, upset that the captain should be so insensitive to intrude on us.

"Lord Raine, forgive me. I believe the princess will wish to speak to these people."

"How so?"

"Sir, beside me stands Lady Sommerfugl's foreparents."

Erika gasped a shivering breath inwards.

"Foreparents?" I asked softly.

"It is the Mother's parents." Erika clarified although I think she would have preferred gnome Snigmorder at that moment.

"Grandparents then?" I asked confused at the strange title.

"No, Grandparents are the Father's Parents. The Mother's parents are foreparents." Erika explained, she looked frightened and I had never seen her frightened, even standing in the face of death she always remained composed.

"Shall I ask them to go? We can do this later." I asked, sensitive to Erika's raw feelings. She nodded yes then shook her head no.

"No let them in. I need to do this now." Erika replied and stood to smooth down her dress. The chameleon suit had absorbed and cleaned away the blood.

I holstered my pistol and touched the security rune carved on the inside of the door, it was the mirror image of the one on the outside. The heavy door swung silently inwards. Captain L'Ussler stood centre and behind Lady Sommerfugl's foreparents. The couple that stood before me comforting each other looked no older that Lady Sommerfugl's own parents. I could see the resemblance immediately, I would have taken the foremother to be her daughter's sister they were so alike. The wife had long golden locks like her daughter and granddaughter, or was it foredaughter; I marked that question away to ask later. The woman had emerald green eyes while her daughter and little Lady Sommerfugl had eyes of pale blue, the type of blue that made the black pupils stand out in startling relief. The forefather had hair as black as my own and his eyes where that startling blue of his daughter.

"Peace to your home, may we enter?" The husband asked in the formal nisse manner. I did not know the reply so I stepped back and bowed slightly indicating with outreached hand that they may enter. It seemed to do the trick.

The foreparents smiled and walked in followed by Captain L'Ussler. Erika and the foremother curtsied at the same time, going down like gently falling leaves. It was proper for the woman to curtsy before the princess but Erika wanted to show respect to the couple. When they came up, they fell about each other's shoulders like long lost sisters. After a long hug, Erika and the woman parted and Erika curtsied low to the husband, who was so taken aback that he forgot to bow in response. No one saw fit to comment.

I extended my hand for a handshake but the forefather hugged me instead. I went along with his nisse familiarity, it was his family we were grieving after all. Erika took the foremother to the settee and sat down with her, they held each other's hands.

"I am so sorry for your loss ..." Erika hesitated, she realised she did not know this woman's name.

"This is Sara and Rialph Andover." Waccaar quickly introduced the grieving pair to spare Erika's embarrassment.

"Lady Sara, I cannot put into words how much I am saddened by your loss." Erika began.

"Your highness. You need not explain. We heard your words from outside these apartments. Forgive us your majesty." Sara said with genuine humility.

"It is I who should ask your forgiveness. If I should have passed this village, this city by, it would have been spared a visit by the Ferryman."

"Your Highness..." Sara began.

"Erika, please." Erika smiled.

I smiled a little myself. Perhaps a little of me was rubbing off on her.

"Princess Erika. No one knows the day or hour the Ferryman visits. My granddaughter was doing that which she was called to do in the service of her country and her king. It was all she lived for and you gave her life fulfilment. She could not have died a happier child." Both women cried together while we men awkwardly stood about trying to think of something constructive to do. I do not know which of us was more grateful for the noise of the commotion outside. Waccaar, Rialph and I drew our swords as one. Erika stood from the settee and drew her own knife as she motioned the woman behind her; it immediately grew to a thin three-foot nisse sword.

Someone pounded the door. It had to be critically important for the guards to allow anyone close to the door, let alone pound on it.

"Captain L'Ussler! Princess!" A voice called from outside. It sounded like the Mayor but I had seen him carried to the healer's house swathed in bloody bandages.

"Vassal is that you?" Waccaar called through the door.

"Captain L'Ussler! I summon the Princess. Please come quickly." The Mayor called back.

"Have you no respect man?" Waccaar shouted back, anger in his voice.

"The Lady Sommerfugl lives yet. She hangs by the finest of threads!" The Mayor's voice was almost in panic.

"She lies upon death as we speak but her spirit has not left her body, she still breathes. The Ferryman is at her doorstep. Hurry my princess! Hurry!" Came his pleading through the door. Erika rushed to the door, the butterfly still upon her back.

"Open the door." She demanded as she strode across the floor. Waccaar deactivated the immolation spell and pulled open the door. Erika stepped through and pushed the mayor to one side, without stopping or offering apology she broke into a run to the side of the pathway three hundred feet in the air. Without stopping, she dived over the edge. I saw her wings explode out as she disappeared out of sight.

Waccaar, the foreparents, and I jumped from path to path to descend to ground level. I followed Waccaar to the healer's tree, the nisse village hospital. We entered the main door as holly bough wearing LandNisse guards took up positions under Waccaar's expert direction. Healers pointed us to the room into which Erika had rushed. She leaned over the Lady Sommerfugl, her hand on her breast. Erika felt for her heartbeat.

"It is there. Very faint but it is there. How could I have missed it?" She cursed herself. The girl was swathed in blood soaked bandages her left arm missing mid forearm. Her face lay open to the bone with three vicious scars across her innocent face down her neck and across her chest. Even in all that gore, she looked peaceful and serene.

"Upon pain of death I demand the presence of all nisse battle wizards and anyone else who remotely thinks he or she has any sort of magic at all. Witches are included." Erika demanded her voice low and menacing. I think I would have preferred to face a troll right then. LandNisse guards ran to do her bidding.

"Jon, to my side quickly!" She called to me. I moved to her side at once. "Darling. Place your hands upon the Lady Sommerfugl." She ordered. It was hard to find a place where there was no blood. Erika placed her hands upon my shoulders. I thought it a bit strange she touched me and not the child. I stiffened in shock as the gushing force of what felt like boiling hot water gushed up my legs to fill my chest only to gush down my arms. Lady Sommerfugl bucked and spasmed on the table as the force poured into her frail little body. The pain was excruciating, the pleasure exquisite.

"Hold on my love. We have her." Erika whispered into my ear. I was barely aware of the battle wizards and other beings of magic that filed into the room. With trained professionalism, they formed a magic circle. I felt the pressure and the pain ease from my body as the wizards, warlocks; sorcerers and witches shared the path for the earth magic that poured into the girl's body. Her body glowed with the power it contained and I wondered if she felt the same pain I just felt.

Erika controlled the efforts of the magic circle; she moved the magic within Lady Sommerfugl. I could feel all of the different cooperating conduits; I could feel Erika directing force, guiding the magic to where it was needed. I was able to open my eyes and to my wonder the girls arm slowly reformed and grew back. The open wounds on her face closed and healed leaving only three fine white diagonal scars across her face. The scarring on her chest and arms remained but reduced to the same fine white lines. Apparently, there were limits to what Erika could do with this power.

Lady Sommerfugl groaned and the glowing reduced and dissipated. She turned her head, opened her eyes to look at the Princess, and smiled.

"How do you feel?" Erika asked as she stroked the girl's forehead.

"I feel like... I feel like I fell off an Ironwood tree; all the way from the top!"

A ripple of gentle laughter went around the room. I looked around to see many nisse battle wizards, as well as those summoned by the princess, there were wood nymphan shaman, elf wizards and a few fae I did not recognise but knew held some level of magic ability. I learned later that a summons was not required, each came willingly.

Erika leaned forward and whispered in the girl's ear.

"How did I do?" I saw her mouth the words.

"You did very well, I think." Little Lady Sommerfugl smiled back.

Chapter 30

Before the sun kissed Sol, our wagon train was packed and ready to set off. Our plan was to take the road to Lugon City and the safety of the Dwarfen Legions stationed there. Prince Hjlink the dwarfen King Olinfad's son had his palace there.

The plan, put together by Waccaar would see us depart Copperstone City in the guise of wool merchants. Erika glamoured a young nisse couple to look like Erika and me. The glamour would last a few weeks and give us plenty of time to journey to Lugon City and the royal protection of the dwarfen prince Hjlink.

I wished my chameleon suit to the form of a nisse wagon driver's garb. I took the reins of the wagon and four and as instructed by the real wagon driver, a click from my mouth, and a flex of the reins, the wide backed mulluks lumbered forward. We travelled back out the road we travelled in. Today there was no cheering; no people lined the roads, not a thing to give us away.

Looking back, we could see our doppelgangers surrounded by a heavy LandNisse guard wave us a royal farewell. The two young volunteers who would remain in the line of danger in the village. For several weeks, the spell would hold and the young couple would enjoy the hospitality of their own village while they impersonated us. To anyone spying on the village, the story was that the royal couple remained in Copperstone City to honeymoon and wait for their RiNisse guard. A detachment of L'Ussler's LandNisse guard surrounded the bogus royal couple; every one of them wore holly boughs to ward against further Snigmorder attack. The city mayor assured Erika that the entire city would have crowns of holly even if they had to use a trollgate to Earth Prime to collect enough to supply everyone.

Through the magical avenue of trees, we travelled without incident to the crossroads that marked the edge of Copperstone City, the vivid fields of flowers stretched out to each side like a multi-coloured patchwork quilt to cover the land and hide the horror of the previous night.

To the right lay the road we travelled yesterday to come to the City; straight ahead would take us nearer the Rhine and to the left we turned to begin our journey south, to the City of Lugon and aid from the dwarfen High Council and King Olinfad, in the person of his son Prince Hjlink.

The summer day warmed quickly, the bright early sun burnt off the morning mists and shone down on us to bless us with its life-giving rays. The journey was warm and pleasant and although we enjoyed the journey by foot that got us to Copperstone City, the wagons and their comfortable spring suspension came as a welcome change for this long journey ahead of us. By midmorning, we were so far from the city that we could no longer see the tall Ironwood trees or the perfumed multi-coloured fields of the Copperstone flowerbeds.

Although our disguises were false, our wagonloads were not. We carried the famous wool of the Copperstone nisse, a fine soft wool woven into bales of differing types of fine fabric, some as fine and soft as the most expensive of silks while others were as tough as mulluk hide yet light and breathable and every grade in between. Copperstone nisse flowers are as renowned as their wool. Used in the dyeing process to make the most vivid of designs and patterns, Copperstone City also sells the dyes and the perfumes made from the flowers. The medium wool is hardwearing and favoured by the working classes for their best dresses and suits of clothes to the sturdy and hardwearing farming and manual labourer's woollens.

The wagons trundled on in the heat of the day, we fell into a long comfortable silence, Erika, I enjoyed the scenery, and each other's company until Erika finally broke that comfortable silence.

"Jon, tell me about your family." Erika asked, and spread out her peasant skirts to settle them on the bench seat. I took an appreciative glance at her voluminous deep blue skirts and her dainty ebony feet contrasted against the snow white under skirts peeping out from beneath.

"What would you like to know, Princess?" I asked. I used Erika's title more like a term of endearment than the stuffy royal title for which the same word held meaning. I felt that Erika liked it because she stopped correcting me to be less formal.

"I fear you will soon hear of my family and their histories both truth and legend, good and bad. I would like to know about your family. Do your parents yet live? How many brothers and sisters do you have? I hear you humans breed rather rapidly."

I paused for a moment to gather my thoughts and nudge the mulluks back in line with the wagon train; they wanted to veer off to the long grass and the rich grazing they would find there.

"Mum is passed away but my father and brothers are all still alive. I am the youngest of four boys the oldest Patrick and Evan are twins and then there is Phillip, the middle one."

"Twins, I have heard of that. The human women give birth to a live litter, sometimes two and sometimes more than that, three or four or more."

"Yes something like that but not as often as you might think. Well, I was the fourth sprog and unlike my brothers, I had black hair while they and my father were all fair-haired. Mum had black hair until it began to turn grey just before she passed away."

"How did your mother die, Jon?" Erika gently probed. I never talked about Mum even to my closest friends, Mum and I were very close and I missed her still.

"Please do not speak if it burdens you so." Erika had caught my melancholy thoughts and hesitation.

"I think I would like to tell you Erika." I replied and Erika squeezed my hand in support and warm comfort.

"It was cancer, cancer of the pancreas, she was so healthy and fit, then she began to lose weight and when she died she was a frail grey haired shadow of herself. There was no time to transplant and no time to grow a replacement from her own stem cells. It was just one of those things that sneak up from behind, and before you know it, it takes your loved one with little warning. She did not suffer. She took the exit option and when she said her goodbyes, father administered the lethal dose by intravenous drip and she fell into sleep and died in comfort a few minutes later. She died with her family about her in peace and comfort with a smile on her lips. She was still a young woman at fifty-five years old and on the day she died; I think something in Dad died inside as well.

About ten years later Dad retired from the AOEUF as a regimental Sergeant Major. He lived with each of us year round, visiting each of the brothers for about three months at a time. He still loved to move around and spent very little time in his retirement accommodation complex. While he could book accommodation on any of the commonwealth worlds, he preferred to keep his living quarters as those he shared with Mum in Saint Patricks Barracks in the Euro State of Ireland.

Just before he began to need care himself, he came to visit me on Sol on my first posting seven years ago. I was able to swing an assignment in New New York on Avalon. It was where York in England was located and it could not be called New York due to the New York in our own world so some pencil pushing nerd called it after a city in an old 2D Vid cartoon series.

Father and I had three very happy months hunting, fishing, and generally getting up to no good together. I am very like my dad and he enjoyed being with me and he said how amazed he was that he could have a son as ugly as me yet remind him so of his wife's beautiful dark looks. I knew he was joking and..."

"Was he?" Erika cut in with a serious expression she held for but a moment before laughing with that sweet voice of hers. I laughed along with her and continued my story.

"My brothers would all tease me that I was adopted until I actually believed it was the family secret and I really was adopted. I did love my parents and my brothers but there was always a thought, a fear in the back of my mind that I was not from this family but from a place very far away."

"And what of your father now?"

"Dad is still alive. It will take a lot more that an illness to bump that guy off. After his second heart attack, he moved into a veteran's rest home in Pompey, a lunar rest settlement on the Moon of Earth Prime."

"Like Epona?" Erika asked with amazement.

"Yes like Epona. The reduced gravity eases his heart condition and he can get about very well indeed up there. Nevertheless, he is not the same man I remember when mum was alive. Now it seems he has nothing to live for and I do think something died inside of him when he pressed that button and mum passed away. No, he is not the soldier I remember. I think he has retired into himself and I believe he counts the days until the Gods send the Ferryman and he can be with Mum again."

Erika hugged me. "I am saddened to hear that Jon. I am sure he was a fine warrior in his best years."

"Yes he sure was that! I really missed him when he was off soldiering across the Cosmos. He was there mostly for the important times and for the most part, we had some fine times when he was home on leave. I loved those times when he was home and it made me miss him all the more when he was away."

Erika hugged me again but said nothing; she allowed me my happy, sad memories and left me to those precious thoughts for a while. I found out later that she empathically shared those thoughts with me and shared in both the happiness and the sadness of my past.

A little later, I broke the comfortable silence.

"I... I remember my mum always read to us at bedtime." I said with a smile. "She read many different types of story books but our favourites were the books my Grandmother Linda wrote. My most favourite of them all was her first ever book titled 'My trollish Prince.' That's Uffe you know. He and my Great Grandmother. Well they... You know... They... Well that

Uffe is my Great Grandfather." I said not believing my own words. "How could she with a troll?"

"She must have loved Uffe Jon." Erika replied.

"No princess I don't mean how could they. I meant how could they... Physically."

"Oh" Erika replied. After a moment, I continued my tale.

"Sometimes Grandmother Linda would spend a few weeks visiting with us and during those times she always read us one of her many famous books."

"Please Jon; tell me more of your Grandmother Linda." Erika asked, and I had an inkling that she had felt my memory and was mind reaming me then.

The way Lieutenant Amanda Stewart and her Psy Corps colleagues mind reamed could be uncomfortable and many times, painful, depending on how deep they went or how urgently they required seeing the memories and thoughts. When Erika mind reamed me, it felt quite euphoric.

"I have over one hundred years' experience." Erika answered my unspoken question. "We nisse use a technique that numbs the pain and releases the chemicals you call endorphins in to your physical mind, your brain as you call it, to ease the metaphysical mind that is you.

Last night you experienced the opposite when you experienced how the gnomes cast their dream weaves. Yes theirs is a very different approach entirely."

"Can you do what they did last night?" I asked. A massive spider, the size of my head, crawled out from beneath the bench on which we sat. It planted one of its hairy legs on my inner thigh. I jumped up, drew my tanto and skewered the beast to the wooden floor. Erika laughed and caught the discarded reins. I looked down again and the big hairy spider had vanished.

"Boo!" Erika laughed and I sat back down and took the reins again. I kept a frown for a few moments then laughed along with my beautiful ebony princess.

"Amongst the fae there are good and bad." Erika went on to volunteer. "It is not divided between race and clan. Most nisse belong to the Seelie Court of which my father the Emperor King presides. The gnomes for the most part belong to the Unseelie court; those are the fae that you would consider the bad fairies. We like to refer to them as the dark fae as your concept of good and evil is not as we understand. There are many shades of grey between light and dark and many fae, through their lives, move through many of those shades." Erika poured a drink form a leather skin hung by the side of the wagon. I took the wooden cup and drank it down. The water tasted sparkling and cold with a hint of elderberry. "Now that is refreshing! How is it so cold? Magic spell?" I asked.

"No, it is the skin of the mulluk. It has properties that prevent heat from moving through its skin. Anything you put in it will stay warm or cold depending on how it is when you pour it in. It needs a good stopper to contain the heat or cold." Erika held out the skin bag to inspect it. "This is a very well made skin indeed."

"This Grandmother of yours, tell me of her." Erika commanded. Well it sounded like a command but I knew it was Erika's way and she was finding it just as hard to adjust as I was.

"Most people thought her quite odd. She was a gifted writer and our family fortune comes from the wealth grandmother made from the sales of her books.

Granny Linda was the only daughter of Great grandmother Annika. She was Danish and she and Granny Linda lived just outside Fredericia in her mother's farm home for the first ten years of her life. They lived alone when Great grandmother's parents passed away and for all accounts, Granny Linda had a very happy childhood. She was full of imagination and often told us of her fantasy trips with her mother to a world of nisse, trolls and faeries.

"She sounds like a woman of a strong mind and fertile imagination." Erika commented, taking a drink from the wooden cup that held the refreshing water.

"She was that indeed." I agreed. "At the age of ten years old, her mother, Great grandmamma came into a significant sum of money and they bought a remote farmhouse in Northumbria, England bordering Scotland to the north. Again, there she had a happy childhood although she never mentioned missing her father at all. Actually, there was never any mention of a Father. Now I know why!

"Back then, it was more acceptable to give birth out of wedlock until the resurgence of the churches due to the revelations of a life after death. With the churches growing in strength and the population explosion that threatened our world, the United European Federation outlawed birth out of wedlock. Such children are now taken from their mothers and placed with families looking for adoption; the women, unless there is good cause, are sterilized and that is not reversed until the woman is married."

"And you call this world barbaric!" Erika exclaimed.

I shrugged my shoulders; being a man, I did not really have very strong thoughts on the matter.

"The farm was remote and Granny Linda continued to have a settled and comfortable life as a child. It was just before she was to go up to University to study Xeno Anthropology at Cambridge that her very first fantasy novel called 'My Trollish Prince' became an overnight eBook sensation. The book was released just one week before the Felix Culpa that caused the gateway between Earth Prime and Sol. The subject matter of the book was so close to the real thing that everyone wanted a copy. It was so successful that it remains a best seller to this day. The publishers even took the rare step of having the book published in paper form and it became a firm favourite of both adults and children.

Granny Linda did not go to university but instead pursued her dream of writing full time and she produced many more novels of her fantasy worlds. Being born a Dane, she was able to own her mother's house back in Fredericia and she lived between the house in Fredericia in which her mother grew up and the remote farmhouse in Northumbria. For the rest of her years she spent most of her time in either Denmark or England writing her famous Chronicles of Sol.

One summer on her remote farm in Northumbria, there happened by a young man, looking for work as he travelled the countryside. He was very handsome and of great physical strength. Granny Linda gave the young man work on her farm. The next summer they wed and they had a long and happy marriage. Granny Linda had five strong sons and one daughter who was the youngest. That daughter was my mother."

"It sounds like your mother had a happy life." Erika commented and removed her nisse peasant scarf to lean her head back and bask in the hot refreshing rays of the summer sun.

"Yes, come to think of it, I suppose she did. Yet the one thing that I feel she missed even though she never spoke of it was that she never knew her father."

Erika gave me a puzzled look and said. "Maybe you do not know your Granny Linda as well as you might think you know her."

"You think she knew?" I asked. The strange reply was, I thought, something Erika had picked up from her reaming of my mind. Something I did not consciously know about my Granny Linda.

Chapter 31

One of the LandNisse guard pulled in to trot his angor beside our wagon. The guards were ordered not to show any deference to us in the open.

"Milady, there is something up ahead on the road. Captain Commander L'Ussler goes to investigate as we speak." The outrider automatically doffed his cap before he caught himself. "Apologies Milady."

I leaned out the side of the wagon to peer beyond the three wagons in front of us.

"I see a handcart with a broken wheel and the guys are helping clear the spillage from the road."

"You suspect an ambush." Said Erika, it was not a question; she had felt my fear and reamed my mind.

We could see for miles and any type of ambush would take a great deal of magical preparation to avoid the Princess's senses.

"I smell nothing." Erika commented. It was an elvin euphemism, which meant that Erika could not sense anything. The saying derived from the troll language that used the same word for smell as it did for sensing.

During their first titanic battles with the Angelic and Cherubim back near the beginning of time, their battle priests endowed the trollish warriors with the power to sense the presence of the Angelic Host so that they could not be ambushed. Through the hundreds of thousands of years, it became the legend that trolls could smell the blood of a Christian. This in reality meant they could sense those that give allegiance to the Christian Gods that commanded the Angels and all types of magic in use.

I trusted Erika's magical enhanced senses but I had a little apprehension as we drew up beside the broken handcart.

A little old man sat by the roadside, a large floppy hat obscured most of his face and beside him he held a long wanderers staff. His colourful patchwork-travelling cloak was the stamp of a travelling peddler and with his tools and pedal operated sharpening stone he looked like a Bruuker, a man that carries out minor repairs and sharpens knives. As soon as he laid eyes on us, he jumped up and shouted while shaking his staff.

"Look what your clumsy wagon guards have done to my fine handcart."

"Milady the old man lies!" Captain Commander L'Ussler protested.

"Your Highness." The old man exclaimed slyly, he made a leg, doffed his floppy hat and bowed with a great flourish of his tattered patchwork cloak. I was immediately alert to the tone of his salutation. He was not nisse he did not have the swept back pointed ears and neither did he have the upward pointed ears of the elvin. From the colour of his dark brown skin, I guessed he was a male wood nymph, I had never seen one before but he fit the male type of the numerous female wood nymphs I have seen. There was only one male to every eight hundred or so female wood nymphs, males were very rarely seen and I do not think one so old as this little man had ever been seen by anyone from Earth Prime.

"How am I to make my living without my goods and a broken cart your guards broke?" he demanded, pointing to Captain Commander L'Ussler.

"Be quiet little man!" Captain Commander L'Ussler lifted his leather gauntlet hand to strike. "You think to make coin from Milady because of your own misfortune! Do you know to whom you address?"

The old man recoiled in fear from L'Ussler's threat, his wizened old arms up to cover his head and face.

"Captain!" Erika commanded and raised her hand both to stop the blow and any further words from the captain's mouth.

"Yes it was he, that one, what broke my sturdy handcart." The old man pointed at the Captain, emboldened by the staying of Erika's hand. "Yes! Humph! This fine cart has served me for years, now your bully of a guard and his big smelly angor has destroyed my whole life. Humph!" The old man pressed his complaint. I thought he was completely exaggerating, even lying.

"It's no more than a pile of sticks!" L'Ussler harrumphed through his bushy drooping, salt and pepper, moustaches.

"Yes now it's not more than a pile of sticks; after you broke it! You oaf!"

Captain L'Ussler ignored the old man's protests and turned to Erika.

"Milady, we found him like this. We have been trying to help him gather his goods and attempt repairs."

"Captain L'Ussler, shame on you." Erika rebuked the captain with a glint in her eye that told the captain he had nothing to fear. "How can you expect me to take your word over the word of a fine and noble craftsman?"

Captain L'Ussler was lost for words. "Milady" He bowed on top of his mulluk. Erika leaned forward and whispered. "Secure the area and check for ambush."

The captain nodded obedience and wheeled his mount away. With silent hand signals, he ordered his men to fan out and secure the immediate area.

Erika nimbly leapt from the cart and alighted beside the little old man, his floppy hat back on his head to cover the few wisps of grey hair he had left.

"My apologies, noble sir. My men can be clumsy brutes at the best of times." Erika spoke softly and touched the old man's hand.

"He he he", the old man cackled like an old witch. The sudden fear that he might be just that, passed through my mind. Erika looked up and shook her head slightly to indicate no.

"Lorna, it is obvious that the cart was broken before the men..." I used Erika's false name we created. Her last name was Sisson the same as the regular wagon mistress, Erika pretended she was family. I stood to look around watching for sudden attack and the progress of the LandNisse guard securing the area. Erika again raised her hand to stop any protest. I could see she was serious about helping this old peddler and accept his obvious manufactured story. Maybe she has a soft spot for those that looked as old as her years; I knew for certain that I was a long way from understanding her at all.

"Noble Artificer what is the cost to replace your sturdy handcart?" Erika asked softly and with a respect I would have believed offered to the highest lord. The little old man was certainly acting like one.

"Humph! Two, no three gold pieces, Your Highness." The little man stated as if trying out the highest price he could get away with. Why did he keep calling Erika 'Your Highness' when 'Milady' was the correct form of address?

"Rubbish. The carts not worth..." I began again only for Erika to stop me once more. "Milady! You could buy a carriage and four for two gold..." I protested.

"Done." Erika interrupted my protest. The little man clapped his wizened old hands, his long staff leaning in the crook of his arm.

"And another gold crown for your troubles good sir."

"Mistress Sissan!"

"And two more for your broken wares." She looked up at me and I knew any further protest would enrich this offensive little man even further.

"You are truly a princess amongst women." The old man bowed and kissed Erika's hand. The comment was too close for my comfort and my hand went to my katana. I hopped down from the cart to stand a little behind Erika. The little old man caught the movement with the side of his sly old eye.

"So you would attack an old man for paying a beautiful young woman a compliment." He shook his fist at me. "Come draw that wicked looking sword and I will teach you a thing or two about fighting. Come and I will vanquish you with my staff. Humph!" The little old man shook his long staff at me. I could not help laughing at his absurd claim.

"Kind Sir. I would that you would spare this foolish man for he is my love." Erika pleaded as if she addressed a general and his armies. Sometimes Erika was too good for her own good. I laughed again at Erika's comment.

"Come on Lorna, you ask him to spare me!" I laughed

"Humph. Okay." The little man stroked his chin. I could see his devious mind working behind those furtive eyes. "I will require transport for myself and my wares to... Where are you going?" He suddenly thought to ask.

"We journey to Lugon city." Erika replied before I could stop her.

"Yes, yes Lugon. I require transport to Lugon for me to spare your love. Not that he deserves it!" He shook his staff at me again. I wanted to take that staff and... Well, I could understand why Captain L'Ussler was so flustered by the time we got to him.

"You are most gracious noble sir." Erika curtsied.

"Mistress Sissan, with all respect, you go too far." I complained, pulling Erika to one side. Captain L'Ussler appeared on his mount.

"The area is secure. Milady." Captain L'Ussler reported.

"No it is not!" The little old man piped up. "I could defeat you all and make away with the beautiful young princess."

The comment startled the captain and he drew his long thin nisse rapier. The old man cowered behind his staff; his cowardly action stayed the captain's hand.

"Captain you would dare attack such a warrior?" Erika asked of the captain. L'Ussler looked as confused as I did. He looked to me for clarity and all I could do was shrug my shoulders.

"Captain L'Ussler, you will apologise for breaking this noble craftsman's sturdy handcart. Then you will pack his cart and its contents into the back of our wagon. We are to take this craftsman's handcart and wares to Lugon with us."

Captain L'Ussler looked from Erika to me and all I could do was shrug my shoulders again. I was glad I was not the only one to feel like a fool.

"Apologies, Master Bruuker." Captain Commander L'Ussler bowed from his mount and puffed through his moustaches. He wheeled his mount and detailed off four of the guards to move the cart and its belongings into the back of our half-empty wagon.

"No, not them! They already broke all my precious things." The old man protested waving that absurd staff at us. "Him!" He pointed at me. "I want the fine gentleman to do it." The last comment was made with such a contemptuous tone that it could not be mistaken for anything other than an insult.

"If you think I am going to lift all that stuff and..."

Erika stood so close before me I could feel her sweet breath on my face.

"Please Jon. Do it for me." Erika whispered and kissed me lightly on the lips.

"Can you see how much is there? And the bloody cart as well." I protested.

"Well if you think you cannot do it then maybe this fine old master craftsman and I will have to do it instead." Erika smiled. She knew she had cornered me and there was no way out.

I rolled my eyes and made for the broken handcart.

"I would start with the heavy things first." Captain L'Ussler suggested from on top of his mount. I shot him a stare that told him what I thought of his comment. L'Ussler harrumphed through his droopy moustaches and wheeled his mount away to attend his guards.

I got to the job of moving the handcarts contents into our wagon, within twenty minutes the cart was empty and the contents packed and strapped down. With my enhanced strength, I was able to lift the handcart, with little effort, into the back of the wagon. I patted the dust from my clothes knowing that the chameleon suit would self-clean anyway.

"Humph! I could have done that in half the time." The old man complained.

I just ignored him. He was along for the ride by the princess's invitation. I just did not know what that girl was thinking.

"Okay you, in the back." I indicated for the old man to climb aboard the back of the wagon. He shuffled up to the back and tried to climb aboard. After three attempts, I lifted him up and over the tailgate.

"Unhand me!" He shouted. "Do you think me a helpless old man?" He demanded as he straightened his clothes in the back of the wagon. I shook my head and walked around the side of the wagon to the front.

There he was, sitting in the middle of the bench with the reins in his hands.

"Bah! I can drive this old wagon better than any man." The Old Man boasted. I missed the detail completely; he used the word man instead of fae.

"Get in the back." I demanded.

"No!" Came the reply.

"I said in the back, old man." I repeated.

"Oh let him be." Erika laughed and nimbly hopped on board and around the old man to sit on the opposite side. I climbed on board knowing that this smelly old peddler was going to sit between my love and I for the entire journey to Lugon city.

We would not be able to speak freely and we would not be able to touch each other. I would have to address Erika by her assumed name and worst of all; I would have to put up with this dirty old peddler jostling against me rather than my beautiful princess.

I drove for about 10 minutes before I tired of the little old man's constant complaining. "You shouldn't do that. It's better to do it this way. You don't want to do that like that." He constantly chimed in. I do not think I could pick my nose without the old man giving me suggestions.

"Would you not rather climb in the back and lie down for a spell?" I asked.

"What and miss sitting beside this beautiful young princess? Bah! You are the fool are you not?" He smiled at me with his idiot grin and missing teeth. I looked back to my mulluks and sighed in exasperation.

"So, Noble Sir. Where do you hail from?" Erika asked.

"Oh around, here and there." Came the old man's obtuse reply.

"And what is it you do exactly?" Erika asked.

"This and that. A little bit of everything."

"And a lot of nothing." I cut in.

"Bah! How rude." The little man crossed his arms in a huff, his staff sticking up from between those folded arms.

"And what is your name little man?" I asked.

Erika glanced at me as if I had uttered a string of profanities.

"It is not little man!" The little man huffed.

"Okay, so let's start again." I sighed.

"What is your name?" I asked with great patience I thought.

"What are your names?" The old man mimicked me.

"I am Carsten Underwood and this is Mistress Lorna Sissan." I picked the name Underwood myself. I though it most appropriate.

"And my name is..." He leaned forward as if to let us into a great secret. "Aiken Drum." He nodded conspiratively.

"I know that name. I used to sing a song about a faerie by that name." I said.

Aiken Drum burst into the chorus.

"And he played upon a ladle, a ladle, a ladle,

And he played upon a ladle,

and his name was Aiken Drum."

He sang the song I remembered from infant school. He laughed aloud, his breath rank with rotten teeth.

He was silent for a glorious moment, and then he had to go and spoil it.

"I have another name you know." He volunteered. "Yes, yes Aiken Drum is my name, the name everyone knows me by. However, people like me have another name. A special name."

"Yeah, I can think of a name or two." I said

"Do you mock me?" Aiken Drum shot me a pointed stare.

"And what would that name be Aiken Drum?" I asked. I just had to know.

"Can you not guess?" He seemed to be mocking me now.

"No I cannot guess your other name." I sighed with exasperation.

Heute back ich, morgen brau ich,
Übermorgen hol ich mir der Königin ihr Kind;
Ach, wie gut, dass niemand weiß,
dass ich Rumpelstilzchen heiß

The German poem from my childhood popped into my head. I got icy shivers up and down my spine.

It was my second elected language. I knew that poem well.

Today I bake, tomorrow I brew,
The day after I get the queen's child,
Oh, how good, that nobody knows that
My name is Rumpelstilzchen.

Well it rhymed in German.

"Rumpelstilzchen?" I said, alarm bells going off in my mind. The legends surrounding both Aiken Drum and more importantly Rumpelstilzchen were not the best character references one would have asked for. Aiken Drum jumped to his feet and pointed a gloved finger at me.

"Bah! goblin mind reamer!" He spat hateful words at me. "You cheated; nobody can guess what I am. You have help, have you not?"

"What kind of help do you think I have then? Mr Rumpelstilzchen. Tell me Mr Rumpelstilzchen, what happens if I get you to say your name backwards?" I asked.

"I don't know." he shrugged his ragged shoulders.

"Can you spin straw into gold then?" I asked.

"Of Course! Not only gold, I can turn wood and stone to gold as well." Aiken Drum volunteered.

"How do you do that then?" I laughed.

"Well I get a piece of wood. Then I cut all the bits off I do not need then I turn it into gold!" He boasted.

It was the most ludicrous rubbish I had ever heard, even above that of the sergeants mess, after a drunken party.

"Will you turn some wood into gold for me?" I asked.

"I might." He replied obtusely, trying to be mysterious.

Chapter 32

"Erika this is ridiculous!" I hissed under my breath. "We can't talk, we can't hold hands. We can't do anything."

The next morning found us stopped so that the Bruuker could climb down from the wagon and make his waters behind a large stone that marked twenty miles to Lugon City. The runes on the stone also marked the border between the nisse territories and the province of Lugon, the province's capital city was one of the dwarfen's greatest cities. Lugon city started life as a dwarfen mining outpost established about three thousand years ago. At first a small mining outpost but with its location to the Rhine that split Europa in two and the rich farmland from long dead volcanic activity, surrounded the city. This once rough mining outpost quickly became a sprawling city and the ever-industrious dwarfen built high walls to contain and protect that first city of Lugon.

Through the ages, the city spread, and the rich and powerful built large mansions to house the wealthy outside the first walls and as money talks in all the worlds, so another set of walls were built to surround and protect the mansions and palaces of those rich and powerful merchants. This expansion repeated itself three more times and now the city stands sprawled across the Valley of Lugon and on both sides of the river. The ruling family feared the province would separate into an independent kingdom or worse still a republic, so they stationed the prince regents palace in Lugon. King Olinfad's son Prince Hjlink and heir to the dwarfen throne had his official residence there.

Five grand stone bridges spanned the Rhine within the city, each but one named in honour of the Queenly wife of the King in power at the time of completion of the bridges. The central bridge, named Tower Bridge, took its name from the three great towers that support it, each tower a mini fortress with its own legion of guard. This bridge would be the last to go in an attack, as all other bridges are able be collapsed or drawn up in a siege. The Tower Bridge would always stay open and only fall when the city fell. The three legions that are based in the towers are named the Tower Legions and they act as city guards and watchmen during times of peace. The first Legion in the first tower closest to the centre of the city and the third Legion furthest away.

* * *

"Don't mind me." Aiken Drum spoke as he walked back from the stone, lacing his pants and balancing that idiot staff in the crook of his arm.

"You just talk away, I am sure you two lovebirds have plenty to say to each other."

"You heard us all the way over there." I asked, amazed that the old man could hear so well.

"Well when you talk with great big outside voices I could not help but over hear. Bah! You should try conversing with inside voices, it is much more civilised." Aiken Drum tried to climb back onto the wagon. While it was easy for him to jump down, the little man found it difficult to climb back on.

"A hand for an old man if you would?" Aiken Drum smirked; I wanted to throw up on him. I pretended not to hear. Erika poked me in the ribs.

"For the sake of the Gods will you all stop doing that?" I ranted.

"Help the poor man, Jon my love." Erika asked with such a sweet smile.

"Ha! Yes help the old man, Jon my love." Aiken Drum smiled his sarcastic crooked smile with every one in three teeth missing; he looked one sorry excuse for a nymphan or for any other decent creature. I reached my hand down and he grabbed it.

"For all the Gods, you haven't washed your hands." I exclaimed in horror.

"What am I to wash my hands with? Do you see a palace or a public spa out there boy?" He growled back as he climbed over me to sit between us once again. I wiped my hand on his dirty patchwork peddler's cloak, as it was the lesser of two evils.

"And we are not lovebirds." I added in disgust. Erika leaned around the old man and asked with genuine concern.

"Aren't we Jon?"

"Of course we are my love. I just meant..."

"What did you mean?" Erika huffed.

"Well just that it's not dirty like the old man suggests."

Aiken Drum saw my discomfort so he pressed me again.

"Bah! It's as plain as your blackened skin." Aiken Drum made a show of looking around. "I see no other Nisse here with black skin except for you two." He pointed at Erika and jabbed his finger into my side. I went for my tanto and Aiken Drum cringed back against Erika. She put her arm protectively around the wretched old man. I was insanely jealous. Erika shook her head no and I was tempted just to knife the old cranky fool and have done with it.

From his protected place beside Erika, he snapped back.

"You have bedded a Nisse and now you are a Changeling." The old man cackled like a witch.

"A Changeling! That's ridiculous, little man." I sneered and snapped the rains to the mulluks. Captain Commander L'Ussler saw the move and called to the lead wagon and his troop of guards to move on.

"Aiken Drum." Aiken Drum stated with a snap.

"What?"

"Aiken Drum is my name. I have told you before; my name is Aiken Drum, not little man. And I am not a man I am a nymphan, a male nymph and you are very fortunate to meet me." Aiken Drum announced and puffed up his chest with pride.

"You are still a little old man and I will call you what I like." I told him without looking away from the mulluks.

Erika cut into the rather frustrating conversation.

"Carsten" she used my false name. "Aiken Drum is a very special person. Within the race of nymph, there is but one male nymph born in every eight hundred children and they are treated with the greatest of respect. They are very rarely seen and we should treat noble Aiken Drum with every civility he deserves."

"Well I don't see why we need to be civil to him if he is not civil to us."

"Aha! Your ladylove is quite correct. I am a very special and important person, very important indeed." Aiken Drum announced smugly.

"Well how come we have the privilege of meeting this one then?" I complained and pointed to the cantankerous old man planted between Erika and me.

"A good point Carsten." Erika agreed and turned to Aiken Drum to ask.

"So Noble one, what brings you to the honourable trade of Bruuker and your travels amongst the races and nations of Sol?"

"Bah, I tired of my life of decadence and luxury. I had everything yet owned nothing. My duty was to bed four or five even ten nymphs every night. Every single night of my life from the age of 17 years, I was destined to make love to different nymphs every night but not to know the love and companionship of a single one. We are but breeding machines like those lowly mulluks." He pointed to the four that pulled our wagon. "Yes, we are pampered and preened but we are more like pets than husbands. We are so treated; we become lazy and good for nothing other than to father the next generation of nymph.

We hold no office and have no say or vote in the government of our nation and race." For the first time since meeting Aiken Drum, I felt that he was sincere and truthful.

"So Aiken, why a Bruuker? As a male nymph, you have limitless wealth and luxury. Why toil for a living?"

"Bah! It's Aiken Drum not just Aiken on its own. Aiken Drum, understand boy?" The old man complained again then shifted in his seat between us and poked me in the ribs again.

I jerked away. "Will you stop doing that?" I demanded.

"Only if you call me Aiken Drum." The little man replied.

"Okay Okay already. Aiken Drum... Why a Bruuker. When you..."

"Bah. I know, I know. I heard you the first time boy!" Aiken Drum cut me off and continued. "As nymphan we are surrounded with the wealth of the nymph race. We need only ask for what we want and it is supplied. We have no need for money and riches and all that wealth is just so much bright metal and pretty baubles to us nymphan.

"Yes, we have everything we want and we want for nothing. In the day we relax and rest, we are allowed no sports or any other activity that may endanger us. Come the night and we must perform with many nymphs, every night, night after night, year after year until we are dead. No two nights is it the same nymphs. There are no nymph half bloods, as the nymph cannot breed outside our race. Every nymph's blood is pure and as male nymphan, we are not tied to any one tree as the females are. Nymphan males have no need to return to their birthing tree to rest and take of life's energy. As males, we can take of life's energy from anything living, trees, and animals, even all of the races. We are moved around nymph habitats, exchanged and traded for like a prize mulluk stud. Sometimes we get to make the choice of where we go next and it is a small privilege we appreciate."

"I know of a few soldiers that would jump at the chance of such a life." I remarked.

"Bah! Then let them have it. If I could have changed places with one of you humans I would have done it in a heartbeat." Aiken Drum replied with a dismissive laugh.

"So how did you leave and why become a Bruuker?" Erika asked enthralled in the old man's story.

"I rebelled. I refused to continue to be a breeding grall, stuffed full of luxury slop through the day and forced to breed all night. Knowing in my heart that the children I sired, I would never know. And if I was fortunate to have a son I would never know him either." Aiken Drum turned to me and added. "I wonder how your soldier friends would feel if they had to do that night after night, year after year, decade after decade. Well?" Aiken Drum demanded.

"I can see your point." I replied flatly. I still thought some of the lads would jump at the chance, even with all of those pitfalls.

"When I got the chance I decided to escape my nymph jailers, to strike off the golden bonds of luxury and idolatry. I waited patiently for it was a nice place to wait. I was in Enlar Forest and there was want of a nymphan in the Forest of Lugon." Aiken Drum began. "Look yonder." Aiken Drum pointed to the tree line North West. That is the Forest of Logon, beyond are the wastes of Arabath and beyond them Enlar Forest. To travel there I had to cross the wastes of Arabath where few trees grow and no nymph live. I never arrived in the Forest of Lugon; that was two hundred and fifty years ago."

"What did you do then noble Aiken Drum?" Erika prompted him to go on. I must admit I was becoming interested in the old fool's story myself.

"I disappeared and became that which I always wished to be. First, I became a peddler. I found that I had a talent with metal. In addition, I discovered I had a small talent with music. So I took to wandering, selling pots and pans. Mending those that need mending, sharpening blades and helping those who cannot help themselves. I would play my music in the taverns and hostelries in towns and cities all about. I put the two together and played music to entertain the drinkers, on pots and pans, and even ladles."

"More like helping yourself to things people could not defend." I commented to myself.

"Bah! I heard that. I do not have to sit here and listen to your insults boy! Let me off this ragtag caravan!" Aiken Drum shouted loud enough that the outriders closed in just in case he tried to injure their princess.

"My pleasure. No one asked you along anyway." I snapped back and pulled on the reins to stop the wagon.

"Carsten, please. You know we invited the noble Aiken Drum to our wagon train. It would be a great insult to me if he left before we made the destination I promised him." Erika scolded.

"Yes a great insult to the Lady." Aiken Drum added.

"Please Carsten, apologise to our guest." Erika pleaded.

"Yes apologise or I leave this very minute." The little old man demanded as if he held a dagger to my throat.

I shook my head in submission to Erika's request. "Okay. Very well I apologise." I agreed.

"Say you apologise to the Noble Aiken Drum." Aiken Drum demanded. I looked to Erika and she pleaded with the nod of her pretty head.

"Very well. I apologise to the noble Aiken Drum." I sighed.

"Aha! Now we are all friends again!" Aiken Drum cracked a wide grin and went to poke me with his finger. My look told him that was a step too far and he did not follow through with his action.

"Shall I continue with my story?" Aiken Drum fished for an excuse to continue.

"Please noble craftsman." Erika asked in kindly tones.

"Well I kept well away from the forests of Sol and eventually when I had to pass through a forest, I kept firmly to the path. All paths through the forests are, as you know, neutral, as are all roads through the open lands.

"I travelled many places and met many peoples. What I worked for I kept, and what is mine is mine. Now I earn a living doing just that." Aiken Drum pointed back onto the wagon to his broken upturned handcart and his possessions secured underneath.

"And that is all you have for all those years work as a Bruuker?" I asked looking back at his meagre possessions in the back of the wagon.

"Oh no, no, no. I have much more than that." The peddler declared.

"Tell us noble Aiken Drum. What more do you have?" I asked with a smirk to await his hollow boasts.

"Hmmm I have... I have a house. A big house. With many servants and... And an Army of fine warriors and... And a whole city. Yes I am the master of a whole city." Aiken Drum declared.

"Yeah right. In that case I am the Emperor of all the world." I laughed.

"And I am Princess Erika Nisse, first daughter of the Emperor King." Erika laughed along with my jest, however I was a little uncomfortable with Erika's bluff by telling the truth disguised as a harmless boast.

"Your Majesty." Aiken Drum doffed his floppy hat and bowed in his seat. "And to you, noble boy emperor of all of the world."

We all laughed together.

"Ha ha ha. Shall I call you...? Ha, ha, ha, Your Majesties or will Jon and Erika do?

The statement rang alarm bells in the back of my mind. We never used our names in his presence. There was no way he could have known. The LandNisse guard disguised as outriders and wagon toughs never used our names either, they always referred to Erika as Milady, a common title for an important woman merchant. I had not called her by name in his presence, so how did he know her name. I looked to Erika for guidance. My hand dropped to my tanto and I was eager to resolve the problem. Erika frowned at me.

Aiken Drum continued his story as if his revelation of knowing our correct names was nothing. "Now that I have a trade and a calling the nymphs leave me alone. They do not speak to me anymore and when they do require communicating with me they send an emissary who is protected by ancient fae law."

I laughed again at Aiken Drum's absurd claims.

"Bah! You think something funny. Emperor of all the world?" Aiken Drum sneered.

"You are telling me that the nymph nation sends an emissary protected by fae law when they want to talk to you, a simple Bruuker and peddler?"

Aiken Drum jumped to his feet and shook his staff at me.

"Bah! You laugh at me! Emperor of all the world. Ha! I am a very important man! A noble artisan and a skilled warrior. Princess Erika has said so herself. Should you mock me again, I will smite you with my staff." Aiken Drum threatened, trying to tower over me by standing in the wagon.

"A Warrior!" I laughed. "You?"

"Yes, I am the greatest warrior in all of the world." The little man boasted.

"Yeah Okay." I laughed again. "You know Aiken Drum, I believed you right up to that point. You just cannot be serious. Listen old man, I am not the Emperor of the world and Erika is not the Princess Royal."

"Bah. What is the Lady's name then?"

"Erika." I replied, "As you rightly know". I was just about keeping my temper.

"There you are then." He declared and added. "Emperor" With an insulting scoff. Erika laughed at Aiken Drum's simple logic.

"You are an idiot." I shouted at Aiken Drum who still stood above me trying to look menacing and intimidate me with his stupid staff. I turned my attention to the mulluks in an attempt to keep my temper from erupting and my tanto to remain in its scabbard. I noticed a quick move from the side of my eye.

"Smite!" The old man shouted and smacked the side of my head with the foot end of his staff.

I opened my eyes to find myself lying on my back in the dirt. Erika was beside me cradling my head in her arms and tending to my head. Two of the LandNisse guard had leapt off their angors, they stood on the backs of the wagon mulluks, their bows stretched, ebony arrows pointed at the old man. Still mounted on his angor, Captain Commander L'Ussler held his long elvin rapier blade at the old man's chest. He was still sat in the wagon, I was sure another blade was held to his back.

I reached up to feel the goose egg of a lump forming above my right ear. "Ouch! That hurts." I exclaimed. My vision not yet quite clear enough to stand. What happened?" I asked, still trying to focus.

"Aiken Drum smitted you." Erika replied, her lips tight to stifle her laugh.

"Very funny! He could have killed me!"

"He nearly did. That was a long fall off that wagon. You were very lucky you landed on your head." Erika burst out laughing.

I touched the goose egg lump again.

"Ouch! That hurts. Aren't you going to magic it away?"

"No."

"What?"

"No."

"Why the hell not? It bloody hurts like hell!"

"We shall call it a lesson in manners and respect for your elders." Erika scolded.

I scrambled to my feet still a bit woozy. Two outriders galloped back to the wagon trail on their fast and sleek angors. They looked puzzled and wary at the scenario before them.

"Report." Waccaar ordered.

"Milady. We have checked the campsite for tonight. It is three miles hence; there is one dwarfen family there. It is quiet."

"Excellent." Erika Replied. "Make your report to your captain." She added then turned to me. "With your permission Emperor of all the world." Erika smiled at me.

"Not you as well." I complained, as I nursed the lump on the side of my head.

"Well, I think you deserve it. You should have more respect for your elders."

I pulled Erika to one side. "Look Erika, he has robbed us of seven gold pieces, enough to buy a wagon and four, feed for a year and all of his possessions ten times over. And he gets a free ride to Lugon City."

"It is only three miles to the camp." She tenderly touched the lump on the side of my head. "If you cannot manage it I can get one of the guards to drive. Maybe Aiken Drum would help us."

Held at sword and arrow point, Aiken Drum doffed his floppy hat and with a flourish of his patchwork cloak, he presented a leg and bowed like a high lord.

"I would be delighted to help the boy, your majesty."

"Milady will do kind sir."

The peddler bowed once more. "Milady." He agreed.

"I think he knows you are the Princess Royal," I whispered into Erika's ear.

"Did I not tell him I am Princess Erika Nisse?"

"Yes but you could be any Erika. Not necessarily the Princess Erika Nisse."

"That is not possible." Erika looked puzzled that I did not understand.

"Why?" I asked confused at her request.

"Erika is the princess's name."

"Yes I know that. So?"

"So that is why I have taken the name Lorna Sissan. I cannot be called Erika as well as the Princess Royal."

"So can't you just be some other Erika?"

"No Jon. Only the first princess; the Princess Royal can be called Erika. No other nisse or any other person living on nisse land or under the Emperor Kings protection can be called Erika."

"Like nobody else at all?" I asked, amazed at this revelation.

"Nobody subject to the nisse crown is called Erika except me."

"So what if someone called Erika moved onto nisse land?"

"Well if they wished to remain on the land then in accordance with nisse common law, they would have nine months to choose a new name."

"And if they don't?"

"First they are removed from nisse land and all possessions are forfeit to the crown." Erika answered casually.

"And if they return."

"The person named Erika is executed as well as any who would call her by that name."

"No way!"

"Way" Erika nodded her head.

"Are you telling me the nisse would execute someone, no, murder someone just because they had the same name as you?"

"That is how it is. How it always has been." Erika stated rather flatly and turned her back on me. I knew she did not want me to broach the subject again.

"Shall I drive Milady? I am an excellent driver, far better than that boy." Aiken Drum pointed down at me from his perch atop the wagon. He picked up the reins and the mulluks, feeling the movement of the reins, shambled forward. Aiken Drum lost his footing and fell over the bench and into the back of the wagon. Captain Commander L'Ussler grabbed the reins to the mulluks and still mounted upon his angor, he brought the mulluks to a standstill. It was a fine show of angor control and I doubted many of our cavalry soldiers could match that skill.

Chapter 33

The angor mounted outrider pointed into the forest to the right and one by one, we turned our lumbering mulluks from the arrow straight dwarfen road and onto the narrow forest trail. I looked around at the nearness of the trees. Our wagons clearly overlapped the sides of the well-worn trail. Branches slid across the thick canvas sides to the wagons.

"Do you think this trail transgresses fae law?" I asked, worried that the bulk of the wagons would breach the neutrality of the forest path and open us up for an attack.

"No, we will be safe here." Erika replied to ease my mind.

"Yes, I will protect you boy, and this fair lady." Aiken Drum chipped in and I sighed in exasperation.

"Do you want I should smite you again?" Aiken Drum threatened.

"That was the first and the last time Aiken Drum." I dismissed his threat with one of my own.

"Did you just threaten me? You did! You just threatened me!" Aiken Drum leaned away from me and into Erika and I knew he did it to wind me up. "Milady you heard him did you not?" He asked, his dirty cheek resting on Erika's delicate bare shoulder. Hidden from Erika's view he smirked a gap toothed grin at me.

"Jon?" Erika warned. I said nothing and concentrated on following the wagon in front. Overhanging branches swept along the side of the wagon and I worried that we had no outriders either side of us until I saw Captain Commander L'Ussler and his LandNisse guard slipping through the close set tree trunks, skipping over the undergrowth and leaping over felled branches. Very few of the dangers of the deep forest would challenge a pack of angors.

The sleek fur of the bipedal angors shimmered in the dappled sunlight. The LandNisse's mastery of their charges had no equal; they looked like two symbiotic life forms moving naturally as one. They swept through the forest ranging far and near and I knew we would be safe from any surprise attack. The manner in which the LandNisse handled their mounts proved to me that they would be a match for any troll let alone a gnome attack. Base animals without abstract thought cannot fall to gnomish or goblin dream weaving and they would not be distracted by phantoms as I was last night. They would only see attacking gnomes or goblins.

The angors were battle beasts and fought just as fiercely as their riders. Their long snouts split with a maw from earlobe to earlobe lined with razor sharp teeth, the points would rend the thickest of hides, and a pack of angors were known to take down the massive Triceratops, even the mighty Tyrannosaurs Rex would fall to an attack of a pack of angors. Their small arms with three fingered hands, and their massive legs ending in three toed clawed feet tipped with deadly talons and prehensile whip like tails, were their natural weapons, which they used well. I have seen our own angors rip the belly out of a troll. Lizard like but covered in sleek black fur, they move with the grace of a cat and the power of a buffalo.

Atop an angor, the rider carried either a long spear not unlike the trollish Yari, or a long sword to engage the enemy. Some of our mounted guards carried lances favoured for fighting trolls. A few of our LandNisse were archers and their elvin recurved bows shot thin black arrows, the white fletching allowing the archer to guide the enchanted arrow to its target by sight alone. Nisse archers, like their elvin cousins, rarely missed their targets.

My scorpion hung in its holster formed out of the chameleon suit to hold the weapon. Now and again, I would finger the handle to feel the comforting weight of the pistol. No one except Erika and I knew of the scorpions power and I kept it that way. It was our unfair advantage.

Soon enough we turned off the forest trail onto another short track that led through an opening in a mound that gave access to the camp clearing. This was not a natural clearing. A lot of work went into this camp. There were many like this dotted all over Europa, some more sophisticated than others and this one looked like one of the better ones.

No, it was not by chance that the wagons fitted snugly through the trees, this was a dwarfen-constructed camp. Roughly circular in shape, it was located in a natural depression and an earthen mound ringed the clearing to give privacy and indicate the boundary within which the First Fae Law of the first Council of the twelve original titans demanded neutrality. A traveller could not be attacked nor tempted into the deep woods while they remained on the forest trails or in these camp clearings. Anyone who wandered away from the neutral tracks and clearings were fair game for those that preyed on others and there were many on Sol that did.

Camps such as these were known as Waystops where travellers individual or in groups, on a quest or like us, a merchant's wagon train, could find shelter from the night and the dangers that lurked in the shadows of the night forest. A fresh stream meandered through the camp and on closer inspection, I could see that the river was manmade to provide water and flush the Jakes that lay downstream where the river left the camp. In the centre of the camp was a well-used fire pit with a tripod and roasting spit. Small Wayhuts dotted the camp; they were rustic, not much bigger than a garden shed with an overhanging porch that allowed a traveller to sit and enjoy the night even in inclement weather. They were identical to those we used on our walk to Copperstone city. Commonly known as Wayhuts, most contained a set of triple bunk beds a small metal wood burning stove and a little further room to move about. All Wayhuts contained flint and steel to light a fire and essential rations to feed a lost soul as standard. These little cabins dotted around the camp all contained the same. The Wayhut would provide a weary traveller somewhere to warm and rest in safety and comfort and allow a night's rest off the cold ground. Tradition demanded that they were treated with respect. While they may be just a night's stay for one set of travellers, they may be lifesavers for the next wandering souls.

About half a mile along the main forest road where we turned onto the forest trail, there was a dwarfen toll bridge and a company of dwarfen warriors that replenished this camp and watched over it and the surrounding countryside. When the guard changed, a patrol would travel to the camp and restock the Wayhuts, chop wood for the central woodpile if needed and check on traveller's wellbeing that stayed at the camp.

Our tolls paid to cross the fortified bridge paid their wages and financed the upkeep of the camp. The camp, as all camps, was free to use with the understanding that the site was left as it was found and to take away only that which was needed. As lives depended on these camps, hefty and almost draconian punishments were meted out for abuse of camp privileges.

Near the fire pit was a well-stocked mini Dutch barn, cut and seasoned wood neatly piled to the roof. There were piles of stacked dried turf briquettes cut from a nearby bog. The LandNisse guard set about dismounting and tying off their angors well away from the centre of the camp.

Already in the camp, a family of dwarfen, parents, grandparents and three young children were already camped to one side of the clearing. They gave us friendly waves as we circled our wagons for the night. In the custom of the Wayfarer camps, they helped us unhook the mulluks from the wagons and settle the shaggy beasts safely away from the angor corral. They, like us, wisely left the angors to their own riders. In turn, as the larger party, we were obliged to invite the dwarfen family to a hot evening meal once the LandNisse guard had the main fire going. Two of the guard Valder and Kaia experienced hunters were dispatched to hunt the small roe like deer, common in the area. We had fresh meat preserved in enchanted chests and some of the wagon drivers prepared some of this meat for roasting. Even before the packed meat was prepared, Valder and Kaia, returned with three of the little deer, we had a veritable feast that night. It was our obligation to provide protection for the family as well as providing the evening meal.

Erika and I were happy with our vegetable dinner. The LandNisse guard, the dwarfen family and unsurprisingly Aiken Drum were all meat eaters. It was not long before the fires glowed and crackled in the falling light of evening. The smell of wood smoke and aromas of roasting meat and vegetables filled the twilight air. By the time of true nightfall, we had a cosy central campfire with a few satellite fires, we all ate our supper around the main fire on the tables and chairs provided.

We could tell that elvin and nisse travellers used the camp quite often; they left many different examples of elvin and nisse sung wood; from the basic minimalist table slabs to the ornate and sometimes whimsical sculpted furniture. It looked as if each elvin or nisse visitor to the camp tried to out-sing the previous visitor's attempts.

I sat on an elvin sung long bench that I would be proud to have in my own living quarters. The dwarfen kids sat upon stools that were sculptures of forest animals, so detailed that they looked like real animals magically changed into wood. With my experiences of enchanted troll Yari's, Erika had to reassure me that they were indeed actual sculptures and not the aforesaid enchanted beasts.

I spied near the shadows of the mound that marked the boundary of the camp, a sculpture of a sleek cat like animal positioned off on its own and facing the camp. Its head was down below its shoulders, I supposed to make the stool. It was a ways off and not likely to be used by anyone. I walked over to it to collect it to add to our eclectic selection of outdoor furniture and sculptures. I got to within ten feet of the sculpture when it turned and bolted towards the surrounding mound.

I drew my katana in a purely reflex action to the sudden unexpected move; at the sound of drawn steel, the cat creature turned at the top of the mound and roared, showing its bright white teeth, startling against its black face. Three of the LandNisse guard were immediately by my side. Yori and Folke with drawn rapier swords and the third with a black arrow notched in her recurved bow, Kaia stood ready to drop the animal.

"SkyggenKat." Yori, the younger nisse said. "They are lone beasts and usually avoid contact. They will not attack unless threatened."

"I thought it was one of the bloody sculptures!" I whispered.

"Well fortunate for you my Lord that you did not try to pick the beast up." Yori replied with a smile. I smiled back and nodded agreement but in reality that was just what I was about to do!

"Jon. Please just Jon." I asked for what I thought was the one hundredth time.

"Yes My Lord" They all replied and I knew they were going to ignore the princess's husband and escort yet again.

"Yori please take Folke and check the perimeter."

"I will take Kaia, if that is permissible my Lord." Yori made a shallow bow of respect. Folke bowed slightly the nisse custom to agree with such a proposal.

"It's Jon. Just Jon." I repeated.

"Yes, My Lord." Yori bowed his head in obedience once more. I knew he was going to ignore me again.

"Yes, take Kaia but check the perimeter out and not each other Okay?" I smiled. Kaia's face reddened in embarrassment but only a blind man would fail to notice the chemistry between the two and I spied those two exchanging kisses when they thought no one was looking.

I walked back to the campfire. The meal over, everyone was heading for bed. Some went to the Wayhuts while others chose to sleep in or under their own wagons. Habits of a lifetime are hard to break.

Erika dropped the tarpaulin of our wagon to provide some privacy and she had laid out our sleeping pads on the ground between the wheels.

"So where is Aiken Drum then?" I asked, looking around for the wizened old fool.

"He went to the jakes then he is taking that Wayhut over there." Erika replied as she helped two of the wagon drivers, Hanni and Sacha put away the supper dishes.

"I want to check on the guard before turning in." I lifted the trunk of clean dishes back onto the second wagon.

"Not too long." Erika smiled at me a smile that held a promise. I smiled back and walked away towards the perimeter, the opposite direction from the jakes. Once out of sight, I doubled back to catch the little man before he made the safety of his hut.

Neither bright Epona nor her lover dark Hekata had risen and the only light came from the stars and our lanterns. My enhanced sight was sharp and clear although lacking the colour range I enjoyed in the daytime. I heard Aiken Drum before I saw him. He came around one of the huts lantern in one hand and his staff in the other. I ducked back into the shadows and waited until he drew closer. I estimated that he would be by me in about 30seconds. When he did not show up, I peeked around the corner of the hut where I had secreted myself. Aiken Drum had changed direction and stood in the middle of an open space. For the first time since meeting him, I saw Aiken Drum put down his walking staff. He moved slightly away from the staff and took up a pose that looked similar to a Ti Chi stance.

He began a series of slow controlled moves rather like Ti Chi only a little faster and more flowing. I could tell from the way he moved that he was well versed in this exercise regime. If it were not for the fact that this routine was executed by an absurd, deceitful joke of a filthy peddler, I would ask him to teach me the form. As I settled down to watch him I noticed that his kata was very similar to the one Erika performed every morning. At the end, Aiken Drum did a cartwheel picking up his staff as he went. With staff in hand, he began another kata, again fluid and controlled. He moved from form to form with a fluid grace that I had to reluctantly accept as being executed with expertise. He has some mastery of martial arts and I would need to be more careful approaching him as planned. I watched Aiken Drum perform his katas for about thirty minutes until he was finished. By this time, I had shifted from the shadows of one hut to another to put myself between Aiken Drum and the hut he had chosen. As he made his way towards me, I slowly withdrew my katana. I wished my chameleon suit to cover all of my body and the sword. I willed myself invisible, the light bent around me in the fabric.

I stood motionless as Aiken Drum walked past totally engrossed in the conversation he was having with himself. He froze when he felt the end of my blade rest upon his shoulder, the tip pressed against the flesh of his scrawny neck.

"What do you want Jon Raine?" The old man asked of the dark shadows that concealed me. I wished my chameleon suit back to the brown and green nisse forest garb I wore to match the others in the wagon train, the fabric retreated up the blade to expose the bright metal.

"For a start how did you know it was me?"

"An easy answer. Two things, one, I could smell you and two, who else except you and that L'Ussler would put a blade to my throat?" Aiken Drum replied moving nothing but his mouth. With my blade resting on his shoulder I should have felt him trembling, I did not.

"You are not afraid of me. Why not?" I asked, puzzled at the lack of fear in the old man.

"If you try to kill me I will smite you again with my staff." Aiken Drum threatened, lifting his staff as if to emphasise the point.

"Over there." I indicated to a couple of chairs sitting on the small porch in front of the Wayhut Aiken Drum had chosen to sleep in. "And try not to smite me while we get there." I smiled at my own jest.

The old man shuffled to one of the chairs whilst I took the other. We sat in silence for a short while. Neither of the moons Epona or Hekata had risen and all was still very dark, the camp lanterns and fires cast flickering shadows against the mound and tree line that surrounded us.

We listened to the camp settle for the night. I caught site of Hocking and Valder moving silently along the edge of the mound. They stayed within the shadows like the seasoned hunters they were. Vigilant, they spotted us sitting in the shadows of the little porch. Hocking had one of his black arrows notched to his recurved bow, while Valder carried his halberd under his arm with the blade in front, low to the ground. Both wore long thin nisse swords.

Valder lifted his halberd in a wave to acknowledge us while Hocking raised his bow a little. I waved back and the little man raised his staff slightly to wave back.

"Do you realise old man that the last time you hit me with that staff of yours, it was a lucky shot and you would be wise to understand that it was the last time you will do that." I warned, still looking out at the stars.

"Bah! You think I cannot defeat you boy. I am the greatest warrior in the whole world and I can smite you when I like!" Aiken Drum protested but did nothing to prove the point.

"Yeah, Yeah, and you have an army and a big palace and a whole village to command." I laughed. "And you spend your time travelling dusty roads on foot, from village to village sharpening peasant's knives and scissors and mending pots and pans."

"I did not say I owned a great big palace." Aiken Drum waved his arms dismissively.

"At last the truth!" I exclaimed.

Aiken Drum shot me an icy stare. "It's a mansion, not a palace." He corrected me.

"Look Aiken Drum, I am not interested in your idiotic boasts. Believe what you like but don't expect us to believe your tall tales."

"Ha! Erika believes them and... And they aren't tall tales." Aiken Drum protested and folded his arms around his staff in a huff.

"Look old man..."

"Aiken Drum!"

Okay... Aiken Drum, Erika is being nice to you and she humours your eccentricities. Only the Gods and Erika know why!" I sighed and lifted my hands in mock supplication; I made the sign of the hammer in the air before me.

"Do not mock the Gods for the Gods will not be mocked." Aiken Drum warned by quoting a passage from one of the elvin holy texts, the Book of the Beginnings.

"She is only being nice to you Aiken Drum." I repeated.

"No she is not. I mean, yes, she is being nice but she is always nice. Erika knows I am the first warrior of Sol and the finest warrior and swordsman in all of the world." Aiken Drum declared and went on without stopping for breath. "And... and she has visited my mansion many times and she has inspected my soldiers and she is respected and loved by all that dwell in my village and lands around."

"Stop! Do you not realise that all I have to do is ask Erika and your foolish boasts will be exposed for what they are, just so many tall tales."

Aiken Drum was silent; he hung his head, his eyes downcast. I realised that I had eventually got through to him. I had at last pierced his inflated delusions. He lifted his eyes to me and I could see the sadness moisten his eyes even in the shadowed darkness.

"They aren't tall tales. They are the truth." He pleaded. A frail old man sitting in the shadows. Wasted and aged in the twilight of his own life, he was not long from the long cold sleep that the Ferryman brings. I realised that these stories, these delusions he rambled on about, were his reality and his bright shining stars in the evening of his life. He had told these faerie stories so many times that he believed them himself. Who was I to rob a silly old man his brief view of happiness in his sad life. I was sure the stories he prattled out entertained the peasants and earned him a sleeping pallet in some wayfarer's inn on a cold and unpleasant night.

"Alright Aiken Drum, maybe there is some truth to your tales." I said in spite of myself. I felt that if I challenged him any further I would break this old man's spirit and Erika would not speak to me for months, she may even withhold her favours, as the elvin say and that would be a bitter hardship, I had no wish to fulfil.

I stood from my chair and Aiken Drum filled a long stemmed corn pipe with a wad of moist tobacco from his leather tobacco bag. He placed his finger on the pipe and sucked at the long stem. The tobacco glowed in the shadowed porch and Aiken Drum blew white tobacco smoke into the still night air.

"Saxicoline magic! Troll magic! How did you do that?" I demanded, now a little wary that this old man had a degree of magic about him.

"It is only called Saxicoline magic when trolls perform it. When the fae use the same magic it is called Saxitile magic, it is the same magic but a small difference in description; it prevents the offended troll from ripping your head off." Aiken Drum lifted a warning finger and puffed another cloud of the sweet smelling smoke. "A small important difference. Yes, I learn many things in my humble travels through the villages. Many things indeed." Aiken Drum warned again as if I should be wary of him.

"Erika, how did you know her name before anyone told you it?" I pressed him.

"I told you. Princess Erika and her father the Emperor King have visited me many times." Aiken Drum spoke to me as if I were a simpleton.

"Okay Aiken Drum." I decided to try another tact. "Let's assume you had not known her before."

"Any child with one eye in his head could work it out!"

"How so?"

"As I have said, I travel from village to village, village to town, town to town, city..."

"Yes, yes, so you travel a lot." I interrupted his travel itinerary recital.

"The Gods gave me two ears and only one mouth and I take that as a divine warning to listen twice as much as I speak! It is not only the nisse villages that are full of the news of the princess's abduction." Aiken Drum leaned forward conspiratively. "The stories say that a Euroforce band of strong-arm cutthroat Snigmorder, led by a man called Theodore 'Dixie' Dixon..."

'Theodore!' I had to remember that.

"... Abducted the Princess just before the Waybomb exploded. They say that the Princess attacked a certain Lieutenant Jon Raine from this band of cutthroats just before the explosion." Aiken Drum eyed me suspiciously. "The Waybomb blew many humans and fae away and injured hundreds more caught in the explosion."

"Do you know who is dead and who survived?" I asked anxiously.

"Those blown away would not be present so none would see which are hurt and which are not. Among the missing, are the Princess Royal, her Lady Sommerfugl and escort. Prince Uffe Jægerblod..."

"Prince Jægerblod?" I interrupted, the facts I discovered coming from another independent source cemented the knowledge I already knew.

"Yes. Prince Uffe is first son to the troll king and heir to the throne of the trollish nations. And Sareal the Princess's SkyggenNisse Captain Commander"

"The lying, scheming...!"

"It was a despicable act Lieutenant Jon Raine." Aiken Drum stated as if he was uncovering a crime and the criminal who committed it.

"We had nothing to do with the bomb or the attack. We were the ones being attacked." I protested.

"If that is so then why did Princess Erika attack you?" Aiken Drum puzzled.

"You make the mistake that she was attacking me."

"What else would she be doing?"

"Saving my life." I replied flatly.

"Aha so you are this Jon Raine and the Lady is Princess Erika!"

I did not reply.

"Your silence speaks volumes." Aiken Drum puffed another sweet smelling smoke cloud. He took the pipe from his mouth and pointed the stem at me.

"And you are not too difficult to work out. Your black skin and the skin of the Princess are both exactly the same shade. Which is either a rare coincidence or you both conceived an infant with other partners at exactly the same time. You are from Earth Prime and while it is not unheard of to see one out here in the back of beyond, it is a very rare occasion that it happens. Yes, any child with one eye that looked twice could easily spot you and your fair lady wife." Aiken Drum sneered.

"Okay Aiken Drum. We take you to Lugon city and our word is fulfilled. We drop you off outside the main gates and I had better never see you ever again. If I find that you have uttered one word, a single word into any ear, I will personally hunt you down and take your own ears, then I will take your life. Do I make myself clear?"

Epona had shown her face at last and the old man's eyes glistened in her silvery light.

"I hear your words." Aiken Drum replied, formally accepting my warning, and I felt ashamed that I had just threatened the life of a frail old man. I had no choice other than to put him to the sword, I did think about it but I am no Snigmorder, I had not sunk that low, not yet anyway.

"We understand each other?" I asked. He nodded his head in silence his frail old eyes watching Epona rise from behind the treetops.

"Then I will bid you goodnight Aiken Drum for the last time. We part company at Lugon city."

"Yes. We part company when we reach Lugon." The old man agreed without taking his eyes from the bright rising moon.

I left the old man to his own thoughts and went to seek the warm and welcoming arms of my wife and lover.

Chapter 34

Morning found us in chaos. Four members of the eight driver pairs were stricken with dysentery like symptoms. Erika, The dwarfen family, the LandNisse guard and Aiken Drum were, like me, unaffected. Erika and the dwarfen women with the women drivers Sacha, Panilla and Ranveg tended the sick; they picked ginger and cinnamon, which they mixed with charcoal from the fire to make a stomach sedative they brewed medicinal herbs on the restocked campfire.

"My Lord, a word." Captain Commander L'Ussler whispered in my ear and motioned me aside.

"Captain?"

"Please my lord. I would be honoured if you would call me Waccaar."

"Very well Waccaar. I would be pleased of you would call me Jon."

Waccaar L'Ussler gave me a surprised look only equalled by the look he gave Erika when she promoted him from captain to captain commander of the royal guard, from that moment on he could officially address himself as a RiNisse, a royal nisse."

Waccaar bowed his head and spoke softly. "I would be honoured... Jon."

"Well Waccaar, speak your thoughts."

"The way I see it, we may have a spy in our camp. Maybe the dwarfen or the old man, maybe one of the LandNisse guard, may the Gods spare us." He made the formal supplication of the hammer in the air. "The drivers have been poisoned, and if not for Princess Erika they would be in a very bad way now." Waccaar took a deep breath as if he found it hard to speak the words. People he had responsibility for had been poisoned. This after the Snigmorder attack on Copperstone city, Waccaar seemed unsure of himself. He took a deep breath and went on.

"The fae law of neutrality is broken in this camp. This is a very serious matter. I have never known the fae law of neutrality ever to be broken before. It will take one of the First

Council of the Twelve to rededicate this space to neutrality again. Maybe even Rhea herself will come here."

"Rhea, she is one of your deities. Is she not?"

"She is a Titan and one of the Twelve Titans of the First Council. This is very bad." Waccaar repeated shaking his head in worry.

"I understand. I had similar suspicions myself, Waccaar."

"My lord... Jon, I think it is of the highest importance that we get you and Princess Erika to Lugon city and the safety of the dwarfen court. There, the Princess Royal can request a larger force to escort you to the safety of the nisse armies moving south."

I considered Waccaar's words for a moment trying to think of alternatives to our problem that avoided splitting us up. I felt as if I had an uncomfortable itch in the back of my mind. Not a doubt, but a suspicion. The problem was that I did not know what I was suspicious about. I knew something was not right.

"You are saying we should leave the other wagons behind? Split our forces?"

"It would be but for a day Jon. We split my Guard and leave five of them with the stricken drivers. They are all handpicked LandNisse guard. The six remaining Guard including myself would escort you and the Princess to Lugon city and with you two in the safety of Prince Hjlink's court we would return with a greater force to relieve those left behind. We could also warn the dwarfen legion at the toll bridge and they could offer temporary security until our return."

"What if you send a smaller dispatch to Lugon city and return with the greater force?" I asked considering alternatives.

"The enemy know we are here. This attack proves it so. If the Princess were not with us, it would take us days to get a royal audience maybe even never. No one in Lugon knows of my royal promotion they would see me as a pretentious country bumpkin. A lower ranking military officer may not see the urgency of my claims and not send sufficient force to see us safely to Lugon."

"I see," I replied.

The Captain Commander must have understood my hesitation as doubt. "Jon it is the best way to relieve the sick and get you two to safety." He admonished. "Also, time is of the essence and I would be happier that the Princess was away from the threat of this unknown assassin."

"Agreed." I nodded my assent.

"The neutrality of the camp is broken and will remain so until one of the First Council of the twelve travels here to rededicate it. I pity the people of this assassin or assassins when the Titans find out who they are."

"A Titan would travel here." I whispered in disbelief. The First Council of the Twelve always referred to but never seen by human eyes. They are the first twelve Titans, brothers and sisters to the first cherubim, and said to have lived many eons before the worlds were made. Memory of them passed down through the millennia years of civilisation by story and legend on both Sol and Earth Prime.

* * *

Leaving behind the rest of the wagons, Erika and I with Aiken Drum, Waccaar L'Ussler with six of the nisse guard, Yori, Folke, Laus, Hocking and Sakso, left with our wagon and the six nisse guard mounted on their angors. Yori and Laus carried long halberds and rode in front of the wagon team of huffing mulluks, their breaths misting against the chill of the morning. Folke and Hocking carried their nisse made recurved bows across their saddles, each had a black enchanted arrow notched to the bowstring and rested the bow against their thighs. They held both reins in one hand and guided the angors mostly with their knees.

Waccaar and Sakso behind the wagon carried a further set of arrow notched bows. I was happier that we had a compliment of six nisse to guard one wagon and they could pay closer attention to just it and nothing else.

We made for Lugon city and our first stop was the fortified toll bridge and the dwarfen legion there. Aiken Drum insisted on taking his previous position between Erika and me, I felt he had done it just to spite me again. I did not rise to his bait and allowed myself some comfort in knowing we would be rid of this old fool when we arrived in Lugon city. I had the Princess's safety to think of. As far as we knew the gnome Snigmorder were still watching the young nisse couple Erika glamoured with a doppelganger spell to make them look like us, and the gnomes were still behind us watching the new nisse city of Copperstone. We hoped that there was no communication between the poisoner and the Snigmorder on our trail.

Twenty minutes from leaving the camp, we were back on the neutral ground of the main forest trail. I felt uneasy that the neutrality of the camp clearing had been breached, but Erika and Waccaar seemed to be happy that the same would not happen on the forest road. About half a mile along the arrow straight road, we could see the towers of the toll bridge and there we would find some relief for the stranded Wagoner's back in camp. All dwarfen roads were arrow straight. The first and last time I asked a dwarf why, he looked at me as if I was a fool and he firmly told me that the shortest distance between two places was a straight line. I found no argument in that.

The forest road we travelled led gently down to a dip then upwards to the toll bridge. Where the land rose and fell like this, the road followed such gentle differences, however when faced with a hill or mountain the path was cut from the land by a tunnel or a narrow cut through the obstacle. Such places were easily defended with dwarfen carved caves high up to allow archers to fire down arrows, drop rocks or burning oil on any foe that dared to attack a dwarfen outpost. In such cuts and tunnels, dwarfen fortified the passages. Usually there were several heavy wooden or rock hewn gateways through either a tunnel or narrow dwarfen made path, that could be closed and defended as required, and tolls demanded for passage. Their bridges were much the same and operated with at least one legion per bridge, path or tunnel.

As the day warmed but far from the heat of midday we reached the toll bridge. The barriers down, we were met by four dwarfen military. They all wore the black boots, grey breeches and olive drab tunic, which were the uniform of the dwarfen military. Two wore the black belt and braces of the regular soldier, just as I was in the Euroforce army of Earth Prime. One of the other two wore the green belt and braces of the dwarfen provost while the last wore white belt and braces indicating him as an official and I suppose could be understood to be their customs officials.

Waccaar greeted the dwarf in white in his native tongue, to me it sounded Italian. The dwarf raised his fist to his white hat to salute the Waccaar then rushed into the guardhouse. The guards and the provost stayed behind the barrier, they kept the six angors on the other side. Even mounted and controlled by its rider, one did not want to venture anywhere close to these angors.

In a moment, the customs official came back out and asked if we would accompany him inside to speak with the guard commander. I jumped down from the wagon while Erika alighted after me. She turned to help Aiken Drum down to come with us.

"Does he have to come?" I whispered in Erika's ear.

"Bah! And why not?" The old man complained. I forgot about his Nymphan ears.

Erika smiled and said. "He comes to protect us all." With that comment, the old man grinned and puffed out his chest. Erika used her winning ways on the old man and he followed her around like an old obedient hound. I let it go as I could only see him making a lot of distracting noise when we needed to get help to our own people and get across the bridge as quickly as possible.

We walked with the dwarfen official to a thick, metal studded wooden door that stood ajar. He bowed slightly and bade us enter. We walked into the large guardroom. Inside there was a large black highly polished guard commanders table, it shone like obsidian. Seated behind the table was the guard commander himself, we could see his reflection in the tabletop. To his right was seated a dwarf dressed in military uniform but all in black, the uniform of the SkyggenDwarf, their elite fighting warriors. Upon his breast, he wore the flame of the legendary Blademasters of Sol. This man was a formidable warrior and at my best with my heightened speed and senses, I would be a poor match for him.

At the sight of us, the SkyggenDwarf jumped to his feet in what seemed like high alert. I placed my hand on my katana in preparation for some sort of confrontation but as quick as he jumped up he relaxed and smiled an easy smile, such a smile I would believe many a fae, goblin, ogre and troll looked upon just before they died. The guard commander looked puzzled at the SkyggenDwarf's reaction but he quickly and professionally recovered to bid us welcome.

Erika and I took the two chairs in front of the large black table. The SkyggenDwarf stood again and brought his chair around for Aiken Drum to sit upon, at the time I was impressed with this elite officer's respect for the elderly. Waccaar stood guard behind the Princess; he had not worn the official sash of the RiNisse guard since before we set out from his village and he presented himself simply as captain of the wagon guard.

Waccaar introduced Erika as Lorna Sissan the wagon merchantwoman and mistress of the wagon train. The Guard Commander knew the real Mistress Sisson well and he passed his best wishes to her through her supposed niece Lorna Sisson. Waccaar introduced me as her escort and confidant, otherwise known as lover, Aiken Drum was the clerk of the caravan.

We learned the names of the guard commander and the man in black after which our first action was to ask for assistance for our stricken companions. When the request was heard and the appropriate amount of gold handed over, a file of twenty-five mounted heavy dwarfen cavalry plus medical aid was immediately dispatched to our companions, it was a highly organised and efficient exercise and I felt comforted that these soldiers and medics were going to the aid of our loyal companions. They looked like they were worth every gold piece we paid for them.

The guard commander asked if we needed additional security to Lugon city but Erika played the canny wagon mistress and suggested we did not have the necessary gold to request such a service. Out of concern, the guard commander offered the escort free as one of the patrols was due to go back to Lugon City in the morning. Waccaar, Aiken Drum and Erika did not want any more attention paid to our little band and a detachment of dwarfen cavalry, they thought, would be an unwelcome addition to our procession. I disagreed; I thought we needed any assistance we could muster. In war and combat, generally the surest way to win a fight is to attack first with superior numbers and overwhelming force. I believed we needed some overwhelming force at the time, and the dwarfen at the bridge fitted the bill exactly. I was out voted and we declined the offer of assistance.

After declining all help with our travel to Lugon city, the black clad SkyggenDwarf offered his sword, without fee, to accompany us, Erika politely declined his offer. I saw some sort of eye contact with Aiken Drum, and the SkyggenDwarf bowed in polite acquiescence and returned to lean against the wall beside the big black desk, a puzzling detail that brought a distrusting light upon the foolish old man again. Was Aiken Drum more than he presented himself to be? As a Rumpelstilzchen, I could not discount anything. Did he have anything to do with the poisoning at the camp? I would keep my eye on this old man. Even with the extra attention, the cavalry escort would cause, as a military man, I reluctantly agreed to this arrangement. I would have preferred all of the military help we could get for the last leg of the journey and we had plenty gold to pay forfeit.

Not long after the meeting with the Guard Commander and help dispatched to our caravan in the camp, we were through the toll bridge with all the necessary documents stamped and tolls paid. I sat in the wagon feeling as if I had missed something important.

Again, we followed an arrow straight road. So close to Lugon city these roads and highways were made from a solid concrete like substance, which made the burden on the mulluks easier and increased our own comfort. We were able to make good headway and in a few hours when the bright sun burned down on us we came to a narrow cliff sided passage cut through a steep set of hills. The road, straight as any dwarfen road, allowed us to see through the pass and onto the valley beyond. The valley was where Lugon city nestled. I believed us through the worst of the danger and after this path; we would have another three miles easy travelling to Lugon City and the help of the dwarfen High Council and Prince Hjlink.

Chapter 35

We entered into the pass with high spirits; the Snigmorder behind us, we had a clear view of our destination and the safety of the dwarfen royal court. We just passed one of the gigantic set of doors that could seal this passage in time of war when we first spotted the four gnome Snigmorder standing in our path. Four dark figures stood in the road to block our way. Their long thin bodies and long arms hanging from wide shoulders told us they were gnome Snigmorder, connected we were sure with the attack on Copperstone city. Each held their curved flat blades, one in each hand. I knew there would be as many if not more hiding amongst the rocks and crevices as standing there in the open before us.

"What do we do now?" Aiken Drum asked.

"We fight." I replied flatly and jumped down from my perch on the wagon. Erika was by my side her hand on the handle of that magical knife of hers. Captain L'Ussler came before us.

"Milady, please forgive us but there will be many Snigmorder hidden in the rocks and cliffs around. We cannot face them all."

"What are you saying Captain?" I demanded. He ignored me and addressed the Princess.

"Milady we are simple farmers and with wives and families. We cannot leave them fatherless even for our Princess Royal." Waccaar explained. He lied, I knew he lied; Waccaar L'Ussler was no poker player.

"I understand Captain." Erika replied, much gentler than I would have expected.

"Erika! They intend leaving us!" I exclaimed. "How could you L'Ussler!" I shouted at the man and moved forward. His angor snarled and snapped at me. "Don't leave us now, Captain." I pleaded. "We are a match for them with your angors. Without you, we will fail."

"I am sorry." Waccaar replied through gritted teeth.

"I know you are an honourable man Captain, do not do this." I pleaded again.

L'Ussler looked to his men who looked as stricken as I, then back to Erika. "Forgive us your majesty." L'Ussler said coldly, bowed and turned his angor to ride back past the wagon. His men reluctantly followed him; there was no mistaking the look of pain in their faces. I could not reconcile their cowardly present actions with their brave and courageous past.

"Come back you coward." I shouted after him. L'Ussler turned in his saddle his hand on his sword. I saw such a conflict in his countenance that I just could not work out his cowardly behaviour and his actions to leave us to a certain death, so close to our goal and place of safety. I could not understand that the rest of these soldiers left with him as well. I thought them friends with a shared conflict. I had gravely mistaken the character of the nisse and now I would pay the price in blood.

"I think we have a fight to go to." Erika spoke without taking her eyes off the gnome Snigmorder in front of the wagon.

"Aiken Drum, get in the back of the wagon and stay there." I ordered.

"Bah! No I will not!" He hissed back at me.

"Old Man, this is not time for argument." I shouted at the old fool.

"That is the first sensible thing I have heard you say so far today." Aiken Drum replied.

"Then go get out of here."

"And leave all my things behind in your wagon for these filthy gnomes to steal! They are as bad as you humans, stealing and breaking things." Aiken Drum replied. "No. I stay and fight. Who else is going to protect you?" he smiled up at me. At least I could not fault him his foolish bravery. These Snigmorder would gut him if he ran and I expected he wanted to face his end like Erika and I. Yes, I overestimated the nisse and underestimated this old romantic fool.

"Well Erika, I did not think it could end like this. You and I murdered on a lonely dust road." I smiled, accepting our fate.

"And me. And me murdered on the lonely dusty road as well?" Aiken Drum added excitedly.

"And you as well noble Aiken Drum." I added.

Erika smiled at me without replying. I put my hand under her chin and drew her to me. I kissed her lightly on the lips.

"Well at lease we go down fighting." I smiled and drew my katana and scorpion. The four gnomes raised their blades above their heads in a formal challenge of a duel. No assassin likes a fair fight and I believed their challenge was in the belief of a sure win. I raised my pistol to drop these four when Erika put her hand upon my wrist and lowered my pistol.

"Jon put that abomination of a weapon away. They have challenged us and we must reply according to ancient fae law."

"Erika, they out number us and there are the Gods know how many hidden in the rocks. We stand a fair chance with this pistol and none without it." I warned her.

"Nevertheless I forbid its use on Sol." Erika answered quietly.

I reluctantly holstered the pistol and drew my tanto in its stead. "A fight it is then." I agreed.

"Bah! I am fed up with all you love birds cooing and clucking. I will go and smite them myself!" Aiken Drum declared and walked off towards the waiting Snigmorder.

"No, Aiken Drum!" I shouted and went to go after him. Erika caught my arm and held me back.

"Let us see where this leads us." She said.

"Are you out of your pretty head woman?" I demanded.

"Do you really think you should speak to your princess like that? Erika replied.

"But he is only an old man. They will butcher him." I pleaded with her.

"Let us watch." She spoke without feeling and I could not fit her cold and calculating answer into any type of impression I had of her, not even the bratty teenager.

The gnomes looked at each other when they saw that we sent the old man and his staff to face them.

"Come you filthy beasts and I shall smite you with my staff." The old man shouted in defiance. The gnomes laughed thinking it some twisted jest. One of the gnomes stepped out to finish the old man off. Aiken Drum took up a fighting stance with his staff. I made to run to his aid but Erika caught my arm again.

"We watch and learn Jon Raine." She ordered.

The gnome came at the old man. The old man shouted "Smite!" and struck the side of the gnome's baldhead with his staff. The gnome went down in a heap. I looked askance at Erika and she smiled a knowing smile at me.

The other three Snigmorder looked at each other for a moment then as the assassins they are, they all rushed the old man at once.

"Smite, Wallop, Smite Ha Ha!" The old man shouted and all four gnomes lay on the ground. The old man leaned on his staff.

"Foolish little gnomes!" He cackled like a witch.

The four gnomes got to their feet and three more joined them from the rocks. They attacked as one.

"Bang, Wallop, Smash, Bonk, Wallop, Smite." The old man shouted and the gnomes fell in rapid succession.

Two gnomish arrows came at him from hidden archers. The old man swiped them out of the air as if he batted away an annoying fly. Four more arrows came quickly and not only did he swat them away but his spinning staff slapped one of the arrows into the shoulder of one of the Snigmorder getting up of the ground, the gnome fell and rolled in pain.

All Snigmorder stepped out of their hiding places. Six carried crossbows; they joined the six able-bodied gnomes, the wounded one slowly crawled away.

I stepped forward to go to the amazing old fool's aid but Erika caught my arm.

"Wait and learn Jon." Erika said again with unnerving calmness.

The Snigmorder surrounded the old man and carefully closed in on their prey. Aiken Drum stood his ground, his staff before him; he scanned his assailants ever watchful for the first attack.

The old man twisted the end of his staff and withdrew a long curved single edged blade cleverly concealed within the straight staff. A cross guard sprang out to complete the weapon and he brandished the sword before him the bright steel glinted in the noon day sun, along each side of the bright blade there were etched licks of flame. The Snigmorder froze gazing at the blade and to my utter amazement and disbelief; they bowed down to the crazy old man.

"What the hell?" I gasped.

"Aiken Drum is the High Blademaster of Sol." Erika smiled.

Words failed me. I looked at Erika and she smiled and nodded.

I looked at Aiken Drum with the Snigmorder arrayed around him. They laid all of their weapons on the ground then dropped on one knee, right fist to chest and left arm raised over their heads they jointly pleaded for mercy. Twelve trained assassins begging for mercy from a crazy old man.

"The slaughterers of the innocents deserve no mercy," The old man barked. "But it is nisse you murdered. For that, you may petition the nisse Emperor King Kennet. While he is far from here, his daughter the Princess Royal is but a few steps away." Aiken Drum called back to us. "Your Majesty, these Snigmorder seek mercy." He spat their name from his lips.

Erika took a few steps forward to make herself visible. I stepped to her side, my katana drawn and readied. Erika held her shoulders back and her head high in regal form. "They have assaulted the Royal Person, foully murdered my loyal subjects."

A dark angry shadow crossed Erika's face, and she added with a voice low and full of menace. "And did grievous harm to the Lady Sommerfugl." A tear of rage rolled down her ebony cheek. "High Blademaster, I request that you carry out the Emperor's will in this matter." She added.

"What's that?" I whispered into her ear keeping my eyes on the Snigmorder before us.

"Death to all Snigmorder." Erika called out, her royal decree echoed off the high walls around us as if the Gods repeated her words.

"The Emperors will be done." Aiken Drum spoke loud and clear.

The Snigmorder attacked immediately and in force in an effort to overrun Aiken Drum at once. They were assassins, highly skilled killing machines and death was their trade, not battles fought with any honour, just death by any means. I stepped forward to lend my blade to the battle. Erika caught my arm and spoke quietly.

"This battle is not for you. You would surely die." She stated as softly as a creeping black widow spider, her calmness caused me to take pause.

The moment the Snigmorder attacked, so Aiken Drum attacked in that same instant. His sword held high with both hands he darted forward in a blur and one gnome fell, cleaved from shoulder to navel. He fell with a sickening moist thwack as his viscera fell to the ground before him. As the gnome fell, Aiken Drum spun, withdrew his blade and cut across another's stomach in one fluid, lightning fast cut. To the normal eye, this would have happened in an instant, however with my enhanced vision I could barely keep up with the old man's killing sword moves. The Snigmorder moved with enhanced speed and years of training and experience. Aiken Drum made them look like clumsy children at swordplay, bloody swordplay. Each clash of blades rang out in the pass, so fast was the swordplay that the ringing sounded like an alarm bell. The Blademaster fell into a rapid succession of cuts and thrusts; I could see the sword forms from Aiken Drum's stick kata he performed the previous evening. These were not the muscle stretching slow controlled dance movements. In the fight, they appeared in an instant, and then moved from one form to the next, even before the armed assassin fell. Two Snigmorder attacked as one, one from the front all loud and distracting while the other attacked silently from the back. Aiken Drum reversed his sword, spun to parry the frontal attack, lay open the throat of the one behind and spun on to come back around to take the head clean from the shoulders of the frontal attacker. To normal eyes, this would have seemed to happen in an instant, too fast even for the enhanced Snigmorder.

In as many seconds as there were attackers, all lay in pools of their own dark blood. Some were not dead but badly wounded. Aiken Drum casually walked around hamstringing the wounded, he cleaned his blade on the cloak of the nearest dead gnome then sheathed his sword into his staff, a flick of his fingers and the cross guard folded forward to slip back into his innocuous looking staff.

There were groans of pain from the wounded but Aiken Drum ignored them. Erika later explained that it was beneath Aiken Drum to dispatch the wounded.

The old man waddled back to us with that gap-toothed grin on his brown wrinkled face.

"Did you see how I smitten them?" Aiken Drum asked Erika.

"My Lord Blademaster." Erika curtsied as gentle as a falling leaf before the old man; he reached out his hand, Erika took it in hers and touched the back of his hand to her forehead, a sign of respect only used between nisse family members.

"It has been too long Your Highness." Aiken Drum spoke as Erika returned to her feet. "You must give my regards to Kennet and tell him he has been away from his Blademasters for too long."

"I will relay your good wishes the next time I see my father, Nobel Sir."

"You call the Emperor King, Kennet?" I asked in amazement.

"Bah! It is his name isn't it?" Aiken Drum replied, he pointed a bony finger at me. "To you he is an Emperor and I can see from your skin that he is to be informed of a new son and grandchild. To me he is a student."

"Am I correct in understanding that you are the High Blademaster?" I asked Aiken Drum. I believed Erika's words. I just did not believe myself.

He nodded. "Now that pretence is over, I can tell you as I have told you before. I am the mightiest warrior in all of Sol." The old man declared and stood a little more erect.

"And what you said about a palace, all the servants and a village and an army?" I asked. Aiken Drum nodded affirmation.

"It is not so much a palace it is a large mansion with many servants. My village is a city and my school and those there, are my warrior army." Aiken Drum confirmed all of his boasts.

"Go on, ask Princess Erika." He added.

I looked to Erika and she simply nodded to affirm all his claims.

"So... So what do I call you?"

"You may call me Aiken Drum."

"Do I shake your hand or bow or what?"

"You are not an official royal prince yet so you are supposed to prostrate yourself and lie face down on the ground." Erika replied to my question.

"Really?" I asked.

"Really." She replied.

I took a deep breath, swallowed my pride, lay down on the dusty path, and put my face to the floor. "Am I doing it right?" I asked. They both burst out laughing.

I got to my feet and tried to dust down my face and clothes.

"Very funny." I snapped.

"The reply to the 'I Love NY' cap I believe." Erika suggested, still laughing along with Aiken Drum.

"Ha Ha" I laughed flatly.

"So young man, you may shake my hand." Aiken Drum volunteered, reaching out his gnarled hand. I reached to take it and he pulled it out of my way. I reached again and he moved his hand once more.

"What is the matter boy? You not fast enough?" Aiken Drum asked.

I tried to grab his hand but he moved it at the last moment. Faster and faster, we went, our hands became blurs. I used all of my enhanced speed and dexterity to catch the old man's hand but no matter how hard I tried, I could not catch him.

We stopped and I still had not captured his hand.

"Only a Blademaster can shake my hand." Aiken Drum smiled and for the first time since I set eyes on him, his smile was kindly.

"Come we have a long way to go." Aiken Drum declared.

"Lugon city is there." I pointed through the gorge and on over the savannah to the high-fortified outer walls barely three miles away.

"You are to visit my little city. Would you like that?" Aiken Drum asked as if I was a child.

"I need to get the Princess to safety." I stated as a matter of urgency.

"She is in a safe place. She is with me." Aiken Drum answered as if I should understand.

"But you are one man. Even you cannot guard the princess all of the time."

"Maybe not but I do not have to." Aiken Drum lifted his hand to his mouth and a booming call like a dragon coughing, rang out and echoed off the high stone cliffs. A moment later, I could hear the padded feet of galloping angor.

Captain Waccaar L'Ussler and his LandNisse guard galloped back up the ravine.

"Has this all been staged?" I asked Erika, anger boiling in my heart. "What part of all of this has been real?" I shouted and Erika flinched back from my raging outburst.

Waccaar moved his angor between the princess and me. The beast snapped and Waccaar held its head back with his reins.

"Lord Raine, please." Waccaar pleaded. It was one request I would grant. I did not think I could take on an angor let alone an experienced angor mounted soldier.

"Okay okay." I raised my hands to forestall any aggression. I paced from side to side, my fists at my waist and arms akimbo. After a few lengths of ten steps or more, I turned to Erika in a more controlled temper.

"Well? Explain yourself and all of this stupid playacting. Was the attack last night staged as well?" I demanded. I knew I had said too much even as the words left my mouth but as if an arrow loosed from a bow, once loosed, it cannot be taken back. There was genuine hurt in Erika's dark eyes. Her full red lips pouted as if she would burst into tears in a moment. Even Aiken Drum and Waccaar looked hurt. I glanced across to Yori mounted on his angor; a slight shake of his head told me my accusations were false.

Cries and groans still came from the wounded Snigmorder, all had either one or both hamstrings severed, some had tried to crawl away to the cover of the rocks on either side.

"Come, we have business to finish." Waccaar L'Ussler ordered his LandNisse guard. Although it may have been beneath the High Blademaster to finish the wounded, it was not beneath Captain L'Ussler and his LandNisse guard from Copperstone city. They cantered past us onto the killing field. Their angors began the grizzly work of savaging first the dead while the wounded watched in horror knowing their fate in a few short moments. The LandNisse guard set about their work with the relish only shared by the kin of the slayed innocent. Bloody cadavers were thrown into the air and caught between the sharp-toothed maws of the ever-hungry angors. The angors stripped the skulls clear of all meat; they even sucked the brains out of the skull. The nisse custom for these skulls is to raise them upon wooden poles with the Emperor King's royal colours as a warning to assassins and bandits alike. The savaged bodies left for the lizards or carrion birds that circled above.

    Erika and I stood in silence as we watched this grizzly spectacle. When the angors turned on the live Snigmorder, the screams filled the pass as they stripped their skulls and faces of all flesh before killing them.

Chapter 36

I kicked my boots into the dust of the road as if that would give me the courage to apologise.

"Erika...Look, I am so sorry." I began. Erika raised her hand.

"No Jon. It is I who should apologise." She said as she turned her head from the bloody display. "I meant to educate, not to deceive. The attack last night was as real as those bloody corpses before us. If I could implore the Gods to make it so and start all over again I would."

"No Erika, you should not think like that. As my mother used to say: If you are fed up starting over again then don't give up in the first place."

We fell to silence again until Malte returned with the poles he was ordered to obtain. He had taken one of the large wagon pulling mulluks and rode back to a copse of trees to cut twelve poles for the Snigmorder skulls. Duly cut and collected, he returned with the bundle strapped to the side of the big mulluk. Each pole was about six inches in diameter and just over 10 foot long. Yori and Hocking placed a stripped skull upon one of the poles along with the yellow and green ribbons of the Emperor King. The pole hoisted vertical, the pair called upon nisse magic and the poles sunk into the ground. They began the nisse song again, it sounded like the elvin and nisse song I had heard before, only this song, held both anger and sadness. I cannot tell you how I knew this except to say that the emotion seemed to be borne in the harmony of the enchanted haunting sound.

Roots pushed out of the base of the pole and into the ground while five slim branches sprouted out from under the base of the skull to grow up and around and back together to form a sung wooden cage. The branches fused together to form the pole once more. The skull would remain encased in the wooden cage of slim branches for years to come.

Folke and Laus repeated the same thing with the second pole, Sakso and Waccaar followed with the third then the task went back to Yori and Hocking to repeat the process until the last skull remained to be hoisted. It sat upon the dusty ground at the tip of the pole it would be mounted on. The LandNisse looked towards Erika and me.

"What's happening?" I whispered to Erika.

"It is for us to finish." She replied. I could do no magic and I regarded her "Us" in her reply to be the royal "We" meaning herself alone. I remained beside the wagon as Erika stepped towards the line of poles.

Aiken Drum poked me hard in my kidney with his staff. I stumbled forward.

"What's the matter boy? Are your ears made of fine Copperstone wool?" He jeered from behind, almost back to his irritating self. "Go on then, this is for the Princess and her Prince to complete." He added in a serious tone.

I walked quickly to Erika and caught up halfway to the line of poles. I took her hand in mine as we walked. Erika looked up at me.

"Jon, my love. This is the first time I do not have to do this alone."

"You will never have to do this alone again." I replied and squeezed her hand in reassurance. "And not very often I hope." I added.

At the pole, we placed our hands on it as the others had on the poles before us. Erika closed her eyes and with my hands around the pole, I closed my own eyes. The pole felt grainy, and the sides of my hands felt Erika's hands touching my own.

"Concentrate on my song and when you feel it inside you, sing it with me."

Erika began to hum the haunting cadence, I listened thinking she meant for me to pick up the tune and hum along with her. A warm tingling crept up my arms towards my body. I was about to pull away in a panic when Erika said.

"Be still Jon. My song fills your body. Allow it to flow through you and sing it with me.

As the tingling reached my chest, I felt that I knew the song well enough to hum along with Erika. Erika whispered.

"That is correct, now feel the song fill your body. Picture the other poles in your mind and will this pole to be the same. I thought the song sounded very like Uffe's song when it grew those Dogrose bushes that day I captured him. I followed Erika's lead and I fixed the picture of the pole in my mind. The tingling moved gently down my legs towards the ground. A picture of the Snigmorder skull caged in slender branches with Dogrose flowers all around came unbidden to my mind.

The tingling went to my feet and when it touched the ground an explosion of force gushed up my legs and burst into my chest. It felt like a torrent of hot boiling water surging through my body. Just like the force that I felt when we saved Little Lady Sommerfugl.

The force found vent through my arms and into the pole. I stood fixed like this for a long minute. I gripped onto the pole not knowing if I should let go or not. I knew Erika would guide me. I realised that I could not feel Erika's hands next to mine. The gushing force stopped as suddenly as it had started, I felt strangely empty yet strongly complete and I knew I wanted to feel that force within me again. I opened my eyes to look for Erika.

The first thing I noticed was the Dogrose flowers. They sprouted from every wooden thing around us. The wagon, the poles, the scrub bushes clinging to the sides of the rocky ravine walls, even the wood of the weapon handles the Nisse held. Their wooden breastplates and wooden helmets all covered in Dogrose flowers. About us fluttered thousands of colourful butterflies.

Waccaar took his helmet off to inspect it. I saw Erika sat a couple of paces away from the pole I still clutched. Her eyes upturned her mouth agape in amazement. I looked up at my pole and instead of the ten foot of pole I expected, I beheld a tree, it stood some thirty feet in height. The Snigmorder skull remained in its wooden cage at the same height as the others. I knew this tree would be how the others would look many years from now. Everywhere, the same Dogrose flowers I had seen Uffe grow.

'Crap what have I done?' I thought standing in this sea of white and yellow flowers. Thousands, if not millions of butterflies filling the air around us.

"Milady, these are Dogrose flowers." Waccaar spoke with amazement and fear in his voice. Erika was on her feet looking around with equal amazement and fear when Sakso raised his arm and pointed along the ravine towards Lugon City. Erika and Aiken Drum walked to the centre of the ravine to get a good look down the path. The Dogrose plants bloomed all along the ravine and out towards Lugon city only to stop at the city walls. I looked up at the macabre skulls housed in their nisse sung cages and wondered how many nisse taboos and sacred laws I had just broken.

I walked over to where Erika and Aiken Drum stood.

"Erika listen..." I started to explain. "This must have something to do with Uffe Jægerblod. These were the flowers I saw him grow when I captured him." I tried to explain. Erika quietened me by putting her delicate ebony fingers to my lips.

Aiken Drum turned to me. "Bah! You captured Uffe Jægerblod? You?" He laughed. "Listen to me. If Uffe Jægerblod did not want to be captured you would not even have seen him." Aiken Drum added and I did not doubt his word.

All of us looked towards Lugon city and back the way we came. Both ways lay under a carpet of the flowers. We could see one end at Lugon City but the other end stretched further than the eye could see.

Aiken Drum quoted in a solemn and reverent tone from one of the Elvin holy books. "From the book of Deliverance Chapter 132 verse 12: 'The Dark Messiah will come to deliver us from the Evil that treads his path. The sign of his coming shall be the Dogrose that leads from the Seat of Kings to the Seat of Kings.'"

"You think this is that sign?" Erika asked.

"Behold Lugon city. It housed the round table that the ancient kings used to meet around. Its shape made circular that everyone should sit at the table as equals. The king's table was then presented to the Emperor King on his two hundredth birthday and sits in his palace as the meeting place of the kings to this day. The meeting place is referred to as..."

"The Seat of the Kings." Erika finished knowing her father's Seelie court.

"I have no doubt where the other end of this path lies."

"At my father's palace?" Erika asked.

"I believe it to be so." Aiken Drum replied. "This is not the work of Uffe Jægerblod; this is far more than he could manage. No... This is the sign of the Black Messiah." Aiken Drum looked at me and I knew what he was getting at.

"The sign of Black Messiah? Can it be true?" Waccaar exclaimed looking about him at the sea of Dogrose.

"Evidently." Aiken Drum replied with what sounded like resigned inevitability. "Do we not have the proclaimed Black Messiah before us?" Aiken Drum raised his hand to indicate me. All turned to me and looked at me as if they had never seen me before. Aiken Drum stepped over to stand before me. He cleared his throat as if to cough out words that would not come.

"Bah!" he exclaimed, and then with a bow he spread his colourful patchwork cloak. "My Lord Messiah." He said his eyes lowered to the ground. The LandNisse guard all arrayed in the Dogrose flower fell to their knees as one. The only one left standing was Princess Erika Nisse. With a smile upon her face, she curtsied and bowed her head to me. She rose again and spoke to the kneeling nisse.

"Arise all, we have work to do."

Waccaar L'Ussler stood before me as the old man climbed onto the wagon.

"Lord Messiah...!" He began.

"Jon. Call me Jon." I insisted.

"Jon." He nodded. "Please forgive me for leaving."

I raised my hand to stop him then put it on his shoulder. "You obeyed your Princess as your oath would have you do. There is no fault in your actions."

"Thank you My Lord." L'Ussler sighed with relief.

"It's Jon. Not My Lord." I reminded him with a smile.

"Yes My Lord." He replied. That is when I gave up trying to change a stone into a tree.

Captain Commander L'Ussler drew his sword and held it up in a formal salute, the cross guard up to his face the long thin blade pointing to the sky. "I swear by my sword and my honour that I shall not leave your side again." The rest of the LandNisse drew their long thin blades and saluted following Waccaar's example. This was the elvin oath salute as I knew it and I was sure it meant the same thing to the nisse. I drew my katana and returned the salute accepting the Captain Commander's oath and promise.

"Comhaontu Comhaontu Comhaontu!" The LandNisse guard cheered three times in the First Tongue, to seal their oath promise to Waccaar's spoken oath. As they chanted, they thrust their swords aloft with each shout.

Erika leapt a standing leap from where she stood to the top of the covered wagon nearly twenty feet in the air, her chameleon suit now a long gossamer gown that flowed in the breeze. She made the jump look gracefully elegant.

"Those of the LandNisse guard, hear my voice and the voice of my Father Emperor and King." Erika called down from atop the wagon. Her translucent gown moved in the breeze, its subtle colours seemed to shift within the fabric. Against the sky, she looked both regal and dramatic.

"From this day forward you are released from all obligations and oaths of allegiance to my Father Emperor and King, the Nisse Crown and to the Seelie Court." All nisse present seemed to recoil as if a tether had been cut. I felt the severing of that tether deep in my own chest, like a tree that had a branch severed. The tree still lives and has many other branches but this branch and the many smaller offshoots and leaves are forever gone. The nisse looked up at the princess then to each other in confused silence. I felt fear and panic rising within the LandNisse guard, as they were the branch severed from the royal nisse tree.

Erika took a breath and spoke again. "I call upon you as free men to give oath to the Black Messiah and his Princess, Princess Erika Nisse daughter of the Emperor King Kennet and mother of the heir to the Emperor's seat. Those that give oath today are foresworn to no others and will foreswear no other oaths except to that of your lawfully wedded partner. Do you so swear?"

"Comhaontu!" The nisse replied almost a cheer. I felt a new pull deep in my body and I knew it was this new oath bond.

"Nisse of the new messianic order; Do you swear by the secret name of the Allfather to be a true and faithful servant and protector to the Lord Messiah, his family, heirs and true successors?"

"Comhaontu." Came the solemn reply.

Erika withdrew her dagger strapped to her thigh.

"Do you swear that you will not know or understand any manner of harm to be done or spoken to the Lord Messiah's person, honour or dignity and you will forswear your lives to sustain this oath?" Erika cut into the skin of her left arm with the razor sharp dagger, red blood bloomed from the cut. Erika held her arm out and the blood fell to the ground. Aiken Drum stepped over to the small pool of royal blood and with his finger; he mixed it with the dirt of the road to make a paste. He scooped up the paste on one hand and walked through the standing nisse, as he passed each one he placed his thumb into the paste and pressed a thumbprint onto the foreheads of every nisse there. As he anointed their heads with the royal nisse blood each one spoke.

"Comhaontu"

When Aiken Drum had finished his anointing, Erika spoke again.

"Do you swear upon your lives that you will, to your utmost, even to the pain of death, bear faithful and true allegiance to the Lord Messiah and will assist and defend all civil and temporal jurisdictions, pre-eminences and authorities taken and presumed by the Lord Messiah? In addition, that you do so as a free and willing subject of the nisse Emperor King and in all things, you do so as a faithful and willing servant of the Lord Messiah and seal this oath by the secret name of the Allfather. Do you so swear?"

"Comhaontu." They replied as one.

The oath bond finished I felt the same pull in my chest but stronger. Erika leapt the twenty feet from on top of the wagon and landed lightly on the ground beside Captain Commander Waccaar L'Ussler. She waved to beckon me over to where they stood. Erika gently pressed Waccaar on the shoulder to bid him kneel.

As I got to them, Erika said. "Please place your hands on the Captains head."

I did as asked and Erika placed her hands upon mine.

"Repeat after me." She whispered, and I repeated her every word.

"I name you as Commander Waccaar L'Ussler, Commander of my personal Messian Guard. You stand above all other nisse in the protection and service to my person and the person of my wife Princess Erika Nisse." As I repeated her words, I felt that gushing torrent of heat rush up my legs and down my arms filling me with the sweet sense of power, power beyond understanding. In reaction, Waccaar stiffened as the torrent of power flowed from my hands to his head. There was a hushed gasp from those around us. I opened my eyes to see Waccaar stand up. His salt and pepper hair and bushy moustache were now snow white, shocking against his dark tanned weather beaten skin.

Waccaar could see his bushy moustache. "Oh My. Oh my, my, my." He exclaimed and we all laughed aloud, all but one. Ranja looked at Waccaar as if she was looking at a new man. I remembered the greying and portly but earnest Captain that puffed up to us after his men to meet Erika and I. The Commander Waccaar that stood before me now looked like a Greek God. I saw Waccaar glance side wards at Ranja before as if she were on a pedestal far beyond his reach, when Erika named him RiNisse he seemed to gain the confidence to grow closer to Ranja. Now as he looked around Ranja was the first person at which he gazed. She coyly lowered her gaze with demure Nisse charm. Ranja was a young maiden no man would feel cheated to have at his side, either in bed or in battle. I think Ranja's reaction was all that Waccaar could hope for. He looked back at me with a smile of thanks that no words could describe.

I repeated a similar exercise on all of the nisse there, each nisse's hair changing from nisse jet black to the startling white first sported by Commander Waccaar. Except for Ranja, all of the female nisse guard were married. I could not help but feel a magnetic attraction to their womanly charms, to all of the nisse maidens present. Inside I became awkward and embarrassed. Erika took me to one side.

"Jon my love, worry not about how you feel. It is the bond that causes the attraction. They feel the same for you as you do for them. It is the same for me."

"You feel the same attraction to all of the men?" I asked not knowing if I should sound interested or angry.

"I do, however any action is forbidden by nisse law and the Holy Books."

"Why is that?" I asked.

"When a nisse maiden gives herself to her husband she gives herself completely. A nisse woman cannot conceive of being unfaithful."

"That's all very well Erika but what if the nisse man is a complete asshole. Is she stuck with him? Surely not every marriage is a complete success."

Erika thought about that as we found a couple of seat-sized boulders to sit upon.

"Not every marriage is a success but very few fail." Erika began to explain. "It is only after a long and involved courtship and very careful consideration that a nisse couple will decide to marry. And when they do she gives herself to him completely."

"What if he abuses her?" I asked.

Erika shook her head and smiled. "Jon my darling, nisse males are not human men." She laughed. "But to answer your question, she dissolves the marriage and looks for another."

"Ah ha! So you do have divorce after all!"

"In a manner of speaking... I suppose yes we do."

"Well then." I formed my question in my little victory. "How is this divorce carried out?"

"The nisse maiden will execute her husband, usually in his sleep, and then begin her search for a new husband." Erika leaned into me and patted the back of my hand as if she comforted a child. "But it very rarely happens."

"So what you are telling me is that if you get bored with me you will execute me in my sleep then go and find somebody else." I exclaimed.

"Oh of course not. I am a Royal Princess; I could never do something like that."

"Thank the Gods." I sighed.

"No, I would have one of my handmaidens do it." Erika added casually. I looked at her horrified. She simply smiled back as if all was right in the world.

"By the Gods nisse males have it hard." I commented in spite of myself.

"They do not think so." Erika replied.

"And why would that be?" I did not think that any reward could make up for a midnight execution.

"Look to Sakso and Santino." Erika pointed at the couple. They both serve in the LandNisse guard and they are married."

"Okay, so they have a common interest."

"Well yes, but Sakso has two other wives back in Copperstone city."

"He has three wives?" I asked, seeing how this arrangement could well indeed make up for any midnight wifely assassination.

"Yes, most nisse males have several wives. Of course, they must show that they are able to cherish and support each wife and the current wives must agree to any marriage that their husband wishes to enter into. The maidens who marry into such a family become sister wives, that is wives to their husbands and sisters to the other wives. Regard Waccaar there." She pointed to the Commander.

"He has no wife; he has been married to the LandNisse guard for decades. But it looks like that may change." Erika indicated to Waccaar and Ranja talking beside the wagon. Waccaar lifted his hand and touched Ranja's cheek, to the nisse it was a very serious show of affection and I could see that Waccaar could be a man of direct action when he wanted to be.

Chapter 37

We travelled for the next six days across gentle green hills with delightful valleys hidden within. The countryside teemed with vibrant life, not just flora and fauna but a myriad of differing faerie.

At the end of the second day following the Dogwood rose path away from Logon we met up with the other wagons. All wagon crews looked healthy, a few lowered their heads, nisse were not known to blatantly lie and the act of deception did not sit well with them.

We rumbled through a dense forest, the massive Ironwood trees as big as New York skyscrapers. Within the forest, we passed through a faerie village as impressive as Copperstone and shared by a number of different fae. We were not anything special; a caravan of trader's wagons with an overabundance of professional looking guards all hid their snow-white hair under their helmets. Waccaar's bushy moustaches could not be hidden, but there was the odd albino nisse and we hoped Waccaar would be dismissed as such.

With so many guards, it would be assumed we carried a valuable cargo. It suited us as we could avoid others eyes under the guise of protecting our cargo.

We moved along a busy avenue, the village residents kept a safe distance from our angors. A small, thin figure flitted out of the shadows to hover before us just above the mulluks. The faerie sustained its flight by two sets of wings like a dragonfly; its body was slim with long thin arms and legs. I felt that it was female even though it had no distinguishing sexual organs. I am sure Asrais can tell the difference. Its large head contained overlarge pale blue intelligent eyes that looked upon us as if it was deciding to trust us or not.

The fae darted closer then away, it halted, looked back and shot off into the trees as quick as a robin. I looked to Erika for an explanation.

"It looks like you have an admirer." She smiled and added. "That is one of those Asrais like the ones we encountered just outside Copperstone city." She explained.

"We saved one like her from the sunlight. I remember." I said to confirm I recalled that time.

"They live within the dense forest; the Ironwood trees give it cover from the sunlight, they cannot abide direct sunshine. An Asrais can drown in sunlight and if exposed for even a short time it will melt into a pool of clear sugary fluid." Erika explained. She pointed the way the Asrais had flown. "Look, she returns."

Sure enough the Asrais flew back with an array of freshly picked wild flowers, she flew over to me and slowly hovered forward holding out the flowers. I reached to take them when Erika leaned into me.

"Remember Jon; take care not to touch her skin." Erika cautioned. I quickly withdrew my hand, it startled the Asrais and she fluttered back a way.

"They are very delicate and the softest touch can bruise, or break a bone." The faerie hovered forward once more as Erika and I smiled at her. "She is so cute. Like an adorable child." I whispered as I eased my hand out for the offered flowers.

"She is probably older that all of us put together. An Asrais is considered an elder when they reach five thousand years or more. From the looks of this one, she would be about two thousand years old. She is a fully grown female."

"It looks so fragile." I replied as I gently took the flowers making sure I did not touch her long thin fingers. The Asrais smiled widely when I held the flowers up to smell them, she quickly darted off again.

"Definitely an admirer. It is remarkable for one to be so forward; I have never seen this behaviour before." Erika smiled. "These Asrais are a sympatric fae. They live in this village not as members of the village but more like the animals and plants that occupy this part of the forest. The fae are always very jealous of their Asrais as they bring happiness, wellbeing and riches to a village or home. They are a simple wholesome faerie; they take from the village in a way that humans might call theft; bright things, odd things like tools, nails and oddly enough, worked timber, sometimes-sugary food, perhaps a needle or a button. They give much more that they take, so they are always welcome everywhere the faerie live.

The Asrais returned holding a deep-dish pie, the rich smell of lamb, or what smelt like lamb, wafted to my nose and I inhaled the mouth-watering aroma. The little Asrais darted in more confidently now and offered me the pie.

"I don't suppose she baked this pie?" I asked.

"No. She will have found it in a fae maiden's oven." Erika advised.

"Should I take it?" I asked remembering my Sol military training. Euroforce Soldiers on Sol were trained never to accept any type of food or beverage offered by a fae; to do so would allow that fae to have control over that soldier. Most of their food would kill or seriously incapacitate a human no matter how well meaning the offer.

"If I take the food it will do me harm." My hesitation obvious and it caused the Asrais to frown. Erika laughed. "Yes it is true, most food the fae eat is not compatible with humans but Jon, you are a human no more. It would be a great insult to the whole village if you did not accept the gift." Erika raised her hand to show me the smiling faerie faces around our wagon, faces full of expectation. I reached out and the Asrais placed the pie on my outstretched hands. I quickly but carefully dropped the dish to the floor.

"By the Gods that was hot!" I exclaimed. This time the Messian guard, including Waccaar, began to laugh aloud. "Yes, although the Asrais are delicate creatures." Erika lectured. "They feel no hot or cold. They have different strengths and weaknesses than us and they should not be underestimated." Erika lifted the pie to place it between us on the wagon seat. "You should give something in return."

"Like what?" I asked. I had nothing but my weapons and my chameleon suit, none of which I would give up any time soon.

"It would be gracious of you to give her a lock of your hair."

"What for?" I demanded, worried that this fae could do me harm with such a possession.

"Are you worried she may make a sympathic doll and stick needles in you?" Erika laughed a musical sweet laughter that infected me and those gathered around the wagon.

"Here let me." Aiken Drum spoke from behind. I felt the rasping snick of his shears and he held out a lock of my hair. It was a bloody big lump of hair and I knew I would be missing a large patch from the back of my head for weeks. I grabbed the lock from him and shot him an angry stare. High Blademaster or no he was still a mischievous old man.

Holding out my hand, I offered my lock of blue-black hair to the Asrais. She leaned in and delicately took the lock from me. Her hand brushed mine and I felt the rush of force like gushing hot water push up my arm. I pulled back heeding Erika's warning.

"She touched me! Is she alright?" I asked feeling my left hand with my right.

"She is fine. Asrais can touch others but cannot be touched. It is very seldom done and you are very fortunate to have an Asrais touch you."

Still feeling my hand, I turned to Erika and spoke low so that no one might hear.

"Erika, I felt the same feeling that comes out of the ground when I do magic stuff only this time I felt it from this Asrais and not from the ground." I explained.

"The Asrais are strong in earth magic. You channelled that magic from her into your arm. See how the Asrais looks at you now?" Erika pointed at the faerie, she still hovered before us but no other part of her body moved, she looked to be in astounded shock. I smiled at her and she did a mid-air curtsy amid gasps of surprise from the on looking faerie folk.

The Asrais lifted the hair in her outstretched hand and blew it into the air. The lock of black hair broke up and strands swirled before her; held in a magically contained whirlwind. The strands coalesced with the dust caught up in the whirlwind to form a little me. The form had the dimensions of the Asrais and with two sets of wings that it used to hover beside its creator. Where the Asrais was completely covered in fine grey dappled fur, my little me was covered in black fur.

"What just happened?" I asked looking worriedly at the little black Asrais that looked just like me.

"She just created an Effigy. I have never seen one created before. And... We'll all Asrais are grey Jon." Erika looked at me confused. "She has just given you a wonderful gift." She indicated the Asrais Effigy.

"What am I supposed to do with it?" I asked still staring at the unsettling black image of me in Asrais form.

"Lean back and support yourself against the Wagon." Erika asked and I followed her request. "Now close your eyes and feel with your mind, reach out for the Effigy." I relaxed and cleared my mind as Erika had previously taught me. I reached out with my mind and I felt the need to open my eyes. I did so but I was not looking out of my eyes but from the eyes of the Effigy. I began to waver from side to side. The wings beat in a motor nerve reaction like a heartbeat or breathing, I did not have to think about it, it just happened. I was as unaware of the wings as I was of my own heartbeat, however hovering in the air was an acquired skill and as I became aware of my surroundings, I found I could not compensate for the slight variations in the air from the light breezes and differing air currents. It was like trying to think to walk it was an impossibility. The Asrais caught my hand and steadied me.

"Fear not Jonraine. Relax and allow your body to make the compensations automatically." The voice came from the Asrais but it was inside my head. The Asrais moved as if she spoke but her mouth did not move. I tried to speak but found that I could utter no words; I had no voice box to form the words.

"Do not try to speak only form the words in your mind and I will hear them."

"Canyouhearme?"

"I cannot make out what you are saying. Form each work individually" She replied.

"CAN ... YOU ... HEAR ... ME?" I tried again.

The Asrais flinched back. "Goodness, I think every Asrais in this forest heard that!" She smiled. I wavered and she darted in to steady me again.

I noticed the wagon and looked over to see Erika and Aiken Drum looking at me. My body slumped as if asleep on the wagon seat. I felt panic well up inside me. Was I caught like this forever?

"Relax Jonraine you are free to return to your body any time you like. I ask that you only remain here for a moment that I might explain." The Asrais spoke inside my head again. I looked to Erika.

"Please listen to the Asrais my love. (Picture of Erika and me under the oak Tree in Denmark of Earth Prime.) You are quite safe. We will look after your body until you wish to return. (Picture of Erika kissing my chest.)." Erika smiled at me her voice and pictures she projected into my head.

"CAN ... YOU ... Hearme to?" I thought to Erika.

"I can hear you my love, just tone it down a little lower." She replied.

"I can hear the Asrais speaking in my head. Can you hear it?"

"No I cannot hear the Asrais. She can communicate only with another Asrais."

"A Ha! So hence the mini-me." I thought back.

"Yes and the volume is much better." Erika replied without speaking.

"You can speak to the Princess?" the Asrais asked.

"ICan"

"What." Erika asked.

"Sorry Erika, I am speaking to Estrid, the Asrais." I explained.

"Oh how delightful." Estrid clapped her hands. I began to waver again and she gently grasped my shoulders to steady me.

"How do I know your name?" I asked Estrid while trying to control this hovering business, it felt like I balanced on a big invisible ball.

"It came with my communication to you. Every time we communicate, we have an individual signature. Your brain interprets that as a normal name and because I am female your brain makes it a female name." Estrid explained and lifted her hands slightly to see if I could control my static hovering. I still swayed but only slightly. "Good enough." Estrid smiled.

"Will you come with me to meet my people?" She asked.

"I do not know if we have time. (Image of Snigmorder's, flashes of attack on Copperstone, Snigmorder heads on poles.)" I replied.

"Oh how dreadful." Estrid cringed under the barrage of uncontrolled images.

Erika heard my reply and correctly assumed the question. "Should she wish to take you to her people it is a very great honour, please accept the invitation. We are happy to wait and refresh ourselves. We will take the greatest care of your body."

"Okay. Just make sure that Aiken Drum doesn't draw on me or tattoo me or something equally foolish. You promise."

Erika laughed. "I promise." She replied verbally.

"You promise what?" Aiken Drum interrupted.

"Lord Raine takes a small journey with the Asrais. We promise to look after his body while he is away with the faeries."

"Yes we will look after your body." Aiken Drum sneered and I felt relieved that Erika promised first.

"It would seem I have the all clear." I thought to Estrid.

"Good! Flying is much easier than hovering." Esrtid instructed. "Just lean your body in the way you wish to go and your body will do the rest." She demonstrated and flew around me then the wagon. "To slow or stop just lean back and feel your body stop. It will obey."

I tried a few unsteady moves. First, I shot off and bounced into a tree. I bounced back but did not lose flight; it seemed as natural as breathing or blinking. I flew around the clearing we were in then up and into the nisse sung treetop paths and avenues. A few minutes of experimentation and I mastered the basic art of faerie flight. There was little difference from it and riding a Segway only there was up and down in faerie flight.

"Come now and follow me." Estrid beckoned me deeper into the forest. I waved goodbye to Erika and the guards and flew directly into a low branch. I bounced back much to the amusement of Aiken Drum and I could see that Erika, Waccaar and the guys, fought to keep their smiles just smiles and not laughter. Gathering myself together, my head still ringing from the strike, coincidentally in the exact same place as Aiken Drum's bash on my other body's head reminded me to be careful and not to underestimate anything.

My Asrais eyes were much bigger than my nisse eyes; I was still struggling not to call myself human and now I was something else entirely. I could see much more detail and further than my enhanced nisse vision but not as good as my chameleon suit. Off in the distance possibly invisible to nisse eyes Estrid hovered playfully, beckoning me to follow.

"Did he really do that?" Estrid asked with an angry frown and started back to the clearing.

"No Estrid. Please let us go, he was only playing around." I tried to distract her.

"You do not play around with the Black Messiah's head with a big stick, even if you are the High Blademaster!" Estrid huffed and folded her little arms.

"Come let us fly!" she suddenly dismissed any thoughts of revenge. I shot off through the trees after Estrid. We ducked and dodged moving ever faster. The tree trunks flashed past and I felt very comfortable weaving around them, over, and under low growing branches. Estrid swooped around a clearing keeping to the shade and I dashed across the clearing to short cut the pursuit. The sun hit me like Thor's hammer and I spun out of control. I could not breathe; I hit the ground and bounced several times feeling every painful knock and roll. I felt like I was drowning.

"Oh my goodness me!" I heard Estrid exclaim as if from a long way away or maybe like under the water.

"Lay still Lord Raine, I am coming." I looked up to see Estrid hovering just at the edge of the clearing; everything shimmered as if I was looking up through water. The whole water description is the only way I can convey my experience of nearly drowning in the sunlight. With the force of my fall, I almost made it across the clearing and Estrid was very near. She moved to a vine and cut it away from its anchors with a small knife that looked long in her tiny hands. Estrid tied a loop to one end and threw that end to me. Her thought images told me to put the loop around myself. It was a struggle to move in the light, it felt like every inch of my body had a great weight pressing down on it.

I managed to get the rope around myself and by the time Estrid began to pull, three other Asrais appeared to give assistance. They soon had me out of the light and safely into the shade.

Estrid and her three new companions, two female and one male, examined me. Sometimes I could hear them speak to each other and sometimes I heard nothing. I learned from Estrid that there was a common frequency for general communication and a private or rather millions of channels for private communications.

Edra the male Asrais spoke to me. "Well it looks like no lasting harm done, but it was a close thing. You could have drowned (Image of dead Asrais dead and melting to sticky goo in the sunlight) out there." Edra pointed out into the clearing basking in the summer sun.

"Apologies" I thought, not the word but the feeling.

They all nodded in kind acceptance. Image of child at play came from their common minds and I flushed with embarrassment.

"Think nothing more of it. Come we have many Asrais to meet. They are all looking forward to see our Black Messiah." Estrid sent an image of Asrais massing deep in the forest. They sat about a clearing, covered with a canopy of heavy treetop foliage. The clearing seemed to be in constant twilight and few ground plants grew between the tree trunks. The telepathic chatter between the Asrais in the image overwhelmed my mind and I fell to the ground dizzy and disorientated. Names rushed at me with overwhelming thoughts of sympathy that nearly drove me insane. I was able to understand that all names ending in rid indicated a female and all names ending with a ra indicated a male.

"That is correct." Estrid commented on my thought. Her voice came at me loud and strong, it drowned out all the others and distracted my mind from the cacophony of mind talk around me.

"Can everybody read my thoughts?" I worried.

"No, just me, it was I that made you, as you grow more accustomed to your Asrais body, so your thoughts become harder to read and eventually I will lose the ability. For now Jonraine, concentrate on my voice only and the noise will eventually sort itself out. Your brain needs time to adjust."

"How long will that take?" I asked, impatient to have my own thoughts private again.

"If you stay in your Asrais body then maybe five hundred years, perhaps a little more." Magrid, one of the other female Asrais replied.

"Come Lord Jonraine, lets us come to our family, they wait in our place of meeting. It is our holy ground. (Image of Asrais all sitting cross-legged on the forest floor, all holding each other's hands, some touching the occasional tree, in the middle of this group of hundreds perhaps thousands sat some Asrais in a wide circle.)"

Chapter 38

In a matter of minutes that would have taken days to travel on foot, we came to the dark forest clearing. I could still hear the jumble of chatter in the back of my mind but Estrid sang constantly to me to keep the chatter from overwhelming me. Being a telepathic song, it was in perfect pitch. The chatter was still nonsense to me but now like a ticking clock it paled into the background. The clearing, shrouded in shadow to my big Asrais eyes, was clear as day.

Estrid and her four companions escorted me to the centre of the ring. Estrid bowed to the set of Asrais before us and I took them to be their elders or priests (Image of these male and female performing sacred acts confirmed them to be the Asrais Elders and Priests.) They seemed to rule or govern as equals, with those in the ring first amongst equals.

One elder, her fur turned completely light grey with age, stood on slender legs her arms outstretched to welcome me.

"Welcome he who must come to free the lands. Hail to the Black Messiah!" She sent with a warm welcoming smile.

"Hail the Black Messiah!" A booming reply came from those seated about the clearing. The reply nearly knocked me off my feet. The conjoined voice seemed to be millions rather than the few hundred I could see. Estrid and Edra grasped my arms to steady me and Atrid the Elder stepped forward to place her hands on my shoulders.

"Fear not Lord Jonraine." Atrid sent. "I would have believed Estrid would have prepared you more." (Image of rebuttal from Atrid.) (Image of sorrow and apology from Estrid.) Estrid lowered her head in shame. I shifted and put my arm around Estrid.

"Estrid did a wonderful job. There is no failure on her part. You must allow me to get used to your form of communication." (I think that Amanda would be so excited at this. Image of Amanda in the elvin bed. Image of Erika under the oak tree) big blue eyes stared at me in surprise.

"Forgive me Elder Atrid. I am new to this mind talk." With my arm around Estrid, she looked up at me with her big blue catlike eyes and an image of Estrid in an elvin bed invaded my mind. There was a ripple of giggling around the gathered Asrais, even the Elders joined in the amusement.

"Help me here Estrid." I pleaded and there was another round of gentle laughter like tinkling elvin bells.

"Jonraine you must not think every thought in the common broadcast mode." Estrid sent but she did not move away from my embrace. "Imagine a room and walk into it. This room is your private place. No Asrais will come in uninvited. You can imagine anything in this room, even those quite pleasant thoughts." Estrid smiled and moved closer to me. When you leave the room, imagine you close and lock the door. In your mind, it will be so."

I sent kind affectionate thanks to Estrid.

Atrid held out her hand and beckoned me into the circle of Elders. I stood within and all around me, thousands of Asrais sat cross-legged on the ground. To each side they held the hand of the one next to them and I noticed that the circle of Elders formed a linked ring around us after I stepped into the centre.

Estrid and Atrid hugged and I felt the message of gratitude and love sent to Estrid from Atrid. No. Not from Atrid but through her, the message of thanks came from all of the Asrais, not just the Asrais gathered here in this hollow but from all Asrais everywhere. I did not know how I knew this, I could not describe it. How can you describe the beauty of a sunset to a person born with no eyes or how can you explain the scent of a pine forest to a goblin. It was as if I had another sense I never knew I had and now that I could use it, I felt as if I always had it.

"Lord Jonraine, the Asrais welcome you to our world." Atrid sent. I felt that she spoke for all Asrais. "We have awaited your appearance since the first human crawled through a trollgate." (Image of a primitive man looking around him at massive Ironwood trees.)

"As you look at us so we look at you. We have never beheld a black Effigy. You are the first." Atrid smiled, she turned to face Estrid. "We are grateful for the skill and gift you bring to the Asrais. Like the Lord Jonraine you are a NiAsrais." (A picture of a pretty nisse maiden dressed in the clothes of a Hofdame, a high lady of the nisse Seelie Court.) The image morphed into Estrid and I knew that this nisse and Estrid were the same. I looked at Estrid and she stood there beside me with a pleased smile on her lips.

"Estrid NiAsrais, for your contribution to the race of Asrais I name you an Asrais and NiAsrais no more." Atrid sent to Astrid. A cheer filled my mind from all around and that tinkling of faerie bells filled the air.

"My child, please take your place amongst the Asrais." Atrid sent.

Estrid fluttered up and across to find a spot amongst the Asrais gathered. She descended into the waiting Asrais and I could feel the emotion of a warm welcome, a welcome for a child lost and found again.

Atrid came to stand in front of me.

"You are doing very well Jonraine." She offered me a drink in a glass cup. I took it from her and drank it down. It tasted sweet and refreshing. "You will need your strength for what is to come." She smiled. I did not feel wary or afraid, I felt that I was amongst friends and they would protect me from any danger.

"Lord Jonraine. Please look up to the tree cover above and close your eyes." Atrid asked of me and I did as she asked. My eyes closed to the leafy rooftop of the tree foliage. In the self-imposed darkness of my closed eyes, I could still feel the Asrais all around us.

"Can you feel the Asrais around you?"

"Yes." I replied.

"Clear your mind from all thoughts. Listen to my voice, only my voice." Atrid's voice felt as if it came from everywhere, all around me and inside my head.

"Keep your mind free and your eyes shut. Focus on my voice and slowly lower your head." She instructed.

I lowered my head to its normal position. To my astonishment, I could see Atrid standing before me. She was not as before, as I saw her with physical eyes. She was the same basic shape but made of a soft glowing light that I could both see and see through, she was a light pastel shade of green. I knew this to be her astral form without her explaining. I could clearly make out her features as easily as I could with my physical eyes. Atrid raised her arms and sent to me.

"Welcome to the Asrais." As she spoke, those Asrais seated around me began to appear like stars in the nighttime sky, they gently came into view and my astral eyes became accustomed to their presence. I looked around at the multi-coloured sea of glowing beings and I instantly spotted the smiling Estrid. I smiled back. I realised that I knew every single name of each Asrais present. Beyond our hollow meeting place, I could see other Asrais. They spread out forever, countless millions of them. I looked up into the sky and there above me I could see the night sky. Millions of stars above my head.

"Jon, you do not see stars but Asrais above you." Atrid explained. "I know you have journeyed the stars of your universe. You have seen life belonging to other worlds. Up there you see Asrais on other worlds. We live throughout the universe from beginning to end."

I felt the immense distance between us; it made me feel so small so insignificant.

"Jon, they are so far away we cannot communicate with them. They remind us of the size of the universe and they remind us of our position in the great wheel of life."

I looked about at the Asrais around me and beyond in the world. I noticed that some in the distance winked on and off.

Atrid understood my unformed question and replied.

"Those on this world, too far away to be seen, need to touch a tree or a bush, any living thing that springs from mother

Sol. When an Asrais does this, we can communicate to any other Asrais touching a plant growing from Sol. Through those standing close to us and touching a tree, we can tunnel our thoughts through them and to our brothers and sisters all over Sol. The lights you see coming on or going off are individual Asrais who touch a plant or release one."

I could understand Atrid's simple explanations to the amazing sights and mental communications I felt. I knew Atrid guided me and kept me under control, but like a young infant beginning to walk I felt myself taking those first few steps into the world of the Asrais, a much bigger and much more complex world than any fae who was not an Asrais could ever understand.

I knew through all the impressions and feelings I received from those countless Asrais around me that I was correct, and that my Asrais friend Estrid would be my companion and guide to this new world, much greater and complex than the physical world that contained it.

"Black Messiah, I welcome you to the Asrais and on behalf of all of us I pledge our united loyalty to you."

Every Asrais within my comprehension agreed with Atrid's sending's. I understood that before me I faced the greatest number of beings that I have ever beheld and everyone without exception, made that loyalty promise.

In that state, I travelled the world of Sol while Estrid accompanied me. I spoke to hundreds even thousands of different Asrais. Everyone told me of their experiences, of what happens in the places they inhabit. I realised that I understood and remembered every one of them. When I wanted to know something, it seemed that I looked out of their eye and saw what they saw. Sometimes I felt that I looked out of millions of eyes and listened to countless noises but with Estrid's guidance and protection, the sensations did not overwhelm me.

Sometimes Estrid brought me back to physical form to partake of the same sugary drink or a warm sweet porridge that tasted delicious. Finally, Estrid urged me to return to partake of a final meal. Upon my return, I found the meeting place with far fewer Asrais within it. I opened my physical eyes and after a moment to compose myself I saw that Estrid stood beside me and around us lay what I immediately recognised as faerie dust.

"Yes Jonraine it is faerie dust." Estrid sent.

I know that the Asrais made faerie dust and Sorcerers sand but I knew how expensive the stuff was in Sol. It was worth ten times its weight in gold and there was plenty of it around us. Several Asrais were there using magic to lift the sand and put it into glass jars, which they sealed tight when full.

"How did all this faerie dust get here?" I asked

"We made it. Watch" Estrid sent, and fluttered up into the air, she gave a little shake and faerie dust fell from her grey dappled fur.

"How did you do that?" I asked amazed.

"When we eat and drink we need to expel our waste. When we do we create this dust." Estrid explained. (Estrid sent to me an image of a nisse sitting on a toilet.)

I laughed with that tinkling sound and Esrtid looked at me with a puzzled frown. I fluttered up into the air and shook as Estrid did. The faerie dust fell from my body and I laughed that tinkling laugh again.

"And what amuses you my love." Estrid asked.

"Faerie dust; it is Asrais Shit." I sent. Estrid fluttered there, the sentence beyond her comprehension. When I explained Estrid laughed aloud and the tinkling laughter came from all around me when the Asrais in the hollow understood my understanding of Asrais waste. I knew in that moment that I had changed the Asrais forever.

"Jonraine, it is time for us to journey back to your companions." Estrid sent. She seemed a little sad to me.

"I do not have to go just yet Estrid. We can dally a little." I suggested.

"No we cannot, you have much to do in the world of fae. We must go back now."

I hugged Estrid and saw that Atrid stood close by. I went to her and hugged her as well.

"Farewell Black Messiah; I wish you well in your journeys. Remember your Asrais friends and come back to us often. We may not be big enough to fight but we are a very powerful ally" She smiled.

"I will remember you always." I replied, and hugged her once more.

Chapter 39

Shortly Estrid and I left with an escort of four other Asrais to see us safely home. We took an indirect route. We flew here and there, Estrid showing me the different flowers we could drink from, their nectar tasted as pleasant as the drink in the hollow. We explored the forest around the village finding various hidden spots the Asrais preferred to dwell in when the sun was up. Near the village, Estrid took me to a small opening in the side of a small mound.

"Is it safe to go in there?" I sent

"It should be we built it." She replied.

In we flew and the narrow tunnel angled down for some distance. It took several turns before opening onto a large natural cave. To one side a fall of water fell into a small lake that took up a full third of the floor below. The whole floor was about the size of a football field and the roof as high as a cathedral. The cave was lighted with floating faerie lights and Asrais sat in groups either on the floor or on shelves of rock that went in to shallow caves. In the walls at all levels there were openings to other passageways that led to other caves just like the one we hovered in or openings to winding passageways to the surface world above.

"This is our place of rest when the sun is in the sky." Estrid explained.

"Are you not afraid that so close to the village your place may be uncovered by the fae or animals?"

"Jonraine, we live beside fae not humans, they love and respect us we fear no ill from them. They know we live in such places and they revere them and treat them with respect and reverence. As for the animals, they come and go but none cause harm. Any that threaten we can repel like this." Estrid let out an ear-splitting whine that pierced my skull; I had to put my hands over my ears to stop the shrill noise. There were many mental complaints and I did not think Asrais swore it was another false assumption.

Estrid sent apologies and explanation. All sent welcome to the Black Messiah and hoped we had a peaceful and quiet stay in their burrow.

We bathed in the clear pool of the cavern floor. We dived down beneath the water to see Asrais there as well. Estrid explained that some Asrais preferred to live beneath the water and many lived in the seas of Sol never coming above the surface. We swam for hours, discovering the fascinating world of their underwater subterranean caverns. Again, much sooner than I wanted Estrid urged me to the surface. She sent that we needed to get back to my nisse self and the travelling I needed to do.

We waited near the mouth of the tunnel we entered by. We waited for the sun to kiss Sol and the night to cover the world with her starry diamond blanket. When the sun sank beneath the horizon, we ventured out. We were only a short distance from the village and in a few short minutes we would be back to our companions and I would feel Erika's loving arms around me again. I even missed the crazy old cantankerous Blademaster. I hoped that the few nights I was away that crazy old man had not been allowed to do anything to my helpless body.

Flying to the village, I felt conflicting feelings of excited expectation of being in my body again, as well as the sadness of leaving this amazing Asrais form. I realized that during my time as an Asrais I did not mind the shadow, gloom and darkness the Asrais lived in, to me in my Asrais form it felt natural and inviting, and the brightness of the Sun held the fear that the darkness did for my nisse form.

When we entered the village, we took direction from other Asrais there and within seconds, we were in the tree top apartments these villages had for visiting dignitaries and noblemen.

There were smiles of welcome from the Messian guard posted at the door to our apartments. It was Malte and Ranja. Malte silently opened the door for us and we fluttered in.

"Jonraine, will you lie with me this night." Erika sent shyly. She looked so cute I could not resist. I resisted my urge to join my body and we looked around for somewhere private to lie. Two of the Messian guards, Folke and Valder stood beside a closed bedroom door and I knew behind that door lay my Princess.

We made signs that we wanted to sleep and Valder showed us a large leather trunk like box that had an Asrais sized door in the side. Folke opened the top and placed a small candle inside. We entered through the door to see a miniature bedroom, it contained a miniature nisse sung bed and a sofa and a set of chairs. I looked up at Folke looking down into the room.

"Hocking has some talent in the song, Lord Raine." He explained the furniture. "Princess Erika made the pillows, sheets and covers. The Princess is also very talented is she not?" Suggested Folke.

We waved our thanks and Folke quietly and gently closed the lid to the trunk. We retired to the bed and made our love as the Asrais do, before long, exhausted and fulfilled, I fell to a deep sleep. I felt a nudge at my side; I thought Estrid moved in her sleep. I opened my eyes to see Erika lying beside me; I could see her open eyes in the darkness of the room.

"Welcome back my love." She smiled softly and I noticed the white flash of her teeth between her dark lips. I smiled back.

"It's nice to be back again." I said softly. It was good to be able to speak again, I did not realise how much I missed it. "I sort of lost track of time Princess. How long have I been away?" I asked.

"Three weeks." Erika whispered.

"Three weeks!" I exclaimed.

Erika put her finger to her lips.

"Shush, my love you will summon the guards, with all that noise."

A knock on the bedroom door. "Your Highness is everything alright?" I recognised Valder's voice.

"All is well. The Lord Raine returns from his journey with the Asrais. He is well." Erika called back. There was a quiet pause then Valder called again.

"Welcome Lord Raine." He called cautiously through the door.

I did not know if I should answer. Erika gestured with her head and mouthed, "Go on."

"Ah... Hello Valder. It is nice to be back. Carry on." I could not think of anything more authorative or commanding to say. We heard Valder and Folke move away from the door to give us privacy. After three weeks away from my princess, they knew what we would be up to next. Erika kissed me passionately and we began to make up for our unintentional three-week separation.

* * *

The weather stayed warm but the first day out of the village storm clouds threatened. We heard the thunder and now and again, we saw a flash of lightning. It would be nice to have a refreshing storm to settle the dust of the previous weeks. Even though the storms threatened from the West and North our journey was pleasant enough. I could almost forget the horror of the Snigmorder attack on Copperstone city but sometimes in the shadows of Erika's eyes, I could see that she would never forget.

Before we left the faerie village, Hocking, a talented singer of wood who made the delightful bed and furniture, made a sort of boxed area within the wagon where we could place the bedroom trunk so that it was protected from all sides and secure away from the rays of the sun. It was a private place Estrid and I could share as a couple without flying away.

We followed the Dogrose path through the forest away from the faerie village for another two days. The storm clouds were always there on the horizon and we seemed to be moving towards them. On the afternoon of the second day, we made the edge of the forest. The path stretched arrow straight North West towards the Emperors Palace and Erika's family home.

On the grassy plain that lay before us, we parted company from the Dogrose path at the edge of the forest.

Within me, I could feel the nisse nation moving further away, it gave me a sort of melancholy that made me feel that I was away from home and that home was with these people. In some way, I was homesick for a place I had never been and a people I had never met.

Mostly during the day, Estrid slept in the tiny bed beside my Effigy. As soon as the sun went down she was able to come out of the cover of the little bedroom trunk. She would hang around trying to be as useful as a twelve inch tall Asrais could be. Everything was a game to her and she willingly helped with the most mundane tasks, she especially liked to peel the root vegetables and wash up the plates. Erika knew to leave out a sugary sweet porridge snack for the Asrais, as was the nisse custom. Estrid and I seemed only to require this one snack once a day to remain fully nourished.

Most evenings with both Erika's encouragement and Estrid's promptings, I would shift my consciousness from my nisse body and into my own Asrais effigy. After the first few attempts, the change became a lot easier. When the company settled for the night, Estrid and I would range away from the wagons to explore the countryside around us. We kept the wagons in sight and with Asrais eyes that gave us a very big field of range and we could be back at the wagon in less than a few minutes. I would partake of the sugary snack and Estrid and sometimes-other Asrais would fly in to share our breakfast or supper depending on whose eyes you looked at it from. The snack in the evenings nourished my effigy and I felt such a sugar rush. I really enjoyed it safe that I would not become obese or diabetic.

After our nightly jaunts, I would expect to be tired when I moved back into my nisse body, however; it always felt like it had a well-rested night. I could do this for several days, after which my brain began to play tricks on me and I would hear voices and begin to daydream in my nisse form. I got a bit worried but Estrid explained that it was normal and the voices and hallucinations were my body's way of saying I needed real sleep. I would take that night's sleep to allow my own mind to reset and my subconscious to sort all the input from my days as a nisse and my nights as an Asrais. I do not mind knowing that the role of Messiah is difficult and fraught with danger, I can do difficult and dangerous, I did not expect it to be so darned complicated.

  On the fourth evening of our journey out from Bridge End Village, Estrid and I shared our sweet evening porridge.

  "I have something to show you." Estrid sent. One benefit of being an Asrais is that because I used mind speak and my mouth to eat, I could do both at the same time. I always did as a soldier but this way I avoided spilling half my meal down my front.

  "I wanted to show you at the hollow, then the burrow, but we just did not have enough time in either." Estrid added.

  "No time?" I laughed that tinkling sound. Hocking and Aiken Drum looked around at us; their keen ears noticed the unusual noise. I waved back at them that all was well. They waved understanding and went back to preparing for bed; neither was on guard duty that night.

  "No time." I said again. "We were there for three bloody weeks Estrid!" I exclaimed. Estrid frowned.

  "You make those uncouth words again." She huffed. Estrid did not like me swearing even if it was only a mild cuss word.

  "Apologies." I sent.

  "We come close to the thing I want to show you tonight." Estrid said.

  "Okay sounds interesting… We will be just one night won't we?" I asked. I did not want to delay the wagon train any longer than I needed. The nisse army had stopped and I could feel them waiting far to the West. Every day we delayed was a day the Army of the UFE dug deeper into Sol and would be all the more difficult to rout.

    I had not thought of the cause of all this since on-board the Klaubautermann's ship. In some ways I wished the whole thing over, the fae returned to the freedom of their own determination and the human blight lifted from Europa, I knew it would not stop at Europa; eventually all of Sol would succumb to the human blight. Humans would call it taming Sol but the fae saw how they tamed America. They did not wish to experience the same taming the Native Americans experienced.

    "Okay I am yours for tonight." I sent.

    "You are always mine for the night." Estrid sent back with her tinkling laugh. The sound suited coming from Estrid. I wished my laugh could sound a little manlier. I sent back an image of Estrid and me in an interesting position. Estrid gasped, surprised at my forwardness. She tinkled again.

    "Jon, would you mind refraining from that until I am at least asleep." Erika sent. I cringed in embarrassment. I completely forgot that Erika could hear my sending's. While multiple wives were permitted in nisse culture, one wife usually did not want to know what went on in the other wives beds and while I was wed to Erika and not to Estrid, I felt myself drawing closer to Estrid.

    The night was warm and with most of the sky covered in cloud, darkness shrouded us. The fires were dampened and backed up for lighting for breakfast in the morning, lanterns and faerie globe lights extinguished save but a few. To our Asrais eyes, the night was bright and clear. Ever since that mind bending experience back at the hollow with the Elder Atrid, every Asrais I now saw had a coloured aura around them as if their physical bodies eclipsed their astral form. Estrid glowed a pale green; the darker the night the brighter the glow, tonight it showed up quite clearly. I could see these auras only in low natural light. If in any form of artificial light including fire or candle light, the aura could not be seen. Sometimes as in our trunk bedroom in complete absence of light, I would see Estrid in her astral form only. I was unsure if I saw Estrid with astral eyes or the glow in the darkness with my physical eyes. Estrid explained it to me and it was quite simple really, when she demonstrated the difference to me.

With my physical eyes, I could not see through solid objects like the walls of the trunk, so if I saw only Estrid I was using my physical eyes. When I used my astral eyes every physical thing I saw in its astral form, these forms are translucent. With astral eyes, I could see through the walls and every Asrais about was shown bright and clear. Every living thing had an astral form, some brighter than others, Erika and Aiken Drum shone bright and clear; the nisse Messian guard had dimmer astral bodies.

All astral bodies are naked and while I appreciated the sights of the female nisse, seeing the men, especially Aiken Drum was slightly disturbing. An astral body shows the health and strength of your mind and subconscious and Aiken Drum shone like Apollo, Erika also looked more ravishing glowing bright and fair, blonde hair falling down over her shoulders she looked like the Princess I first beheld, within her stomach shone another sun, bright and strong. Before we came out for our evening porridge Astrid blew out the candle and I noticed Astrid's stomach. Within her womb, I saw two glows, one stronger than the other, one glowed a pale blue and the other a deep green.

Our porridge eaten we flew into the night. Around us, the Savannah grasslands spread before us like a dark ocean. Epona made a brief appearance between two clouds and lights rose from the grasslands, millions of Asrais came up to bask in the moonlight.

"That is amazing." I sent to Estrid. "How many Asrais are there?" I asked.

"Many." She sent.

"What do we seek?" I asked while we sped inches from the top of the long grass. I was even beginning to speak like one of these Asrais.

"Not far." Estrid sent. "We seek a burrow, within is the thing I want to show you." She added.

"Just what is this wondrous thing?" I needed to know, the suspense was too much for me to bear.

Erika sent an image of a nisse sitting on a toilet.

"We are going to find an Asrais toilet." I laughed.

"It is not just a toilet. You will see." Came Estrid's enigmatic reply.

We swerved to the East; in the distance, we could see a more concentrated gathering of Asrais. They flashed into and out of a low mound and instinctively I knew this was the same type of burrow we saw back outside Bridge End Village.

We streaked across the grasslands like a pair of loosed arrows. This Asrais flight was more adrenaline pumping than a space re-entry jump in a Para Drop Suit. We swerved down and in through one of the entrances. Down we snaked, deeper into the womb of mother Sol. The earth magic was so strong in the burrows it was almost overcoming. We entered a massive cathedral like cavern. We shot across the expanse in seconds. I worried we moved too fast but I stayed close to Estrid and allowed her to take the lead. Before I panicked, I saw the opening in the far wall and we sped towards it. When we got to it, I found that it was reassuringly wide. Through that opening and along an arrow straight tunnel we emerged in another immense cavern. Sitting in the middle was a great wooden wheel like a water wheel. Asrais darted about and in a moment I realised I was looking at an Asrais toilet.

The wheel remained stationary and on it hung smoked glass jars. They looked like they swivelled when the wheel turned. To one side was a great vertical funnel. Asrais darted to the mouth of the funnel, a quick shake, a dart in a different direction and faerie dust fell from their grey dappled fur. The dust slowly fell into the funnel and down into the mouth of the dark glass jar beneath. The wheel moved slightly. After our meal, Astrid and I felt the need of a quick dump of faerie dust. Together we flew to the mouth of the funnel gaping beneath us.

I did that shake thing, I did not trust myself to do the darting manoeuvre, and I feared getting faerie dust over everything. Erika did a dart in and out and left almost a faerie dust image of herself.

"Very cleverly done." I sent.

"I will teach you how." She replied.

I heard a tinkle of glass upon glass and we shot to the other side of the great wooden wheel to see a full glass jar stoppered by a very clever device and the jar automatically unhooked from its position on the wheel. The glass jar, now full with about a pound of faerie dust, slid along a sloping platform to clink gently against identical glass jars. A few feet above where the jar was unhooked an empty glass jar stood ready and the rising hooks of the slowly moving wheel slid up and into handles fashioned on the sides of the jar. It picked up and swivelled to a vertical position while the wheel inched ever so slowly and moved on.

"Now that is the most interesting crap I have ever taken." I sent. Estrid frowned again.

"Is that another uncouth word Jonraine?" She sent her little fists on her waist.

"No." I lied. Estrid did not seem to want to challenge me.

Two Asrais fluttered down to lift one of the jars from the hopper.

"Come Jonraine, let us help. Should we use the device then we should help if needed. The hoppers look quite busy so we need to help." Estrid explained.

"A bit like flushing the loo." I smiled. (An image of a nisse flushing a toilet.)

"Yes, something like that, I suppose." Estrid sent back, a little puzzled.

We fluttered down and gripped a jar each side by the handles. I went to fly up but Estrid sent.

"No, my love. The jar is much too heavy for us to lift; a little magic is needed to lighten the load." Estrid made a wave of her hand and I felt a little earth magic slide past me towards Estrid. The magic passed around the jar and Estrid sent that we should lift. This time it lifted effortlessly as if we held a balloon between us.

We followed the Asrais before us out a wide opening, a short snaking run and we found ourselves in another chamber. There was a flat floor and on it sat several small wagons. They were immense to us; a full sized nisse would find them small but functional. Upon one of the carts sat many of the glass jars and we followed the lead of the other Asrais and placed our jar down in the cart.

"I take it this cart is going somewhere?" I sent to Estrid.

"Yes, would you like to see?" Estrid sent back.

I nodded yes.

"We will dally a little. The cart is almost full and then we can help with the move." Estrid explained.

I looked around but I could see no mulluks to hitch to the cart.

"We are Asrais; we need no beasts of burden." Estrid said to my unsent question.

We took one of the rock ledges high up on the wall and watched the cart being filled with glass jars. The cart full, we dived off the ledge and down to floor level. The flat floor led to a wide incline that sloped gently upwards. Including us, about ten Asrais surrounded the cart. One took the driver's seat and he made gestures similar to Estrid's. The cart lurched forward under a gentle push and all the Asrais pushed the cart up the slope. At the top, the floor levelled off again and the cart came to a stop before a pair of heavy wooden doors.

"What happens now?" I sent, eager to see the next part of the process.

"That is where we finish." Estrid sent back. "The cart will remain here until the morning. When the sun kisses Sol, merchants will come for the cart; they will take it and leave an empty cart with payment for the goods."

"That must be a lot of gold." I sent.

"It is many gold coins but we do not need the gold. We want for nothing and need nothing that the gold buys."

"So why do you do it then?" I sent, puzzled over the whole process.

"When we live amongst the fae, we watch and see what they do. Those that do good deeds we reward if they need it. Where a good farmer shows kindness to a passing traveller, the farmer might find gold coins on his kitchen table the following day. It is not always so. We do not want the fae just to be good for the coin we give. Those that give without expectation of receiving receive the most." Estrid explained.

"How do you know what they are thinking?" I asked.

"We are Asrais." Came the enigmatic reply.

Estrid went on to explain. "When fae children lose a tooth or a tusk, they leave it by their bedroom window and in the morning it is gone and in its place is a shiny gold piece. Again it must be done with the correct heart or no gold will appear." Estrid warned with a wagging finger.

"So you are the tooth faerie!" I laughed that tinkling chime.

"Yes we all are." Estrid held out her arms to indicate all the Asrais around us.

"Outstanding!" I laughed.

"Jonraine we must away from here." Estrid became suddenly serious.

"Why is that my love?" I asked.

"The sun rises shortly and we must be within the wagon and be about our bed."

"By the Gods, time flies when I am with you Estrid." I exclaimed.

"It is always so. Time is different for us. For me it seems only a short while ago I was a nisse Hofdame in the court of my King." Estrid looked a little melancholy.

"If you got the chance to return, to be nisse again; would you return?" I held Estrid by the waist and looked into her eyes.

"Would you take me to wife?" She asked in return.

I nearly said yes but I stopped myself.

"Estrid I am married to the Princess." I stated. Estrid looked puzzled.

"For me it is hard to get my head around having more than one wife. I am not Muslim or one of our church's fundamental factions, so I did not know how to answer that. I am used to one man, one wife." I tried to explain.

"How positively barbaric." Estrid frowned. "Is that a human thing?"

"Yes it is." I replied. I could see Estrid did not comprehend.

"I have heard of this, you humans breed like the goblins. You take only one wife then ruin your women's bodies by making them have many children." Estrid shivered at the thought and left a dusting of faerie dust on the ground around her.

"Pardon me." She sent embarrassed.

"Come on Estrid, let's get back before we are caught here." I suggested.

Chapter 40

We darted through the tunnels and out from a different exit from which we entered the burrow. The sky was lightening in the West and we knew we did not have much time to get back. We streaked across the grasslands towards our camp. The dawn lightened the sky and we felt the pressure of the heaver light upon our bodies. We were cutting it very fine. Ever faster, we flew, the sky turned pale blue to the West. I knew we had moments before we heeded to take cover. Like rockets, we skimmed across the grassy plains. At last, we saw out camp in the distance.

"Will we make it?" I sent a desperate message to Estrid.

"I do not know my love." Estrid sent back, she had a determined look upon her face, it must have reflected mine.

The camp came closer and we aimed for the rear opening, to our right and west, the yellow spot brightened where the globe of the sun would burst upon us. Our target so close, so very close, the sun burst upon the grassy plains as we shot in through the rear opening of the wagon. Half a moment longer and we would have had the full force of the sun drill into us with no protection. We shot into the wagon and bounced off the front wall to fall on the floor. We were safe but I felt the pain I felt that time in the forest. It was just a moment this time but just as painful. Estrid lay panting on the floor beside me.

"Estrid, Estrid are you okay?" I asked as I reached for her shoulder. She lifted her head and looked into my eyes.

"Wow! What a ride!" She sent, high on the adrenaline rush and we laughed our tinkling laughter.

"Take me to bed my Black Prince." She demanded. We crept low to avoid the sun's rays streaming across the savannahs. Into our bedroom, we crept and I worried how I was going to keep both Estrid and Erika happy like this.

* * *

Every morning and evening Aiken Drum trained the Messian guard in his Ti Chi like katas, slow fluid and controlled it took over half an hour to complete each kata. While my own katas were snappy and powerful, a greater effort was needed to perform the slower more involved katas Aiken Drum taught. I could see in his graceful forms the sword stances he used in his one-sided battle with the twelve Snigmorder in the ravine.

In the morning, they performed the empty-handed katas, in the evening they performed the sword katas with wooden practice swords sung and shaped from the trees on the first night of our journey away from Logon City. As with everything practical and marshal some excelled faster than others. Malte became an exceptional student and one evening over dinner Aiken Drum requested that we consider releasing Malte from the Messian guard as he thought the nisse would be an asset to the school. It is an honour to be considered for Blademaster and we would never think to stand in the way of Malte's progression.

Erika spoke to Malte about the opportunity to train in Læringsted. While he was excited about the prospect of becoming a Blademaster, he fretted over leaving the company and relinquishing his oath to us. Erika discussed the problems with Aiken Drum and Malte. I listened in, trusting Erika's decades of experience in deal making. Eventually they came to an agreement where Malte remained a Messian guard but assigned under personal order from Erika and me to attend the Læringsted. Once a Blademaster, Malte would be a welcome bonus to our personal Messian guard. Malte was overjoyed with the agreement and became keen to get to the Læringsted to begin his training.

Six more days' journey and we moved up into the mountainous ranges before us. The air became colder and I was glad of the change into the Asrais, as I was impervious to the cold of the night. On one of our nightly jaunts, Estrid flew up to a frost-covered ridge and looked down into the valley beyond. I flew up to her to see what she was looking at. Before us spread in a neat valley of tidy farmland laid out in a patchwork quilt of colours. The earth quilt led up to a sprawling city which looked very affluent with buildings roofed in red clay tiles and white painted walls, with beautiful tended gardens they gave the impression of rich Mediterranean villas. Beyond the city, the valley ran into wasteland and further still dunes of the great eastern desolation spread on to the horizon.

"What a beautiful place." I sent to Estrid.

"Læringsted." She replied.

END